MYSTERY AND SUSPENSE

Great Stories from THE SATURDAY EVENING POST

Other books in this series

GREAT WESTERNS
from *The Saturday Evening Post*
GREAT LOVE STORIES
from *The Saturday Evening Post*

MYSTERY AND SUSPENSE

Great Stories from THE SATURDAY EVENING POST

EDITED BY JULIE EISENHOWER

THE CURTIS PUBLISHING COMPANY   INDIANAPOLIS, INDIANA

GREAT STORIES OF MYSTERY AND SUSPENSE
FROM *THE SATURDAY EVENING POST*

Copyright © 1910, 1919, 1930, 1933, 1935, 1937,
1943, 1946, 1947, 1959, 1960, 1961, 1966 by
The Curtis Publishing Company.

Printed in the United States of America.
All rights reserved. No part of this book
may be used or reproduced in any manner
whatsoever without written permission
except in the case of brief quotations
embodied in critical articles and reviews.
For information address
The Curtis Publishing Company,
1100 Waterway Boulevard,
Indianapolis, Indiana 46202

Copyright © 1976 The Curtis Publishing Company
Library of Congress Catalog Card Number 76-41561
I.S.B.N.: 0-89387-005-6

CONTENTS

Secret Service, *F. Britten Austin*	1
Master of the Hounds, *Algis Budrys*	25
October Corn, *Sigman Byrd*	50
The Hammer of God, *G.K. Chesterton*	65
The Dream, *Agatha Christie*	80
The End of Devil Hawker, *Arthur Conan Doyle*	99
The Evil Eye, *Alfred Gillespie*	123
The Sea Devil, *Arthur Gordon*	147
Motive for Murder, *John & Ward Hawkins*	155
A Caballero of the Law, *Ben Hecht*	176
When the World Was Young, *Jack London*	194
Hit and Run, *John MacDonald*	208
The Black Cat, *Edgar Allan Poe*	219
The Murderer, *Joel Townsley Rogers*	228
Pen in Hand, *Ben Ames Williams*	244

NOVELETTE

Method Three for Murder, *Rex Stout*	258

INTRODUCTION

The reader of the *Post* anthology of mystery and suspense has one vivid first impression—the tremendous galaxy of famous authors: Edgar Allan Poe ("The Black Cat" appeared in the *Post* in 1843), Agatha Christie, Jack London, Arthur Conan Doyle, G.K. Chesterton, Rex Stout, John D. MacDonald. The majority of stories in this volume were selected from the magazine's golden years of literature, 1930 to 1960, when almost all the great authors of the twentieth century were *Post* contributors.

Although the *Post* was founded by Benjamin Franklin in Philadelphia forty-eight years before the American Revolution, it was not until Cyrus Curtis bought the property in 1897 that the magazine became a mecca for good short stories. Curtis decided to make his five-cent weekly better than the literary monthlies. He accomplished his goal simply by instituting a policy of decisions on manuscripts within days rather than the customary four to six weeks, and by immediate payment to authors for their work. As the fame of the magazine grew, the public called for more and more stories which would take them out of their favorite reading chairs into the world of the unknown, for an hour of outguessing a sleuth. This volume captures the very best of the mystery-suspense stories of those years.

The fiction in the *Post* anthology is a compendium of three elements: suspense, mystery, and the pure detective story. Suspense is defined by Hitchcock, the master of minute detail and excruciating expectation, as "uncertainty accompanied by apprehension."

"The Sea Devil," Arthur Gordon's powerful story of one man's desperate struggle with a giant eel against death, represents the ultimate in the suspense story. Horror is an important factor in several of the suspense selections in this volume and, indeed, greatly heightens the tension and "apprehension" Hitchcock describes. For example, "The Evil Eye" by Alfred Gillespie is a torturous saga of horror, in which a father becomes convinced his nine-year-old stepdaughter is systematically plotting his death.

Post author John D. MacDonald, a past president of Mystery Writers of America and a novelist with sales of over thirty million books, recently defined the difference between the suspense and detective story. He stated that the pure suspense story is concerned "with what is going to happen and moves forward, often towards catastrophe... the detective story, however, is concerned with what has happened and moves backward through time in search of an explanation." MacDonald's own story in this anthology, "Hit and Run," is a detective story which evokes the response from the reader, "It could have happened to me." As MacDonald skillfully tells his story of a police detective's attempt to solve a hit-and-run death, one marvels at the hero's skill and tenacity. It is just this quality of strong reader identification with the character solving the crime that gives the detective story such tremendous appeal. An incredible example of the public's very real identification with a character was the refusal by many to believe that the *Post*'s fictional lawyer "Mr. Tutt," created by Arthur Train, was not a real person. In the 1930's, *Who's Who* listed "Mr. Tutt" in its pages, and the *Saturday Review of Literature* called him the "best-known American lawyer."

The third and final element in *Great Stories of Mystery and Suspense* is the classic mystery story which combines the best of two worlds: an unexplained occurrence and a suspenseful solution. For a fast-paced beautifully intricate mystery, one can read "A Caballero of the Law" by Ben Hecht, author of *The Front Page*. And the great storyteller, G.K. Chesterton, confronts the subject of evil and the fate of men in his mystery "The Hammer of God."

The *Post* collection of detective, suspense, and mystery stories is a volume with tremendous variety in mood and style of writing by many of the masters of the genre. It is a book to be read and reread many times.

In the course of researching over one hundred years of literature in the archives of the *Post*, the following members of *The Saturday Evening Post* staff aided me in finding stories and "missing" authors.

Jep Cadou
Roberts Ehrgott
Rosalyn Fox
Astrid Henkels
Jean White

MYSTERY AND SUSPENSE

Great Stories from THE SATURDAY EVENING POST

SECRET SERVICE

F. BRITTEN AUSTIN

"But, *Excellenz!*"

The entreaty, from such a man, was oddly and strikingly sincere. About forty years of age, sprucely dressed in a well-cut lounge suit, spats over patent boots—he was the type to be seen any day gazing rather aimlessly into the shop windows of Piccadilly or the Rue de la Paix; the type that haunts the hotels frequented by the best society and yet is not of that society; the type that drifts behind the chairs of every gambling casino in the world. A dark mustache carefully trimmed curled over lips whose fine curves were unpleasantly thin and clear-cut. His complexion was sallow; his dark eyes, fixed on his companion in an accentuation of his entreaty, implored now with an expression of genuine truthfulness which was certainly not habitual to them. He gesticulated with a white and exquisitely manicured hand.

"But rubbish!"

The speaker was an oldish thickset man in evening dress. His round red face barred with a clipped white mustache, lit with a pair of small gray eyes, vivacious behind pince-nez, was set upon a short apoplectic neck which rucked into folds above his collar. The scalp showed pink through close-cropped white hair. He stood warming himself with his back to the fire—a very large fire for Berlin in the winter of early 1918—and glared angrily at the younger man. He spoke with the irascibility of a brutal superior whose impunity is of long date and unquestioned.

"Are you mad, Kranz? Do you take me for an imbecile old woman? Am I feeble-minded? Do I look feeble-minded—that you should dare to—to play such a trick upon me?" He was obviously working himself up into one of his official rages. "You—you tell me that you have an infallible means of obtaining secret information, no matter how hidden. You persuade me to come and test it—me! I give you credit for your impudence! And this is what it is!" He almost choked with offended dignity. "Be careful, Kranz! You have traded this once upon your record with us—you will never do it again! To bring me—me!—to this absurdity! To expect me to listen to the hypnotic ravings of that idiot girl! I wonder you didn't offer me crystal gazing!"

"But, *Excellenz!*"

The old man waved a hand at him. "My dear Kranz," he said, dropping suddenly into a tone of tolerant contempt, "I forgive you this once. I dare say you have been the victim of a genuine hallucination. You would not have dared else. You don't drug, do you?"

The question was asked with a disconcertingly sudden sharpness. The younger man made a gesture of emphatic denial, defying the piercing gray eyes that probed him. The old man grunted:

"Keep your sanity, Kranz—or the bureau will lose a valued servant. Drop this nonsense. I know what I am talking about—I studied psychology under Wundt of Leipzig. The whole thing is a hallucination, the raving of the dream-self released from control. *Dummes Zeug!* Give me my coat!"

"*Excellenz*, I implore you!"

The old man looked at him with a snarl of savage mockery.

"Don't waste any more of my time, Kranz! Look at her! Is it even probable that an imbecile creature like that can be of use in our business? Look at her, I say!"

He flung out a hand toward a young girl, who stood with obvious reluctance in the center of the luxuriously furnished apartment. She was perhaps eighteen, but her youth had neither beauty nor charm. Her features were soft and heavy—the nose thick, the chin receding, the eyes weak and protuberant. Her personality was of the feeblest. Her face flooded scarlet with shame and her eyes swam with tears at this brutal insult. Yet evidently she did not dare to rush away. Only she looked beseechingly toward Kranz, like a dog that awaits a sign from its master.

His sallow face blanched. The thin lips under the dark mustache lost their curves, became a straight line.

"Agathe," he said, and his voice of command was strangely in contrast with the tone in which he had entreated the old man, "go into the next room and wait!"

The girl vanished without a word. Kranz waited until she had closed the door, and then he turned once more to his superior.

"I implore Your Excellency to listen!" he said with a desperate gesture. "I stake my reputation upon it——"

The old man grunted scornfully:

"Your reputation!"

The dark eyes flashed.

"My reputation with you, *Excellenz*," he corrected in a gentle voice of complete cynicism.

The old man stared at him.

"Well, go on!" he said brutally after a short pause which was eloquent of his appraisement. He cleaned his pince-nez to mark his contemptuous indifference to anything that might be said.

"You remember Karl Wertheimer, *Excellenz*?"

The old man swung round on him, replaced the pince-nez.

"Shot by the English. You'll never equal him, Kranz."

Kranz shrugged his shoulders.

"*Excellenz*, I believe in neither God nor devil. Until the other day I believed that death finished us completely; but I assure you solemnly upon my—upon anything which you think will bind me—that the soul, or whatever you choose to call it, of Karl Wertheimer speaks through that girl!"

There was a pause of silence in which the old man's eyes probed him to the depths. He proffered no comment and Kranz continued, his voice intensely earnest: "The English shot Karl Wertheimer in London—but they did not kill him. His—his soul is here, in Berlin, in that room, alive as ever, as eager as ever to work for the Fatherland!"

"He always had patriotic notions," murmured the old man, with a sly smile at the obviously cosmopolitan Kranz. "That is why he was such an invaluable agent. Go on with your little romance."

"It is no romance, *Excellenz*, I assure you—it is living fact. Karl Wertheimer was a useful agent while he lived upon this earth, but he is immeasurably more useful now that he is a—a spirit. There are no walls that can keep him out; there is nothing he cannot see if he chooses to; there is no conversation he cannot overhear."

"H'm!" grunted the old man; "admitted that if he is a spirit he can do all this—how can he convey it to us?"

"Through this girl!"

"Who is she, this girl?"

"The daughter of some shopkeeper or other. I followed her ankles one evening in the park—she was ahead of me, and I could not see her face." He smiled cynically. "I won't trouble Your Excellency with the details. I brought her in here, and no sooner had she sat down in that chair than she swooned off.

"I was just cursing my luck—I saw her face for the first time then!—and wondering how I was going to get rid of her, when Karl spoke to me. I confess, *Excellenz*, it gave me a pretty bad turn. It was so utterly unexpected—his voice coming from her lips. However, I pulled myself together—and we had a most interesting conversation."

"He could answer your questions?" interjected the old man sharply.

"Just as if he himself were sitting in the chair. So, naturally, I kept a tight hold on the girl. She has not been allowed out since."

"H'm!" The old man grunted again and looked at his watch. "Well, I have missed my appointment," he said with the factitious bad temper he owed to his dignity. "I may as well see her performance. Fetch her in!"

Kranz went to the door and called:

"Agathe!"

The girl entered, stood with her eyes fixed timorously on him. He pointed to a large armchair by the fireplace.

"Sit down!" he commanded.

The girl obeyed dully, one little apprehensive glance at him the only sign of any mental life in her. She sat upright, her hands on her lap, staring stupidly into the fire. Two heavy tears collected themselves in her protuberant eyes, rolled down her cheeks; they seemed but to emphasize her degradation. Her tyrant stood over her, his dark eyes hard.

"Lean back and go to sleep!"

She sank back among the cushions. Obviously she had no will at all of her own. Her eyes closed. Her expressionless face twitched for a moment and then was as still as a mask. Her bosom heaved in the commencement of deep and heavy breathing, which continued in the normality of slumber. The old man watched her keenly and contemptuously, alert for any sign of simulation.

Kranz pulled a little table across to the fireplace. A telephone instrument, incongruously utilitarian in this luxurious room, and writing materials were on it.

"You should note down what is said, *Excellenz*," he said earnestly in a low voice.

The old man ignored him, his eyes on the girl. Suddenly he

shuddered in a rush of cold air. The paper on the table fluttered as in a draft. He turned to Kranz in savage irritation:

"Shut that window!"

Kranz shook his head.

"They are all shut, *Excellenz!*" His whisper was one of genuine awe. "Hush! It's beginning! He's come!"

The old man favored him with a glance of inexpressible contempt. The scorn was till in his eyes when he jerked round to the girl again in an involuntary start of surprise at a sudden greeting:

"Good evening, *Excellenz!*"

The words issued from that expressionless mask of the deeply breathing girl, but they were uttered in a tone of easy jocularity, followed by a little good-humored laugh, which was uncanny in its contrast with her degraded personality. Despite the feminine vocal cords which had articulated the phrase the timbre and intonation were vividly those of a man of the world.

The old man stared speechlessly. His faculties seemed inhibited under the shock. The red faded out of his round face, left it ashen gray under the close-cropped white hair. Kranz watching him feared for his heart. He made a brusque little gesture as though seizing control of himself.

"*Herr Gott!* It's—it's his voice!" he gasped.

His eyes turned to Kranz and there was fear in them, a primitive fear of the supernatural. Trembling he reeled rather than walked to the chair by the table with the telephone, dropped heavily into it. Kranz broke the oppressive silence, posed himself as master of the situation.

"Good evening, Karl!" he said, as though welcoming an everyday acquaintance into the room.

"Hello, Kranz!" came the easy jocular voice through the lips of the entranced girl. "*Wie geht's?* I am glad you persuaded His Excellency to come. Now we can start!"

The old man pulled himself together, moistened his lips for speech.

"Is—is that really you, Karl?" he asked unevenly.

The merry little laugh, so uncanny from the only origin visible, preceded the answer:

"Really I, *Excellenz*. Karl Wertheimer, shot six months ago by the English in the Tower of London, and as alive in this room as ever I was." The tone changed to that of a humorously bantering introduction. "Karl Wertheimer, *Excellenz*, the terror of the English counter-espionage department; at your service—still!"

The old man fumblingly produced a handkerchief and mopped at the perspiration on his brow. He hesitated for an appropriate remark.

"Why?" he asked falteringly and stopped.

The merry little laugh rang out again in the silent room.

"Why, *Excellenz*? Because in my earth life I had only one passion—and it is as strong as ever it was. Stronger, for I owe our enemies a grudge for that little early-morning shooting party in the Tower. You've no idea how I long for a really good cigar, *Excellenz*," he finished in a tone of jesting complaint.

The old man stared into the empty air beyond the girl.

"And you can really obtain information and convey it?"

He was recovering his poise. The question was asked in the brusque tone familiar to his subordinates.

"Test me, *Excellenz!*"

"I assure you, *Excellenz*——" interjected Kranz eagerly.

His superior waved him aside. The brow under the short white hair had recovered its normal ruddiness, was wrinkled in cogitation. He felt in his pocket and produced a letter in a sealed envelope.

"Tell me from whom this comes."

He proffered the letter as though expecting it to be taken out of his fingers. Then, as it was not, he dropped his hand with a gesture of hopeless bafflement. There was so real a feeling of the actual presence of Karl Wertheimer in the room that the quite normal fact of the letter remaining untouched emphasized suddenly the uncanny nature of this conversation.

"Permit me, *Excellenz*," said Kranz politely. He took the letter and laid it on the girl's brow. Her lips moved at once.

"This purports to be from the firm of Wilson & Staunton, Boston, to the firm of Jensen & Auerstedt, Christiania, with reference to an overdue account." The voice was still the chuckling voice of Karl Wertheimer. "Actually it is a communication in code to you from Heinrich Biedermann at New York. Do you wish me to read the message? I still remember the old code, *Excellenz!*"

"No, no!" interposed the old man. "Never mind!"

"Perhaps you would like me to tell you what Heinrich Biedermann is doing at this moment, *Excellenz?*"

"But he is in New York! You can't be here and there too!"

Again came the merry little laugh.

"Time and space are an illusion of matter, *Excellenz*. I half forget that you are still subject to it. Well, Heinrich Biedermann is sitting with a young woman in a restaurant, having tea. They are both very cheerful, for he has just received a remittance from you, and he has bought her a new hat. The sun is just setting, and he is lost in admiration of the glow of her red hair against the background of the illuminated sky which he can perceive through the window. He is hopelessly in love with her, which is unfortunate, as the lady happens to be a spy, by name Desiree Rochefort, in the pay of the French Secret Service."

"The devil!" ejaculated the old man.

"But," said Kranz in a puzzled tone, "sunset? It is nearly midnight!"

The old man turned on him.

"Fool! There is a difference of six hours in time between here and America. That proves it—if anything can be proof of such wild improbability!"

"Test me again!" said the amused and confident voice of Karl Wertheimer. "Something really difficult this time!"

The old man leaned back in his chair and pondered. Then the gleam of an idea came into his malicious gray eyes.

"Right!" he said emphatically. "You know the library in my house?"

"Certainly, *Excellenz!*"

"Go into my library. Read me the fifteenth line of the ninety-first page of the sixth volume on the third shelf of the right-hand side, without opening the book. Can you do that?"

"You shall see, *Excellenz*," replied the voice cheerfully. "The sixth volume counting from the left, I presume?"

"Yes."

"I will note that," said Kranz, coming to the table. He wrote the particulars and looked up to his superior. "Do you know what the line is, *Excellenz?*" he asked.

"I don't even know what the book is!" replied the old man harshly. He wrinkled his brows in impatience at the silence, which prolonged itself through several seconds. The girl seemed quite normally asleep.

"Here you are, *Excellenz!*" It was again the mocking voice of Karl Wertheimer which issued from her lips. "The book is Shakespeare. The line is 'England, bound in with the triumphant sea.' Can you interpret the omen, *Excellenz?*"

"The U-boat war," murmured Kranz, as if to himself.

"Write it down!" commanded the old man. Kranz wrote the line. His Excellency took up the telephone receiver.

"Hello! Hello!" he gave a number and waited. "Hello! Is Wolff there? . . . Tell him I want him at once! . . . Yes. . . . A thousand devils! Wolff, my secretary! Are you all deaf?" he vociferated irascibly. "Hello! Is that you, Wolff? Yes, of course it is I speaking! You ought to know my voice by this time! Go into the library and get——" He hesitated. Kranz passed him the sheet of paper. "Get the sixth volume from the left on the third shelf of the right-hand side. Bring it to the telephone. Hurry now!"

Again he waited. There was a tense silence in the room, a silence that was emphasized by the heavy and regular breathing of the sleeping girl.

"Hello! Are you there? Is that you, Wolff? . . . Be quiet! Answer my questions! Have you got the book? . . . Right! what is it? . . . An English book? . . . Shakespeare—right! Now turn up page—page ninety-one. Got it? Count to the fifteenth line." He turned from the telephone to Kranz. "Write down what I repeat!" Then again speaking into the telephone: "Yes? . . . Read out the line! . . . What? . . . 'England, bound in with the triumphant sea.' A thousand devils! Wolff! Wolff! Wait a minute! Where did you find the book? On the shelf? . . . Had it been touched? . . . You are sure that it had not been touched—not opened? . . . Oh, you have been in the library all the evening, working——"

"Tell him that the love poem he has been writing to Fräulein Mimi in your library tonight is not only banal but it does not scan," interjected Karl Wertheimer. "The line *Unsere Herzen schlagen rhythmisch* is particularly bad."

The old man glanced toward the vacant air over the girl and grinned. He repeated the message into the telephone. He waited a moment—and then burst into chuckling laughter.

"*Famos!* He's smashed the receiver. Scared out of his life! I heard him yell." He put down the instrument and turned again to the chair. "Karl Wertheimer, I believe in your reality—I believe in your powers." His voice was solemn. "The Fatherland has work for you to do."

"That is why I am here, *Excellenz*." The voice came jauntily through the expressionless lips of the unconscious girl. The old man pursed his mouth under the clipped white mustache and pondered. Kranz watched him with acute interest.

"Listen!" said the old man, looking up in a sudden decision. "At the present time the Allied military missions in Washington are negotiating with the United States Government with regard to the dispatch of the American Army to Europe for the coming campaign. We know this—we know that any day now they may come to an agreement. It is of the utmost importance to us that we should know immediately the numbers promised and the schedule of sailings. The fate of the world depends upon it. The secret will be most jealously guarded—triply locked out of reach of any ordinary agent. Can you read it as you read the line in that closed book?"

"I can, *Excellenz*—if you can give me some indication where to look," replied the voice. "We must, so to speak, focus ourselves. I can't now explain the conditions with us, but you will understand what I mean. Spirit pervades——" For the first time in the colloquy the voice spoke with hesitation, as though despairing of explaining the inexplicable. "Direction—definite direction—is essential."

"H'm," the old man grunted. "Well, I suggest Forsdyke—you know, the permanent undersecretary of department—as the man most likely to prepare the schedule. You know where he lives?"

"The very house in Washington!" replied the voice triumphantly. "Good enough! I will do my best, *Excellenz*."

"Today is the twenty-first of February," said the old man. "We must know by the end of the month. Vast issues depend on it. Can you do it?"

"I will try." The voice came feebly and as from far away. "I must go now, *Excellenz*. The power—the power is failing—fast. Good-bye—good-bye, Kranz. Take—take care of the girl. She—she is the—only means—of—communication." The last words came in a whisper, ceased. The girl appeared to be in normal slumber.

The old man turned to Kranz, spoke out of a preoccupation which otherwise ignored him.

"Give me my hat and coat!"

A sudden anxiety paled the sallow face.

"Your Excellency remembers what Karl said," he murmured as he assisted his chief into the heavy fur-lined garment. "The girl is the only means of communication. I need not remind Your Excellency that the girl is my——"

"You need not remind me of anything, Kranz," interrupted the old man harshly. "You will not be forgotten. Good night!"

Kranz accompanied him obsequiously to the door.

On that evening of the twenty-first of February a cheerful little party was assembled round the dinner table of Henry Forsdyke, chief of a certain department in the United States Administration. The large room, which had been built by a Southern magnate who led Washington society in pre-Civil War days, was illumined only by the shaded lights of the table, and beyond the dazzling shirt fronts of the men it lapsed into a gloom that was intensified by the dark curtains over the long windows and was scarcely relieved by the glinting gilt frames of the pictures spaced on the walls hung in a dull tint. In that half light the servants moved, scarcely real. Only the party within the illuminated ellipse of white napery, sparkling glass and gleaming silver was vividly actual, plucked out of shadow. It was a fad of the host's, this concentration of the light upon the table. He alleged that it emphasized the personalities of his guests. His daughter, who was irreverent, accused him of an atavistic tendency that craved for the candlelight of his ancestors.

Within the magic ellipse the party exchanged lighthearted talk that effervesced every now and then into merry laughter where a young girl's voice predominated. All were in evident good spirits. The host himself, a man of between fifty and sixty years, with shrewd gray eyes looking out of a face characterized by a pointed and neatly clipped iron-gray beard, set the tone. He smiled down the table with a contentment that seemed to spring from a secret satisfaction, the contentment of a man who has completed an anxious and difficult task and can now relax. He was in his best vein of sententious humor.

The same undertone of relief could have been discerned by the acute in the gaiety of young Jimmy Lomax, Forsdyke's private secretary, though one alone of the little glances between him and his host's daughter, if intercepted, might have seemed sufficient reason.

Captain Sergeantson, Jimmy Lomax's chum, had obvious cause for cheerfulness. Attached to a special service department, he had just returned from Europe, where he had fulfilled an extremely difficult mission with conspicuous success. His homecoming had provided the excuse for this little dinner party.

As for Professor Lomax, Jimmy's father, no one had ever seen him other than in high spirits. The author—after a lifetime of profound and exact scientific research that had earned him a worldwide reputation—of an inquiry into the possible survival of human personality, which was the controversial topic of that winter and which threatened to deprive him of that reputation, he was in striking contrast with the idea of him propagated by the sensational press. There was nothing of the visionary about those clear-cut features. A stranger would have diagnosed him as a lawyer—a lawyer whose judicial perception of evidence was clarified by a sense of humor. The mobile mouth even in silence hinted at this latter quality. The eyes twinkled, eminently sane, under a well-balanced brow. He joked like a schoolboy with his host's daughter, exciting—for the secretly selfish pleasure of hearing it—her gay young laugh. Occasionally he glanced across to his son, approbation in his eyes.

Hetty Forsdyke, the only woman of the party, was a typical specimen of the self-reliant college-bred American girl. Good to look upon, her beauty hinted at a race which had been proud of its exclusiveness long after Napoleon had sold Louisiana to the States. Her vivacity and charm had roots perhaps in the same stock, but the cool levelheaded understanding of life, which she expressed in a slang that provoked her father to vain rebuke, and the genuineness of which was vouched for by her clear gray eyes, was an attribute of the Forsdykes and the North.

The dinner was nearly at an end. Forsdyke, launched on a story of a presidential campaign in the Middle West a generation ago, had arrived at the stage where the chuckles of his hearers were on the point culminating in the final burst of laughter. Hetty, her glass between her fingers, halfway to her mouth, was looking at him with a smile that pretended the story was quite new to her. Suddenly her expression changed. She stared as if spellbound at the dark curtains, from which her father's oval face detached itself in the illumination of the table. The glass slipped from her fingers, smashed.

Forsdyke's story ceased abruptly. Four pairs of alarmed eyes focused themselves upon his daughter. Jimmy involuntarily had half risen from his chair. The movement seemed to recall the girl to her surroundings. She shuddered, and then with an evident effort of will brought back her gaze to the table. Her smile routed the momentary anxiety of her companions.

"How careless of me!" she said easily, quelling with quiet self-control her confusion ere it could well be remarked. "I don't know what I was thinking of! Do go on, papa! It was just getting interesting."

She signaled composedly to a servant to pick up the broken glass and settled herself for the familiar story.

"What a hostess she is!" thought her father. "Just like——" He did not finish the complementary clause, and stifled another which began "I wonder what I shall do when——" He picked up his story again and was rewarded by his need of laughter. But his eyes rested uneasily on his daughter, and he promised himself a later inquiry into this abnormality.

The party withdrew into the drawing room, where, since Forsdyke was a widower of many years' masculine supremacy, the men lit their cigars. Hetty at a request from her father seated herself at the grand piano in the far corner and commenced the soft chords of a Chopin prelude. Jimmy Lomax stood over her. There was already something proprietary in his air. But the girl after one glance up at him seemed to forget his presence in the spell of the music. Her position commanded a full view of the room and she looked dreamily across to where the three men were gathered by the white-marble fireplace.

Suddenly the music stopped on a crashing discord. The girl had jumped to her feet, was trembling violently. Young Lomax clutched at her.

"Hetty! What——"

She broke away from him, came swiftly across the room to his father.

"Professor!" she said. "You were once in practice as a doctor, weren't you?"

The twinkling eyes went grave as they met hers. There was unmistakable seriousness in her question.

"Yes, my dear."

"Then I want you to examine me right here, professor!" she said. "Tell me if I've got fever!"

She met the amazed eyes of the other men with a look which announced that she knew her own business.

Without a word the professor lifted up her wrist and felt her pulse.

"Now show me your tongue!"

She obeyed. He nodded his head, and placed his hand upon her brow. His eyes plunged into hers for one second of searching scrutiny, and then he nodded his head again, satisfied.

"My dear," he said, "I haven't a thermometer here, but I should say you are absolutely normal in every way. Your pulse is a shade rapid perhaps."

The girl took a long breath.

"Thank you, professor," she said simply. She turned to the others. "You heard what the professor said? There's no fever about me. Now—listen! I want to tell you something. I've been wanting to tell you ever since we sat down to dinner—and now I must tell you! And you mustn't laugh! Papa, this is serious!"

The four men, puzzled at her demeanor, grouped themselves round her. She assured herself of their gravity.

"This evening," she began, "between five and six o'clock I suddenly developed a dreadful headache. It was so bad that I just had to go to my room and lie down. I went to sleep straight off. And then—then I had a—a—dream. Only," she interposed quickly, to hold their interest, "it wasn't like an ordinary dream. It was so vivid that I felt all the time it meant something. I dreamed that someone or something that I could feel was sort of loving and kind and earnest—very earnest; I could feel that strongly—took me into a room. And somehow I knew that the room was in Berlin. It seemed quite a nice room, but I don't remember much about the details of it. I only remember that I saw myself there with two men, one young and dark, the other old and white, who were staring at a girl sleeping in a big armchair. They took not the faintest notice of me, and I didn't worry much about them. The girl was the interesting thing to all of us—and yet, though I was staring at her with a sort of fascination I couldn't shake off, I didn't know why.

"Then a strange thing happened: The girl kind of faded away. I don't know how to describe it, because I felt all the time she was still there; and as she faded there came up the figure of a man. He seemed to grow out of her, to take her place. It was really uncanny. This man that grew out of the girl like a—like a ghost, was somehow more living than any of us. It was as if he were in the limelight and we were in the shadow. I shall never forget his face. It was handsome but wicked—mocking—malicious—like a devil. And he had a scar over the right eyebrow, which made him look even more devilish."

"What color was his hair?" interposed Captain Sergeantson. "Any mustache?"

The girl looked at him in surprise at the question.

"Fair; sticking up straight. No mustache. Why?"

Captain Sergeantson nodded.

"I only wondered. Go on, Miss Forsdyke."

The girl resumed.

"Well—it seemed that we were all looking at this man and not at the girl at all. She had disappeared behind him, or into him, I don't know which. The other two men were talking to him, talking earnestly. And it seemed to me that it was extremely—oh, immensely important that I should understand what they were saying. I listened with all my soul. It almost hurt me to listen as hard as I did. And yet I couldn't get a word of it. What they said was somehow just out of reach—like people you see talking on the bioscope. And then all of a sudden I heard—one sentence—as clearly as possible: 'Forsdyke is the man who prepares the schedule!'"

Jimmy Lomax uttered a sharp cry of amazement.

"What!" He turned to Forsdyke. "Chief, that's strange!"

Forsdyke imposed silence with a gesture.

"Go on, Hetty," he said calmly. "What then?"

"Then I woke up. The words were ringing in my ears. They haunted me all the time I was dressing for dinner. I wondered if I ought to tell you. Something was whispering to me that I should. But I was afraid you would laugh at me. But that's not all. You remember at dinner I dropped a glass. Papa"—her voice suddenly became very earnest—"I saw that man, the man who had grown out of the girl, standing behing you. His eyes were fixed on you as though trying to read into you; so evilly that I went cold all over."

The professor gave her a sharp glance.

"No vision of the room in Berlin—or wherever it was?" he queried. She shook her head.

"No, just the man. But even that's not all. Just now when I was playing and looking across to you I distinctly saw him again, close behind papa! He moved this time, moved with a funny little limp; just like a real man with a bad leg. I jumped up—and—and then he had disappeared and was gone!"

She looked round apprehensively, as though expecting to see him still.

"Your liver's out of order, my dear," said her father. "Take a pill when you go to bed tonight."

"No," said the girl. "It's not that. I knew you would say I was ill. That is why I asked the professor to examine me. I am sure it means something!"

Captain Sergeantson threw the end of his cigar into the fireplace and took a wallet out of his pocket. The wallet contained photographs. He handed them to the girl.

"Miss Forsdyke," he said gravely, "would you mind telling me if you have ever seen any of these people?"

The girl examined them.

Suddenly she uttered a cry and held up one of the prints.

"This!" she said. Her eyes were wide with astonishment. "This is the man I saw! There's the scar too—exactly! Who is he? Do you know him?"

"That man," replied Captain Sergeantson sententiously, "is Karl Wertheimer, about the cutest spy the German Secret Service ever had. I was going to tell Jimmy a story about him and brought his picture along with me," he added in explanation. "I sort of recognized him from your description."

The girl stared at the photograph.

"Of course," continued Sergeantson, "he made up over that scar. He was an extraordinarily clever actor, by the way. They cleaned off the makeup when they took the photograph."

"And he is a German spy!" mused the girl, still staring at the picture.

"He was!" replied Sergeantson grimly. "The British shot him in the Tower when I was in London six months ago."

The girl looked up sharply.

"I'm sure I've never seen his photograph before!" she said, as though answering an allegation she felt in the silence of the others. "How could I?"

"I can't imagine, Miss Forsdyke. The extraordinary thing is that you should have got his limp. That's what gave him away to the

British. He broke his leg dropping over a wall in an exceedingly daring escape at the beginning of the war. But how you should know about it beats me all to pieces."

"I didn't know! I saw——"

"You saw his ghost, I guess, Miss Forsdyke. And that's all there is to it."

Captain Sergeantson lit himself another cigar by way of showing how cold-blooded he could be in the possible presence of a specter.

Jimmy shuddered. "It's uncanny," he said. "I don't like it."

"But why?" puzzled Hetty, wrinkling her brows. She turned to her father. "Papa——"

Forsdyke shook his head smilingly.

"I'm out of this deal. Ask the professor. He's the authority on spooks. What does it all mean, Lomax? Can you give an explanation that doesn't outrage common sense?"

The professor smiled. The eyes in that clean-cut face twinkled.

"Common sense?" He shrugged his shoulders. "We want to start by defining that—by defining all our senses; and we should never finish." He looked with his challenging smile round the group. "I see you are inviting me to throw away my last little shred of reputation as a sane man," he said humorously. "Well, I will not venture on any explanation of my own. The evidence, with all respect to Hetty here, is insufficient. We only know that she had a dream and a hallucination twice repeated. We know that the hallucination corresponds to a photograph in Captain Sergeantson's pocket. We do not know what basis there is, if any, for her dream. But I will give you two alternative explanations that might be suggested by other people. Will that satisfy you?"

"Go ahead, professor," said Forsdyke. "Don't ask me to believe in ghosts, that's all!"

"I don't ask you to believe in anything," replied the professor. "I don't ask you to believe in the reality of your presence and ours in this room. If you have ever read old Bishop Berkeley you will know that you would find it exceedingly difficult to evade the thesis that it may all be an illusion. Your consciousness—whatever that is—builds up a picture from impressions on your senses. You can't test the reality of the origins of those impressions—you can only collate the subjective results. Everything—time and space—may be an illusion for all you or I know!"

"I heard that in my dream!" Hetty broke in. "Someone said it: 'Time and space are an illusion!' I remember it so clearly now!" Her eyes glistened with excitement.

"All right, Hetty," said her father. "Let the professor have his say.

It's his turn. And don't take us out of our depth, Lomax. You know as well as I do what I mean by common sense."

The professor laughed.

"Well, I'm not going to guarantee either of the explanations, Forsdyke. I merely put them before you. The first is the out-and-out spiritualist explanation. Let us see what we can make of that. You must assume, with the spiritualists, that man has a soul which survives with its attributes of memory, volition and a certain potentiality for action upon what we know as matter. Captain Sergeantson here vouches for the fact that a certain German spy, Karl Wertheimer, was shot in London six months ago. The spiritualist would allege that it is possible—under certain conditions which are very imperfectly under human command—for the soul—we'll call it that—of Karl Wertheimer to put itself into communication with his old associates who still remain in the world of the living. There is an enormous mass of human testimony—which you may reject as worthless if you like—to the possibility of such a thing. Assume it is possible.

"Karl Wertheimer was a spy so successful, according to Captain Sergeantson, that it is reasonable to suppose that spying was his natural vocation, his life passion, as much as painting pictures is the life passion of an artist. It may be assumed that if anything survives, one's life passion survives. Now suppose that Karl Wertheimer's late employers believe in the possibility of communication with their late agent; that they find a medium—in this case, the young girl that Hetty saw in her dream—who can be controlled by the defunct Karl Wertheimer, through whom they can speak to him and receive communications from him. What is more natural than that they should do so? Admitting the premises, difficult as they are, it appears to me that the discarnate soul of Karl Wertheimer would be an extremely valuable secret agent——"

"Yes, suppose! Suppose!" said Forsdyke. "It is all supposition. And it doesn't explain Hetty's dream."

"I am coming to that," pursued the professor. "Grant me, for the sake of argument, all my suppositions. Karl Wertheimer's employers are communicating with him and setting him tasks. One of those tasks, we will assume, concerns you. Now it may be, Forsdyke, that in the unseen world of discarnate spirits there is one who watches over you, guards you from danger. Someone, perhaps, who loved you in this life."

Forsdyke glanced up to the portrait of his wife upon the wall.

"I leave the suggestion to you," said the professor delicately. "We will merely pursue it as a hypothesis. Such a spirit would seek to warn you. It is obviously futile to discuss the means it might or might not employ. We know nothing of the conditions of discarnate life—nothing, at any rate, with scientific certainty. But we will assume that such a spirit, desirous of communicating, finds that Hetty here is temporarily in a mediumistic condition; and by 'mediumistic' I mean merely that she is in that abnormal state which, in all ages and in all countries, induces persons to declare that they see and hear things imperceptible to others. She certainly had an abnormal headache. She goes to sleep and dreams.

"We won't analyze dream consciousness now. I will only point out that in a clearly remembered dream the events of that dream are as real to consciousness as the events of waking life, and that the perception of time is enormously modified—you dream through hours of experience while the hand marks minutes on the clock. You are subject to a different illusion of time—and as time and space are but two faces of the same phenomenon it may be said that you are subject to a different illusion of space as well. The spiritualist uses this undoubted fact to support his assertion that in dream sleep the spirit of the living person is freed from the conditions of matter and is in a condition at least approximating to that of a person who is dead; that it can and does accompany the spirits of those who in this life were linked to it.

"The spiritualist, then, endeavoring to explain our present problem, would allege that a spiritual agency concerned with your welfare led Hetty's spirit into a room in Berlin where Karl Wertheimer's employers were indicating him to you for some special purpose; that Hetty, being then pure spirit, could actually perceive Karl Wertheimer as a living being when perhaps those in the room—if there was such a room—could not perceive the girl through whom he was speaking; that she could actually hear the significant phrase of their conversation.

"Further, the spiritualist would assert as a possibility that Karl Wertheimer, ordered to obtain information in your possession, is actually here—shadowing you more effectively than any mortal spy could do; and that Hetty, still retaining her mediumistic power, has actually seen him. That is a spiritualistic explanation. I apologize for its length, Forsdyke. Give me another of your very excellent and material cigars!"

"It is a fantastic explanation. I don't believe a word of it," said Forsdyke, passing him the box. "Let us have the other one."

"The other one," replied the professor, cutting the tip of his cigar and lighting it carefully, with a critical glance at its even burning, "is shorter. It is the explanation of those who are determined to explain a great mass of well-attested and apparently abnormal facts by normal agency. Their explanation in one word is—telepathy. You know the idea—the common phenomenon of two people who utter a remark, unconnected with previous conversation, at the same moment. Living minds unconsciously act upon each other; that is experimentally proved. Why, therefore, drag in dead ones? That is the argument that they always use.

"Let us apply their theory. Hetty is in an abnormal condition. Captain Sergeantson is coming to dinner. In his pocket he has a photograph of the notorious German spy, Karl Wertheimer. In his mind he has a story about him that he intends to relate. Now, there are well-documented cases of hallucinations of persons actually on their way to a house where they were not expected appearing to their destined hostesses. I could quote you dozens of examples. The telepathist says this is because the guest forms in his mind a vivid picture of himself in that house, which is projected forward to the hostess' mind and causes her to think she sees him. Now, Captain Sergeantson's mind is not full of himself—it is full of the story about Karl Wertheimer that he is going to tell. Hetty's mind somehow picks this up. She goes to sleep, and as in sleep, notoriously, the human mind has a faculty for building up pictures and a story, Hetty dreams this story about Karl Wertheimer. It is true that she has never seen Karl Wertheimer. But Captain Sergeantson presumably has a visualization of him, including the limp, in his mind.

"The subsequent hallucinations are explained by the tendency to automatic repetition of any vivid impression upon the nervous centers, which excite a picture in consciousness. It is a more or less tenable theory, but it would be gravely shaken if it happened that, unknown to Hetty or Captain Sergeantson, you actually had something to do with a secret schedule which would interest our friends the enemy."

There was a silence. Forsdyke's brow wrinkled as he stared into the fire. Suddenly he switched round to the professor.

"That's the devil of it, Lomax!" he exclaimed. "I have! A most secret schedule. Thank God, it will be out of my possession tomorrow morning, when I——"

"Don't, papa!" cried Hetty, clapping her hand over his mouth. She stared wildly around her. "I feel sure that someone is listening!"

Forsdyke freed himself with a gesture that expressed his impatience of this absurdity.

"What do you make of that, Lomax?" he asked.

"Of course," murmured the professor, "Hetty's mind may be

influenced by a dominant anxiety in yours. I should not like to say, Forsdyke!" His tone was emphatic. "Personally I have never heard of a spectral spy—but—well, you are, on your own showing, worth spying on. And 'there are more things in heaven and earth, Horatio,' you know! If it is possible—then there are things more improbable than that this means of acquiring information should be used. Your schedule would, I take it, be priceless?"

"The fate of the world may be involved in it," replied Forsdyke. "But I can't believe——"

"I am certain!" exclaimed Hetty. "I feel there's something uncanny round us now!" She shuddered. "Oh, do take care, papa!"

"But what can he do?" asked Jimmy, who had been listening anxiously to the professor's explanation. "What do you suggest, Sergeantson? You're the authentic spy catcher. How can you defeat the ghost of one?"

"I pass!" replied Sergeantson laconically. "Professor, the word's to you!"

Forsdyke looked genuinely worried.

"Of course I don't believe it, Lomax," he said. "But supposing—supposing there were something like you suggest. What could I do?"

The professor's eyes twinkled.

"Assuming the objective reality of our supposition, my dear Forsdyke," he replied, "I can think of only one effective counterstroke."

He held their interest for a moment in suspense.

"And that is——"

"To drop a bomb on the girl!"

"A bomb—on the girl," puzzled Jimmy slowly. "Why?"

"Because when you break the telephone receiver it doesn't matter what the fellow at the other end says. You can't hear!"

"But we can't get at her," said Sergeantson. "We don't even know who she is, or where. We should never find out—in time."

"That's just it," agreed the professor. "You would have no time. Assuming that a ghostly spy is haunting our friend Forsdyke, the moment he reads that schedule, or even indicates where it is, the spy reads it, too, and possibly communicates it instantaneously. As Forsdyke is going to do something with that schedule tomorrow morning, well"—he shrugged his shoulders—"my money would be on the ghost!"

"My God!" said Forsdyke, thoroughly alarmed, "if it's true—it's maddening! One can do nothing!"

"Nothing," agreed the professor. "There would be no time."

The men stared at each other, exasperated at the hopelessness of the problem. If—they scarcely dared admit it to their sanity—it really were the case?

Hetty startled them by a sudden cry.

"Didn't you hear? Didn't you hear?" she exclaimed. "Someone laughing at us—close behind! Oh, look! Look!" She pointed to empty space. "There he is again! Don't you see?"

She fainted in Jimmy's ready arms.

The next morning Hetty found her father already at breakfast.

"Well," he asked, his dry smile mildly sarcastic, "any more dreams?"

"Horrid!" she replied with a little shudder as she poured herself some coffee. "But I don't remember them."

"You will see the doctor today, young woman," observed her father in a tone which indicated his verdict on the happenings of the previous night.

Hetty was docility itself, a phenomenon not altogether lost on her experienced parent.

"Very well, papa," she agreed demurely. "What are you going to do this morning?"

"I am going to the office to get some papers."

"The papers?" She checked herself with a little frightened glance round the room.

Her father laughed—a good healthy commonsense laugh.

"The papers!" he said. "No more nonsense about ghosts, Hetty. I'm going to get the papers from my office and take them round to the conference. So now you know. And there's an automatic in the pocket of the automobile if anyone tries tricks on the way."

Hetty nodded her head sagely.

"Guess you've a place for me in that automobile, papa," she said. "I'll come with you to the office, wait while you get the papers, and go on with you to the conference building; and while you're there I'll go on to see that doctor. I shall be back in time to pick you up before you are finished with your old conference."

Her father saw no objection to this, was, in fact, secretly glad to have her under his eye as long as possible.

"Mind, no tricks about the doctor!" he said with an assumption of severity.

"Sure, papa!" was her equable reply.

A few minutes later saw them speeding through the keen air of a frosty morning toward Forsdyke's office. But the interior of the limousine was warm and Hetty, snug in her furs, looked a picture of young healthy beauty; looked——a memory came to Henry Forsdyke in a pang that brought a sigh. He thought of the professor's suggestion of last night. Of course the whole thing was absurd—but he wondered——

The car swung in to the sidewalk in front of the government building, stopped before the big doorway with the marble steps. Forsdyke got out.

"I shall be back in a few minutes," he said.

Hetty watched him go across the pavement, ascend the marble steps. He looked neither to right nor left. Then who was that with him? Hetty felt her heart stop. Who was that who passed into the doorway with him? No one had been on the steps—she was suddenly sure of it. Yet—her heart began to pump again—certainly two figures had passed through the swing doors! She sat chilled and paralyzed for the moment in which she visualized the memory of those two figures passing into the shadow of the interior; tried to think when she had first perceived the second. A certitude shot through her, a wild alarm.

She jumped to her feet and with a blind instinctive desire for a weapon pulled the automatic out of the pocket of the limousine and thrust it into her muff. A moment later she was running across the pavement and up the marble steps. The janitor pulled open the swing door for her.

She fixed him with excited eyes. "Who was that who came in with Mr. Forsdyke just now?" she asked breathlessly.

The janitor stared.

"No one, miss. Mr. Forsdyke was alone."

Alone! She repressed an impulse to scream out, dashed to the elevator, which had just come to rest after its descent. The attendant opened the gate at her approach.

"Did you take Mr. Forsdyke up just now?" she asked.

"Yes, miss."

"Was he alone?"

"Sure! He came in alone."

"Take me up!" She trembled so that she could scarcely stand. Her eyes closed in a sickening anxiety as she swayed back against the wall of the elevator.

She shot upward. Another moment and she found herself racing along the corridor to her father's rooms, twisting at the handle of the door.

She almost fell into the anteroom occupied by Jimmy Lomax. He jumped to his feet.

"Hetty!"

"Father!" She had scarcely breath enough for utterance. "Father! I must see father!"

"Hetty, you can't! He's busy in his private room. No one dare——"

"I must!" she gasped. "Quick! The ghost!"

He stared in astonishment. She dodged past him and flung open the door into the next room.

Henry Forsdyke was standing, checking over a sheaf of papers in his hand, in front of the swung-open wall of the room, now revealed as a safe divided into many compartments. Hetty perceived him at the first glance; perceived, standing at his side, a man with a sardonic mocking face and a scar over the right eye, who peered over his shoulder.

In a blind whirl of impulse she whipped out the automatic, rushed up close, and fired—into thin air!

Her father swung round on her in a burst of anger.

"Good God, Hetty, are you mad?"

She looked wildly at him.

"The ghost! The ghost!"

He laughed despite his genuine wrath. "What are you thinking of? You can't shoot a ghost!"

But Hetty had sunk onto a chair and was sobbing hysterically.

In the luxuriously furnished room in Berlin Kranz was speaking excitedly into the telephone.

"*Excellenz!*" he called. "*Excellenz!* Are you there? Quickly! . . . Karl says he will tell us in ten minutes!" He glanced toward the girl sleeping in the big chair. "Quickly!"

He listened for a moment and then put down the receiver with a satisfied air. He rose from his seat and began to pace nervously up and down the room. From time to time he threw a glance at the still figure stretched back among the cushions. She slept with a regular deep breathing. He listened anxiously, alert for any change.

The minutes passed, slowly enough to his impatience. He looked at his watch. It marked ten minutes of four. A thought occurred to him—he amplified it deliberately, to occupy his mind. Ten minutes of four! What time would it be in Washington? Six hours—ten minutes of ten in the morning. What would be happening at ten minutes of ten? What was Karl looking at?

The raucous hoot of an automobile horn startled him out of these meditations. He ran to the window, looked out. A familiar motorcar was drawing up by the pavement. His Excellency had lost no time!

A few moments later the dreaded chief stood in the room, formidable still despite his dwarfed appearance in the great fur coat turned up to his ears. The clipped white mustache bristled more than ever, it seemed, as he glared at Kranz through the pince-nez with a ferocity that was but the expression of his excitement.

"Yes!" he cried ere the door had closed after him. "What has happened? Speak, man!"

"Nothing yet, *Excellenz!*" Kranz hastened to assure him. "The girl swooned off suddenly at about a quarter of four. I have not let her out of my sight since last night. And then Karl spoke. He said—and it sounded as though he meant it—that he would give us the information in ten minutes. I telephoned you at once."

"Right! Quite right!" snapped His Excellency. "Ten minutes! The time must be up."

"Good afternoon, *Excellenz!*"

The old man jumped. The familiar mocking voice came from the lifeless mask of the sleeping girl. "Your suggestion was correct—Forsdyke! He is taking me to it now!" The derisive laugh rang out, uncanny in the silent room. "Patience for a few minutes!"

The old man made an effort of his will.

"Where are you now, Karl?" he asked.

"In a motorcar. Funny story—tell you later. Patience." The voice sounded far away and faint. "Look to the girl, Kranz. Not breathing properly. Can't speak—if—power—fails."

Kranz went to the sleeping girl. Her head had fallen forward and she was breathing stertorously. He rearranged the cushions, posed her head so that she once more breathed deeply and evenly.

They waited in a tense silence. The her lips moved again.

"Listen—now! Take it down as I read it!" Karl's voice rang with an unholy triumph.

"Quick, Kranz! Write!" commanded the old man.

His subordinate leaped to the table, settled himself, pen in hand. The girl's lips trembled in the commencement of speech, opened.

"Schedule of Sailings of American Army to Europe!" began the triumphant voice.

There was a pause.

"Yes—yes!" cried the old man impatiently. "Go on!"

"Numbers for March——" Karl Wertheimer's voice came with a curious deliberation as though he were memorizing figures. "Ah-h!" The voice broke in a wild unearthly cry that froze the blood.

They waited. There was no sound. They heard their hearts beat in a growing terror.

Suddenly the old man spoke:

"The girl! Look, Kranz! She does not breathe!"

Kranz sprang to her, lifted her hand, bent suddenly down to her face. He looked up with the eyes of a balked demon.

"She is dead!" he said hoarsely.

He turned to her again and with a frenzied rage tore away the clothes from her throat and chest. Just over her heart was a small round dark spot staining the unbroken skin.

"Look!" he cried.

The old man peered down at the mark and round the room.

"What has happened?" The wild cry quavered with the terror of the unseen.

No answer came from the silence.

THE MASTER OF THE HOUNDS

ALGIS BUDRYS

The white sand road led off the state highway through the sparse pines. There were no tire tracks in the road, but, as Malcolm turned the car onto it, he noticed the footprints of dogs, or perhaps of only one dog, running along the middle of the road toward the combined general store and gas station at the intersection.

"Well, it's far enough away from everything, all right," Virginia said. She was long and lean and had dusty black hair. Her face was long, with high cheekbones. They had been married ten years ago, when she had been girlish and very slightly plump.

"Yes," Malcolm said. Just days ago, when he'd been turned down for a Guggenheim Fellowship that he'd expected to get, he had quit his job at the agency and made plans to spend the summer, somewhere as cheap as possible, working out with himself whether he was really an artist or just had a certain commercial talent. Now they were here.

He urged the car up the road, following a line of infrequent and weathered utility poles that carried a single strand of power line. The real-estate agent already had told them there were no telephones. Malcolm had taken that to be a positive feature, but somehow he did not like the looks of that one thin wire sagging from pole to pole. The wheels of the car sank in deeply on either side of the dog prints, which he followed like a row of bread crumbs through a forest.

Several hundred yards farther along they came to a sign at the top of a hill:

ALGIS BUDRYS

MARINE VIEW SHORES! NEW JERSEY'S NEWEST,
FASTEST-GROWING RESIDENTIAL COMMUNITY.
WELCOME HOME! FROM $9,990. NO DN PYT FOR VETS.

Below them was a wedge of land—perhaps ten acres altogether—that pushed out into Lower New York Bay. The road became a gullied, yellow gravel street, pointing straight toward the water and ending in three concrete posts, one of which had fallen and left a gap wide enough for a car to blunder through. Beyond that was a low drop-off where the bay ran northward to New York City and, in the other direction, toward the open Atlantic.

On either side of the roughed-out street, the bulldozed land was overgrown with scrub oak and sumac. Along the street were rows of roughly rectangular pits—some with half-finished foundation walls in them—piles of excavated clay, and lesser quantities of sand, sparsely weed-grown and washed into ravaged mounds like Dakota Territory. Here and there were houses with half-completed frames, now silvered and warped.

There were only two exceptions to the general vista. At the end of the street, two identically designed, finished houses faced each other. One looked shabby. The lot around it was free of scrub, but weedy and unsodded. Across the street from it stood a house in excellent repair. Painted a charcoal gray and roofed with dark asphalt shingles, it sat in the center of a meticulously green and level lawn, which was in turn surrounded by a wire fence approximately four feet tall and splendid with fresh aluminum paint. False shutters, painted stark white, flanked high, narrow windows along the side Malcolm could see. In front of the house, a line of whitewashed stones the size of men's heads served as curbing. There wasn't a thing about the house and its surroundings that couldn't have been achieved with a straight string, a handsaw, and a three-inch brush. Malcolm saw a chance to cheer things up. "There now, Marthy!" he said to Virginia. "I've led you safe and sound through the howlin' forest to a snug home right in the shadder of brave Fort Defiance."

"It's orderly," Virginia said. "I'll bet it's no joke, keeping up a place like that out here."

As Malcolm was parking the car parallel to where the curb would have been in front of their house, a pair of handsome young Doberman pinschers came out from behind the gray house across the street and stood on the lawn with their noses just short of the fence, looking out. They did not bark. There was no movement at the window, and no one came out into the yard. The dogs simply stood there, watching, as Malcolm walked over the clay to his door.

The house was furnished—that is to say, there were chairs in the living room, although there was no couch, and a chromium-and-plastic dinette set in the area off the kitchen. Though one of the bedrooms was completely empty, there was a bureau and a bed in the other. Malcolm walked through the house quickly and went back out to the car to get the luggage and groceries. Nodding toward the dogs, he said to Virginia, "Well! The latest thing in iron deer." He felt he had to say something light, because Virginia was staring across the street.

He knew perfectly well, as most people do and he assumed Virginia did, that Doberman pinschers are nervous, untrustworthy, and vicious. At the same time, he and his wife did have to spend the whole summer here. He could guess how much luck they'd have trying to get their money back from the agent now.

"They look streamlined like that because their ears and tails are trimmed when they're puppies," Virginia said. She picked up a bag of groceries and carried it into the house.

When Malcolm had finished unloading the car, he slammed the trunk lid shut. Although they hadn't moved until then, the Dobermans seemed to regard this as a sign. They turned smoothly, the arc of one inside the arc of the other, and, keeping formation, trotted out of sight behind the gray house.

Malcolm helped Virginia put things away in the closets and in the lone bedroom bureau. There was enough to do to keep both of them busy for several hours, and it was dusk when Malcolm happened to look out through the living-room window. After he had glanced that way, he stopped.

Across the street, floodlights had come on at the four corners of the gray house. They poured illumination downward in cones that lighted the entire yard. A crippled man was walking just inside the fence, his legs stiff and his body bent forward from the waist, as he gripped the projecting handles of two crutch-canes that supported his weight at the elbows. As Malcolm watched, the man took a precise square turn at the corner of the fence and began walking along the front of his property. Looking straight ahead, he moved regularly and purposefully, his shadow thrown out through the fence behind the composite shadow of the two dogs walking at his pace immediately ahead of him. None of them was looking in Malcolm's direction. He watched as the man made another turn, followed the fence toward the back of his property, and disappeared behind the house.

Later Virginia served cold cuts in the little dining alcove. Putting the house in order seemed to have a good effect on her morale.

"Listen, I think we're going to be all right here, don't you?" Malcolm said.

"Look," she said reasonably, "any place you can get straightened out is fine with me."

This wasn't quite the answer he wanted. He had been sure in New York that the summer would do it—that in four months a man would come to *some* decision. He had visualized a house for them by the ocean, in a town with a library and a movie and other diversions. It had been a shock to discover how expensive summer rentals were and how far in advance you had to book them. When the last agency they saw described this place to them and told them how low the rent was, Malcolm had jumped at it immediately. But so had Virginia, even though there wasn't anything to do for distraction. In fact, she had made a point of asking the agent again about the location of the house, and the agent, a fat, gray man with ashes on his shirt, had said earnestly, "Mrs. Lawrence, if you're looking for a place where nobody will bother your husband from working I can't think of anything better." Virginia had nodded decisively.

It had bothered her, his quitting the agency; he could understand that. Still, he wanted her to be happy, because he expected to be surer of what he wanted to do by the end of the summer. She was looking at him steadily now. He cast about for something to offer her that would interest her and change the mood between them. Then he remembered the scene he had witnessed earlier that evening. He told her about the man and his dogs, and this did raise her eyebrows.

"Do you remember the real-estate agent telling us anything about him?" she asked. "I don't."

Malcolm, searching through his memory, did recall that the agent had mentioned a custodian they could call on if there were any problems. At the time he had let it pass, because he couldn't imagine either agent or custodian really caring. Now he realized how dependent he and Virginia were out here if it came to things like broken plumbing or bad wiring, and the custodian's importance altered accordingly. "I guess he's the caretaker," he said.

"Oh."

"It makes sense—all this property has got to be worth something. If they didn't have someone here, people would just carry stuff away or come and camp or something."

"I suppose they would. I guess the owners let him live here rent-free, and with those dogs he must do a good job."

"He'll get to keep it for a while, too," Malcolm said. "Whoever started to build here was a good ten years ahead of himself. I can't see anybody buying into these places until things have gotten completely jammed up closer to New York."

"So, he's holding the fort," Virginia said, leaning casually over the table to put a dish down before him. She glanced over his shoulder toward the living room window, widened her eyes, and automatically touched the neckline of her housecoat, and then snorted at herself.

"Look, he can't possibly see in here," Malcolm said. "The living room, yes, but to look in here he'd have to be standing in the far corner of his yard. And he's back inside his house." He turned his head to look, and it was indeed true, except that one of the dogs was standing at that corner looking toward their house, eyes glittering. Then its head seemed to melt into a new shape, and it was looking down the road. It pivoted, moved a few steps away from the fence, turned, soared, landed in the street, and set off. Then, a moment later, it came back down the street running side by side with its companion, whose jaws were lightly pressed together around the rolled-over neck of a small paper bag. The dogs trotted together companionably and briskly, their flanks rubbing against one another, and when they were a few steps from the fence they leaped over it in unison and continued across the lawn until they were out of Malcolm's range of vision.

"For heaven's sake! He lives all alone with those dogs!" Virginia said.

Malcolm turned quickly back to her. "How do you come to think that?"

"Well, it's pretty plain. You saw what they were doing out there just now. They're his servants. He can't get around himself, so they run errands for him. If he had a wife, she would do it."

"Did you notice how happy they were?" Virginia asked. "There was no need for that other dog to go meet its friend. But it wanted to. They can't be anything but happy." Then she looked at Malcolm, and he saw the old, studying reserve coming back into her eyes.

"For Pete's sake! They're only dogs—what do they know about anything?" Malcolm said.

"They know about happiness," Virginia said. "They know what they do in life."

Malcolm lay awake for a long time that night. He started by thinking about how good the summer was going to be, living here and working, and then he thought about the agency and about why he didn't seem to have the kind of shrewd, limited intuition that let a man do advertising work easily. At about four in the morning he wondered if perhaps he wasn't frightened, and had been frightened for a long time. None of this kind of thinking was new to him, and he knew that it would take him until late afternoon the following day to reach the point where he was feeling pretty good about himself.

When Virginia tried to wake him early the next morning he asked her to please leave him alone. At two in the afternoon, she brought him a cup of coffee and shook his shoulder. After a while, he walked out to the kitchen in his pajama pants and found that she had scrambled up some eggs for the two of them.

"What are your plans for the day?" Virginia said when he had finished eating.

He looked up. "Why?"

"Well, while you were sleeping, I put all your art things in the front bedroom. I think it'll make a good studio. With all your gear in there now, you can be pretty well set up by this evening."

At times she was so abrupt that she shocked him. It upset him that she might have been thinking that he wasn't planning to do anything at all today. "Look," he said, "you know I like to get the feel of a new thing."

"I know that. I didn't set anything up in there. I'm no artist. I just moved it all in."

When Malcolm had sat for a while without speaking, Virginia cleared away their plates and cups and went into the bedroom. She came out wearing a dress, and she had combed her hair and put on lipstick. "Well, you do what you want to," she said. "I'm going to go across the street and introduce myself."

A flash of irritability hit him, but then he said, "If you'll wait a minute, I'll get dressed and go with you. We might as well both meet him."

He got up and went back to the bedroom for a T-shirt and blue jeans and a pair of loafers. He could feel himself beginning to react to pressure. Pressure always made him bind up; it looked to him as if Virginia had already shot the day for him.

They were standing at the fence, on the narrow strip of lawn between it and the row of whitewashed stones, and nothing was happening. Malcolm saw that although there was a gate in the fence, there was no break in the little grass border opposite it. And there was no front walk. The lawn was lush and all one piece, as if the house had been lowered onto it by helicopter. He began to look closely at the ground just inside the fence, and when he saw the regular pockmarks of the man's crutches, he was comforted.

"Do you see any kind of bell or anything?" Virginia asked.

"No."

"You'd think the dogs would bark."

"I'd just as soon they didn't."

"Will you look?" she said, fingering the gate latch. "The paint's hardly scuffed. I'll bet he hasn't been out of his yard all summer." Her touch rattled the gate lightly, and at that the two dogs came out from behind the house. One of them stopped, turned, and went back. The other dog came and stood by the fence, close enough for them to hear its breathing, and watched them with its head cocked alertly.

The front door of the house opened. At the doorway there was a wink of metal crutches, and then the man came out and stood on his front steps. When he had satisfied himself as to who they were, he nodded, smiled, and came toward them. The other dog walked beside him. Malcolm noticed that the dog at the fence did not distract himself by looking back at his master.

The man moved swiftly, crossing the ground with nimble swings of his body. His trouble seemed to be not in the spine, but in the legs themselves, for he was trying to help himself along with them. It could not be called walking, but it could not be called total helplessness either.

Although the man seemed to be in his late fifties, he had not gone to seed any more than his property had. He was wiry and clean-boned, and the skin on his face was tough and tanned. Around his small blue eyes and at the corners of his thin lips were many fine, deep-etched wrinkles. His yellowish-white hair was brushed straight back from his temples in the classic British military manner. And he even had a slight mustache. He was wearing a tweed jacket with leather patches at the elbow, which seemed a little warm for this kind of day, and a light flannel, pale-gray shirt with a pale-blue bow tie. He stopped at the fence, rested his elbows on the crutches, and held out a firm hand with short nails the color of old bones.

"How do you do," he said pleasantly, his manner polished and well-bred. "I have been looking forward to meeting my new neighbors. I am Colonel Ritchey." The dogs stood motionless, one to each side of him, their sharp black faces pointing outward.

"How do you do," Virginia said. "We are Malcolm and Virginia Lawrence."

"I'm very happy to meet you," Colonel Ritchey said. "I was prepared to believe Cortelyou would fail to provide anyone this season."

Virginia was smiling. "What beautiful dogs," she said. "I was watching them last night."

"Yes. Their names are Max and Moritz. I'm very proud of them."

As they prattled on, exchanging pleasantries, Malcolm wondered why the Colonel had referred to Cortelyou, the real-estate agent, as a provider. There was something familiar, too, about the colonel.

Virginia said, "You're the famous Colonel Ritchey."

Indeed he was, Malcolm now realized, remembering the big magazine series that had appeared with the release of the movie several years before.

Colonel Ritchey smiled with no trace of embarrassment. "I am the famous Colonel Ritchey, but you'll notice I certainly don't look much like that charming fellow in the motion picture."

"What in hell are you doing *here*?" Malcolm asked.

Ritchey turned his attention to him. "One has to live somewhere, you know."

Virginia said immediately, "I was watching the dogs last night, and they seemed to do very well for you. I imagine it's pleasant having them to rely on."

"Yes, it is, indeed. They're quite good to me, Max and Moritz. But it is much better with people here now. I had begun to be quite disappointed in Cortelyou."

Malcolm began to wonder whether the agent would have had the brass to call Ritchey a custodian if the colonel had been within earshot.

"Come in, please," the colonel was saying. The gate latch resisted him momentarily, but he rapped it sharply with the heel of one palm and then lifted it. "Don't be concerned about Max and Moritz—they never do anything they're not told."

"Oh, I'm not the least bit worried about them," Virginia said.

"Ah, to some extent you should have been," the colonel said. "Dobermans are not to be casually trusted, you know. It takes many months before one can be at all confident in dealing with them."

"But you trained them yourself, didn't you?" Virginia said.

"Yes, I did," Colonel Ritchey said, with a pleased smile. "From imported pups." The voice in which he now spoke to the dogs was forceful, but as calm as his manner had been to Virginia. "Kennel," he said, and Max and Moritz stopped looking at Malcolm and Virginia and smoothly turned away.

The colonel's living room, which was as neat as a sample, contained beautifully cared-for, somewhat old-fashioned furniture. The couch, with its needlepoint upholstery and carved framing, was the sort of thing Malcolm would have expected in a lady's living room. Angling out from one wall was a Morris chair, placed so that a man might relax and gaze across the street or, with a turn of his head, rest his eyes on the distant lights of New York. Oil paintings in heavy gilded frames depicted landscapes, great eye-stretching vistas of rolling, open country. The furniture in the room seemed sparse to Malcolm until it occurred to him that the colonel needed extra clearance to get around in and had no particular need to keep additional chairs for visitors.

"Please do sit down," the colonel said. "I shall fetch some tea to refresh us."

When he had left the room, Virginia said, "Of all people! Neighborly, too."

Malcolm nodded. "Charming," he said.

The colonel entered holding a silver tray perfectly steady, its edges grasped between his thumbs and forefingers, his other fingers curled around each of the projecting black-rubber handgrips of his crutches. He brought tea on the tray and, of all things, homemade cookies. "I must apologize for the tea service," he said, "but it seems to be the only one I have."

When the colonel offered the tray, Malcolm saw that the utensils were made of the common sort of sheet metal used to manufacture food cans. Looking down now into his cup, he saw it had been enameled over its original tinplate, and he realized that the whole thing had been literally made from a tin can. The teapot—handle, spout, vented lid, and all—was the same. "Be damned—you made this for yourself at the prison camp, didn't you?"

"As a matter of fact, I did, yes. I was really quite proud of my handiwork at the time, and it still serves. Somehow, living as I do, I've never brought myself to replace it. It's amazing, the fuddy-duddy skills one needs in a camp and how important they become to one. I find myself repainting these poor objects periodically and still taking as much smug pleasure in it as I did when that attitude was quite necessary. One is allowed to do these things in my position, you know. But I do hope my *ersatz* Spode isn't uncomfortably hot in your fingers."

Virginia smiled. "Well, of course, it's trying to be." Malcolm was amazed. He hadn't thought Virginia still remembered how to act so coquettish. She hadn't grown apart from the girl who'd always attracted a lot of attention at other people's gallery openings; she had simply put that part of herself away somewhere else.

Colonel Ritchey's blue eyes were twinkling in response. He turned to Malcolm. "I must say, it will be delightful to share this summer with someone as charming as Mrs. Lawrence."

"Yes," Malcolm said, preoccupied now with the cup, which was distressing his fingers with both heat and sharp edges. "At least, I've always been well satisfied with her," he added.

"I've been noticing the inscription here," Virginia said quickly, indicating the meticulous freehand engraving on the tea tray. She read out loud, " 'To Colonel David N. Ritchey, R.M.E., from his fellow officers at *Oflag* XXXI*b*, on the occasion of their liberation, May 14, 1945. Had he not been there to lead them, many would not have been present to share of this heartfelt token.' " Virginia's eyes shone, as she looked up at the colonel. "They must all have been very fond of you."

"Not all," the colonel said, with a slight smile. "I was senior officer over a very mixed bag. Mostly younger officers gathered from every conceivable branch. No followers at all—just budding leaders, all personally responsible for having surrendered once already, some apathetic, others desperate. Some useful, some not. It was my job to weld them into a disciplined, responsive body, to choose whom we must keep safe and who was best suited to keeping the Jerries on the jump. And we were in, of course, from the time of Dunkirk to the last days of the war, with the strategic situation in the camp constantly changing in various ways. All most of them understood was tactics—when they understood at all."

The colonel grimaced briefly, then smiled again. "The tray was presented by the survivors, of course. They'd had a tame Jerry pinch it out of the commandant's sideboard a few days earlier, in plenty of time to get the inscription on. But even the inscription hints that not all survived."

"It wasn't really like the movie, was it?" Virginia said.

"No, and yet——" Ritchey shrugged, as if remembering a time when he had accommodated someone on a matter of small importance. "That was a question of dramatic values, you must realize, and the need to tell an interesting and exciting story in terms recognizable to a civilian audience. Many of the incidents in the motion picture are literally true—they simply didn't happen in the context shown. The Christmas tunnel was quite real, obviously. I did promise the men I'd get at least one of them home for Christmas if they'd pitch in and dig it. But it wasn't a serious promise, and they knew it wasn't. Unlike the motion picture actor, I was not being fervent; I was being ironic.

"It was late in the war. An intelligent man's natural desire would be to avoid risk and wait for liberation. A great many of them felt exactly that way. In fact, many of them had turned civilian in their own minds and were talking about their careers outside, their families—all that sort of thing. So by couching in sarcasm trite words about Christmas tunnels, I was reminding them what and where they still were. The tactics worked quite well. Through devices of that sort, I was able to keep them from going to seed and coming out no use to anyone." The colonel's expression grew absent. "Some of them called me 'the Shrew,'" he murmured. "*That* was in the movie, too, but they were all shown smiling when they said it."

"But it was your duty to hold them all together any way you could," Virginia said encouragingly.

Ritchey's face twisted into a spasm of tension so fierce that there might have been strychnine in his tea. But it was gone at once. "Oh, yes, yes, I held them together. By lying and cajoling and tricking them. But the expenditure of energy was enormous. And demeaning. It ought not to have made any difference that we were cut off from higher authority. If we had all still been home, there was not a man among the prisoners who would have dared not jump to my simplest command. But in the camp they could shilly-shally and evade; they could settle down into little private ambitions. People will do that. People will not hold true to common purposes unless they are shown discipline." The colonel's uncompromising glance went from Virginia to Malcolm. "It's no good telling people what they ought to do. The only surety is in being in a position to tell people what they *must* do."

"Get some armed guards to back you up. That the idea, Colonel? Get permission from the Germans to set up your own machine-gun towers inside the camp?" Malcolm liked working things out to the point of absurdity.

The colonel appraised him imperturbably. "I was never quite that much of my own man in Germany. But there is a little story I must tell you. It's not altogether off the point." He settled back, at ease once again.

"You may have been curious about Max and Moritz. The Germans, as you know, have always been fond of training dogs to perform all sorts of entertaining and useful things. During the war the Jerries were very much given to using Dobermans for auxiliary guard duty at the various prisoner-of-war camps. In action, Mr. Lawrence, or simply in view, a trained dog is far more terrifying than any soldier with a machine pistol. It takes an animal to stop a man without hesitation, no matter if the man is cursing or praying.

"Guard dogs at each camp were under the charge of a man called the *Hundführer*--the master of the hounds, if you will—whose function, after establishing himself with the dogs as their master and director, was to follow a few simple rules and to take the dogs to wherever they were needed. The dogs had been taught certain patrol routines. It was necessary only for the *Hundführer* to give simple commands such as 'Search' or 'Arrest,' and the dogs would know what to do. Once we had seen them do it, they were very much on our minds, I assure you.

"A Doberman, you see, has no conscience, being a dog. And a trained Doberman has no discretion. From the time he is a puppy, he is bent to whatever purpose has been preordained for him. And the lessons are painful—and autocratic. Once an order has been given, it must be enforced at all costs, for the dog must learn that all orders are to be obeyed unquestioningly. That being true, the dog must also learn immediately and irrevocably that only the orders from one particular individual are valid. Once a Doberman has been trained, there is no way to retrain it. When the American soldiers were seen coming, the Germans in their machine-gun towers threw down their weapons and tried to flee, but the dogs had to be shot. I watched from the hospital window, and I shall never forget how they continued to leap at the kennel fencing until the last one was dead. Their *Hundführer* had run away...."

Malcolm found that his attention was wandering, but Virginia asked, as if on cue, "How did you get into the hospital—was that the Christmas tunnel accident?"

"Yes," the colonel said to Virginia, gentleman to lady. "The sole purpose of the tunnel was, as I said, to give the men a focus of attention. The war was near enough its end. It would have been foolhardy to risk actual escape attempts. But we did the thing up brown, of course. We had a concealed shaft, a tunnel lined with bed slats, a trolley for getting to and from the tunnel entrance, fat lamps made from shoe blacking tins filled with margarine—all the normal appurtenances. The Germans at that stage were quite experienced in ferreting out this sort of operation, and the only reasonable assurance of continued progress was to work deeply and swiftly. Tunneling is always a calculated risk—the accounts of that sort of operation are biased in favor of the successes, of course.

"At any rate, by the end of November, some of the men were audibly thinking it was my turn to pitch in a bit, so one night I went down and began working. The shoring was as good as it ever was, and the conditions weren't any worse than normal. The air was breathable, and as long as one worked—ah—unclothed, and brushed down immediately on leaving the tunnel, the sand was not particularly damaging to one's skin. Clothing creates chafes in those circumstances. Sand burns coming to light at medical inspections were one of the surest signs that such an operation was under way.

"However that may be, I had been down there for about an hour and a half, and was about to start inching my way back up the tunnel feet first on the trolley like some Freudian symbol, when there was a fall of the tunnel roof that buried my entire chest. It did not cover my face, which was fortunate, and I clearly remember my first thought was that now none of the men would be able to feel the senior officer hadn't shared their physical tribulations. I discovered, at once, that the business of clearing the sand that had fallen was going to be extremely awkward. First, I had to scoop some extra clearance from the roof over my face. Handfuls of sand began falling directly on me, and all I could do about that was to thrash my head back and forth. I was becoming distinctly exasperated at that when there was another slight fall behind the original collapse. This time, the fat lamp attached to the shoring loosened from its fastenings and spilled across my thighs. The hot fat was quite painful. What made it rather worse was that the string wick was not extinguished by the fall, and accordingly, the entire lower part of my body between navel and knees, having been saturated with volatile fat. . . ." The colonel grimaced in embarrassment.

"Well, I was immediately in a very bad way, for there was nothing I could do about the fire until I had dug my way past the sand on my chest. In due course, I did indeed free myself and was able to push my way backward up the tunnel after extinguishing the flames. The men at the shaft head had seen no reason to become alarmed—tunnels always smell rather high and sooty, as you can imagine. But they did send a man down when I got near the entrance shaft and made myself heard.

"Of course, there was nothing to do but tell the Jerries, since we had no facilities whatever for concealing my condition or treating it. They put me in the camp hospital, and there I stayed until the end of the war with plenty of time to lie about and think my thoughts. I was even able to continue exercising some control over my men. I shouldn't be a bit surprised if that hadn't been in the commandant's mind all along. I think he had come to depend on my presence to moderate the behavior of the men.

"That is really almost the end of the story. We were liberated by the American Army, and the men were sent home. I stayed in military hospitals until I was well enough to travel home, and there I dwelt in hotels and played the retired, invalided officer. After that journalist's book was published and the dramatic rights were sold, I was called to Hollywood to be the technical adviser for the movie. I was rather grateful to accept the employment, frankly—an officer's pension is not particularly munificent—and what with selectively lending my name and services to various organizations while my name was still before the public, I was able to accumulate a sufficient nest egg.

"Of course, I cannot go back to England, where the Inland Revenue would relieve me of most of it, but having established a relationship with Mr. Cortelyou and acquired Max and Moritz, I am content. A man must make his way as best he can and do whatever is required for survival." The colonel cocked his head brightly and regarded Virginia and Malcolm. "Wouldn't you say?"

"Y—es," Virginia said slowly. Malcolm couldn't decide what the look on her face meant. He had never seen it before. Her eyes were shining, but wary. Her smile showed excitement and sympathy, but tension too. She seemed caught between two feelings.

"Quite!" the colonel said, smacking his hands together. "It is most important to me that you fully understand the situation." He pushed himself up to his feet and, with the same move, brought the crutches out smoothly and positioned them to balance him before he could fall. He stood leaning slightly forward, beaming. "Well, now, having heard my story, I imagine the objectives of this conversation are fully attained, and there is no need to detain you here further. I'll see you to the front gate."

"That won't be necessary," Malcolm said.

"I insist," the colonel said in what would have been a perfectly pleasant manner if he had added the animated twinkle to his eyes. Virginia was staring at him, blinking slowly.

"Please forgive us," she said. "We certainly hadn't meant to stay long enough to be rude. Thank you for the tea and cookies. They were very good."

"Not at all, my dear," the colonel said. "It's really quite pleasant to think of looking across the way, now and then, catching glimpses of someone so attractive at her domestic preoccupations. I cleaned up thoroughly after the last tenants, of course, but there are always little personal touches one wants to apply. And you will start some planting at the front of the house, won't you? Such little activities are quite precious to me—someone as charming as you, in her summer things, going about her little fussings and tendings, resting in the sun after weeding—that sort of thing. Yes, I expect a most pleasant summer. I assume there was never any question you wouldn't stay all summer. Cortelyou would hardly bother with anyone who could not afford to pay him that much. But little more, eh?" The urbane, shrewd look returned to the colonel's face. "Pinched resources and few ties, eh? Or what would you be doing here, if there were somewhere else to turn?"

"Well, good afternoon, Colonel," Virginia said with noticeable composure. "Let's go, Malcolm."

"Interesting conversation, Colonel," Malcolm said.

"Interesting and necessary, Mr. Lawrence," the colonel said, following them out onto the lawn. Virginia watched him closely as she moved toward the gate, and Malcolm noticed a little downward twitch at the corners of her mouth.

"Feeling a bit of a strain, Mrs. Lawrence?" the colonel asked solicitously. "Please believe that I shall be as considerate of your sensibilities as intelligent care of my own comfort will permit. It is not at all in my code to offer offense to a lady, and in any case—" the colonel smiled deprecatingly "—since the mishap of the Christmas tunnel, one might say the spirit is willing but. . . ." The colonel frowned down absently at his canes. "No, Mrs. Lawrence," he went on, shaking his head paternally, "is the flower the less for being breathed of? And is the cultivated flower, tended and nourished, not more fortunate than the wild rose that blushes unseen? Do not regret your present social situation too much, Mrs. Lawrence—some might find it enviable. Few things are more changeable than points of view. In the coming weeks your viewpoint might well change."

"Just what the hell are you saying to my wife?" Malcolm asked.

Virginia said quickly, "We can talk about it later."

The colonel smiled at Virginia. "Before you do that, I have something else to show Mr. Lawrence." He raised his voice slightly: "Max! Moritz! Here!"—and the dogs were there. "Ah, Mr. Lawrence, I would like to show you first how these animals respond, how discriminating they can be." He turned to one of the dogs. "Moritz," he said sharply, nodding toward Malcolm. "Kill."

Malcolm couldn't believe what he had heard. Then he felt a blow on his chest. The dog was on him, its hind legs making short, fast, digging sounds in the lawn as it pressed its body against him. It was inside the arc of his arms, and the most he could have done was to clasp it closer to him. He made a tentative move to pull his arms back and then push forward against its rib cage, but the minor shift in weight made him stumble, and he realized if he completed the gesture he would fall. All this happened in a very short time, and then the dog touched open lips with him. Having done that, it dropped down and went back to stand beside Colonel Ritchey and Max.

"You see, Mr. Lawrence?" the colonel asked conversationally. "A dog does not respond to literal meaning. It is conditioned. It is trained to perform a certain action when it hears a certain sound. The cues one teaches a dog with pain and patience are not necessarily cues an educated organism can understand. Pavlov rang a bell and a dog salivated. Is a bell food? If he had rung a different bell, or said, 'Food, doggie,' there would have been no response. So, when I speak in a normal tone, rather than at command pitch, 'kill' does not mean 'kiss,' even to Moritz. It means nothing to him—unless I raise my voice. And I could just as easily have conditioned him to perform that sequence in association with some other command—such as, oh, say, 'gingersnaps'—but then you might not have taken the point of my little, instructive jest. There is no way anyone but myself can operate these creatures. Only when I command do they respond. And now you respond, eh, Mr. Lawrence? I dare say.... Well, good day. As I said, you have things to do."

They left through the gate, which the colonel drew shut behind them. "Max," he said, "watch," and the dog froze in position. "Moritz, come." The colonel turned, and he and the other dog crossed the lawn and went into his house.

Malcolm and Virginia walked at a normal pace back to the rented house, Malcolm matching his step to Virginia's. He wondered if she wasn't being so deliberate because she wasn't sure what the dog would do if she ran. It had been a long time since Virginia hadn't been sure of something.

In the house, Virginia made certain the door was shut tight, and then she went to sit in the chair that faced away from the window. "Would you make me some coffee, please?" she said.

"All right, sure. Take a few minutes. Catch your breath a little."

"A few minutes is what I need," she said. "Yes, a few minutes, and everything will be fine." When Malcolm returned with the coffee, she continued, "He's got some kind of string on Cortelyou, and I bet those people at the store down at the corner aren't too happy about those dogs walking in and out of there all the time. He's got us. We're locked up."

"Now, wait," Malcolm said, "there's the whole state of New Jersey out there, and he can't——"

"Yes, he can. If he thinks he can get away with it, and he's got good reasons for thinking he can. Take it on faith. There's no bluff in *him*."

"Well, look," he said, "just what can he do to us?"

"Any damn thing he pleases."

"That can't be right." Malcolm frowned. "He's got us pretty well scared right now, but we ought to be able to work out some way of——"

Virginia said tightly, "The dog's still there, right?" Malcolm nodded. "Okay," she said. "What did it feel like when he hit you? It looked awful. It looked like he was going to drive you clear onto your back. Did it feel that way? What did you *think?*"

"Well, he's a pretty strong animal," Malcolm said. "But, to tell you the truth, I didn't have time to believe it. You know, a man just saying 'kill' like that is a pretty hard thing to believe. Especially just after tea and cookies."

"He's very shrewd," Virginia said. "I can see why he had the camp guards running around in circles. He deserved to have a book written about him."

"All right, and then they should have thrown him into a padded cell."

"Tried to throw," Virginia amended.

"Oh, come on. This is his territory, and he dealt the cards before we even knew we were playing. But all he is is a crazy old cripple. If he wants to buffalo some people in a store and twist a two-bit real-estate salesman around his finger, fine—if he can get away with it. But he doesn't own us. We're not in his army."

"We're inside his prison camp," Virginia said.

"Now, look," Malcolm said. "When we walk in Cortelyou's door and tell him we know all about the colonel, there's not going to be any trouble about getting the rent back. We'll find someplace else, or we'll go back to the city. But whatever we do to get out of this, it's going to work out a lot smoother if the two of us think about it. It's not like you to be sitting there and spending a lot of time on how we can't win."

"Well, Malcolm. Being a prisoner certainly brings out your initiative. Here you are, making noises just like a senior officer. Proposing escape committees and everything."

Malcolm shook his head. Now of all times, when they needed each other so much, she wouldn't let up. The thing to do was to move too fast for her.

"All right," he said, "let's get in the car." There was just the littlest bit of sweat on his upper lip.

"*What?*" He had her sitting up straight in the chair, at least. "Do you imagine that the dog will let us get anywhere near the car?"

"You want to stay here? All right. Just keep the door locked. I'm going to try it, and once I'm out I'm going to come back here with a nice healthy state cop carrying a nice healthy riot gun. And we're either going to do something about the colonel and those two dogs, or we're at least going to move you and our stuff out of here."

He picked up the car keys, stepped through the front door very quickly, and began to walk straight for the car. The dog barked sharply, once. The front door of Ritchey's house opened immediately, and Ritchey called out, "Max! Hold!" The dog on the lawn was over the fence and had its teeth thrust carefully around Malcolm's wrist before he could take another eight steps, even though he had broken into a run. Both the dog and Malcolm stood very still. The dog was breathing shallowly and quietly, its eyes shining. Ritchey and Moritz walked as far as the front fence. "Now, Mr. Lawrence," Ritchey said, "in a moment I am going to call to Max, and he is to bring you with him. Do not attempt to hold back, or you will lacerate your wrist. Max! Bring here!"

Malcolm walked steadily toward the colonel. By some smooth trick of his neck, Max was able to trot alongside him without shifting his grip. "Very good, Max," Ritchey said soothingly when they had reached the fence. "Loose now," and the dog let go of Malcolm's wrist. Malcolm and Ritchey looked into each other's eyes across the fence, in the darkening evening. "Now, Mr. Lawrence," Ritchey said, "I want you to give me your keys." Malcolm held out the keys, and Ritchey put them into his pocket. "Thank you." He seemed to reflect on what he was going to say next, as a teacher might reflect on his reply to a child who has asked why the sky is blue. "Mr. Lawrence, I want you to understand the situation. As it happens, I also want a three-pound can of Crisco. If you will please give me all the money in your pocket, this will simplify matters."

"I don't have any money on me," Malcolm said. "Do you want me to go in the house and get some?"

"No, Mr. Lawrence, I'm not a thief. I'm simply restricting your radius of action in one of the several ways I'm going to do so. Please turn out your pockets."

Malcolm turned out his pockets.

"All right, Mr. Lawrence, if you will hand me your wallet and your address book and the thirty-seven cents, they will all be returned to you whenever you have a legitimate use for them." Ritchey put the items away in the pockets of his jacket. "Now, a three-pound can of Crisco is ninety-eight cents. Here is a dollar bill. Max will walk with you to the corner grocery store, and you will buy the Crisco for me and bring it back. It is too much for a dog to carry in a bag, and it is three days until my next monthly delivery of staples. At the store you will please tell them that it will not be necessary for them to come here with monthly deliveries any longer—that you will be in to do my shopping for me from now on. I expect you to take a minimum amount of time to accomplish all this and to come back with my purchase, Mr. Lawrence. Max!" The colonel nodded toward Malcolm. "Guard. Store." The dog trembled and whined. "Don't stand still, Mr. Lawrence. Those commands are incompatible until you start toward the store. If you fail to move, he will grow increasingly tense. Please go now. Moritz and I will keep Mrs. Lawrence good company until you return."

The store consisted of one small room in the front of a drab house. On unpainted pine shelves were brands of goods that Malcolm had never heard of. "Oh! You're with one of those nice dogs," the tired, plump woman behind the counter said, leaning down to pat Max, who had approached her for that purpose. It seemed to Malcolm that the dog was quite mechanical about it and was pretending to itself that nothing caressed it at all. He looked around the place, but he couldn't see anything or anyone that offered any prospect of alliance with him.

"Colonel Ritchey wants a three-pound can of Crisco," he said, bringing the name out to check the reaction.

"Oh, you're helping him?"

"You could say that."

"Isn't he brave?" the woman said in low and confidential tones, as if concerned that the dog could overhear. "You know, there are some people who would think you should feel sorry for a man like that, but I say it would be a sin to do so. Why, he gets along just fine, and he's got more pride and spunk than any whole man I've ever seen. Makes a person proud to know him. You know, I think it's just wonderful the way these dogs come and fetch little things for him. But I'm glad he's got somebody to look out for him now. 'Cept for us, I don't think he sees anybody from one year to the next—'cept summers, of course."

She studied Malcolm closely. "You're summer people too, aren't you? Well, glad to have you, if you're doin' some good for the colonel. Those people last year were a shame. Just moved out one night in September, and neither the colonel nor me or my husband seen hide nor hair of them since. Owed the colonel a month's rent, he said when we was out there."

"Is he the landlord?" Malcolm asked.

"Oh, sure, yes. He owns a lot of land around here. Bought it from the original company after it went bust."

"Does he own this store, too?"

"Well, we lease it from him now. Used to own it, but we sold it to the company and leased it from them. Oh, we was all gonna be rich. My husband took the money from the land and bought a lot across the street and was gonna set up a real big gas station there—figured to be real shrewd—but you just can't get people to live out here. I mean, it isn't as if this was *ocean*-front property. But the colonel now, he's got a head on his shoulders. Value's got to go up someday, and he's just gonna hold on until it does."

The dog was getting restless, and Malcolm was worried about Virginia. He paid for the can of Crisco, and he and Max went back up the sand road in the dark. There really, honestly, didn't seem to be much else to do.

At his front door, he stopped, sensing that he should knock. When Virginia let him in, he saw that she had changed to shorts and a halter. "Hello," she said, and then stood aside quietly for him and Max. The colonel, sitting pertly forward on one of the chairs, looked up. "Ah, Mr. Lawrence, you're a trifle tardy, but the company has been delightful, and the moments seemed to fly."

Malcolm looked at Virginia. In the past couple of years, a little fat had accumulated above her knees, but she still had long, good legs. Colonel Ritchey smiled at Malcolm. "It's a rather close evening. I simply suggested to Mrs. Lawrence that I certainly wouldn't be offended if she left me for a moment and changed into something more comfortable."

It seemed to Malcolm that she could have handled that. But apparently she hadn't.

"Here's your Crisco," Malcolm said. "The change is in the bag."

"Thank you very much," the colonel said. "Did you tell them about the grocery deliveries?"

Malcolm shook his head. "I don't remember. I don't think so. I was busy getting an earful about how you owned them, lock, stock and barrel."

"Well, no harm. You can tell them tomorrow."

"Is there going to be some set time for me to run your errands every day, Colonel? Or are you just going to whistle whenever something comes up?"

"Ah, yes. You're concerned about interruptions in your mood. Mrs. Lawrence told me you were some sort of artist. I'd wondered at your not shaving this morning." The colonel paused and then went on crisply, "I'm sure we'll shake down into whatever routine suits best. It always takes a few days for individuals to hit their stride as a group. After that, it's quite easy—regular functions, established duties, that sort of thing. A time to rise and wash, a time to work, a time to sleep. Everything and everyone in his proper niche. Don't worry, Mr. Lawrence, you'll be surprised how comfortable it becomes. Most people find it a revelation." The colonel's gaze grew distant for a moment. "Some do not. Some are as if born on another planet, innocent of human nature. Dealing with that sort, there comes a point when one must cease to try; at the camp, I found that the energy for overall success depended on my admitting the existence of the individual failure. No, some do not respond. But we needn't dwell on what time will tell us."

Ritchey's eyes twinkled. "I have dealt previously with creative people. Most of them need to work with their hands; do stupid, dull, boring work that leaves their minds free to soar in spirals and yet forces them to stay away from their craft until the tension is nearly unbearable." The colonel waved in the direction of the unbuilt houses. "There's plenty to do. If you don't know how to use a hammer and saw as yet, I know how to teach that. And when from time to time I see you've reached the proper pitch of creative frustration, then you shall have what time off I judge will best serve you artistically. I think you'll be surprised how pleasingly you'll take to your studio. From what I gather from your wife, this may well be a very good experience for you."

Malcolm looked at Virginia. "Yes. Well, that's been bugging her for a long time. I'm glad she's found a sympathetic ear."

"Don't quarrel with your wife, Mr. Lawrence. That sort of thing wastes energy and creates serious morale problems." The colonel got to his feet and went to the door. "One thing no one could ever learn to tolerate in a fellow *Kriegie* was pettiness. That sort of thing was always weeded out. Come, Max. Come, Moritz. Good night." He left.

Malcolm went over to the door and put the chain on. "Well?" he said.

"All right, now, look——"

Malcolm held up one finger. "Hold it. Nobody likes a quarrelsome *Kriegie*. We're not going to fight. We're going to talk and we're going to think." He found himself looking at her halter and took his glance away. Virginia blushed.

"I just want you to know it was exactly the way he described it," she said. "He said he wouldn't think it impolite if I left him alone in the living room while I went to change. And I wasn't telling him our troubles. We were talking about what you did for a living, and it didn't take much for him to figure out——"

"I don't want you explaining," Malcolm said. "I want you to help me tackle this thing and get it solved."

"How are you going to solve it? This is a man who always uses everything he's got! He never quits! How is somebody like *you* going to solve that?"

All these years, it occurred to Malcolm, at a time like this, now, she finally had to say the thing you couldn't make go away.

When Malcolm did not say anything at all for a while but only walked around frowning and thinking, Virginia said she was going to sleep. In a sense, he was relieved; a whole plan of action was forming in his mind, and he did not want her there to badger him.

After she had closed the bedroom door, he went into the studio. In a corner was a carton of his painting stuff, which he now approached, detached but thinking. From this room he could see the flood lights on around the colonel's house. The colonel had made his circuit of the yard, and one of the dogs stood at attention, looking across the way. The setting hadn't altered at all from the night before. Setting, no, Malcolm thought, bouncing a jar of brown tempera in his hand; mood, *si*. His arm felt good all the way down from his shoulder, into the forearm, wrist and fingers.

When Ritchey had been in his house a full five minutes, Malcolm said to himself aloud, "Do first, analyze later." Whipping open the front door, he took two steps forward on the bare earth to gather momentum and pitched the jar of paint in a shallow arc calculated to end against the aluminum fence.

It was going to fall short, Malcolm thought, and it did, smashing with a loud impact against one of the white-washed stones and throwing out a fan of gluey, brown spray over the adjacent stones, the fence, and the dog, which jumped back, but, lacking orders to charge, stood its ground, whimpering. Malcolm stepped back into his open doorway and leaned in it. When the front door of Ritchey's house opened, he put his thumbs to his ears and waggled his fingers, "*Gute Nacht, Herr Kommandant*," he called, then stepped back inside and slammed and locked the door, throwing the spring-bolt latch. The dog was already on its way. It loped across the yard and scraped its front paws against the other side of the door. Its breath sounded like giggling.

Malcolm moved over to the window. The dog sprang away from the door with a scratching of toenails and leaped upward, glancing off the glass. It turned, trotted away for a better angle, and tried again. Malcolm watched it; this was the part he'd bet on.

The dog didn't make it. Its jaws flattened against the pane, and the whole sheet quivered, but there was too much going against success. The window was pretty high above the yard, and the dog couldn't get a proper combination of momentum and angle of impact. If he did manage to break it, he'd never have enough momentum left to clear the break; he'd fall on the sharp edges of glass in the frame while other chunks fell and cut his neck, and then the colonel would be down to one dog. One dog wouldn't be enough; the system would break down somewhere.

The dog dropped down, leaving nothing on the glass but a wet brown smear.

It seemed to Malcolm equally impossible for the colonel to break the window himself. He couldn't stride forward to throw a small stone hard enough to shatter the pane, and he couldn't balance well enough to heft a heavy one from nearby. The lock and chain would prevent him from entering through the front door. No, it wasn't efficient for the colonel any way you looked at it. He would rather take a few days to think of something shrewd and economical. In fact, he was calling the dog back now. When the dog reached its master, he shifted one crutch and did his best to kneel while rubbing the dog's head. There was something rather like affection in the scene. Then the colonel straightened up and called again. The other dog came out of the house and took up its station at the corner of the yard. The colonel and the dirty dog went back into the colonel's house.

Malcolm smiled, then turned out the lights, double-checked the locks, and went back through the hall to the bedroom. Virginia was sitting up in bed, staring in the direction from which the noise had come.

"What did you do?" she asked.

"Oh, changed the situation a little," Malcolm said, grinning. "Asserted my independence. Shook up the colonel. Smirched his neatness a little bit. Spoiled his night's sleep for him, I hope. Standard *Kriegie* tactics. I hope he likes them."

Virginia was incredulous. "Do you know what he could do to you with those dogs if you step outside this house?"

"I'm not going to step outside. Neither are you. We're just going to wait a few days."

"What do you mean?" Virginia said, looking at him as if he were the maniac.

"Day after tomorrow, maybe the day after that," Malcolm explained, "he's due for a grocery delivery I didn't turn off. Somebody's going to be here with a car then, lugging all kinds of things. I don't care how beholden those storekeepers are to him; when we come out the door he's not going to have those dogs tear us to pieces right on the front lawn in broad daylight and with a witness. We're going to get into the grocery car, and sooner or later we're going to drive out in it, because *that* car and driver would have to turn up in the outside world again."

Virginia sighed. "Look," she said with obvious control, "all he has to do is send a note with the dogs. He can stop the delivery that way."

Malcolm nodded. "Uh-huh. And so the groceries don't come. Then what? He starts trying to freight flour and eggs in here by dog back? By remote control? What's he going to do? All right, so it doesn't work out so neatly in two or three days. But we've got a fresh supply of food, and he's almost out. Unless he's planning to live on Crisco, he's in a bad way. And even so, he's only got three pounds of that." Malcolm got out of his clothes and lay down on the bed. "Tomorrow's another day, but I'll be damned if I'm going to worry any more about it tonight. I've got a good head start on frustrating the legless wonder, and tomorrow I'm going to have a nice clear mind, and I'm going to see what other holes I can pick in his defense. I learned a lot of snide little tricks from watching jolly movies about clever prisoners and dumb guards." He reached up and turned out the bed light. "Good night, love," he said. Virginia rolled away from him in the dark. "Oh, my God," she said in a voice with a brittle edge around it.

It was a sad thing for Malcolm to lie there thinking that she had that kind of limitation in her, that she didn't really understand what had to be done. On the other hand, he thought sleepily, feeling more relaxed than he had in years, he had his own limitations. And she had put up with them for years. He fell asleep wondering pleasantly what tomorrow would bring.

He woke to a sound of rumbling and crunching under the earth, as if there were teeth at the foundations of the house. Still sleeping in large portions of his brain, he cried out silently to himself with a madman's lucidity, "Ah, of course, he's been tunneling!" And his mind gave him all the details—the careful transfer of supporting timber for falling houses, the disposal of the excavated clay in the piles beside the other foundations. Perhaps there were tunnels leading toward those other foundations, too, for when the colonel had more people. . . .

Now one corner of the room showed a jagged line of yellow, and Malcolm's hands sprang to the light switch. Virginia jumped from sleep. In the corner was a trap door, its uneven joints concealed by boards of different lengths. The trap door crashed back, releasing a stench of body odor and soot.

A dog popped up through the opening and scrambled into the bedroom. Its face and body were streaked, and it shook itself to get the sand from its coat. Behind it, the colonel dragged himself up, naked, and braced himself on his arms, half out of the tunnel mouth. His hair was matted down with perspiration over his narrow-boned skull. He was mottled yellow-red with dirt, and half in the shadows. Virginia buried her face in her hands, one eye glinting out between spread fingers, and cried to Malcolm, "Oh my God, what have you done to us?"

"Don't worry, my dear," the colonel said crisply to her. Then he screamed at Malcolm, "I will not be abused!" Trembling with strain as he hung on one corded arm, he said to the dog at command pitch, pointing at Malcolm, "Kiss!"

OCTOBER CORN

SIGMAN BYRD

The things folks said about one another in Bluespring had a way of sticking until almost everybody in the community had a special adjective that was as much a part of him as his name or his face.

Young Jim Witton, for example, was smart, folks said; too smart for his own good, they amplified, when he did something like tell the gov'ment man to his face that he'd be damned if he'd plow under a single stalk of his cotton, even if President Roosevelt himself got down on his knees and begged him to.

Hugh Brame, they said, was hard. Guy Peters was mean, although his daughter, Donna, was sweet and pretty—sweet as pie and pretty as a picture. Nobody thought it necessary to say much about Rudy Cates, but when they did say anything, it was simply that he was crazy.

Actually, Rudy was an imbecile, a more or less physically adult by-product of the careless inbreeding of generations of pork-eating, malarial cousins. But somewhere in the past the weary plasm had got the germ of an idiotic kind of genius. Rudy was a mimic.

Slouching on the sagging boards before Buck Simmons's store, chawing a succulent quid of tobacco, Rudy peered through his ropy hair at the other men and listened to their drawled talk with the acute concentration of the monomaniac. Wanting only tobacco, and having tobacco, he was content; life had balance. Sounder minds were confused by the new order.

"But looky, Jim," Hugh Brame was saying. "Sposin' you'd plowed up twenty acre at twelve dollar a acre. That there'd be—'d be——"

"That's not the point," Jim Witton said pleasantly, puffing amusement from his pipe. "As long as I'm a cotton farmer I aim to raise all the cotton I can and sell it for the best price I can get. That Government feller tried to soft-soap me with a lot of hooey about having to control production to eliminate the surplus and raise the price. I told him there hadn't ever been any such thing as a surplus yet, and that the thing for the Government to do was control the market until we get a real surplus. He called me a Communist."

"Communist," repeated Rudy, grinning toothily.

Guy Peters decided that he could think of a better word. His impatience spread to both the other men now. Hugh Brame was mean, and Jim was full of such fool notions as organizing cooperatives and community canneries, not to mention the fact that he wanted to marry Donna.

Right now Jim was stretching his smooth brown neck so he could look across the sandy roadway into the window of the telephone office over the bank, where Donna Peters was making connections for the long-talking women on the lines. Pretty as a picture! Well, yes, and rather like one, even at such a distance, framed in profile by the open window, an electric glint of the steel headset in her dark hair.

Rudy's grin widened maniacally as his pale eyes tracked down Jim's softening gaze. Deep in his blighted brain lay words these two had spoken one night while he lay still as a varmint behind the blackberry vines in the Peterses' front yard.

"But he won't let us, Jim. You know what he'll say."

"Look here, Donna. You love me, don't you?"

"Oh, Jim!"

"All right, sweetheart, look. I'm going to see him one more time, and if he says anything against it we'll run away. Then we'll come back and say we're married. He can't do anything then."

"All right. We'll run away."

"When, darling?"

"Oh, soon. Soon!"

Rudy tried to halt the quickening words, but, like the tears of a hurt child, they came in spite of him.

"Oh, soon. Soon!" It was as though Donna had spoken, and Jim jumped like a rabbit, then glared at the idiot until Rudy already felt the kick he knew was coming. But he grew crafty-eyed. "Number, please," he crooned placatingly, exaggerating Donna's voice. "Line is busy. . . . Number, please."

Jim's look of anger turned slowly to amusement. "Shut up, you parrot, you!"

The two older men started talking about corn raising. Corn was one of the reasons why they hated each other. The other reason was peaches, but they never talked about peaches, for there lay a deeper, meaner hatred.

"Looks like that Golden Beauty you planted ain't agoin' to do so good," said Hugh Brame.

"What ye mean, ain't agoin' to do so good?" Peters scorned.

"Looks ragged, to me."

"Ragged! That crow feed o' yourn——"

"Jiss the same, it'll hang in the bank again, come harvest."

"Maybe, maybe. But not next year. An' maybe not this year. Look at this."

Guy was always fishing seed corn from his trousers pockets to show to anybody who would look, expounding the virtues of this or that variety, prophesying his own winning, with some new breed, of the yield contest conducted by the county agent each year. The prize ears were displayed in the bank until another harvest; and the festoon of Southern White hanging above the map of Texas between Joel Perkins' desk and the teller's window across the street had come from Hugh Brame's last crop. For three years running, Hugh had won the prize.

"Look at that!" Guy challenged, holding out a palm full of grain.

Hugh turned to see, hiding his curiosity behind weary condescension; Jim Witton leaned forward with interest, and the lackwit crept nearer on all fours. The grains were large and had a mottled purple color. Guy knew that they were larger than any corn Hugh had ever seen.

"What is it?" asked Hugh. "Looks like pod."

"Pod! That's all you know. This here's pod." Another hand dug into another pocket, came out with a dozen unhusked kernels. "I been 'sperimentin' with it, but it ain't worth the fodder."

Nobody paid much attention to the pod grains. The big purplish ones drew all eyes, like lumps of uncut amethyst.

"What is it?" asked Jim.

Guy swaggered in his cane-bottomed chair. "Hit's a new kind of a hybrid. Different kinds of dent crossed with Cuzco. Comes from Pee-ru."

"Pee-ru," echoed Rudy, ogling the grain.

"Whereabouts you git it at?" asked Hugh carelessly.

"At the gittin' place," answered Guy, and put the seed back into his pockets.

OCTOBER CORN

Joel Perkins, the banker, came across the road to buy some pipe tobacco at the store, and Guy had to show him the new corn and the pod. "He couldn't tell one from t'other," said Guy, pointing his chin at Hugh.

Mr. Perkins had looked at Guy's seed samples before, and he seemed to be in a hurry, but he gave these a brief businesslike scrutiny. "Well, anyway, it's too late to plant it, I reckon."

"Maybe so," said Guy. "Maybe not."

The banker turned to Brame. "By the way, Hugh, you might bring a couple of bushels of those yellow clings around to the house one day this week. My wife wants to do some canning."

Hugh stirred himself. "I'll bring 'em tomorrow, Mr. Perkins. They're jiss right for cannin'. Thank ye."

Guy glared. Hugh's poppish eyes reflected the old hatred. The yellow clings meant trouble.

Guy's paw had planted the quarter-mile row of trees on his side of the worm-crumbled snake fence that separated the Peters farm from the Brame acres, figuring that when the fence fell to punk, the growing trees would mark the boundary and bear fruit besides.

The first year the trees bore, Hugh scratched his head and did some figuring. Then he drove to the county seat and brought back the county surveyor. Guy was gathering the ripe clings when Hugh and the man in khaki breeches came into view through the green leaves, each at one end of a glittering steel tapeline. The tape came straight down a Brame cotton row to the snake fence, and the two men climbed over, throwing the reel between the rails. Khaki breeches thrust a stake into the soil on Guy's side of the peach row and stamped it deep. "There she is," he said, and scribbled in a notebook.

Hugh Brame's beady eyes glittered like the steel tape. Seeing Guy coming his way, bony fists tight, he reached ponderously for a ripe peach and bit into it greedily, letting the juice run out the corners of his mouth and drip from his outstuck chin.

"Too bad Old Man Peters ain't here," drawled Hugh. "I'd like to 'a thanked him for plantin' these fine trees on my land."

Guy Peters froze. "Yore land!"

"You Mr. Peters?" asked the surveyor. "Well, I'm afraid the trees are on Mr. Brame's property, all right, by several feet."

Guy thawed, then flared. He strode to the surveyor's stake, pulled it up like a weed, and held it clubwise before Hugh's juicy face. "Get out!" he cried. "Or I'll——"

But Brame was bigger than he, with the law on his side to boot. The bigger man bit the last flesh from the peach and dropped the stone into the hole the stake had left. "You can have that tree when she comes up," he leered.

Thereafter the ripe peaches belonged to whoever got up first in the morning.

To Hugh the trees were a windfall; so for a while he let Guy gather enough fruit for his own use and some for peddling. It was the canning fruit that started the trouble.

One year when the clings were canning size, Hugh, his two womenfolks and a hired Negro came at the crack of dawn to gather peaches. They stripped the trees of all but the very hardest and greenest, while Guy watched from his cow lot, cursing his dead paw for the old man's stupid prodigality. Rudy Cates, hiding goodness knows where, heard the cursing and repeated it damn for damn in front of Buck Simmons's store.

That night Guy made Donna pedal the grindstone while he put an edge on his ax. Then he went forth like a drunken if shriveled Paul Bunyan and felled the largest tree without once stopping to wipe the sweat from his eyes. He had started to work on the second one when, without warning, a shotgun blazed out thirty yards away and the shot clipped through the leaves like hail. Guy dropped his ax and scampered.

Another time Guy came in the dark of the moon with an arsenic spray, although there were no borers that year, and sprayed not the trees but the fruit.

Hugh got a bad attack of colic that time, but, being a hard man, he recovered quickly. Thereafter, whenever he gathered peaches he washed them carefully.

When Donna got the job as telephone operator, her father stopped most of his peddling, still taking ripe peaches when his mouth watered, and became interested in corn. The fat chain of Southern White ears hanging in the bank became the new symbol of his hatred for his neighbor. He sent for seed catalogues; he'd show that Hugh Brame!

And Hugh, seeing Guy apparently losing interest in the peaches, seemed to consider the trees finally his alone. Folks who didn't have orchards of their own placed orders with Hugh and conceded him the nine points of the law.

One day Guy had gone to the trees with a water bucket and found Hugh having a time finding enough ripe fruit to fill a bushel basket. Hugh was mad.

"I've stood enough o' yore peach swipin'," he said, "I got a order for a bushel, so you better take that bucket back home before I stick yore head in it."

Angry tears burned Guy Peters's eyelids, and he had to go to hide them.

Now, sitting in front of Buck Simmons's store, the banker's order for two bushels of the clings still warming his ears, Guy felt the brine of helpless anger in his eyes again. When he could no longer glare back, he reached for his plug of tobacco, bit savagely, and spat as though the ground were Hugh's porky face.

The late C-shaped moon was setting as Rudy Cates scampered through the woods like a satyr, inhaling the aromatic wind that roared through the pines. Above him an owl hooted. "Whoo—whoo-whoo!"

"Whoo—whoo-whoo!" answered Rudy, and the owl flew down to a lower branch to contemplate the runner.

When the east began to gray and the mocking birds started whistling, Rudy crossed the road and followed a fringe of the woods until he came in sight of Guy Peters's house. Smoke trickled from the clay chimney, lamplight yellowed a window. Snaking through a wire fence into a patch of ragweeds, he crept on palms and kneecaps, silent as death, toward the house. At the end of the patch he waited awhile before he darted across the open yard to the window and edged one eye over the sill.

Donna was moving between the stove and the kitchen table, pouring her father's coffee, frying eggs. Guy Peters arched his thin back over his plate, making appetizing noises. The noises and the smells made Rudy hungry.

Donna said, "Paw, Jim's coming to talk to you this morning."

Guy put down his knife. "What for?"

"I reckon he'll tell you."

"He don't need to. I know. Y'all young uns don't think about me. I'm a old man. You're all I got."

"We're young. I guess you've forgotten what that means."

Guy slurped coffee from his saucer. Finally he said, "He cain't have ye, Donna."

Donna gave him a look. "I don't see what objection you've got to Jim. He's——"

"He's crazy. Crazy as Rudy Cates!"

Hearing his name, Rudy walked around to the back gallery and knocked. Donna opened the door. "Speak o' the devil!" she said.

Rudy grinned.

"You hungry?"

He nodded joyously.

Guy said nothing while Donna took a cup of coffee out to the half-wit and came back to break two eggs into the sizzling skillet and lay in a cut of sowbelly. But when she had set the cooked food on the wash bench and hurried out to the yard to start the car, he got to his feet, picking his teeth with a fork. As Donna drove away, Guy came out of the kitchen, scowling.

"Git out o' here," he commanded sullenly.

Rudy's eggy mouth hung open.

"Git out, I say!" His flying brogan landed on the overalled rear as Rudy fled, terror in every line.

A spur of woods behind the barn promised safety, but before he reached the trees, Rudy knew that he was unfollowed and unnoticed. He lay down in the grass beside the pigpen, peering back toward the house.

Guy came out and pottered around in the tool shed until the rattly rumble of another car was heard. A minute later Jim Witton drove into the yard and hallooed loudly. Guy walked stiff-legged toward the car.

Wriggling along the pen's edge to the north corner of the barn, Rudy looked over the rise and down the long cotton rows, yellow-blossomed against the green, to where the yellower fruit showed from far through the paler green of peach leaves. Beyond the leaves he made out the bulk of Hugh Brame's head and shoulders, the movement of his great hands, gathering peaches.

When he tired of watching Hugh, Rudy crept back to the pigpen. Jim had started his motor, and Guy was turning away, calling back something mean-mouthed over his plow-bent shoulder. He took a bucket from the wash bench and disappeared around the barn in the direction of the peach trees, leaving Jim sitting there in his car, frowning through the windshield.

This was what Rudy had been waiting for. He ran noiselessly around the barn and scurried across the yard to the porch, where the plate of fried eggs and bacon still sat on the wash bench, hid by a corner of the house from Jim's hard-studying eyes. Shooing away the flies, Rudy spooned the food greedily into his mouth.

It was 1:26 in the afternoon by the clock in the telephone office over the bank. Donna Peters was plugging in to see whether Mrs. Carter was through telling Mrs. Simmons about the Presbyterian ice-cream sociable when One Seven rang.

One Seven was her own home, but, plug in the jack, she said, "Number, please."

Her father's voice: "Donna—is that you, Donna?"

Something in the tone frightened her. "Yes, paw."

"He got me, Donna! He's killed me, I reckon. It was Jim Witton. He—he——"

OCTOBER CORN

She heard the receiver thump against the wall, half heard a sound like a sack of flour dropped from a tired shoulder. This was the nearest she had ever come to fainting, she thought. The switchboard was blank as a wall, and turning black. Her own action brought her back. She rang One Seven long and hard, knowing the hook was up. Then she tore the headset and transmitter harness from her and ran down the hall to the room where the night operator slept.

"Pete," she called, "I'm going home! Get Doc Fowler and tell him to follow me! I—I guess you better tell Sam McManus to come too!" Sam McManus was the deputy sheriff.

The car balked, but she got it going. There was a brief glimpse of the loafers in Simmons's doorway, gawking at the dust she raised.

No answer followed her call as she braked the car at the Peters gate. "Paw! Paw!" she cried again at the door. In the dining room the telephone receiver hung on its taut cord, that was all.

The rooms were empty, the backyard too. She ran from the tool shed to the barn, climbing up to the loft, down to the stables. "Paw! Oh, paw!" she called, like a lost child.

When she started back to the house, having heard the sound of a motor on the road, she saw his hat lying in the path to the cotton patch. She stooped to pick it up. Outside it was soiled and familiar, somehow suddenly very dear. Inside was what made her drop it again. A smear of blood, stranded with gray hair, and the torn hole she had not seen before.

The doctor found her there, staring at the dropped hat. "Where's the patient?" he asked.

"I don't know," she said simply, like a child again.

Deputy McManus came on the doctor's heels; two other men on his. The three stayed only to hear about the telephone call. Then they stalked grimly to their car and drove off toward Jim Witton's farm.

They brought him back, in overalls and wide-brimmed straw hat, the sweat of cotton chopping still on him. Donna shrank from him, clutching Doc Fowler's arm.

"Donna!" he exclaimed. "You don't think I—did it, do you? Surely——"

"Where was ye between one an' half past?" asked Sam McManus.

"I told you. I was in the cotton patch, where you found me."

"Can ye prove it?"

Jim looked the officer in the eye. "I don't need to prove it. You've known me all my life. I'm not a murderer."

"Then what d'ye reckon made Guy say what he done on the phone?"

57

"I don't know. He—he didn't like me."

Sam McManus tried to look Jim back in the eye, but had a time of it. "Reckon you didn't like him neither, did ye?"

Jim clamped his mouth shut.

"You said you seen Guy this mornin'. What about?"

"I—well, let Donna tell you."

Donna came a few steps nearer him then; there were tears in her eyes. "I guess everybody knows about that. He—he was trying to get paw to let us get married, Sam. But, Jim"—her hands moved toward him, clenched came back—"What happened?"

"Nothing. We argued, and he told me——Well, he said I'd better stay away from you. I sat in the car while he started off through the cotton patch, yonder, carrying a bucket. Then I drove off. That's the last I saw of him."

"We got to find him," said the deputy sheriff. "Wherever he's at."

They found the bucket at the edge of the cottonfield, a blotch of dark mud on the bottom rim. "Funny," said Doc Fowler, "how he could talk on the phone after gettin' hit that hard with a bucket."

"You reckon he's dead?" asked the deputy.

"Show him to me," said the doctor dourly, "and I'll tell ye."

Doc Fowler stayed with Donna while the men went over every acre of the Peters farm, Jim helping, finding nothing.

"Better see Hugh Brame," reckoned the deputy, and the others reckoned so too. They crossed the peach row through the gap where Guy had chopped down the tree, and trudged up the cotton rows to the Brame house. At the back door the officer knocked.

Mrs. Brame, chewing her snuff brush, squinted at the visitors.

"Where's Hugh?" Sam McManus asked.

"Left two three hour back. He was a-takin' some peaches to Miz Perkins. Ort to be back pretty soon."

"You by yourself between 'bout one o'clock an' half past?"

"Me an' Nancy, that's all. Why?"

"Some-un happened to Guy Peters. Looks kind o' like somebody might 'a' killed him. You didn't hear nothin'—like a fight, maybe?"

The woman's eyes widened. "Ye don't say! No, sir, nary a sound. Hit's too fur, anyways. Whereabouts is he at?"

That was the question. Whereabouts?

Back at the Peters house, Doc Fowler met them at the door. "I gave her something to make her sleep," he said. "I'll stay here till y'all get somebody to stay with her. Better get Mrs. Buck Simmons."

"I'll stay too," said Jim, but this time Sam McManus was hard-eyed.

"You better come along with us," he said firmly.

OCTOBER CORN

In Bluespring the word was going around that Jim Witton had killed Guy Peters because the old man had put his foot down on Jim's marrying Donna—bashed his head in with an iron bucket; the dead man had said so himself.

But Sam McManus said he wasn't going to lock Jim up—not yet awhile, anyway. The women raised horrified eyebrows at that, and some of the men tried to raise the dickens with Sam. But the deputy read them the law.

"Ye cain't arrest a man for a killin' without ye can prove somebody was killed."

"Well!"

Well, where was your dead man? Had anybody seen Guy laid out cold? Had Doc Fowler closed his eyelids and folded his arms? And where was the preacher who could say "dust to dust"? There wasn't any dust!

So Jim went free, technically, if not from the hard eyes of his fellows. It was Donna Peters who was prisoner.

She had moved in at Buck Simmons's house as a boarder and had gone back to work at the telephone office. But she was a different Donna. There was a dim bewilderment in her eyes, and a look on her face, Mrs. Simmons said, like a person lost in life.

All Bluespring knew about the night when Jim had come calling at the Simmons house and Mrs. Simmons had had to send him away because Donna was crying and could not see him. What folks didn't know was whether she was crying for her father or for Jim Witton.

The men of the community, led by Sam McManus, organized one last searching party and went on an all-day hunt for the body of the man who said he had been killed, probing in haystacks and barn lofts and smokehouses and creek bottoms for miles around. At the Brame farm Hugh told them to search their blamed heads off, but he couldn't see why they didn't start at Jim Witton's place.

Jim was there too. He looked at Hugh level-eyed. "The last time I saw Guy Peters, he was going off toward your place carrying that bucket. Looked like he might be going to try to get a few of his peaches."

A sneer began on Hugh's face, but he grinned it away. "Looks like he didn't git far, judgin' from where the bucket an' his hat was found."

Jim's jaw muscles tightened, but he didn't say anything.

Sam McManus said. "You didn't see or hear anything while you was gittin' peaches that mornin', Hugh?"

"You can jiss see the top o' Guy's house from where the tree is," replied Hugh. "It's too far to hear anything."

"What time was it you was gittin' peaches?" Sam asked.

" 'Bout half-past seven."

Jim's jaw loosened. "What were you doing between then and the time you took the peaches to Mrs. Perkins?" he demanded.

Hugh tongued a quid of chewing vaguely but suggestively in Jim's direction. "I don't reckon," he answered, "that's any o' your business, young squirt."

Sam scratched his head. This wasn't getting anywhere.

The Brame farm yielded nothing but Hugh, who saddled a horse and joined the others, a few on horseback, most of them in cars; and the queer procession moved down the dirt road toward Jim Witton's farm.

They found nothing there, nothing anywhere. Guy Peters, dead or living, had been swallowed up by the red earth where the Piney Woods dug its roots. Dust to dust, after all.

It was Jim who, that night, reported the fruitless search to Donna Peters. Mrs. Buck Simmons admitted that she watched the pair from behind a curtained window as they sat in a willow yard seat under the magnolia trees, figuring, she explained, that she'd better keep an eye on the girl.

That she kept her ears open, too, was understood, but she heard only Donna's words, after a long while: "Don't, Jim, please! I—I can't. Not until I know. Don't you see?"

A muttered protestation, and then again, as from the verge of agony: "But why did he say it was you?"

Shortly afterward came the rattle of Jim's car and the slam of the door.

After that Jim came less often, and finally not at all. Bluespring began to forget Guy Peters, but the bewilderment and the lost look remained on Donna's face. Who could blame her? Every day her pretty head wore the metal-and-rubber thing through which her father's voice had come: "He got me, Donna.... It was Jim Witton."

As for Jim, he kept to his lonely farm, busy with the first picking of cotton, even sending the wagons to gin by one of his workers. He, too, was a prisoner, after all.

The hot months went by, and in September Hugh Brame again won the county agent's prize for the best corn yield in the Bluespring district. The finest of his new ears of Southern White were hung again in the bank, and Banker Perkins reckoned that Hugh was a plumb corn-raising fool.

The October harvest moon made poor Rudy Cates wilder than ever. When it was full and bright, he could no more sleep than he could make up words of his own. He had picked a little cotton for Hugh Brame, but the third time Hugh found him asleep in the wagon in broad daylight, the farmer had kicked him awake and taken the empty sack away from him and chased him off the patch without paying him.

Tonight his moon-mad feet flew with him along a familiar cowpath skirting the pine forest, until he saw a clean-picked cotton patch that belonged to Hugh Brame. Crawling through a fence, he came into the open and bent almost as low as the empty stalks as he slunk wolfwise up the long row. The bending hurt, for Hugh's feet had been heavy.

Hugh Brame's two barns, one new, one old with a swayback roof, stood very close together. The space between them had once been used for a poultry pen, as Rudy knew about as well as he knew anything. One night he had raided a Brame hen house, and when the fowls set up a fuss that brought Hugh and his shotgun out of the house, he had lain flat in the dark chicken run and cackled and crowed as loudly as any, until Hugh went back to bed. Now the narrow space, fenced in at both ends with boards as high as a man's head, was not in use.

Coming up behind the buildings, Rudy grasped the upper edge of the high board and pulled himself up to look over. It was the second time he had peered into the empty area lately. The first time, when he should have been on his knees in the cotton patch, he had seen something that interested him. Now he threw an overalled leg across the board wall and climbed down inside.

Next to Rudy Cates, Joel Perkins probably had more imagination than anyone in Bluespring. There are some who would have placed Jim Witton before both the idiot and the banker, he having literally, they would say, got away with murder. But then murder is probably fathered oftener by impulse than by fancy or theory.

Banker Perkins had a theory; he admitted it was just that, but on the strength of it, he let Rudy Cates ride agog in the rear seat of his shining new two-door sedan to the home of Deputy Sheriff Sam McManus. Here he leaned heavily on the horn button.

"You'd swear I was as crazy as Rudy here, Sam," the banker said, when the deputy had come out, "if I told you what I'm thinking. So I won't tell you just yet. Get your car and meet me in front of Buck Simmons's store in twenty minutes. Tell Buck we'll want him too. And—oh, yes, bring a spade, Sam."

"A spade?" The deputy looked suggestively at Mr. Perkins, and then at Rudy.

"That's right," answered the banker, and drove away.

He found Jim Witton at home, washing his noonday plates and pans. "What you need is a wife," Joel said thoughtfully, and repeated what he had told Sam McManus. "And bring a spade."

"What for?"

No, Jim hadn't the imagination of these other two.

From Buck's store the Perkins car led the way in a new direction. "Now which way?" asked Mr. Perkins when the road forked, and Rudy grinned and pointed a crooked finger.

It was fantastic—four sane men following the whimsies of a crazy fool! Or three men and two fools, as Buck suggested to the deputy. But they didn't have far to go.

Before Hugh Brame's house the cars stopped, and when Joel Perkins climbed out, the others got their first glimpse of the twin bulges in the banker's hip pockets.

"Guns?" guessed Buck

"Mortgages," Sam thought rather sardonically.

The only gun that appeared was Hugh's double-barreled shotgun as the corn champion slammed out the back door to see what was going on in his yard. But he held it hunting-fashion, explaining, "Jiss goin' after squirrel. What you-all—what——"

"Now where, Rudy?" asked Mr. Perkins casually.

Rudy became a jack-out-of-the-box. He pointed again and ran through an open gate toward Hugh's barns, shinning up the boards of the abandoned chicken pen, and sitting there astraddle the short fence, grinning like a possum.

The banker speculated, with his eyes on Brame's face. "Hugh," he said carefully, "I guess you'll side with the other boys here in thinking that Rudy and I are crazy. But I've got a kind of a theory I'd like to try out, if you don't mind. It's about"—he reached for the bulges in his hip pockets—"it's about corn."

Hugh smelled a rat—a dead one, from the look on his face. "Corn?" he said, "Well——"

"I've got some interesting ears here," Mr. Perkins went on, not taking his eyes from the farmer's face. "This one"—he held it out for everybody to see—"is pod. You don't see much of it around here, or anywhere else, anymore. This other one I'm not so sure about, but I remember seeing something like it once before."

The ear in his left hand was pod, all right. The other one, shucked, was a size and a half larger, with mottled grains, purple-white. "Rudy brought these to me this morning. It seems he found them growing together somewhere around here—on your place, Hugh. Behind that fence, yonder, I imagine. . . . Jim, suppose you have a look."

They all went through the gate and had a look, chinning themselves on the boards the loony was straddling. But Jim had no patience with the boards. He laid hold and wrenched them away with a terrible shrieking of rusty nails, and then stood back staring.

In the sunless space between the barn walls the two hills of corn stood pale and naked for them to see, etiolated and dwarfed, unplowed and unhoed, yet finally ripened in the vertical glare of many summer noons. One hill was pod, the stalks hung with clumsy, husky ears; one bore larger ears, big-grained, purple where the shucks were parted. And the oddest thing was that the two hills were no farther apart than the width of a man's body.

The width of a man's body! Even unimagining Jim, wrecking the fence, must have guessed the meaning of that.

"You wouldn't mind if we dug up those stalks, would you, Hugh?" asked Mr. Perkins.

Hugh sagged as though a weight had been hung on his shoulders. He shifted the shotgun to his right hand. "Go ahead," he said grimly.

Sam and Buck did the digging, with Rudy grinning like a demon from the fence. A dozen spadefuls of the soft earth were enough, and the labor was not lovely. The corn's roots were deep in the loins of what had been Guy Peters, he who had carried seed corn in his pockets as some men carry symbols and emblems.

"Well, Sam——" suggested Joel Perkins.

Hugh Brame had seen. His big face quivered, seeming to borrow the yellow pallor of ground corn from what he saw. His teeth rattled, but he was still a hard man. "Well, what ye goin' to do? He was buried on my land, but I didn't kill him. He said himself it was Jim Witton."

Sam McManus didn't know what to do any more than the others. The five of them stood rooted like cornstalks, Hugh deeper than the rest.

It was Rudy who rooted them deeper, speaking suddenly, terribly, with the yet-remembered voice of the dead man: "Donna—is that you, Donna? . . . He got me, Donna! He's killed me, I reckon. It was Jim Witton. He—he——"

There was terror in their arms and legs; and then suddenly, in their minds, understanding—almost.

Rudy was delighted with the effect. Squinting merrily at Hugh, laughter and mischief bright in his wild eyes, he mocked the man who had kicked him for resting at his labors. Aping Hugh's meaty voice, speaking again, as always, the words of less-pure-minds than his own, the fool on the fence was now the judge on the bench:

"Say them words, Rudy, jiss like I said 'em, only say 'em like you was Guy Peters. Say 'em into that little black thing, an' I'll give ye this. See? Money, Rudy!"

The roar of the shotgun came too late. Rudy knew what a gun meant; he had seen woods animals fall lifeless from their trees, and so he fell first. The charge tore through thin air he had quitted not a second too soon, while he somersaulted with ridiculous laughter to the soft heap of fresh-piled earth.

Jim Witton didn't need imagination now; he was an arrow from his own bow. He had the gun out of Hugh's hands and the muzzle in the fat stomach of Guy Peters's murderer before Rudy could get to his feet. Nobody, seeing him now, would have called Hugh Brame hard.

Sam McManus had stirred his stumps too. Relieving Jim of the gun, he got down to business.

"All right, Hugh," he said quietly; "let's go to town."

After a while Joel Perkins put his hand on Jim Witton's shoulder. "I've got to get back to the bank, Jim," he said. "I don't reckon you'd be wanting a lift to the telephone office, would you?"

Jim reckoned he would.

THE HAMMER OF GOD

G. K. CHESTERTON

The little village of Bohun Beacon was perched on a hill so steep that the tall spire of its church seemed only like the peak of a small mountain. At the foot of the church stood a smithy, generally red with fires and always littered with hammers and scraps of iron; opposite to this, over a rude cross of cobbled paths, was "The Blue Boar," the only inn of the place. It was upon this crossway, in the lifting of a leaden and silver daybreak, that two brothers met in the street and spoke; though one was beginning the day and the other finishing it. The Rev. and Hon. Wilfred Bohun was very devout, and was making his way to some austere exercises of prayer or contemplation at dawn. Colonel the Hon. Norman Bohun, his elder brother, was by no means devout, and was sitting in evening dress on the bench outside "The Blue Boar," drinking what the philosophic observer was free to regard either as his last glass on Tuesday or his first on Wednesday. The colonel was not particular.

The Bohuns were one of the very few aristocratic families really dating from the Middle Ages, and their pennon had actually seen Palestine. But it is a great mistake to suppose that such houses stand high in chivalric tradition. Few except the poor preserve traditions. Aristocrats live not in traditions but in fashions. The Bohuns had been Mohocks under Queen Anne and Mashers under Queen Victoria. But like more than one of the really ancient houses, they had rotted in the last two centuries into mere drunkards and dandy degenerates, till there had even come a whisper of insanity. Certainly there was something hardly human about the colonel's wolfish pursuit of pleasure, and his chronic resolution not to go home till morning had a touch of the hideous clarity of insomnia. He was a tall, fine animal, elderly, but with hair still startlingly yellow. He would have looked merely blond and leonine, but his blue eyes were sunk so deep in his face that they looked black. They were a little too close together. He had very long yellow mustaches; on each side of them a fold or furrow from nostril to jaw, so that a sneer seemed cut into his face. Over his evening clothes he wore a curious pale yellow coat that looked more like a very light dressing-gown than an overcoat, and on the back of his head was stuck an extraordinary broad-brimmed hat of a bright green color, evidently some oriental curiosity caught up at random. He was proud of appearing in such incongruous attires—proud of the fact that he always made them look congruous.

His brother the curate had also the yellow hair and the elegance, but he was buttoned up to the chin in black, and his face was clean-shaven, cultivated, and a little nervous. He seemed to live for nothing but his religion; but there were some who said (notably the blacksmith, who was a Presbyterian) that it was a love of Gothic architecture rather than of God, and that his haunting of the church like a ghost was only another and purer turn of the almost morbid thirst for beauty which sent his brother raging after women and wine. This charge was doubtful, while the man's practical piety was indubitable. Indeed, the charge was mostly an ignorant misunderstanding of the love of solitude and secret prayer, and was founded on his being often found kneeling, not before the altar, but in peculiar places, in the crypts or gallery, or even in the belfry. He was at the moment about to enter the church through the yard of the smithy, but stopped and frowned a little as he saw his brother's cavernous eyes staring in the same direction. On the hypothesis that the colonel was interested in the church he did not waste any speculations. There only remained the blacksmith's shop, and though the blacksmith was a Puritan and none of his people, Wilfred Bohun had heard some scandals about a beautiful and rather celebrated wife. He flung a suspicious look across the shed, and the colonel stood up laughing to speak to him. "Good morning, Wilfred," he said. "Like a good landlord I am watching sleeplessly over my people. I am going to call on the blacksmith."

Wilfred looked at the ground, and said: "The blacksmith is out. He is over at Greenford."

"I know," answered the other with silent laughter; "that is why I am calling on him."

"Norman," said the cleric, with his eye on a pebble in the road, "are you ever afraid of thunderbolts?"

"What do you mean?" asked the colonel. "Is your hobby meteorology?"

"I mean," said Wilfred, without looking up, "do you ever think that God might strike you in the street?"

"I beg your pardon," said the colonel; "I see your hobby is folklore."

"I know your hobby is blasphemy," retorted the religious man, stung in the one live place of his nature. "But if you do not fear God, you have good reason to fear man."

The elder raised his eyebrows politely. "Fear man?" he said.

"Barnes the blacksmith is the biggest and strongest man for forty miles round," said the clergyman sternly. "I know you are no coward or weakling, but he could throw you over the wall."

This struck home, being true, and the lowering line by mouth and nostril darkened and deepened. For a moment he stood with the heavy sneer on his face. But in an instant Colonel Bohun had recovered his own cruel good humor and laughed, showing two doglike front teeth under his yellow mustache. "In that case, my dear Wilfred," he said quite carelessly, "it was wise for the last of the Bohuns to come out partially in armor."

And he took off the queer round hat covered with green, showing that it was lined within with steel. Wilfred recognized it indeed as a light Japanese or Chinese helmet torn down from a trophy that hung in the old family hall.

"It was the first hat to hand," explained his brother airily; "always the nearest hat—and the nearest woman."

"The blacksmith is away at Greenford," said Wilfred quietly; "the time of his return is unsettled."

And with that he turned and went into the church with bowed head, crossing himself like one who wishes to be quit of an unclean spirit. He was anxious to forget such grossness in the cool twilight of his tall Gothic cloisters; but on that morning it was fated that his still round of religious exercises should be everywhere arrested by small shocks. As he entered the church, hitherto always empty at that hour, a kneeling figure rose hastily to its feet and came toward the full daylight of the doorway. When the curate saw it he stood still with surprise. For the early worshipper was none other than the village idiot, a nephew of the blacksmith, one who neither would nor could care for the church or for anything else. He was always called "Mad Joe," and seemed to have no other name; he was a dark, strong, slouching lad, with a heavy white face, dark straight hair, and a mouth always open. As he passed the priest, his moon-calf countenance gave no hint of what he had been doing or thinking of. He had never been known to pray before. What sort of prayers was he saying now? Extraordinary prayers surely.

Wilfred Bohun stood rooted to the spot long enough to see the idiot go out into the sunshine, and even to see his dissolute brother hail him with a sort of avuncular jocularity. The last thing he saw was the colonel throwing pennies at the open mouth of Joe, with serious appearance of trying to hit it.

This ugly sunlight picture of the stupidity and cruelty of the earth sent the ascetic finally to his prayers for purification and new thoughts. He went up to a pew in the gallery, which brought him under a colored window which he loved and always quieted his spirit; a blue window with an angel carrying lilies. There he began to think less about the half-wit, with his livid face and mouth like a fish. He began to think less of his evil brother, pacing like a lean lion his horrible hunger. He sank deeper and deeper into those cold and sweet colors of silver blossoms and sapphire sky.

In this place half an hour afterward he was found by Gibbs, the village cobbler, who had been sent after him in some haste. He got to his feet with promptitude, for he knew that no small matter would have brought Gibbs into such a place at all. The cobbler was, as in many villages, an atheist, and his appearance in church was a shade more extraordinary than Mad Joe's. It was a morning of theological enigmas.

"What is it?" asked Wilfred Bohun rather stiffly, but putting out a trembling hand for his hat.

The atheist spoke in a tone that, coming from him, was quite startlingly respectful, and even, as it were, huskily sympathetic.

"You must excuse me, sir," he said in a hoarse whisper, "but we didn't think it right not to let you know at once. I'm afraid a rather dreadful thing has happened, sir. I'm afraid your brother——"

Wilfred clenched his frail hands. "What devilry has he done now?" he cried in involuntary passion.

"Why, sir," said the cobbler, coughing, "I'm afraid he's done nothing, and won't do anything. I'm afraid he's done for. You had really better come down, sir."

The curate followed the cobbler down a short winding stair, which brought them out at an entrance rather higher than the street. Bohun saw the tragedy in one glance, flat underneath him like a plan. In the yard of the smithy were standing five or six men mostly in black, one in an inspector's uniform. They included the doctor, the Presbyterian minister, and the priest from the Roman Catholic chapel, to which the blacksmith's wife belonged. The latter was speaking to her, indeed, very rapidly, in an undertone, as she, a magnificent woman with red-gold hair, was sobbing blindly on a bench. Between these two groups, and just clear of the main heap of hammers, lay a man in evening dress, spread-eagled and flat on his face. From the height above Wilfred could have sworn to every item of his costume and appearance, down to the Bohun rings upon his fingers; but the skull was only a hideous splash, like a star of blackness and blood.

Wilfred Bohun gave but one glance, and ran down the steps into the yard. The doctor, who was the family physician, saluted him, but he scarcely took any notice. He could only stammer out: "My brother is dead. What does it mean? What is this horrible mystery?" There was an unhappy silence; and then the cobbler, the most outspoken man present, answered: "Plenty of horror, sir," he said, "but not much mystery."

"What do you mean?" asked Wilfred, with a white face.

"It's plain enough," answered Gibbs. "There is only one man for forty miles round that could have struck such a blow as that, and he's the man that had most reason to."

"We must not prejudge anything," put in the doctor, a tall, black bearded man, rather nervously; "but it is competent for me to corroborate what Mr. Gibbs says about the nature of the blow, sir; it is an incredible blow. Mr. Gibbs says that only one man in this district could have done it. I should have said myself that nobody could have done it."

A shudder of superstition went through the slight figure of the curate. "I can hardly understand," he said.

"Mr. Bohun," said the doctor in a low voice, "metaphors literally fail me. It is inadequate to say that the skull was smashed to bits like an eggshell. Fragments of bone were driven into the body and the ground like bullets into a mud wall. It was the hand of a giant."

He was silent a moment, looking grimly through his glasses; then he added: "The thing has one advantage—that it clears most people of suspicion at one stroke. If you or I or any normally made man in the country were accused of this crime, we should be acquitted as an infant would be acquitted of stealing the Nelson Column."

"That's what I say," repeated the cobbler obstinately; "there's only one man that could have done it, and he's the man that would have done it. Where's Simeon Barnes, the blacksmith?"

"He's over at Greenford," faltered the curate.

"More likely over in France," muttered the cobbler.

"No; he is in neither of those places," said a small and colorless voice, which came from the little Roman priest who had joined the group. "As a matter of fact, he is coming up the road at this moment."

The little priest was not an interesting man to look at, having stubbly brown hair and a round and stolid face. But if he had been as splendid as Apollo no one would have looked at him at that moment. Everyone turned round and peered at the pathway which wound across the plain below, along which was indeed walking, at his own huge stride and with a hammer on his shoulder, Simeon the smith. He was a bony and gigantic man, with deep, dark, sinister eyes and a dark chin beard. He was walking and talking quietly with two other men; and though he was never specially cheerful, he seemed quite at his ease.

"My God!" cried the atheistic cobbler, "and there's the hammer he did it with."

"No," said the inspector, a sensible-looking man with a sandy moustache, speaking for the first time. "There's the hammer he did it with over there by the church wall. We have left it and the body exactly as they are."

All glanced round, and the short priest went across and looked down in silence at the tool where it lay. It was one of the smallest and the lightest of the hammers, and would not have caught the eye among the rest; but on the iron edge of it were blood and yellow hair.

After a silence the short priest spoke without looking up, and there was a new note in his dull voice. "Mr. Gibbs was hardly right," he said, "in saying that there is no mystery. There is at least the mystery of why so big a man should attempt so big a blow with so little a hammer."

"Oh, never mind that," cried Gibbs, in a fever. "What are we to do with Simeon Barnes?"

"Leave him alone," said the priest quietly. "He is coming here of himself. I know those two men with him. They are very good fellows from Greenford, and they have come over about the Presbyterian chapel."

Even as he spoke the tall smith swung round the corner of the church, and strode into his own yard. Then he stood there quite still, and the hammer fell from his hand. The inspector, who had preserved impenetrable propriety, immediately went up to him.

"I won't ask you, Mr. Barnes," he said, "whether you know anything about what has happened here. You are not bound to say. I hope you don't know, and that you will be able to prove it. But I must go through the form of arresting you in the King's name for the murder of Colonel Norman Bohun."

"You are not bound to say anything," said the cobbler in officious excitement. "They've got to prove everything. They haven't proved yet that it is Colonel Bohun, with the head all smashed up like that."

"That won't wash," said the doctor aside to the priest. "That's out of the detective stories. I was the colonel's medical man, and I knew his body better than he did. He had very fine hands, but quite peculiar ones. The second and third fingers were the same in length. Oh, that's the colonel right enough."

As he glanced at the brained corpse upon the ground the iron eyes of the motionless blacksmith followed them and rested there also.

"Is Colonel Bohun dead?" said the smith quite calmly. "Then he's damned."

"Don't say anything! Oh, don't say anything," cried the atheist cobbler, dancing about in an ecstasy of admiration of the English legal system. For no man is such a legalist as the good secularist.

The blacksmith turned on him over his shoulder the august face of a fanatic.

"It's well for you infidels to dodge like foxes because the world's law favors you," he said; "but God guards His own in His pocket, as you shall see this day."

Then he pointed to the colonel and said: "When did this dog die in his sins?"

"Moderate your language," said the doctor.

"Moderate the Bible's language, and I'll moderate mine. When did he die?"

"I saw him alive at six o'clock this morning," stammered Wilfred Bohun.

"God is good," said the smith. "Mr. Inspector, I have not the slightest objection to being arrested. It is you who may object to arresting me. I don't mind leaving the court without a stain on my character. You do mind, perhaps, leaving the court with a bad setback in your career."

The solid inspector for the first time looked at the blacksmith with a lively eye; as did everybody else, except the short, strange priest, who was still looking down at the little hammer that had dealt the dreadful blow.

"There are two men standing outside this shop," went on the blacksmith with ponderous lucidity, "good tradesmen in Greenford whom you all know, who will swear that they saw me from before midnight till daybreak and long after in the committee room of our Revival Mission, which sits all night, we save souls so fast. In Greenford itself twenty people could swear to me for all that time. If

I were a heathen, Mr. Inspector, I would let you walk on to your downfall. But as a Christian man I feel bound to give you your chance, and ask you whether you will hear my alibi now or in court."

The inspector seemed for the first time disturbed, and said, "Of course I should be glad to clear you altogether now."

The smith walked out of his yard with the same long and easy stride, and returned to his two friends from Greenford, who were indeed friends of nearly everyone present. Each of them said a few words which no one ever thought of disbelieving. When they had spoken, the innocence of Simeon stood up as solid as the great church above them.

One of those silences struck the group which are more strange and insufferable than any speech. Madly, in order to make conversation, the curate said to the Catholic priest:

"You seem very much interested in that hammer, Father Brown."

"Yes, I am," said Father Brown; "why is it such a small hammer?"

The doctor swung round on him.

"By George, that's true," he cried; "who would use a little hammer with ten larger hammers lying about?"

Then he lowered his voice in the curate's ear and said: "Only the kind of person that can't lift a large hammer. It is not a question of force or courage between the sexes. It's a question of lifting power in the shoulders. A bold woman could commit ten murders with a light hammer and never turn a hair. She could not kill a beetle with a heavy one."

Wilfred Bohun was staring at him with a sort of hypnotized horror, while Father Brown listened with his head a little on one side, really interested and attentive. The doctor went on with more hissing emphasis:

"Why do these idiots always assume that the only person who hates the wife's lover is the wife's husband? Nine times out of ten the person who most hates the wife's lover is the wife. Who knows what insolence or treachery he had shown her—look there?"

He made a momentary gesture toward the red-haired woman on the bench. She had lifted her head at last and the tears were drying on her splendid face. But the eyes were fixed on the corpse with an electric glare that had in it something of idiocy.

The Rev. Wilfred Bohun made a limp gesture as if waving away all desire to know; but Father Brown, dusting off his sleeve some ashes blown from the furnace, spoke in his indifferent way.

"You are like so many doctors," he said; "your mental science is really suggestive. It is your physical science that is utterly impossible. I agree that the woman wants to kill the corespondent much more than the petitioner does. And I agree that a woman will always pick up a small hammer instead of a big one. But the difficulty is one of physical impossibility. No woman ever born could have smashed a man's skull flat like that." Then he added reflectively, after a pause: "These people haven't grasped the whole of it. The man was actually wearing an iron helmet, and the blow scattered it like broken glass. Look at that woman. Look at her arms."

Silence held them all up again, and then the doctor said rather sulkily: "Well, I may be wrong; there are objections to everything. But I stick to the main point. No man but an idiot would pick up that little hammer if he could use a big hammer."

With that the lean and quivering hands of Wilfred Bohun went up to his head and seemed to clutch his scanty yellow hair. After an instant they dropped, and he cried: "That was the word I wanted; you have said the word."

Then he continued, mastering his discomposure: "The words you said were, 'No man but an idiot would pick up the small hammer.'"

"Yes," said the doctor. "Well?"

"Well," said the curate, "no man but an idiot did." The rest stared at him with eyes arrested and riveted, and he went on in a febrile and feminine agitation.

"I am a priest," he cried unsteadily, "and a priest should be no shedder of blood. I—I mean that he should bring no one to the gallows. And I thank God that I see the criminal clearly now—because he is a criminal who cannot be brought to the gallows."

"You will not denounce him?" inquired the doctor.

"He would not be hanged if I did denounce him," answered Wilfred with a wild but curiously happy smile. "When I went into the church this morning I found a madman praying there—that poor Joe, who has been wrong all his life. God knows what he prayed; but with such strange folk it is not incredible to suppose that their prayers are all upside down. Very likely a lunatic would pray before killing a man. When I last saw poor Joe he was with my brother. My brother was mocking him."

"By Jove!" cried the doctor, "this is talking at last. But how do you explain——"

The Reverend Wilfred was almost trembling with the excitement of his own glimpse of the truth. "Don't you see; don't you see," he cried feverishly; "that is the only theory that covers both the queer things, that answers both the riddles. The two riddles are the little hammer and the big blow. The smith might have struck the big blow, but would not have chosen the little hammer. His wife would have chosen the little hammer, but she could not have struck the big blow.

But the madman might have done both. As for the little hammer—why, he was mad and might have picked up anything. And for the big blow, have you never heard, doctor, that a maniac in his paroxysm may have the strength of ten men?"

The doctor drew a deep breath and then said, "By golly, I believe you've got it."

Father Brown had fixed his eyes on the speaker so long and steadily as to prove that his large gray, oxlike eyes were not quite so insignificant as the rest of his face. When silence had fallen he said with marked respect: "Mr. Bohun, yours is the only theory yet propounded which holds water every way and is essentially unassailable. I think, therefore, that you deserve to be told, on my positive knowledge, that it is not the true one." And with that the old little man walked away and stared again at the hammer.

"That fellow seems to know more than he ought to," whispered the doctor peevishly to Wilfred. "Those popish priests are deucedly sly."

"No, no," said Bohun, with a sort of wild fatigue. "It was the lunatic. It was the lunatic."

The group of the two clerics and the doctor had fallen away from the more official group containing the inspector and the man he had arrested. Now, however, that their own party had broken up, they heard voices from the others. The priest looked up quietly and then looked down again as he heard the blacksmith say in a loud voice:

"I hope I've convinced you, Mr. Inspector. I'm a strong man, as you say, but I couldn't have flung my hammer bang here from Greenford. My hammer hasn't any wings that it should come flying half a mile over hedges and fields."

The inspector laughed amicably and said: "No, I think you can be considered out of it, though it's one of the rummiest coincidences I ever saw. I can only ask you to give us all the assistance you can in finding a man as big and strong as yourself. By George! you might be useful, if only to hold him! I suppose you yourself have no guess at the man?"

"I may have a guess," said the pale smith, "but it is not at a man." Then, seeing the scared eyes turn toward his wife on the bench, he put his huge hand on her shoulder and said: "Nor a woman either."

"What do you mean?" asked the inspector jocularly. "You don't think cows use hammers, do you?"

"I think no thing of flesh held that hammer," said the blacksmith in a stifled voice; "mortally speaking, I think the man died alone."

Wilfred made a sudden forward movement and peered at him with burning eyes.

THE HAMMER OF GOD

"Do you mean to say, Barnes," came the sharp voice of the cobbler, "that the hammer jumped up of itself and knocked the man down?"

"Oh, you gentlemen may stare and snigger," cried Simeon; "you clergymen who tell us on Sunday in what a stillness the Lord smote Sennacherib. I believe that One who walks invisible in every house defended the honor of mine, and laid the defiler dead before the door of it. I believe the force in that blow was just the force there is in earthquakes, and no less."

Wilfred said, with a voice utterly undescribable: "I told Norman myself to beware of the thunderbolt."

"That agent is outside my jurisdiction," said the inspector with a slight smile.

"You are not outside His," answered the smith; "see you to it," and, turning his broad back, he went into the house.

The shaken Wilfred was led away by Father Brown, who had an easy and friendly way with him. "Let us get out of this horrid place, Mr. Bohun," he said. "May I look inside your church? I hear it's one of the oldest in England. We take some interest, you know," he added with a comical grimace, "in old English churches."

Wilfred Bohun did not smile, for humor was never his strong point. But he nodded rather eagerly, being only too ready to explain the Gothic splendors to someone more likely to be sympathetic than the Presbyterian blacksmith or the atheist cobbler.

"By all means," he said; "let us go in at this side." And he led the way into the high side entrance at the top of the flight of steps. Father Brown was mounting the first step to follow him when he felt a hand on his shoulder, and turned to behold the dark, thin figure of the doctor, his face darker yet with suspicion.

"Sir," said the physician harshly, "you appear to know some secrets in this black business. May I ask if you are going to keep them to yourself?"

"Why, doctor," answered the priest, smiling quite pleasantly, "there is one very good reason why a man of my trade should keep things to himself when he is not sure of them, and that is that it is so constantly his duty to keep them to himself when he is sure of them. But if you think I have been discourteously reticent with you or anyone, I will go to the extreme limit of my custom. I will give you two very large hints."

"Well, sir?" said the doctor gloomily.

"First," said Father Brown quietly, "the thing is quite in your own province. It is a matter of physical science. The blacksmith is mistaken, not perhaps in saying that the blow was divine, but certainly in saying that it came by a miracle. It was no miracle, doctor, except in so far as a man is himself a miracle, with his strange and wicked and yet half-heroic heart. The force that smashed that skull was a force well known to scientists—one of the most frequently debated of the laws of nature."

The doctor, who was looking at him with frowning intentness, only said: "And the other hint!"

"The other hint is this," said the priest. "Do you remember the blacksmith, though he believes in miracles, talking scornfully of the impossible fairy tale that his hammer had wings and flew half a mile across country?"

"Yes," said the doctor, "I remember that."

"Well," added Father Brown, with a broad smile, "that fairy tale was the nearest thing to the real truth that has been said today." And with that he turned his back and stumped up the steps after the curate.

The Reverend Wilfred, who had been waiting for him, pale and impatient, as if this little delay were the last straw for his nerves, led him immediately to his favorite corner of the church, that part of the gallery closest to the carved roof and lit by the wonderful window with the angel. The little Latin priest explored and admired everything exhaustively, talking cheerfully but in a low voice all the time. When in the course of his investigation he found the side exit and the winding stair down which Wilfred had rushed to find his brother dead, Father Brown ran not down but up, with the agility of a monkey, and his clear voice came from an outer platform above.

"Come up here, Mr. Bohun," he called. "The air will do you good."

Bohun followed him, and came out on a kind of stone gallery or balcony outside the building, from which one could see the illimitable plain in which their small hill stood, wooded away to the purple horizon and dotted with villages and farms. Clear and square, but quite small beneath them, was the blacksmith's yard, where the inspector still stood taking notes and the corpse still lay like a smashed fly.

"Might be the map of the world, mightn't it?" said Father Brown.

"Yes," said Bohun very gravely, and nodded his head.

Immediately beneath and about them the lines of the Gothic building plunged outward into the void with a sickening swiftness akin to suicide. There is that element of Titan energy in the architecture of the Middle Ages that, from whatever aspect it be seen, it always seems to be rushing away, like the strong back of some maddened horse. This church was hewn out of ancient and silent stone, bearded with old fungoids and stained with the nests of birds. And yet, when they saw it from below, it sprang like a fountain at the stars; and when they saw it, as now, from above, it poured like a cataract into a voiceless pit. For these two men on the tower were left alone with the most terrible aspect of the Gothic; the monstrous foreshortening and disproportion, the dizzy perspectives, the glimpses of great things small and small things great; a topsy-turvydom of stone in the mid-air. Details of stone, enormous by their proximity, were relieved against a pattern of fields and farms, pygmy in their distance. A carved bird or beast at a corner seemed like some vast walking or flying dragon wasting the pastures and villages below. The whole atmosphere was dizzy and dangerous, as if men were upheld in air amid the gyrating wings of colossal genii; and the whole of that old church, as tall and rich as a cathedral, seemed to sit upon the sunlit country like a cloudburst.

"I think there is something rather dangerous about standing on these high places even to pray," said Father Brown. "Heights were made to be looked at, not to be looked from."

"Do you mean that one may fall over?" asked Wilfred.

"I mean that one's soul may fall if one's body doesn't," said the other priest.

"I scarcely understand you," remarked Bohun indistinctly.

"Look at that blacksmith, for instance," went on Father Brown calmly; "a good man, but not a Christian—hard, imperious, unforgiving. Well, his Scotch religion was made up by men who prayed on hills and high crags, and learned to look down on the world more than to look up at heaven. Humility is the mother of giants. One sees great things from the valley; only small things from the peak."

"But he—he didn't do it," said Bohun tremulously.

"No," said the other in an odd voice; "we know he didn't do it."

After a moment he resumed, looking tranquilly out over the plain with his pale grey eyes. "I knew a man," he said, "who began by worshipping with others before the altar, but who grew fond of high and lonely places to pray from, corners or niches in the belfry or the spire. And once in one of those dizzy places, where the whole world seemed to turn under him like a wheel, his brain turned also, and he fancied he was God. So that though he was a good man, he committed a great crime."

Wilfred's face was turned away, but his bony hands turned blue and white as they tightened on the parapet of stone.

"He thought it was given to *him* to judge the world and strike down the sinner. He would never have had such a thought if he had been kneeling with other men upon a floor. But he saw all men walking about like insects. He saw one especially strutting just below him, insolent and evident by the bright green hat—a poisonous insect."

Rooks cawed round the corners of the belfry; but there was no further sound till Father Brown went on.

"This also tempted him, that he had in his hand one of the most awful engines of nature; I mean gravitation, that mad and quickening rush by which all earth's creatures fly back to her heart when released. See, the inspector is strutting just below us in the smithy. If I were to toss a pebble over this parapet it would be something like a bullet by the time it struck him. If I were to drop a hammer—even a small hammer——"

Wilfred Bohun threw one leg over the parapet, and Father Brown had him in a minute by the collar.

"Not by that door," he said quite gently; "that door leads to hell."

Bohun staggered back against the wall, and stared at him with frightful eyes.

"How do you know all this?" he cried. "Are you a devil?"

"I am a man," answered Father Brown gravely; "and therefore have all devils in my heart. Listen to me," he said after a short pause. "I know what you did—at least, I can guess the great part of it. When you left your brother you were racked with no unrighteous rage to the extent even that you snatched up a small hammer, half inclined to kill him with his foulness on his mouth. Recoiling, you thrust it under your buttoned coat instead, and rushed into the church. You pray wildly in many places, under the angel window, upon the platform above, and on a higher platform still, from which you could see the colonel's Eastern hat like the back of a green beetle crawling about. Then something snapped in your soul, and you let God's thunderbolt fall."

Wilfred put a weak hand to his head, and asked in a low voice: "How did you know that his hat looked like a green beetle?"

"Oh, that," said the other with the shadow of a smile, "that was common sense. But hear me further. I say I know all this; but no one else shall know it. The next step is for you; I shall take no more steps; I will seal this with the seal of confession. If you ask me why, there are many reasons, and only one that concerns you. I leave things to you because you have not yet gone very far wrong, as assassins go. You did not help to fix the crime on the smith when it was easy; or on his wife, when that was easy. You tried to fix it on the imbecile because you knew that he could not suffer. That was one of the gleams that it is my business to find in assassins. And now come down into the village, and go your own way as free as the wind; for I have said my last word."

They went down the winding stairs in utter silence, and came out into the sunlight by the smithy. Wilfred Bohun carefully unlatched the wooden gate of the yard, and going up to the inspector, said: "I wish to give myself up; I have killed my brother."

THE DREAM

AGATHA CHRISTIE

Hercule Poirot gave the house a steady, appraising glance. His eyes wandered to its surroundings—the shops, the big factory building opposite, the blocks of cheap mansion flats.

Then his eyes returned to Northway House, relic of an earlier age of space and leisure, when green fields had surrounded its well-bred arrogance. Now it was an anachronism, submerged and forgotten in the sea of modern London.

Few people could have told you to whom it belonged, though its owner's name would have been recognized as one of the world's richest men. But money can quench publicity as well as flaunt it. Benedict Farley, that eccentric millionaire, chose not to advertise his choice of residence. He himself was rarely seen. From time to time he appeared at board meetings, his lean figure, beaked nose and rasping voice easily dominating the assembled directors. Apart from that, he was just a well-known figure of legend.

There were his strange meannesses, his incredible generosities, his famous patchwork dressing gown, now reputed to be twenty-eight years old, his invariable diet of cabbage soup and caviar, his hatred of cats. All these things the public knew.

Hercule Poirot knew them also. It was all he did know of the man he was about to visit. The letter in his coat pocket told him little more.

He pressed the bell, glancing as he did so at the neat wristwatch which had at last replaced the large turnip-faced watch of earlier days. Yes, it was exactly 9:30.

THE DREAM

The door opened after just the right interval. A perfect specimen of the genus butler stood outlined against the lighted hall.

"Mr. Benedict Farley?" asked Hercule Poirot.

The impersonal glance surveyed him from head to foot, inoffensively but effectively.

En gros et en detail, thought Hercule Poirot to himself with appreciation.

"You have an appointment, sir?" asked the suave voice.

"Yes."

"Your name, sir?"

"M. Hercule Poirot."

The butler bowed and drew back. But there was yet one more formality before the deft hands took hat and stick from the visitor.

"You will excuse me, sir. I was to ask for a letter."

With deliberation, Poirot took from his pocket the folded letter and handed it to the butler. The latter gave it to a mere glance, then returned it with a bow. Its contents were simple:

Northway House, W.8.

M. Hercule Poirot.

Dear Sir: Mr. Benedict Farley would like to have the benefit of your advice. If convenient to yourself, he would be glad if you would call upon him at the above address at 9:30 tomorrow (Thursday) evening.

Yours truly,
Hugo Cornworthy,
Secretary.

P.S.: Please bring this letter with you.

The butler said: "Will you please come up to Mr. Cornworthy's room?" and led the way up the broad staircase. Poirot followed him, looking with appreciation at such objets d'art as were of an opulent and florid nature. His own taste in art was always of a bourgeois nature.

On the upper floor, the butler knocked on a door.

Hercule Poirot's eyebrows rose very slightly. It was the first jarring note. For the best butlers do not knock at doors, and yet, indubitably, this was a first-class butler.

A voice from within called out something. The butler threw open the door. He announced—and again Poirot sensed the deliberate departure from orthodoxy: "The gentleman you are expecting, sir."

It was a fair-sized room, very plainly furnished in a workmanlike fashion. Filing cabinets, books of reference, a couple of easy chairs, and an imposing desk covered with neatly docketed papers. The only light came from a big green-shaded reading lamp which stood on a small table by the arm of one of the easy chairs. It was placed so as to cast its full light on anyone approaching from the door. Hercule Poirot blinked, realizing that the lamp bulb was at least one hundred and fifty watts. In the armchair sat a thin figure in a patchwork dressing gown—Benedict Farley. His head was stuck forward in a characteristic attitude, his beaked nose projecting like that of a bird. A crest of white hair like that of a cockatoo rose above his forehead. His eyes glittered behind thick lenses as he peered suspiciously at his visitor.

"Hey," he said at last, and his voice was shrill and harsh. "So you're Hercule Poirot, hey?"

"At your service," said Poirot politely, and bowed, one hand on the back of a chair.

"Sit down—sit down," said the old man testily.

Hercule Poirot sat down in the full glare of the lamp. From behind it the old man seemed to be studying him attentively.

"How do I know you're Hercule Poirot, hey?" he demanded fretfully. "Tell me that, hey?"

Once more Poirot drew the letter from his pocket and handed it to Farley.

"Yes," admitted the millionaire grudgingly. "That's it. That's what I got Cornworthy to write." He folded it up and tossed it back. "So you're the fellow, are you?"

With a little wave of his hand, Poirot said, "I assure you there is no deception."

Benedict Farley chuckled suddenly. "That's what the conjurer says just before he takes the goldfish out of the hat. Saying that is part of the trick, you know."

Poirot did not reply.

Farley said suddenly, "Think I'm a suspicious old man, hey? So I am. Don't trust anybody! That's my motto. Can't trust anybody when you're rich. No, no, it doesn't do."

"You wished," Poirot hinted gently, "to consult me?"

The old man nodded. "That's right. Always buy the best. That's my motto. Go to the expert and don't count the cost. You'll notice, M. Poirot, I haven't asked you your fee. Send me in the bill later. I shan't cut up rough over it. Damned fools at the dairy thought they could charge me two and nine for eggs when two and seven's the market price. Lot of swindlers! I won't be swindled. But the man at the top's different. He's worth the money. I'm at the top myself; I know."

THE DREAM

Hercule Poirot made no reply. He listened attentively, his head poised a little on one side.

Behind his impassive exterior he was conscious of a feeling of disappointment. He could not exactly put his finger on it. So far, Benedict Farley had conformed to the popular idea of himself, and yet Poirot was disappointed.

"The man," he said disgustedly to himself, "is a mountebank; nothing but a mountebank."

He had known other millionaires, eccentric men, too, but in nearly every case he had been conscious of a certain force, an inner energy that had commanded his respect. If they had worn a patchwork dressing gown, it would have been because they liked wearing such a dressing gown. But the dressing gown of Benedict Farley, or so it seemed to Poirot, was essentially a stage property. And the man himself was essentially stagy.

He repeated again, unemotionally, "You wished to consult me, Mr. Farley?"

Abruptly, the millionaire's manner changed. He leaned forward. His voice dropped to a croak:

"Yes. Yes. I want to hear what you've got to say—what you think. Go to the top! That's my way! The best doctor—the best detective—it's between the two of them."

"As yet, monsieur, I do not understand."

"Naturally," snapped Farley. "I haven't begun to tell you."

He leaned forward once more and shot out an abrupt question: "What do you know, M. Poirot, about dreams?"

The little man's eyebrows rose. Whatever he had expected, it was not this.

"For that, Monsieur Farley, I should recommend Napoleon's *Book of Dreams*, or the latest practicing psychologist from Harley Street."

Benedict Farley said soberly, "I've tried both."

There was a pause, then the millionaire spoke; at first almost in a whisper, then with a voice growing higher and higher:

"It's the same dream, night after night. And I'm afraid. It's always the same. I'm sitting in my room next door to this. Sitting at my desk, writing. There's a clock there, and I glance at it and see the time—exactly twenty-eight minutes past three. Always the same time, you understand. And when I see the time, M. Poirot, I know I've got to do it. I don't want to do it, but I've got to."

Unperturbed, Poirot said, "And what is it that you have to do?"

Benedict Farley said hoarsely, "At twenty-eight minutes past three I open the second drawer down on the right of my desk, take out the revolver that I keep there, load it and walk over to the window. And then—and then——"

"Yes?"

Benedict Farley said, in a whisper, "Then I shoot myself."

There was a silence; then Poirot said, "That is your dream? The same every night?"

"Yes."

"What happens after you shoot yourself?"

"I wake up."

Poirot nodded his head slowly and thoughtfully. "As a matter of interest, do you keep a revolver in that particular drawer?"

"Yes."

"Why?"

"I have always done so. It is as well to be prepared."

"Prepared for what?"

Farley said irritably, "All rich men have enemies."

Poirot remained silent for a moment or two, then he said, "Why exactly did you send for me?"

"I will tell you. First of all, I consulted a doctor—three doctors, to be exact. The first told me it was all a question of diet. He was an elderly man. The second was a young man of the modern school. He assured me that it all hinged on a certain event that took place in infancy at that particular time of day—three twenty-eight. I am so determined, he says, not to remember that event that I symbolize it by destroying myself. That is his explanation."

"And the third doctor?"

Benedict Farley's voice rose in shrill anger, "He's a young man too. He has a preposterous theory! He asserts that my life is so unbearable to me that I deliberately want to end it! But since to acknowledge that fact would be to acknowledge that essentially I am a failure, I refuse in my waking moments to face the truth. But when I am asleep, all inhibitions are removed, and I proceed to do that which I really wish to do. I put an end to myself."

Poirot said, "His view is that you really wish, unknown to yourself, to commit suicide?"

Benedict Farley cried shrilly: "And that's impossible—impossible! I'm perfectly happy! I've got everything I want—everything money can buy! It's fantastic, unbelievable, even to suggest a thing like that!"

Poirot looked at him with interest. Perhaps something in the shaking hands, the trembling shrillness of the voice, warned him that the denial was too vehement. He contented himself with saying: "And where do I come in, monsieur?"

THE DREAM

Benedict Farley calmed down suddenly. He tapped with an emphatic finger on the table beside him.

"Because there's another possibility. And if it's right, you're the man to know about it! You're famous, you've had hundreds of cases—fantastic, improbable cases! You'd know if anyone does."

"Know what?"

Farley's voice dropped to a whisper. "Supposing someone wants to kill me. Could they do it this way? Could they make me dream that dream night after night?"

"Hypnotism, you mean?"

"Yes."

"It would be possible, I suppose," Poirot said at last. "It is more a question for a doctor."

"You don't know of such a case in your experience?"

"Not precisely on those lines, no."

"You see what I'm driving at? I'm made to dream the same dream, night after night, night after night, and then one day the suggestion is too much for me, and I act upon it. I do what I've dreamed of so often—kill myself!"

Slowly, Hercule Poirot shook his head.

Farley said, "You don't think that is possible?"

"Possible?" Poirot shook his head. "That is not a word I care to meddle with."

"But you think it improbable."

"Most improbable."

Benedict Farley murmured, "The doctor said so, too." Then, his voice rising shrilly again, he cried out, "But why do I have this dream? Why? Why?"

Hercule Poirot shook his head.

Benedict Farley said abruptly, "You're sure you've never come across anything like this in your experience?"

"Never."

"That's what I wanted to know."

Delicately, Hercule Poirot cleared his throat. "You permit," he said, "a question?"

"What is it? What is it? Say what you like."

"Who is it you suspect of wanting to kill you?"

"Nobody. Nobody at all."

Poirot persisted, "But the idea presented itself to your mind?"

"I wanted to know if it was a possibility."

"Speaking from my own experience, I should say, no. Have you ever been hypnotized, by the way?"

"Of course not. D'you think I'd lend myself to such tomfoolery?"

"Then I think one can say that your theory is definitely improbable."

"But the dream, you fool—the dream!"

"The dream is certainly remarkable," said Poirot thoughtfully. "I should like to see the scene of this drama—the desk, the clock and the revolver."

"Of course. I'll take you next door."

Wrapping the folds of his dressing gown round him, the old man half rose from his chair. Then suddenly he resumed his seat.

"No," he said. "There's nothing to see there. I've told you all there is to tell."

"But I should like to see for myself."

Benedict Farley snapped out, "There's no need. You've given me your opinion."

Poirot shrugged his shoulders. "As you please." He rose to his feet. "I am sorry, M. Farley, that I have not been able to be of assistance to you."

Benedict Farley was staring straight ahead of him.

"Don't want a lot of hanky-pankying around," he growled out. "I've told you the facts; you can't make anything of them. That closes the matter. You can send me in a bill for a consultation fee."

"I shall not fail to do so," said the detective dryly. He walked toward the door.

"Stop a minute." The millionaire called him back. "That letter—I want it."

Poirot's eyebrows rose. He drew out a folded sheet and handed it to the old man. The latter scrutinized it, then put it down on the table beside him with a nod.

Once more Hercule Poirot walked to the door. He was puzzled. His busy mind was going over and over the story he had been told. Yet in the midst of his mental preoccupation, a nagging sense of something wrong obtruded itself. And that something had to do with himself, not with Benedict Farley.

With his hand on the doorknob, his mind cleared. He, Hercule Poirot, had been guilty of an error! He turned back once more.

"A thousand pardons! In the interest of your problem, I have committed a folly! That letter I handed to you—by mischance I put my hand into my right-hand pocket——"

"What's all this? What's all this?"

"The letter that I handed you just now—an apology from my laundress concerning the treatment of my collars." Poirot was smiling, apologetic. He dipped into his left-hand pocket. "This is your letter."

THE DREAM

Benedict Farley snatched at it, grunted: "Why the devil don't you mind what you're doing?"

Poirot retrieved his laundress' communication, apologized gracefully once more, and left the room.

The butler was in the hall below, waiting to let him out.

"Can I get you a taxi, sir?"

"No, I thank you. The night is fine. I will walk."

Herecule Poirot paused a moment on the sidewalk, waiting for a pause in the traffic to cross the busy street.

A frown creased his forehead. "No," he said to himself. "I do not understand at all. Nothing makes sense. Regrettable to have to admit it, but I, Hercule Poirot, am completely baffled."

The second act followed a week later. It opened with a telephone call from one John Stillingfleet, M.D.

He said, with a lack of medical decorum, "That you, Poirot, old horse? Stillingfleet here."

"Ah, yes, my friend. What is it?"

"I'm speaking from Northway House—Benedict Farley's."

"Ah, yes?" Poirot's voice quickened with interest. "What of Mr. Farley?"

"Farley's dead. Shot himself this afternoon."

There was a pause, then Poirot said, "Yes."

"I notice you're not overcome with surprise. Know something about it, old horse?"

"Why should you think that?"

"Well, it isn't brilliant deduction or telepathy or anything like that. We found a note from Farley to you, making an appointment about a week ago. Perhaps you'd come round?"

"I will come immediately."

"Good for you, old boy. Some dirty work at the crossroads, eh?"

Poirot merely repeated that he would set forth immediately.

"Don't want to spill the beans over the telephone? Quite right. So long."

A quarter of an hour later, Poirot was sitting in the library, a low long room at the back of Northway House, on the ground floor. There were five other persons in the room: Inspector Barnett; Doctor Stillingfleet; Mrs. Farley, the widow of the millionaire; Joanna Farley, his only daughter; and Hugo Cornworthy, his private secretary.

Doctor Stillingfleet, whose professional manner was entirely different from his telephonic style, was a tall, long-faced young man of thirty. Mrs. Farley was obviously much younger than her husband. She was a handsome dark-haired woman. Her mouth was hard and her black eyes gave no clue to her emotions. She appeared perfectly self-possessed. Joanna Farley had fair hair and a freckled face. The prominence of her nose and chin was clearly inherited from her father. Her eyes were intelligent and shrewd. Hugo Cornworthy was a somewhat colorless young man, very correctly dressed. He seemed intelligent and efficient.

Poirot narrated simply the circumstances of his visit and the story told him by Benedict Farley. He could not complain of any lack of interest.

"Most extraordinary story I've ever heard!" said the inspector. "A dream, eh? . . . Did you know anything about this, Mrs. Farley?"

She bowed her head. "My husband mentioned it to me. It upset him very much. I—I told him it was indigestion—his diet, you know, was very peculiar—and suggested his calling in Doctor Stillingfleet."

That young man shook his head. "He didn't consult me. From M. Poirot's story, I gather he went to Harley Street."

"I would like your advice on that point, doctor," said Poirot. "Mr. Farley told me that he consulted three specialists. What do you think of the theories they advanced?"

Stillingfleet frowned. "It's difficult to say. You've got to take into account that what he passed on to you wasn't exactly what had been said to him. It was a layman's interpretation."

"You mean he had got the phraseology wrong?"

"Not exactly. I mean they would put a thing to him in professional terms, he'd get the meaning a little distorted and then recast it in his own language."

"So that what he told me was not really what the doctors said."

"He's just got it all a little wrong, if you know what I mean."

"Is it known whom he consulted?" Poirot asked.

Mrs. Farley shook her head.

Joanna Farley spoke up: "None of us had any idea he had consulted anyone."

Poirot said, "Did he speak to you about his dream?"

The girl shook her head.

"And you, Mr. Cornworthy?"

"No, he said nothing at all. I took down a letter to you at his dictation, but I had no idea as to why he wished to consult you. I thought it might possibly have something to do with some business irregularity."

Poirot asked, "And now as to the actual facts of Mr. Farley's death?"

When no one spoke, Inspector Barnett took upon himself the role of spokesman:

THE DREAM

"Mr. Farley was in the habit of working in his own room on the first floor every afternoon. I understand that there was a big merger of businesses in prospect——"

He looked at Hugo Cornworthy, who said, "Consolidated Coach Lines."

"In connection with that," continued Barnett, "Mr. Farley had agreed to give an interview to two members of the press. He seldom did anything of the kind, I understand. Accordingly, two reporters arrived at a quarter past three by appointment. They waited outside Mr. Farley's door—which was the customary place for people to wait who had an appointment with Mr. Farley. At twenty past three, a messenger arrived from the office of Consolidated Coach Lines with some urgent papers. On his leaving, Mr. Farley accompanied him to the door of the room, and from there spoke to the two members of the press.

"He said, 'I am sorry, gentlemen, to have to keep you waiting, but I have some urgent business to attend to. I will be as quick as I can.'

"The two gentlemen, Mr. Adams and Mr. Stoddart, assured Mr. Farley that they would await his convenience. He went back into his room, shut the door, and was never seen alive again."

"Continue," said Poirot.

"At a little after four o'clock," went on the inspector, "Mr. Cornworthy here came out of his room, which is next door to Mr. Farley's, and was surprised to see the two reporters still waiting. He wanted Mr. Farley's signature to some letters and thought he had also better remind him that these two gentlemen were waiting. He accordingly went into Mr. Farley's room. To his surprise, he at first thought the room was empty. Then he caught sight of a boot sticking out behind the desk, which is placed in front of the window. He found Mr. Farley lying there dead, a revolver beside him.

"Mr. Cornworthy hurried out of the room and directed the butler to ring up Doctor Stillingfleet. By the latter's advice, Mr. Cornworthy also informed the police."

Poirot asked, "Was the shot heard by anyone?"

"No. The traffic is very noisy here, the landing window was open. It would be most unlikely if it had been noticed."

Poirot nodded thoughtfully. "What time is it supposed he died?" he asked.

Stillingfleet said, "I examined the body as soon as I got here—that is, at thirty-two minutes past four. Mr. Farley had been dead at least an hour."

Poirot's face was very grave. "So then, it seems possible that his death could have occurred at twenty-eight minutes past three."

"Exactly," said Stillingfleet.

"Any finger marks on the revolver?"

"Yes, his own."

"And the revolver itself?"

The inspector took up the tale: "Was one which he kept in the drawer of his desk, just as he told you. Mrs. Farley has identified it positively. Moreover, you understand, there is only one entrance to the room—the door giving onto the landing. The two reporters were sitting exactly opposite that door, and they swear that no one entered the room from the time Mr. Farley spoke to them until Mr. Cornworthy went in at a little after four o'clock."

"So that there is every reason to suppose that Mr. Farley committed suicide?"

Inspector Barnett smiled a little. "There would have been no doubt at all, but for one point."

"And that?"

"The letter written to you."

Poirot smiled too. "I see! Where Hercule Poirot is concerned, immediately the suspicion of murder arises!"

"Precisely," said the inspector dryly. "However, after your clearing up of the situation——"

Poirot interrupted him, "One little minute." He turned to Mrs. Farley. "Had your husband ever been hypnotized?"

"Never."

"Had he studied the question of hypnotism? Was he interested in the subject?"

She shook her head. "I don't think so." Suddenly her self-control seemed to break down: "That horrible dream! It's uncanny! That he should have dreamed that, night after night, and then—and then—— It's as though he were—hounded to death!"

Poirot remembered Benedict Farley saying, "I proceed to do that which I really wish to do. I put an end to myself."

He said, "Had it ever occurred to you that your husband might be tempted to do away with himself?"

"No—at least—sometimes he was very queer."

Joanna Farley's voice broke in, clear and scornful: "Father would never have killed himself. He was far too careful of himself."

Doctor Stillingfleet said, "It isn't the people who threaten to commit suicide who usually do it, you know, Miss Farley. That's why suicides sometimes seem unaccountable."

Poirot rose to his feet. "Is it permitted," he asked, "that I see the room where the tragedy occurred?"

The doctor accompanied Poirot upstairs.

THE DREAM

Benedict Farley's room was a much larger one than the secretary's next door. It was luxuriously furnished with deep leather-covered armchairs, a thick pile carpet, and a superb outsize writing desk.

Poirot passed behind the latter to where a dark stain on the carpet showed just before the window. He remembered the millionaire saying, "At twenty-eight minutes past three I open the second drawer down on the right of my desk, take out the revolver that I keep there, load it and walk over to the window. And then—and then I shoot myself."

He nodded slowly. Then he said, "The window was open like this?"

"Yes. But nobody could have got in that way."

Poirot put his head out. There was no sill or parapet and no pipes near. Not even a cat could have gained access that way. Opposite rose the blank wall of the factory, a dead wall with no windows in it.

Stillingfleet said, "Funny room for a rich man. It's like looking out onto a prison wall."

"Yes," said Poirot. He drew his head in and stared at the expanse of solid brick. "I think," he said, "that that wall is important."

Stillingfleet looked at him curiously.

"You mean, psychologically?"

Poirot had moved to the desk. Idly, or so it seemed, he picked up a pair of what are usually called lazy tongs. He pressed the handles; the tongs shot out to their full length. Delicately, Poirot picked up a burned match stump with them from beside a chair some feet away and conveyed it carefully to the wastepaper basket.

He murmured, "An ingenious invention"—and replaced the tongs neatly on the writing table. Then he asked, "Where were Mrs. Farley and Miss Farley at the time of the—death?"

"Mrs. Farley was resting in her room on the floor above this. Miss Farley was painting in her studio at the top of the house."

Hercule Poirot drummed idly with his fingers on the table for a minute or two. Then he said, "I should like to see Miss Farley."

Stillingfleet glanced at him curiously, then left the room. In another minute or two the door opened and Joanna Farley came in.

"You do not mind, mademoiselle, if I ask you a few questions?"

She returned his glance coolly. "Please ask anything you choose."

"Did you know that your father kept a revolver in his desk?"

"No."

"Where were you and your mother—that is to say, your stepmother—that is right?"

"Yes, Louise is my father's second wife. She is only eight years older than I am. You were about to say——?"

"Where were you and she on Thursday of last week? That is to say, on Thursday night."

"Thursday? Let me see. Oh, yes, we had gone to the theater. To see *Little Dog Laughed*."

"Your father did not suggest accompanying you?"

"He never went out to theaters."

"He was not a very sociable man?"

The girl looked at him directly.

"My father," she said, "had a singularly unpleasant personality. No one who lived in close association with him could possibly be fond of him."

"That, mademoiselle, is a very candid statement."

"I am saving you time, M. Poirot. I realize quite well what you are getting at. My stepmother married my father for his money. I lived here because I had no money to live elsewhere. There is a man I wish to marry—a poor man—my father saw to it that he lost his job. He wanted me, you see, to marry well—an easy matter, since I was to be his heiress!"

"Your father's fortune passes to you?"

"Yes. That is, he left Louise, my stepmother, a quarter of a million free of tax, and there are other legacies, but the residue goes to me." She smiled suddenly. "So, you see, M. Poirot, I had every reason to desire my father's death!"

"I see, mademoiselle, that you have inherited your father's intelligence."

She said thoughtfully, "Father was clever. One felt that with him—that he had force, driving power, but it had all turned sour—bitter. There was no humanity left."

Hercule Poirot said softly, "*Grand Dieu*, but what an imbecile I am."

Joanna Farley turned toward the door. "Is there anything more?"

"Two little questions. These tongs here"—he picked up the lazy tongs—"were they always on the table?"

"Yes. Father used them for picking up things. He didn't like stooping."

"One other question: Was your father's eyesight good?" She stared at him. "Oh, no, he couldn't see at all. I mean he couldn't see without his glasses. His sight had always been bad from a boy."

"But with his glasses?"

"Oh, he could see all right then, of course."

"He could read newspapers and fine print?"

"Oh, yes."

"That is all, mademoiselle." As she went out of the room, Poirot murmured, "I was stupid. It was there all the time, under my nose. And because it was so near I could not see it."

He leaned out of the window once more.

Below, in the narrow way between house and factory, he saw a small dark object.

Hercule Poirot nodded, satisfied. He went downstairs again. The others were still in the library. Poirot addressed himself to the secretary:

"I want you, Mr. Cornworthy, to recount to me in detail the exact circumstances of Mr. Farley's summons to me. When, for instance, did Mr. Farley dictate that letter?"

"On Wednesday afternoon about five-thirty."

"Were there any special directions about posting it?"

"He told me to post it myself, and I did."

"Did he give any special instructions to the butler about admitting me?"

"Yes. He told me to tell Holmes—Holmes is the butler—that a gentleman would be calling at nine-thirty. He was to ask the gentleman's name. He was also to ask to see the letter."

"Rather peculiar precautions, don't you think?"

Cornworthy shrugged. "Mr. Farley," he said carefully, "was rather a peculiar man."

"Any other instructions?"

"Yes. He told me to take the evening off, and immediately after dinner I went to the cinema."

"When did you return?"

"I let myself in about a quarter past eleven."

"Did you see Mr. Farley again that evening?"

"No."

"And he did not mention the matter the next morning?"

"No."

Poirot paused a moment, then resumed, "When I arrived, I was not shown into Mr. Farley's own room."

"No. He told me that I was to tell Holmes to show you into my room."

"Why was that? Do you know?"

Cornworthy shook his head. "I never questioned any of Mr. Farley's orders," he said dryly. "He would have resented it if I had."

"Did he usually receive visitors in his own room?"

"Usually, but not always. Sometimes he saw them in my room."

"Was there any reason for that?"

Hugo Cornworthy considered. "No, I hardly think so. I've never really thought about it."

Turning to Mrs. Farley, Poirot asked, "You permit that I ring for your butler?"

"Certainly, M. Poirot."

Very correct, very urbane, Holmes answered the bell. Mrs. Farley indicated Poirot with a gesture.

"What were your instructions, Holmes, on the Thursday night when I came here?"

Holmes cleared his throat, then said, "After dinner, Mr. Cornworthy told me that Mr. Farley expected a Mr. Hercule Poirot at nine-thirty. I was to ascertain the gentleman's name, and I was to verify the information by glancing at a letter. Then I was to show him up to Mr. Cornworthy's room."

"Were you also told to knock on the door?"

An expression of distaste crossed the butler's countenance.

"That was one of Mr. Farley's orders. I was always to knock when introducing visitors—business visitors, that is," he added.

"Ah, that puzzled me! Were you given any other instructions concerning me?"

"No, sir. When Mr. Cornworthy had told me what I have just repeated to you, he went out."

"What time was that?"

"Ten minutes to nine, sir."

"Did you see Mr. Farley after that?"

"Yes, sir, I took him up a glass of hot water as usual at nine o'clock."

"Was he then in his own room or in Mr. Cornworthy's?"

"He was in his own room, sir."

"You noticed nothing unusual about that room?"

"Unusual? No, sir."

"Where were Mrs. Farley and Miss Farley?"

"They had gone to the theater, sir."

"Thank you, Holmes."

Holmes bowed and left the room.

Poirot turned to the millionaire's widow.

"One more question, Mrs. Farley: Had your husband good sight?"

"No. Not without his glasses."

"He was very shortsighted?"

"Oh, yes, he was quite helpless without his spectacles."

"He had several pairs of glasses?"

"Yes."

"Ah," said Poirot. He leaned back. "I think that that concludes the case."

There was silence in the room. They were all looking at the little

THE DREAM

man who sat there complacently stroking his mustaches. On the inspector's face was perplexity; John Stillingfleet was frowning; Cornworthy merely stared uncomprehending; Mrs. Farley gazed in blank astonishment; Joanna Farley looked eager.

Mrs. Farley broke the silence. "I don't understand, M. Poirot." Her voice was fretful. "The dream——"

"Yes," said Poirot. "That dream was very important."

Mrs. Farley shivered. She said, "I've never believed in anything supernatural before, but now—to dream it night after night beforehand——"

"It's extraordinary," said Stillingfleet. "Extraordinary! If Mr. Farley himself hadn't told that story——"

"Exactly," said Poirot. His eyes, which had been half closed, opened suddenly. They were very green. "If Benedict Farley hadn't told me——"

He paused a minute, looking round at a circle of blank faces.

"There are certain things, you comprehend, that happened that evening which I was quite at a loss to explain. First, why make such a point of my bringing that letter with me?"

"Identification," suggested Cornworthy.

"No, no, my dear young man. Really, that idea is too ridiculous. There must be some much more valid reason. For not only did Mr. Farley require to see that letter produced but he definitely demanded that I should leave it behind me. And, moreover, even then he did not destroy it! It was found among his papers this afternoon. Why did he keep it?"

Joanna Farley's voice broke in, "He wanted, in case anything happened to him, that the facts of his strange dream should be made known."

Poirot nodded approvingly.

"You are astute, mademoiselle. That must—that can only be the point of the keeping of the letter. When Mr. Farley was dead, the story of that strange dream was to be told! That dream was very important. That dream, mademoiselle, was vital!"

He went on: "I will come now to the second strange point. After hearing his story, I asked Mr. Farley to show me the desk and the revolver. He seemed about to get up to do so, then suddenly refused. Why did he refuse?"

This time no one advanced an answer.

"I will put that question differently. What was there in that next room that Mr. Farley did not want me to see?"

There was still silence.

"Yes," said Poirot, "it is difficult, that. And yet there was some reason—some urgent reason. There was something in that room he could not afford to have me see.

"And now I come to the third inexplicable thing. Mr. Farley, as I was leaving, requested me to hand him the letter I had received. By inadvertence I handed him a communication from my laundress. He glanced at it and laid it down beside him. Just before I left the room, I discovered my error, and rectified it."

He looked round from one to the other. "You do not see?"

Stillingfleet said: "I don't really see how your laundress comes into it, Poirot."

"My laundress," said Poirot, "was very important. That miserable woman who ruins my collars was, for the first time in her life, useful to somebody. Surely, you see. Mr. Farley glanced at that communication—one glance would have told him that it was the wrong letter—and yet he knew nothing. Why? Because he could not see it properly!"

Inspector Barnett said sharply, "Didn't he have his glasses on?"

Hercule Poirot smiled. "Yes," he said, "he had his glasses on. That is what makes it so very interesting." He leaned forward. "Mr. Farley's dream was very important. He dreamed, you see, that he committed suicide. And a little later on, he did commit suicide. That is to say, he was alone in a room and was found there with a revolver by him, and no one entered or left the room at the time that he was shot. It means, does it not, that it must be suicide?"

"Yes," said Stillingfleet.

Hercule Poirot shook his head. "On the contrary," he said. "It was murder. An unusual and a very cleverly planned murder."

Again he leaned forward, tapping the table, his eyes green and shining.

"Why did Mr. Farley not allow me to go into his own room that evening? What was there in there that I must not be allowed to see? I think, my friends, that there was Benedict Farley himself!"

He smiled at the blank faces.

"Yes, yes, it is not nonsense, what I say. Why could the Mr. Farley to whom I had been talking not realize the difference between two totally dissimilar letters? Because, *mes amis*, he was a man of normal sight, wearing a pair of very powerful glasses. Those glasses would render a man of normal eyesight practically blind. . . . Isn't that so, doctor?"

Stillingfleet murmured, "That's so, of course."

"Why did I feel that in talking to Mr. Farley I was talking to a mountebank, to an actor playing a part? Because he was playing a part! Consider the setting. The dim room, the green-shaded light

THE DREAM

turned blindingly away from the figure in the chair. What did I see—the famous patchwork dressing gown, the beaked nose—faked with that useful substance, nose putty—the white crest of hair, the powerful lenses concealing the eyes. What evidence is there that Mr. Farley ever had a dream? Only the evidence of Mrs. Farley. What evidence is there that Benedict Farley kept a revolver in his desk? Only the word of Mrs. Farley. Two people carried this fraud through—Mrs. Farley and Hugo Cornworthy. Cornworthy wrote the letter to me, gave instructions to the butler, went out, ostensibly to the cinema, but let himself in again immediately with a key, went to his room, made himself up, and played the part of Benedict Farley.

"And so we come to this afternoon. The opportunity for which Mr. Cornworthy has been waiting arrives. There are two witnesses on the landing to swear that no one goes in or out of Benedict Farley's room. Cornworthy waits until a particularly heavy batch of traffic is about to pass. Then he leans out of his window, and with the lazy tongs which he has purloined from the desk next door, he holds an object against the window of that room. Benedict Farley comes to the window. Cornworthy snatches back the tongs, and as Farley leans out and the lorries are passing outside, Cornworthy shoots him with the revolver that he has ready. There is a blank wall opposite, remember. There can be no witness of the crime. Cornworthy waits for over half an hour, then gathers up some papers, conceals the lazy tongs and the revolver between them and goes out onto the landing and into the next room. He replaces the tongs on the desk, lays down the revolver after pressing the dead man's fingers on it and hurries out with news of Mr. Farley's 'suicide.'

"He arranges that the letter to me shall be found and that I shall arrive with my story—the story I heard from Mr. Farley's own lips—of his extraordinary dream—the strange compulsion he felt to kill himself! A few credulous people will discuss the hypnotism theory, but the main result will be to confirm without a doubt that the actual hand that held the revolver was Benedict Farley's own."

Hercule Poirot's eyes went to the widow's face—the dismay, the ashy pallor, the blind fear.

"And in due course," he finished gently, "the happy ending would have been achieved. A quarter of a million and two hearts that beat as one."

Stillingfleet and Poirot walked along the side of Northway House. On their right was the towering wall of the factory. Above them, on their left, were the windows of Benedict Farley's and Hugo Cornworthy's rooms. Hercule Poirot stooped and picked up a small object—a black stuffed cat.

"*Voilà*," he said. "That is what Cornworthy held in the lazy tongs against Farley's window. You remember, he hated cats? Naturally, he rushed to the window."

"Why on earth didn't Cornworthy come out and pick it up after he'd dropped it?"

"How could he? To do so would have been definitely suspicious. After all, if this object were found, what would anyone think? Only that some child had wandered round here and dropped it."

"Yes," said Stillingfleet with a sigh. "D'you know, old horse, up to the very last minute I thought you were leading up to some subtle theory of highfalutin psychological suggested murder? I bet those two thought so too! Nasty bit of goods, the Farley. Goodness, how she cracked! I rather like the girl. Grit, you know, and brains. I suppose I'd be thought to be a fortune hunter if I had a shot at her."

"You are too late, my friend. There is already someone *sur le tapis*. Her father's death has opened the way to happiness."

"Take it all round, she had a pretty good motive for bumping off the unpleasant parent."

"Motive and opportunity are not enough, doctor," said Hercule Poirot. "There must also be the criminal temperament."

"I wonder if you'll ever commit a crime, Poirot," said Stillingfleet. "I bet you could get away with it all right. As a matter of fact, it would be too easy for you. I mean the thing would be off, as definitely too unsporting."

"That," said Poirot, "is a typically English idea."

THE END OF DEVIL HAWKER

ARTHUR CONAN DOYLE

There is a fascinating little print shop around the corner of Drury Lane. When you pass through the old oaken doorway and into the dim dusty interior, you seem to have wandered into some corridor leading back through time, for on every side of you are the pictures of the past. But very specially I value that table on the left where lies the great pile of portrait prints heaped up in some sort of order of date. There you see the pictures of the men who stood round the throne of the young Victoria, of Melbourne, of Peel, of Wellington, and then you come on the D'Orsay and Lady Blessington period, and the long and wonderful series of H.B., the great, unknown John Doyle, who, in his day, was a real power in the land. Farther back still you come on the bucks and prize fighters of the Regency—the pompous Jackson, the sturdy Cribb, the empty Brummell, the chubby Alvanley. And then you may chance upon a face which you cannot pass without a second and a longer look. It is a face which Mephistopheles might have owned, thin, dark, keen, with bushy brows and fierce, alert eyes which glare out from beneath them. There is a full-length colored print which shows him to be tall and magnificently proportioned, with broad shoulders, slim waist, clad in a tightly buttoned green coat, buckskin breeches and high Hessian boots. Below is the inscription: "Sir John Hawker"—and that is the Devil Hawker of the legends.

In his short but vivid career, the end of which is here outlined, Hawker was the bully of the town. The bravest shrank away from the angry, insolent glare of those baleful eyes. He was a famous swordsman and a remarkable pistol shot—so remarkable that three times he starred the kneecap of his man: the most painful injury which he could inflict. But above all, he was the best amateur boxer of his day, and had he taken to the ring, it is likely that he would have made a name. His hitting is said to have been the most ferocious ever seen, and it was his amusement to try out novices at Cribb's rooms, which were his favorite haunt, and to teach them how to stand punishment. It gratified his pride to show his skill, and his cruel nature to administer pain to others. It was in these very rooms of Cribb that this little sketch of those days opens, where, as on a marionette stage, I would try to show you what manner of place it was and what manner of poeple walked London in those full-blooded, brutal and virile old days.

First, as to the place. It is at the corner of Panton Street, and you see over a broad, red-curtained door the sign: *Thomas Cribb. Dealer in Liquor and Tobacco*, with the Union Arms printed above. The door leads into a tiled passage which opens on the left into a common bar behind which, save on special evenings, a big, bull-faced, honest John Bull of a man may be seen with two assistants of the sparring-partner type, handing out refreshment and imbibing gratis a great deal more than was good for their athletic figures. Already Tom is getting a waistline which will cause his trainer and himself many a weary day at his next battle; if, indeed, the brave old fellow has not already come to the last of his fights, when he defended the honor of England by breaking the cast-iron jaw of Molyneaux, the black.

If, instead of turning into the common bar, you continue down the passage, you find a green-baize door with the word "Parlor" printed across one upper panel of glass. Push it open and you are in a room which is spacious and comfortable. There is sawdust on the floor, numerous wooden armchairs, round tables for the card players, a small bar presided over by Miss Lucy Stagg, a lady who had been accused of many things, but never of shyness, in the corner, and a fine collection of sporting pictures round the walls. At the back were swing doors with the words "Boxing Saloon" printed across them, leading into a large bare apartment with a roped ring in the center, and many pairs of gloves hanging upon the walls, belonging, for the most part, to the Corinthians who came up to have lessons from the champion, whose classes were only exceeded by those of Gentleman Jackson in Bond Street.

It was early in the particular evening of which I speak, and there was no one in the parlor save Cribb himself, who expected the quality that night, and was cleaning up in anticipation. Lucy wiped glasses languidly in her little bar. Beside the entrance door was a small, shriveled weasel of a man, Billy Jakes by name, who sat behind a green-baize table, in receipt of custom as a bookmaker, dog fancier or cock supplier—a privilege for which he paid Tom a good round sum every year. As no customers had appeared, he wandered over to the little bar.

"Well, things are quiet tonight, Lucy."

She looked up from polishing her glasses. "I expect they will be more lively soon, Mr. Jakes. It is full early."

"Well, Lucy, you look very pretty tonight. I expect I shall have to marry you yet."

"La, Mr. Jakes, how you do carry on!"

"Tell me, Lucy; do you want to make some money?"

"Everyone wants that, Mr. Jakes."

"How much can you lay your hands on?"

"I daresay I could find fifty pounds at a pinch."

"Wouldn't you like to turn it into a hundred?"

"Why, of course I would."

"It's Saracesca for the Oaks. I'd give you two to one, which is better than I give the others. She's a cert if ever there is one."

"Well, if you say so, Mr. Jakes. The money is upstairs in my box. But if you can really turn it into——"

Fortunately, honest Tom Cribb had been within earshot of this little debate, and he now caught the man roughly by the sleeve and twirled him in the direction of his table.

"You dirty dog; doing the poor girl out of her hard-earned savings!"

"All right, Tom. Only a joke! Only Billy Jakes' little joke! ... I wouldn't have let you lose, Lucy!"

"That's enough," said Tom. "Don't you heed him, Lucy. Keep your money in your box."

The green swing door opened and a number of bucks, in black coats, brown coats, green coats and purple, came filing into the room. The shrill voice of Jakes was at once uplifted and his clamor filled the air.

"Now, my noble sportsmen," he cried, "back your opinions! There is a bag of gold waiting, and you have only to put your hands in. How about Woodstock for the Derby? How about Saracesca for the Oaks? Four to one! Four to one! Two to one, bar one!"

The Corinthians gathered for a moment round the bookie's table, for his patter amused them.

"Lots of time for that, Jakes," said Lord Rufton, a big bluff county magnate and landowner.

"But the odds are shorter every day. Now's your time, my noble gamesters! Now's the time to sow the seed! Gold to be had for the asking, waitin' there for you to pick up. I like to pay it. It pleases me to see happy faces round me. I like to see them smiling. Now's your time."

"Why, half the field may scratch before the race," said Sir Charles Trevor—the smiling imperturbable Charles—whose estate has been sucked dry by its owner's wild excesses.

"No race, no pay. The old firm gives every gamester a run for his money. The knowing ones are all on to it. Sir John Hawker has five hundred on Woodstock."

"Well, Devil Hawker knows what he is about," said Lord Annerley, a dashing young Corinthian.

"Have fifty on the filly for the Oaks, Lord Rufton. Four to one?"

"Very good, Jakes," said the nobleman, handing out a note. "I suppose I shall find you after the race."

"Sitting here at this table, my lord. Old established place of business. You've got a certainty, my lord."

"Well," said a young Corinthian, "if it is as certain as that, I'll have fifty too."

"Right, my noble sportsman. I book it at three to one."

"I thought it was four."

"It was four. Now it is three. You're lucky to get in before it is two. Will you take your winnings in paper or gold?"

"Well, in gold."

"Very good, sir. You'll find me waiting at this table with a bag of gold at ten by the clock on the day after the race. It will be in a green-baize bag with a grip, so as you can easily carry it. By the way, I've got a fighting cock that's never been beat. Would any of you gentlemen——"

But the door had swung open and Sir John Hawker's handsome figure and sinister face filled the gap. The others moved toward the small bar. Hawker paused for a moment at the bookie's table.

"Hullo, Jakes; doing some fool out of his money as usual?"

"Tut, tut, Sir John, you should know me by now."

"Know you, you rascal! You have had a cool two thousand out of me from first to last. I know you too well."

"All you want is to persevere. You'll soon have it all back, Sir John."

"Hold your tongue, I say. I have had enough."

"No offense, my noble sportsman. But I've a brindled terrier down at the stables that's the best at rats in the whole of London."

"I wonder he hasn't had a nip at you then. . . . Hello, Tom."

Cribb had come forward as usual to greet his Corinthian guests.

"Good evening, Sir John. Going to put them on tonight?"

"Well, I'll see. What have you got?"

"Half a dozen up from old Bristol. That place is as full of milling coves as a bin is of bottles."

"I may try one of them over."

"Then play light, Sir John. You cracked the ribs of that lad from Lincoln. You broke his heart for fighting."

"It may as well be broke early as late. What's the use of him if he can't take punishment?"

Several more men had come into the room; one of them exceedingly drunk, another just a little less so. They were two of the Tom and Jerry clique who wandered day and night on the old round from the Haymarket to Panton Street and St. James, imagining that they were seeing life. The drunken one—a young hawbuck from the shires—was noisy and combative. His friend was trying to put some term to their adventures.

"Come, George," he coaxed, "we'll just have one drink here. Then one at the Dive and one at the Cellars, and wind up with broiled bones at Mother Simpson's."

The name of the dish started ideas in the drunken man's brain. He staggered in the direction of the landlord.

"Broiled bones!" he cried. "D'you hear? I want broiled bones! Fetch me dish—large dish—of broiled bones this instant—under pain—displeasure."

Cribb, who was well accustomed to such visitors, continued his conversation with Hawker without taking the slightest notice. They were discussing a possible opponent for old Tom Shelton, the navvy, when George broke in again.

"Where the devil's those broiled bones? Here, landlord! Ole Tom Cribb! Tom, give me large dish broiled bones this instant, or I punch your old head." As Cribb still took not the faintest heed, George became more bellicose.

"No broiled bones!" he cried. "Very good! Prepare defend yourself!"

"Don't hit him, George!" cried his more sober companion in alarm. "It's the champion."

"It's a lie. I am the champion. I'll give him smack in the chops. See if I don't."

For the first time Cribb turned a slow eye in his direction.

"No dancin' allowed here, sir," he said.

"I'm not dancing. I'm sparring."

"Well, don't do it, whatever it is."

"I'm going to fight you. Going to give old Tom a smack in the chops."

"Some other time, sir. I'm busy."

"Where're those bones? Last time of asking."

"What bones? What is he talkin' of?"

"Sorry, Tom, but have to give you good thrashing. Yes, Tom, very sorry, but must have lesson."

He made several wild strokes in the air, quite out of distance, and finally fell upon his knees. His friend picked him up.

"What d'you want to be so foolish for, George?"

"I had him nearly beat."

Tom looked reproachfully at the soberer friend. "I am surprised at you, Mr. Trelawney."

"Couldn't help it, Tom. He would mix port and brandy."

"You must take him out."

"Come on, George; you've got to go out."

"Got to go! No, sir; round two. Come up smilin'. Time!"

Tom Cribb gave a sign and a stalwart potman threw the pugnacious George over his shoulder and carried him out of the room, kicking violently, while his friend walked behind. Cribb laughed.

"There's seldom an evening that I don't have that sort of nuisance."

"They would not do it twice to me," said Hawker. "I'd send him home, and his wench wouldn't know him."

"I haven't the heart to touch them. It pleases the poor things to say they have punched the champion of England."

The room had now begun to fill up. At one end a circle had formed round the bookie's table. On the other side there was a group at the small private bar where very broad chaff was being exchanged between some of the younger bucks and Lucy, who was well able to take care of herself. Cribb had gone inside the swing doors to prepare for the boxing, while Hawker wandered from group to group, leaving among these fearless men, hard-riding horsemen of the shires and daredevils at every sport, a vague feeling of repulsion which showed itself in a somewhat formal response to his brief greetings. He paused at one chattering group and looked sardonically at a youth who stood somewhat apart listening to, but not joining in, the gay exchange of repartee. He was a well-built young man with a singularly beautiful head, crowned by a mass of auburn curls. His figure might have stood for Adonis, were it not that one foot was slightly drawn up, which caused him to wear a rather unsightly boot.

THE END OF DEVIL HAWKER

"Good evening, Hawker," said he.

"Good evening, Byron. Is this one of your hours of idleness?"

The allusion was to a book of verse which the young nobleman had just brought out, and which had been severely handled by the critics.

The poet seemed annoyed, for he was sensitive on the point.

"At least I cannot be accused of idleness today," said he. "I swam three miles downstream from Lambeth, and perhaps you have not done so much."

"Well done!" said Hawker. "I hear of you at Angelo's, and Jackson's too. But fencing needs a quick foot. I'd stick to the water if I were you." He glanced down at the malformed limb.

Byron's blue-gray eyes blazed with indignation.

"When I wish your advice as to my personal habits, Sir John Hawker, I will ask for it."

"No harm meant," said Hawker carelessly. "I am a blunt fellow and always say what I think."

Lord Rufton plucked at Byron's sleeve. "That's enough said," he whispered.

"Of course," added Hawker, "if anyone does not like my ways, they can always find me at White's Club or my lodgings in Charles Street."

Byron, who was utterly fearless, and ready, though he was still only a Cambridge undergraduate, to face any man in the world, was about to make some angry reply, in spite of the well-meant warnings of Lord Rufton, when Tom Cribb came bustling in and interrupted the scene.

"All ready, my lords and gentlemen. The fighting men are in their places. Jack Scroggins and Ben Burn will begin."

The company began to move toward the door of the sparring saloon. As they filed in, Hawker advanced quietly and touched the reckless baronet, Sir Charles Trevor, upon the shoulder.

"I must have a word with you, Charles."

"I want to get a ringside seat, John."

"Never mind that. I must have a word."

The others passed in. Devil Hawker and Sir Charles had the room to themselves, save for Jakes, counting his money at his distant table, and the girl, Lucy, coming and going in her little alcove. Hawker led Sir Charles to a central seat.

"I have to speak to you, Charles, of that three thousand you owe me. It pains me vastly, but what am I to do? I have my own debts to settle, and it is no easy matter."

"I have the matter in hand, John."

"But it presses."

"I'll pay it all right. Give me time."

"What time?"

"We are cutting the oaks at Selincourt. They should all be down by the fall. I can get an advance then that will clear all that I owe you."

"I don't want to press you, Charles. If you would like a sporting flutter to clear your debt, I'm ready to give it to you at once."

"What do you mean?"

"Well, double or quits. Six thousand or nothing. If you're not afraid to take a chance, I'll let you have one."

"Afraid, John. I don't like that word."

"You were always a brave gamester, Charles. Just as you like in the matter. But you might clear yourself with a turn of the card, while, on the other hand, if all the Selincourt timber is going, six thousand will be no more to you than three."

"Well, it's a sporting offer, John. You say the turn of a card. Do you mean one simple draw?"

"Why not? Sudden death. Win or lose. What say you?"

"I agree."

A pack of cards was lying on a nearby table. Hawker stretched out a long arm and picked them up.

"Will these do?"

"By all means."

He spread them out with a sweep of his hand.

"Do you care to shuffle?"

"No, John. Take them as they are."

"Shall it be a single draw?"

"By all means."

"Will you lead?"

Sir Charles Trevor was a seasoned gambler, but never before had three thousand pounds hung upon the turn of a single card. But he was a reckless plunger, and roared with laughter as he turned up the queen of clubs.

"That should do you, John."

"Possibly," said Hawker, and turned the ace of spades.

"I thought I had cleared myself, and now it is six thousand," cried Trevor, and staggered as he rose from his seat.

"To wait until the oaks are cut," said Hawker. "In September I shall present my little bill. Meanwhile, perhaps a note of hand——"

"Do you doubt my word, John?"

"No, no, Charles, but business is business. Who knows what may happen? I'll have a note of hand."

THE END OF DEVIL HAWKER

"Very good. You'll have it by the post tomorrow. Well, I bear no grudge. The luck was yours. Shall we have a glass upon it?"

"You were always a brave loser, Charles." The two men walked together to the little bar in the corner.

Had either looked back he would have seen a sight which would have surprised him. During the whole incident the little bookmaker had sat absorbed over his accounts, but with a pair of piercing eyes glancing up every now and then at the two gamblers. Little of their talk had been audible from where he sat, but their actions had spoken for themselves. Now, with amazing, but furtive, speed he stole across, picked up one card from the table and hurried back to his perch, concealing it inside his coat. The two gentlemen, having taken their refreshment, turned toward the boxing saloon; Sir Charles disappearing through the swing doors, from behind which came the thud of heavy blows, the breathing of hard-spent men, and every now and then a murmur of admiration or of criticism.

Hawker was about to follow his companion when a thought struck him and he returned to the card table, gathering up the scattered cards. Suddenly he was aware that Jakes was at his elbow and that two very shrewd and malignant eyes were looking up into his own.

"Hadn't you best count them, my noble sportsman?"

"What d'you mean?" The Devil's great black brows were drawn down and his glance was like a rapier thrust.

"If you count them you'll find one missing."

"Why are you grinning at me, you rascal?"

"One card missing, my noble sportsman. A good winning card, too—the ace of spades. A useful card, Sir John."

"Where is it then?"

"Little Billy Jakes has it. It's here"—and he slapped his breast pocket. "A little playing card with the mark of a thumbnail on one corner of the card."

"You infernal blackguard!"

Jakes was no coward, but he shrank away from that terrible face. "Hands off, my noble sportsman! Hands off, for your own sake! You can knock me about. That's easily done. But it won't end there. I've got the card. I could call back Sir Charles and fill this room in a jiffy. There would be an end of you, my beauty."

"It's all a lie—a lie."

"Right you are. Say so, if you like. Shall I call in the others, and you can prove it a lie? Shall I show the cards to Lord Rufton and the rest?"

Hawker's dark face was moving convulsively. His hands were

twitching with his desire to break the back of this little weasel across his knee. With an effort, he mastered himself.

"Hold on, Jakes. We have always been great friends. What do you want? Speak low, or the girl will hear."

"Now, that's talking. You got six thousand just now. I want half."

"You want three thousand pounds. What for?"

"You're a man of sense. You know what for. I've a tongue, and I can hold it if it's worth my while."

Hawker considered for a moment. "Well, suppose I agree."

"Then we can fix it so."

"Say no more. We will consider it as agreed."

He turned away, his mind full of plans by which he could gain time and disavow the whole business. But Jakes was not a man so easily fooled. Many people had found that to their cost.

"Hold on, my noble sportsman. Hold on an instant. Just a word of writing to settle it."

"You dog, is my word not enough?"

"No, Sir John, not by a long way. . . . No, if you hit me I'll yell. Keep your hands off. I tell you I want your signature to it."

"Not a word."

"Very good then. It's finished." Jakes started for the saloon door.

"Hold hard! What am I to write?"

"I'll do the writing." He turned to the little alcove where Lucy, who was accustomed to every sort of wrangling and argument, was dozing among her bottles. "Here, my dear; wake up! I want pen and ink."

"Yes, sir."

"And paper?"

"There is a billhead. Will that do? Dearie me, it's marked with wine!"

"Never mind; that will do."

Jakes seated himself at a table and scribbled while Hawker watched him with eyes of death. Jakes walked over to him with the scrawl completed. Hawker read it over in a low mutter:

" 'In consideration of your silence——' " He paused and glared.

"Well, that's true, ain't it? You don't give me half for the love of William Jakes, Esquire, do you now?"

"Curse you, Jakes! Curse you to hell!"

"Let it out, my noble sportsman. Let it out or you'll bust. Curse me again. Then sign that paper."

" 'The sum of three thousand pounds, to be paid on the date when there is a settlement between me and Sir Charles Trevor.' Well, give me the pen and have done. There! Now give me that card."

Jakes had thrust the signed paper into his inner pocket.

"Give me the card, I say!"

"When the money is paid, Sir John. That's only fair."

"You devil!"

"Can't find the right word, can you? It's not been invented yet, I expect."

Jakes may have been very near his death at that moment. The furious passions of the bully had reached a point when even his fears of exposure could hardly hold him in check. But the saloon door had swung open and Cribb entered the room. He looked with surprise at the ill-assorted couple.

"Now, Mr. Jakes, time is up, you know. You've passed your hours."

"I know, Tom, but I had an important settling up with Sir John Hawker. Had I not, Sir John?"

"You've missed the first bout, Sir John. Come and see Jack Randall take a novice."

Hawker took a last scowl at the bookmaker and followed the champion into the saloon. Jakes gathered up his papers into his professional bag and went across to the little bar.

"A double brandy, my dear," said he to Lucy. "I've had a good evening, but it's been a bit of a strain upon my nerves."

It was late in September that the grand old ancestral oaks of Selincourt were given over to the contractor, and that their owner, having at last a large balance at his bankers', was able to redeem the more pressing of his debts. It was only a day later that Sir John Hawker, with Sir Charles's note of hand for six thousand pounds in his pocket, found himself riding down the highroad at Six-Mile Bottom near Newmarket. His mount was a great black stallion as powerful and sinister as himself. He was brooding over his own rather precarious affairs, which involved every shilling which he could raise, when there was the click of hoofs beside him and there was Billy Jakes upon his well-known chestnut cob.

"Good evening, my noble sportsman," said he. "I was looking out for you at the stables, and when I saw you ride away, I thought it was time to come after you. I want my settlement, Sir John."

"What settlement? What are you talking of?"

"Your written promise to pay three thousand. I know you have had your money."

"I don't know what you are talking about. Keep clear of me or you will get a cut or two from this hunting crop."

"Ho, that's the game, is it? We will see about that. Do you deny your signature upon this paper?"

"Have you the paper on you?"

"What's that to you?"

It was not wise, Billy Jakes, to trust yourself alone upon a country road with one of the most dangerous men in England. For once your cupidity has been greater than your shrewdness.

A quick glance of those deadly, dark eyes to right and to left, and then the heavy hunting crop came down with a crash upon the bookmaker's head. With a cry, he dropped from the cob, and he had hardly reached the ground before the Devil had sprung from the saddle, and with his left arm through his bridle rein to hold down his plunging horse, he was rapidly running his right hand through the pockets of the prostrate man. With a bitter curse, he realized that however imprudent Jakes had been, he had not been such a fool as to carry his papers about with him.

Hawker rose, looked down at his half-conscious enemy, and then slowly drew his spur across his face. A moment later he had sprung into his saddle and was on his way London-wards, leaving the sprawling and bleeding figure in the dust of the highway. He laughed with exultation as he rode, for vengeance was sweet to him, and he seldom missed it. What could Jakes do? If he took him into the criminal courts, it was only such an assault as was common enough in those days of violence. If, on the other hand, he pursued the matter of the card and the agreement, it was an old story now, and who would take the word of the notorious bookmaker against that of one of the best known men in London? Of course, it was a case of forgery and blackmail. Hawker looked down at his bloody spur and felt well content with his morning's work.

Jakes was raised to his feet by some kindly traveler and was brought back, half conscious, to Newmarket. There, for three days, he kept his room and nursed both his injuries and his grievance. Upon the fourth day he reached London, and that night he made his way to the Albany and knocked at a door which bore upon a shining brass plate the name of Sir Charles Trevor.

It was the first Tuesday of the month, the day on which the committee of Watier's Club was wont to assemble. Half a dozen of them had sauntered into the great board room, decorated with heavy canvases on the walls, and with highly polished dark mahogany furniture, which showed up richly against the huge expanse of red Kidderminster carpet. The Duke of Bridgewater, a splendid, rubicund old gentleman, gray-haired but virile, leaning heavily upon an amber-headed cane, came hobbling in and bowed affably to the waiting committeemen.

"How is the gout, Your Grace?"

"A little sharp at times. But I can still get my foot into the stirrup. Well, well, I suppose we had better get to work." He took his seat in the center of a half-moon table at one end of the room. Raising his quizzing glass he looked round him.

"Where is Lord Foley?"

"He is racing, sir. He will not be here."

"The dog! He takes his duties too lightly. I would rather be on the Heath myself."

"I expect we all would."

"Ah, is that you, Lord Rufton?...How are you, Colonel D'Acre! ... Bunbury, Scott, Poyntz, Vandeleur, good day to you! Where is Sir Charles Trevor?"

"He is in the members' room," said Lord Rufton. "He said he would wait Your Grace's pleasure. The fact is that he has a personal interest in a case which comes before us, and he thought he should not have a hand in judging it."

"Ah, very delicate! Very delicate indeed!" The Duke had taken up the agenda paper and stared at it through his glass. "Dear me, dear me! A member accused of cheating at cards! And Sir John Hawker too! One of the best known men in the club. Too bad! Too bad! Who is the accuser?"

"A bookmaker named Jakes, Your Grace!"

"I know him. Has a stance at Tom Cribb's. A rascal if ever I saw one. However, we must look into it. Who has the matter in hand?"

"I have been asked to attend to it," said Lord Rufton.

"I am not sure," said the Duke, "that we are right in taking notice of what such a person says about a member of this club. Surely, the law courts are open."

"I entirely agree with Your Grace," said a solemn man upon the Duke's left. He was General Scott, who was said to live on toast and water, and win ten thousand a year from his less sober companions.

"I would point out to you, sir, that the alleged cheating was at the expense of Sir Charles Trevor, a member of the club. It was not Sir Charles, however, who moved in the matter. There was a violent quarrel between the man Jakes and Sir John Hawker, and this is the result."

"Then the bookmaker has brought the case before us for revenge," said the Duke. "We must move carefully in this matter. I think we had best see Sir Charles first. Call Sir Charles."

The tall red-plushed footman at the door disappeared. A moment later, Sir Charles, debonair and smiling, stood before the committee.

"Good day, Sir Charles," said the Duke. "This is a very painful business."

"Very, Your Grace."

"I understand from what is on the agenda paper that on May third, of this year, you met Sir John at Cribb's Parlor and you cut cards with him at three thousand pounds a cut."

"A single cut, Your Grace."

"And you lost?"

"Unfortunately."

"Well, now, did you in any way suspect foul play at the time?"

"Not in the least."

"Then you have no charge against Sir John?"

"None on my own behalf. Other people have something to say."

"Well, we can listen to them in their turn. Won't you take a chair, Sir Charles? Even if you do not vote, there can be no objection to your presence. Is Sir John in attendance?"

"Yes, sir."

"And the witness?"

"Yes, sir."

"Well, gentlemen, it is clearly a very serious matter, and I understand that Sir John is a difficult person to deal with. However, we can make no exceptions, and we are numerous enough and have, I trust, sufficient social weight to carry this affair to a conclusion." He rang for the footman. "Place a chair in the center, please! Now tell Sir John Hawker the committee would be honored if he would step this way."

A moment later the formidable face and figure of the Devil had appeared at the door. With a scowl at the members present, he strode forward, bowed to the Duke, and seated himself opposite the semicircle formed by the committee.

"In the first place, Sir John," said the Duke, "you will allow me to express my regret and that of your fellow members that it should be our unpleasant duty to ask you to appear before us. No doubt the matter will prove to be a mere misunderstanding, but we felt that it was due to your own reputation as well as to that of the club that no time should be lost in setting the matter right."

"Your Grace," said Hawker, leaning forward and emphasizing his remarks with his clenched hand, "I protest strongly against these proceedings. I have come here because it shall never be said that I was shy of meeting any charge, however preposterous. But I would put it to you, gentlemen, that no man's reputation is safe if the committee of his club is prepared to take up any vague slander that may circulate against him."

THE END OF DEVIL HAWKER

"Kindly read the terms of the charge, Lord Rufton."

Lord Rufton picked up the agenda paper. "The assertion is," he read, "that at ten o'clock on the night of Thursday, May third, in the parlor of Tom Cribb's house, the Union Arms, Sir John Hawker did, by means of marked cards, win money from Sir Charles Trevor, both being members of Watier's Club."

Hawker sprang from his chair. "It is a lie—a damned lie!" he cried.

The Duke held up a deprecating hand. "No doubt—no doubt. I think, however, Sir John, that you can hardly describe it as a vague slander."

"It is monstrous. What is to prevent such a charge being leveled at Your Grace? How would you like, sir, to be dragged up before your fellow members?"

"Excuse me, Sir John," said the Duke urbanely. "The question at present is not what might be preferred against me, but what actually is preferred against you. You will, I am sure, appreciate the distinction. What do you propose, Lord Rufton?"

"It is my unpleasant duty, Sir John," said Lord Rufton, "to array the evidence before the committee. You will, I am sure, acquit me of any personal feeling in the matter."

"I look on you, sir, as a damned mischievous busybody."

The Duke put up his pudgy many-ringed hand in protest.

"I am afraid, Sir John, that I must ask you to be more guarded in your language. To me, it is immaterial, but I happen to know that General Scott has an objection to swearing. Lord Rufton is merely doing his duty in presenting the case."

Hawker shrugged his broad shoulders.

"I protest against the whole preceedings," he said.

"Your protest will be duly entered in the minutes. We have heard, before you entered, the evidence of Sir Charles Trevor. He has no personal complaint. So far as I can see, there is no case."

"Ha! Your Grace is a man of sense. Was ever an indignity put upon a man of honor on so small a pretext?"

"There is further evidence, Your Grace," said Lord Rufton. "I will call Mr. William Jakes."

At a summons the gorgeous footman swung open the massive door and Jakes was ushered in. It was a month or more since the assault, but the spur mark still shone red across his sallow cheek. He held his cloth cap in his hand, and rounded his back as a tribute to the company, but his cunning little eyes, from under their ginger lashes, twinkled as knowingly, not to say impudently, as ever.

"You are William Jakes, the bookmaker?" said the Duke.

"The greatest rascal in London," interpolated Hawker.

"There is one greater within three yards of me," the little man snarled. Then, turning to the Duke: "I'm William Jakes, Your Worship, known as Billy Jakes at Tattersall's. If you want to back a horse, Your Worship, or care to buy a gamecock or a ratter, you'll get the best price——"

"Silence, sir," said Lord Rufton. "Advance to this chair."

"Certainly, my noble sportsman."

"Don't sit. Stand beside it."

"At your service, gentlemen."

"Shall I cross-examine, Your Grace?"

"I understand, Jakes, that you were in Cribb's back parlor on the night of May third of this year?"

"Lord bless you, sir, I'm there every night. It's where I meet my noble Corinthians."

"It is a sporting house, I understand."

"Well, my lord, I can't teach you much about it." There was a titter from the committee, and the Duke broke in.

"I dare say we have all enjoyed Tom's hospitality at one time or another," he said.

"Yes, indeed, Your Grace. Well I remember the night when you danced on the crossed 'baccy pipes."

"Keep your witness to the point," said the smiling Duke.

"Tell us now what you saw pass between Sir John Hawker and Sir Charles Trevor."

"I saw all there was to see. You can trust little Billy Jakes for that. There was to be a cutting game. Sir John reached out for the cards, which lay on another table. I had seen him look over those cards in advance and turn the end of one or two with his thumbnail."

"You liar!" cried Sir John.

"It's an easy trick to mark them so that none can see. I've done—I know another man that can do it. You must keep your right thumbnail long and sharp. Well, look at Sir John's now."

Hawker sprang from his chair. "Your Grace, am I to be exposed to these insults?"

"Sit down, Sir John. Your indignation is most natural. I suppose it is not a fact that your right thumbnail——"

"Certainly not."

"Ask to see!" cried Jakes.

"Perhaps you would not mind showing your nail?"

"I will do nothing of the kind."

"Of course you are quite within your rights in refusing—quite!" said the Duke. "Whether your refusal might in any way prejudice

THE END OF DEVIL HAWKER

your case is a point which you have no doubt considered. . . . Pray continue, Jakes."

"Well, they cut and Sir John won. When he turned his back, I got the winning card, and saw that it was marked. I showed it to Sir John when we were alone."

"What did he say?"

"Well, my lord, I wouldn't like to repeat before such select company as this some of the things he said. He carried on shocking. But after a bit he saw the game was up and he consented to my having half shares."

"Then," said the Duke, "you became, by your own admission, the compounder of a felony."

Jakes gave a comical grimace.

"No beaks here! This ain't a court, is it? Just a private house, as one might say, with one gentleman chatting easylike with other ones. Well, then, that's just what I did do."

The Duke shrugged his shoulders. "Really, Lord Rufton, I do not see how we can attach any importance to the word of such a witness. On his own confession he is a perfect rascal."

"Your Grace, I'm surprised at you!"

"I would not condemn any man—far less the member of an honorable club—on this man's word."

"I quite agree, Your Grace," said Rufton. "There are, however, some corroborative documents."

"Yes, my noble sportsmen," cried Jakes, in a sort of ecstasy, "there's lots more to come. Billy's got a bit up his sleeve for a finish. How's that?" He pulled a pack of cards from his pocket and singled one out. "That's the pack. Look at the ace. You can see the mark yet."

The Duke examined the card. "There is certainly a mark," he said, "which might well be made by a sharpened nail."

Sir John was up once more, his face dark with wrath.

"Really, gentlemen, there should be some limit to this foolery. Of course these are the cards. Is it not obvious that after Sir Charles and I had left, this fellow gathered them up and marked them so as to put forward a blackmailing demand? I only—I only wonder that he has not forged some document to prove that I admitted this monstrous charge."

Jakes threw up his hands in admiration.

"By George, you have a nerve! I always said it. Give me Devil Hawker for nerve. Grasp the nettle, eh? Here's the document he talks about." He handed a paper to Lord Rufton.

"Would you be pleased to read it?" said the Duke.

Rufton read: " 'In consideration of services rendered, I promise William Jakes three thousand pounds when I settle with Sir Charles Trevor. Signed, John Hawker.' "

"A palpable forgery! I guessed as much," cried Sir John.

"Who knows Sir John's signature?"

"I do," said Sir Charles Bunbury.

"Is that it?"

"Well, I should say so."

"Tut, the fellow is a born forger!" cried Hawker.

The Duke looked at the back of the paper, and read: " 'To Thomas Cribb, Licensed Dealer in Beer, Wine, Spirits and Tobacco.' It is certainly paper from the room alluded to."

"He could help himself to that."

"Exactly. The evidence is by no means convincing. At the same time, Sir John, I am compelled to tell you that the way in which you anticipated this evidence has produced a very unpleasant impression in my mind."

"I knew what the fellow was capable of."

"Do you admit being intimate with him?"

"Certainly not."

"You had nothing to do with him?"

"I had occasion recently to horsewhip him for insolence. Hence this charge against me."

"You knew him very slightly?"

"Hardly at all."

"You did not correspond?"

"Certainly not."

"Strange, then, that he should have been able to copy your signature, if he had no letter of yours."

"I know nothing of that."

"You quarreled with him recently?"

"Yes, sir. He was impertinent and I beat him."

"Had you any reason to think you would quarrel?"

"No, sir."

"Does it not seem strange to you then, that he should have been keeping these cards all these weeks to buttress up a false charge against you, if he had no idea that an occasion for such a charge would ever arise?"

"I cannot answer for his actions," said Hawker in a sullen voice.

"Of course not. At the same time, I am forced to repeat, Sir John, that your anticipation of this document has seemed to me exactly what might be expected from a man of strong character who knew that such a document existed."

"I am not responsible for this man's assertions, nor can I control Your Grace's speculations, save to say that so far as they threaten my honor, they are contemptible and absurd. I place my case in the hands of the committee. You know, or can easily learn, the character of this man Jakes. Is it possible that you can hesitate between the words of such a man and the character of one who has for years been a fellow member of this club?"

"I am bound to say, Your Grace," said Sir Charles Bunbury, "that while I associate myself with every remark which has fallen from you, I am still of the opinion that the evidence is of so corrupt a character that it would be impossible for us to take action upon it."

"That is also my opinion," came from several of the committee, and there was a general murmur of acquiescence.

"I thank you, gentlemen," said Hawker, rising. "With your permission, I shall bring this sitting to an end."

"Excuse me, sir; there are two more witnesses," said Lord Rufton. "Jakes, you can withdraw. Leave the documents with me."

"Thank you, my lord. Good day, my noble sportsmen. Should any of you want a cock or a terrier——"

"That will do. Leave the room." With many bows and backward glances, William Jakes vanished from the scene.

"I should like to ask Tom Cribb one or two questions," said Lord Rufton. "Call Tom Cribb."

A moment later the burly figure of the champion came heavily into the room. He was dressed exactly like the pictures of John Bull, with blue coat with shining brass buttons, drab trousers and top boots, while his face, in its broad, bovine serenity, was also the very image of the national prototype. On his head he wore a low-crowned, curly-brimmed hat, which he now whipped off and stuffed under his arm. The worthy Tom was much more alarmed than ever he had been in the ring, and looked helplessly about him like a bull who finds himself in a strange enclosure.

"My respects, gentlemen all!" he repeated several times, touching his forelock.

"Good morning, Tom," said the Duke affably. "Take that chair. How are you?"

"Damned hot, Your Grace. That is to say, very warm. You see, sir, I do my own marketing these days, and when you've been down to Covent Garden and then on to Smithfield, and then trudge back here, and you two stone above your fighting weight——"

"We quite understand. The chief steward will see to you presently."

"I want to ask you, Tom," said Lord Rufton, "do you remember the evening of May third last in your parlor?"

"I heard there was some barney about it, and I've been lookin' it up," said Tom. "Yes, I remember it well, for it was the night when a novice had the better of old Ben Burn. Lor', I couldn't but laugh. Old Ben got one on the mark in the first round, and before he could get his wind——"

"Never mind, Tom. We'll have that later. Do you recognize these cards?"

"Why, those cards are out of my parlor. I get them a dozen at a time, a shilling each, from Ned Summers of Oxford Street; the same what——"

"Well, that's settled then. Now, do you remember seeing Sir John here and Sir Charles Trevor that evening?"

"Yes, I do. I remember saying to Sir John that he must play light with my novices, for there was one cove, Bill Summers by name, out of Norwich, and when Sir John——"

"Never mind that, Tom. Tell us, now, did you see Sir John and the bookmaker, Jakes, together that night?"

"Jakes was there, for he says to the girl in the bar, 'How much money have you, my lass?' And I said, 'You dirty dog——'"

"Enough, Tom. Did you see the man Jakes and Sir John together?"

"Yes, sir; when I came into the parlor after the bout between Shelton and Scroggins. I saw the two of them alone, and Jakes, he said that they had done business together."

"Did they seem friendly?"

"Well, now you ask it, Sir John didn't seem too pleased. But, Lord love you, I'm that busy those evenings that if you dropped a shot on my head I'd hardly notice it."

"Nothing more to tell us?"

"I don't know as I have. I'd be glad to get back to my bar."

"Very good, Tom. You can go."

"I'd just remind you gentlemen that it's my benefit at the Five Court, St. Martin's Lane, come Tuesday week." Tom bobbed his bullethead many times and departed.

"Not much in all that," remarked the Duke. "Does that finish the case?"

"There is one more, Your Grace. Call the girl Lucy. She is the girl of the private bar."

"Yes, yes, I remember," cried the Duke. "That is to say, by all means. What does this young person know about it?"

"I believe that she was present." As Lord Rufton spoke, Lucy, very nervous, but cheered by the knowledge that she was in her best Sunday clothes, appeared at the door.

"Don't be nervous, my girl. Take this chair," said Lord Rufton kindly. "Don't keep on curtsying. Sit down."

The girl sat timidly on the edge of the chair. Suddenly her eyes caught those of the august chairman.

"Why, Lord bless me!" she cried. "It's the little Duke!"

"Hush, my girl, hush!" His Grace held up a warning hand.

"Well, I never!" cried Lucy, and began to giggle and hide her blushing face in her handkerchief.

"Now, now!" said the Duke. "This is a grave business. What are you laughing at?"

"I couldn't help it, sir. I was thinking of that evening down in the private bar when you bet you could walk a chalk line with a bottle of champagne on your head."

There was a general laugh, in which the Duke joined.

"I fear, gentlemen, I must have had a couple in my head before I ventured such a feat. Now, my good girl, we did not ask you here for the sake of your reminiscences. You may have seen some of us unbending, but we will let that pass. . . . You were in the bar on May the third?"

"I'm always there."

"Cast your mind back and recall the evening when Sir Charles Trevor and Sir John Hawker proposed to cut cards for money."

"I remember it well, sir."

"After the others had left the bar, Sir John and a man named Jakes are said to have remained behind."

"I saw them."

"It's a lie! It's a plot!" cried Hawker.

"Now, Sir John, I must really beg you!" It was the Duke who was cross-questioning now. "Describe to us what you saw."

"Well, sir, they began talking over a pack of cards. Sir John up with his hand, and I was about to call for West Country Dick—he's the chucker-out you know, sir, at the Union Arms—but no blow passed and they talked very earnestlike for a time. Then Mr. Jakes called for paper and wrote something, and that's all I know, except that Sir John seemed very upset."

"Did you ever see that piece of paper before?" The duke held it up.

"Why, sir, it looks like Mr. Cribb's billhead."

"Exactly. Was it a piece like that which you gave to these gentlemen that night?"

"Yes, sir."

"Could you distinguish it?"

"Why, sir, now that I come to think of it, I could."

Hawker sprang up with a convulsed face. "I've had enough of this nonsense. I'm going."

"No, no, Sir John. Sit down again. Your honor demands your presence. . . . Well, my good girl, you say you could recognize it?"

"Yes, sir, I could. There was a mark, sir. I drew some burgundy for Sir Charles, sir, and some slopped on the counter. The paper was marked with it on the side. I was in doubt if I should give them so soiled a piece."

The Duke looked very grave. "Gentlemen, this is a serious matter. There is, as you see, a red stain upon the side of the paper. Have you any remark to make, Sir John?"

"A conspiracy, Your Grace! An infernal, devilish plot against a gentleman's honor."

"You may go, Lucy," said Lord Rufton, and with curtsies and giggles, the barmaid disappeared.

"You have heard the evidence, gentlemen," said the Duke. "Some of you may know the character of this girl, which is by all accounts excellent."

"A drab out of the gutter."

"I think not, Sir John; nor do you improve your position by such assertions. You will each have your own impression as to how far the girl's account seemed honest and carried conviction with it. You will observe that had she merely intended to injure Sir John, her obvious method would have been to have said she overheard the conversation detailed by the witness, Jakes. This she has not done. Her account, however, tends to corroborate——"

"Your Grace," cried Hawker, "I have had enough of this!"

"We shall not detain you much longer, Sir John Hawker," said the chairman, "but for that limited time we must insist upon your presence."

"Insist, sir?"

"Yes, sir, insist."

"This is strange talk."

"Be seated, sir. This matter must go to a finish."

"Well!" Hawker fell back into his chair.

"Gentlemen," said the Duke, "slips of paper are before you. After the custom of the club, you will kindly record your opinion and hand to me. Mr. Poyntz? I thank you. Vandeleur! Bunbury! Rufton! General Scott! Colonel Tufton! I thank you." He examined the papers. "Exactly. You are unanimous! I may say that I entirely agree with your opinion." The Duke's rosy, kindly face had set as hard as flint.

"What am I to understand by this, sir?" cried Hawker.

"Bring the club book," said the Duke. Lord Rufton carried across a large brown volume from the side table and opened it before the chairman.

"C, D, E, F, G. Ah, here we are—H. Let us see! Houston, Harcourt, Hume, Duke of Hamilton—I have it—Hawker. Sir John Hawker, your name is forever erased from the book of Watier's Club." He drew the pen across the page as he spoke. Hawker sprang frantically to his feet.

"You cannot mean it! Consider, sir; this is social ruin! Where shall I show my face if I am cast from my club? I could not walk the streets of London. Take it back, sir! Reconsider it!"

"Sir John Hawker, we can only refer you to Rule 19. It says: 'If any member shall be guilty of conduct unworthy of an honorable man, and the said offense be established to the unanimous satisfaction of the committee, then the aforesaid member shall be expelled from the club without appeal.' "

"Gentlemen," cried Hawker, "I beg you not be precipitate! You have had the evidence of a rascal bookmaker and of a serving wench. Is that enough to ruin a gentleman's life? I am undone if this goes through."

"The matter has been considered and is now in order. We can only refer you to Rule 19."

"Your Grace, you cannot know what this will mean. How can I live? Where can I go? I never asked mercy of man before. But I ask it now. I implore it, gentlemen. Reconsider your decision!"

"Rule 19."

"It is ruin, I tell you—disgrace and ruin."

"Rule 19."

"Let me resign. Do not expel me."

"Rule 19."

It was hopeless, and Hawker knew it. He strode in front of the table.

"Curse your rules! Curse you, too, you silly, babbling jackanapes. Curse you all—you, Vandeleur, and you, Poyntz, and you, Scott, you doddering toast-and-water gamester. You will live to mourn the day you put this indignity upon me. You will answer it—every man of you! I'll set my mark on you. By the Lord I will! You first, Rufton. One by one, I'll weed you out! I've a bullet for each. I'll number 'em!"

"Sir John Hawker," said the Duke, "this club is for the use of members only. May I ask you to take yourself out of it?"

"And if I don't—what then?"

The Duke turned to General Scott. "Will you ask the hall porters to step up?"

"There! I'll go!" yelled Hawker. "I will not be thrown out—the laughingstock of Jermyn Street. But you will hear more, gentlemen. You will remember me yet. Rascals! Rascals everyone!"

And so it was, raving and stamping, with his clenched hands waving above his head, that Devil Hawker passed out from Watier's Club and from the social life of London.

For it was his end. In vain he sent furious challenges to the members of the committee. He was outside the pale, and no one would condescend to meet him. In vain he thrashed Sir Charles Bunbury in front of Limmers' Hotel. Hired ruffians were put upon his track and he was terribly thrashed in return. Even the bookmakers would have no more to do with him, and he was warned off the turf. Down he sank, and down, drinking to uphold his spirits until he was but a bloated wreck of the man that he had been.

And so, at last, one morning in his rooms in Charles Street, that dueling pistol which had so often been the instrument of his vengeance was turned upon himself, and that dark face, terrible even in death, was found outlined against a blood-sodden pillow in the morning.

So put the print back among the pile. You may be the better for having honest Tom Cribb upon your wall, or even the effeminate Brummell. But Devil Hawker never, in life or death, brought luck to anyone. Leave him there where you found him, in the dusty old shop of Drury Lane.

THE EVIL EYE

ALFRED GILLESPIE

The first sentence he typed was filled with mistakes: "El;zab eth is probsbly circlin g the biulding right now like a lonne Shoshone circling a burning wagoon."

"*Wagoon?*" Charlie said aloud, and snorted out a laugh that in turn led him to spill some gin on his bathrobe.

It was only ten-thirty at night, but Charlie had had half a dozen Martinis by six o'clock (such was his despair), and then another three or four by eight-thirty, when he'd tucked El;zab eth into her bed and repaired to the studio with a bottle of gin cradled in his arm. He'd stripped to his underwear, removed his aluminum leg, tossed it away from him, and fallen back onto the day bed in a deep and dreadful sleep.

He woke up, soaked with sweat, at half-past ten, his head wracked with pain in at least four vital places, and he knew he would have to see the night through in a sitting position somewhere. As the leg was out of reach halfway across the room and Charlie was in no condition to crawl after it, he struggled to the edge of the bed, somehow got the robe around him, and hopped heavily to the table on which his electric typewriter crouched like a cannon. Surprisingly, he fell only once en route.

And now he sat, the cigarette pendant at his lip, letting out clouds of smoke, and pecked at the typewriter. Each character was whacked home electronically—*zzkak zzkak*. It gave him a certain feeling of permanence; it was all damn-the-torpedoes-full-speed-ahead, and no changing anything, not even with a string of obliterating x's. His right eye wept continually.

I have (he wrote) drunk a wagoonful of gin tonight so that I would have no trouble sleeping, and you see where it's got me. Exactly five jumps across the floor to the alphabet machine. I shall set down the story of me and that monster child out there in the night, and the camera, if it exists—and I think it does—and all the rest of it. I shall set it down neatly in the straight he-said—she-said manner of Homer, and you'll get no boozy philosophy out of me, no soul searchings, no dialects—in a's and q's and other precise symbols like *c@½?%$. I think *c@½?%$ is a much better expression than the stuff you hear in barracks rooms and school buses.

Elizabeth.

Outside my window somewhere, I'm convinced, a small, nine-year-old bat girl named Elizabeth, my stepdaughter, is circling and circling and circling in for the kill. Why the *c@½?%$ would she want to kill a sweet, middle-aged, forty-year-old bindle stiff like me?

I haven't the foggiest; that's the truth.

Last night, which is when I brought the camera home as a peace token after having been away for two days and one night—well, last night, under a purpling sky, I drove north out of New York City and skimmed like a bee with a sore rear end through Westchester County. The light was on in Elizabeth's room. That's her window just over the front door—the window from which she threw herself on one impressive occasion. My Volkswagen came scrunching up the driveway off the dirt lane to the house, and into the carport that connects the frame house to the studio, where I make my living designing book jackets and things. The darkness by then had become a large black something of some kind kneeling over the two buildings. It was leaning on its forearms and breathing warmly on us. Through a front window, I could see Mrs. Cleary back in the kitchen preparing dinner. I beeped the horn and came grunting out of the car, pulling the camera and the portfolio after me.

Mrs. Cleary dried her long fingers on her apron as I came swinging into the kitchen, the prodigal returned, and gave me the full benefit of her thin face and her eyes, dead and dry as a cigarette ash. Then she ticked off her report, flatly and quickly. There was stew for dinner, Mr. McLenahan, she said, ready in about twenty minutes. The potatoes were ready now. The peas were in their pot. Elizabeth, she reported, seemed a bit pale tonight, though Mrs. Cleary had run her hand over the child's forehead and it seemed cool. (It's a wonder the child hadn't taken a bite at the hand.) Liz was in her room now, the dearie, doing her homework. There had been no trouble at school today, for a welcome change. Oh, but the light on the stairs was burned out, had Mr. McLenahan noticed? (Mrs. Cleary, as you've observed, has as much vivacity as the early Rosalind Russell.) The little James boy, Pete, had stopped by to see if Elizabeth had wanted to hunt frogs across the way, but, of course, she hadn't. Oh, yes, Mrs. C wouldn't be eating with Liz and me that night because her sister, Miss Kelly, was staying with her in town through the week. And she wouldn't be in tomorrow (meaning today) if that was OK with me, because she and her sister planned on journeying up to Mrs. Cleary's brother-in-law Henry's place in North Salem for the day. Well, sir, she would see me in a couple of days, then, and good night. Rosalind Russell, I hope, never had a first-act soliloquy like *that* one to get off.

Good-bye, Ol' Pussycat Cleary! And good sailing!

I need a drink to salute her going. Wait while I make myself a bone-dry cocktail. That's a Martini without vermouth, ice cubes, or glass, and you take it directly from the bottle. Cheers.

Charlie McLenahan shuddered at the sudden onslaught of gin but gulped it down manfully and then squinted off into the night. There was no moon, no stars to illuminate the small figure of Elizabeth (perhaps) standing quite still out there by the young elm, or stepping soundlessly across the gravel. He went back to his typing.

I heard the old woman's car leaving the driveway (he wrote) and turning down the road. As the silence closed in like a black, collapsing parachute in the dark, the time was at hand to summon the child to dinner. "Child!" I cried. "Dinner!" But there was no reply.

I clicked the light switch on the wall, but nothing happened. The bulb, as Mrs. Cleary had reported, was *kaput*. As I climbed the stairs to Elizabeth's room—the slow way some one-legged men do, two actions to a step—the swinging door to the kitchen quite suddenly swang, or swung, or maybe swinged a little shut, as it was in the habit of doing, cutting off all the light but that thin, bright strip under the bedroom door. I was breathing the way a bulldog will after a roughhousing. "Hello, puff puff!" I called aloud at about the half-way point. "Liz! Soup's on!" And in answer the thin line of light vanished silently. I said to myself, "The little &%$?@¢." But I hobbled on, muttering, "Come on now, puff, puff, Liz," as I neared the top of the stairs.

I knew, at least, that she couldn't lock the door, because I'd done away with the key weeks ago after she'd succeeded in locking herself in for the day. My hand was on the doorknob and I paused a moment. The back of my neck had gone a bit cold. "Liz!" I called again, getting an edge of paternal authority into my voice. But after

I'd given her a count of one-two-three-four-five, I said, "I'm comin' in," maybe a bit gruffly, and opened the door and stepped inside.

The blackness of the bedroom wasn't quite as *total* as what I'd walked out of, and I was able, without too much trouble, to get to the desk by the window. "Honey, that's no way to fire off a great welcome to the guy who keeps you in Nancy Drew books, and Jujyfruits, and all," I said. Or something equally effective. The desk lamp, which was the only implement of electrification in the room, was gone. "Give me the lamp, huh?" I said. Then I struck a match and saw her standing in the corner with the frilly little-girl's lamp in her hands. I let the match burn out and lit a second one, but she was already returning the lamp to the desk and plugging it into the wall. The room seemed to burst into light. Liz stood and, giving her grand old stepfather a wide berth, made for the door. "Hold on," I said, and grabbed hold of her hand before she could get it away. I pulled her after me to the bed. It hardly seemed the hand of a nine-year-old. More like five.

"Come on!" I said. "You're giving the fellow who's in love with you a damned rough time, do you know that?"

She said nothing. Her eyes, which are dark brown, are terribly large—too large for beauty, too round and wide and moist and lifeless. Usually her hair is parted in the middle and pulled back tightly into long, black pigtails. Her skin, you know, is white as a shell. I remember holding a buttercup under her chin once, not long ago, and her whole face seemed to turn gold in its reflection. I took the buttercup away, and she was chalk once more.

As I sat holding her on the edge of the bed, I touched her face with my finger just below her right eye and then just below her left. "What," I asked her as gravely as I could, "did one eye say to the other?"

I waited, but she said nothing, only looked away from me with a petulant shrug. "Do you know?" I asked.

"No," she whispered.

"No?" I inquired rather loudly.

"No!" she shouted.

"Something has come between us and it smells."

She looked quickly up at me and then away again, but no smile came within three city blocks of her lips.

"That's a pretty lousy joke," I said, "but I've known nine-year-olds to throw up laughing at it. Do you know about elbows?" I asked her.

She shook her head.

"Well, then, pinch your elbow."

THE EVIL EYE

She touched her left elbow with her right hand.

"Go ahead, *pinch* it. Pinch the skin behind it."

"No, hard!"

She gave it a good one.

"There, you see? You can pinch your elbow all you want, any time, and it'll never hurt. But that's a secret, and I don't want you blabbing it all over the place to Pete James or Mrs. Cuthbert or Mrs. Cleary or Sister Angela Marie."

"I don't tell secrets," she muttered.

"What?"

"*I don't tell secrets!*"

"Oh. Like what?"

"If I told you——"

"*What?*"

"*If I told you*——"

"Yes?"

"Then it would . . . be *told*."

"It *what?*"

"*Would be told!*"

She struggled to get away.

"Hold on! Whoa!" I said. "Look. I'll let you go if you answer one question. OK?"

"Maybe," she whispered.

"Do you like me?"

"No."

And she dug her elbow hard in my ribs to give her leverage enough to get across the room. But I still held fast, idiot that I was.

"But that's only half the question."

"No fair!" she complained.

"Shh. *Why* don't you like me?"

"*I don't know.*"

And she struggled again, her eyes going blurry in the angry tears.

"Why?"

"Because you're a cripple," she said.

"Ah, go on, I just walk a little funny. What's the reason, Liz?"

"You killed her, you killed her," she said in a whimper.

I let the girl go. At the door, before sliding out into the darkness, she turned and looked at me directly with a look so full of hate that the dimes and quarters melted in my pocket. But I noticed that she was, quite unthinkingly, pinching her left elbow between two fingers of her right hand. Earlier, when, of course, I should have released her immediately, I'd held onto her; and now, when I should have been drawing the whole story out of her, I was letting her go. To go mulling off behind the house. To go brooding among the night trees. But I'm basically—and metabolically—an ignorant man.

When I had the dinner dished out, I called to her, "Liz!"

Nothing.

"Liz! Dinner! Come on, old woman!"

Nothing.

"I got you something, did you know?"

Nothing.

"A camera!"

She came slowly out of the shadowed carport and into the kitchen.

"Yes," I said, "a camera, Liz. Now sit down and eat your dinner, because you won't be getting the camera until the morning, when the sun is out. People don't give cameras in the dark. That sort of thing has a curse attached to it."

Charlie stopped typing because a long ash had fallen from his cigarette into the typewriter and in blowing it away he had sent a cloud of ash up into his face. He rubbed his eyes with his knuckles and decided he wanted to walk around a bit. In a kind of diving motion, he bent sideways off the chair until the palms of his hands came flat against the floorboards. Then he allowed his rump to come crashing down, sending the chair flying. He crawled, lurching, to the aluminum leg, an elaborate contraption he would buckle onto his half-thigh and around his hips. It took him a full, exhausting three minutes on his back to get into the thing. Then he had a devil of a time climbing to a standing position. He hobbled quite eccentrically to a far corner where a cane stood, then circumnavigated the room almost with a swagger, peering out of the windows set in the southern and western walls; unlocking and opening the door leading (north) into the carport; and leaning out into the night. He was surprised that it was so chilly, and was about to close the door quickly behind him when, just beyond the hunched automobile, he thought he saw the vague silhouette of a small girl standing still as a snow sculpture in the night.

"Liz?" he said softly.

But suddenly he found himself back inside the studio, sagged against the closed door, and breathing deeply and rapidly. He thought he'd heard, very faintly but nearby, a giggle. And it frightened him.

Charlie righted the chair and slumped back into it, slept for half a minute with his fingers jammed into his eyes, awakened considerably refreshed, and recommenced his account of his life with Liz—yes, and Ann too, and Agnes the beagle, and the camera.

The camera (he tippy-tapped, *zzkak*, *zzkak*, ever so lightly on the infernal machine).

Actually, I bought the camera (I'm told) the day before yesterday. Norb Hutchinson was the fellow who told me, and he should know, because he was present at the ceremony. Norb is a hell of a fine guy, all ear and no lip, and I am as fond as I can be of that long, sallow, crumpled face of his. He has a high tolerance for other people's witticisms and sad confidences, a quality I am too twitchy to share. I guess I'd never told anybody about my malignant stepdaughter (that's the word I used—malignant) until the day before yesterday at lunchtime with Norb Hutchinson at the bar of the Plume Rouge on East Forty-sixth Street.

The Plume's usual circle of art directors, copywriters, printer's representatives and magazine editorial people gave us a large hello when we entered. I get a reception in the Plume each time I enter that would be the envy of a king. (The fact that I am still only six or seven weeks widowed may add to the glamour, of course, but I doubt it.)

It's all a matter of style, y'see.

I come in with the end of a cigarette in my mouth, sending up enough smoke to blot out New Jersey. I go like a dump truck to the coat room to prop my portfolio against one wall and let the owner's wife pull the topcoat off me. Because ol' Charlie—or "the old man," as many of my friends, including my late wife, have referred to me—has never learned to remove a garment correctly, one sleeve comes off inside out, and the black arm band falls slackly about my left wrist in the entanglement. I run a hand swiftly through my pepper-and-salt hair, which has the consistency of kelp, and then pull the arm bend up above my elbow. I'm a slightly-less-than-pretty fellow—a Dylan Thomas, I've been told, and without the poetry. I've put on weight in recent months, especially in the weeks since Ann was killed. My breathing is violent at times—"like the snorts that would escape through the blow hole of an asthmatic whale," as one of my friends put it. My clothes are too tight in some places and too baggy in others. And my limp, which was never slight, now seems more pronounced than ever, as though some tinsmith were trimming the old metal leg by a quarter inch every Tuesday. Now I know—and it isn't immodesty, I swear—that the lunch crowd at the Plume, men with whom I've been working, drinking and jawing for years, love me almost extravagantly. They love me for my style, because in a stylish way I seem to be going to the dogs for *them*. They can smoke too much, get into debt too deeply, risk the jobs by staying too long at lunch each day, and sink ever more quickly into the bad habits of middle age, and somehow not show a mark for it all. I'm their own picture of Dorian Gray, coughing away into my cupped hand (a final hurrah before something definitive strikes) or showing up in the art department of some swanky-danky magazine with eyes glowing red like exit signs, and then blowing my nose into a handkerchief that is already weighing down my hip pocket the way a revolver would. The unregenerate regulars at the Plume know that no matter how sickly they might feel, or how conscience-stricken, I feel even worse, and I have more, each morning, to regret.

"You need a haircut, old man," one of the regulars said that day.

"Old man, when's your cookbook coming out?"

"Move over, Jack, and make room for the old man."

I thanked my companions and hoisted myself onto a stool.

"Old man, what'll you have today?" (This from François, the bartender—the upstart!)

Old man this, old man that; it's just a case of sweet, boozy camaraderie, that's all.

I remember the talk was about my being forty, which is no age to be, and then about putting on weight.

"Ah, I eat like a bird. A pelican."

I sank into a reverie and the conversations struck up once more around me. I glared into my Martini as an important thought struck into me like a javelin out of nowhere at all:

I wonder if Elizabeth thinks that I killed her mother! That it was none other than me—Charlie McLenahan!—over there in the park letting fly with the pistol! Eh? That the "old man" with the gun, who was simply described as "the old man" in the radio report—the only report Liz heard!—was really me!?!

Masculine intuition—that's what it was. And hardly more than twenty-four hours before the little gargoyle said it herself! "You killed her, you killed her."

By two o'clock, the Plume regulars were off at their tables putting away great heaps of *osso buco* and eggplant *parmigiana*, and only Norb and I sat hunched at the bar. Ann Carmody McLenahan, I was telling him in the slick tones of a newscaster, was shot to death one afternoon, a little short of two months ago, as she was about to cross Fifty-ninth Street to enter the swank Plaza Hotel on the arm of a former bit player in Tarzan movies ("See here, ape man, you show us the elephant graveyard or we will kill the monkey, *comprenez*?"). Mention of the square-rigged young actor was news to Norb, as the

THE EVIL EYE

chap had not been cited in the newspaper accounts except as a detached witness. The accident, of course, was an awful, terrible, monstrous freak. It was even bad melodrama. An old man, preparing to blow his brains out in Central Park across the way, had fired his lousy pistol prematurely and by accident, and the stray bullet tore into Ann's back, killing her instantly. The wild improbability of the event slapped it squarely on the front pages of the evening papers and the next morning's one tabloid. "Blonde socialite" and "mainstem beauty" were the archaic descriptions of Ann used most frequently by the reporters. But because the story had no mystery to it—the old man turned himself in to a mounted policeman minutes after the shot—the papers dropped poor Ann, as they'd drop a poorly fought welterweight fight, within hours.

I told Norb I knew the actor pretty well, and he was a good-enough joker. Probably he'd already strolled casually into half a dozen affairs of this kind and would take that walk again because—well, he's who he is, and the world is full of good-looking, well-bred women who become jelly at the sound of a British accent. After her first husband died, Ann went a long time without men, and she was a girl who needed a baritone voice and a hairy leg around the house. Here I'd gone forty years without marriage. Thirty-eight, anyway. Didn't know what it was. Wasn't even sure I wanted it. Then there was Ann with her beagle dog, Agnes, on a leash, and her darlin' little daughter, Liz, skipping along behind. How could a hedgehog like me *not* want to have that creamy face of Ann's—that green-eyed, intelligent, alive, *pretty* face—looking at me all the time and kissing my ugly mug and cleaning up the crumbs I left behind?

I had a damn good marriage, I told Norb. It had a run of only two years—two years and a couple of months and a couple of days—but it was good while it lasted. And I was a gentle and constant lover, and I think Ann rather loved me too. Oh, I had my slouchy side. I was gone a good bit. Holed up here at the Plume. Or at the Font. Or at Tim's. And I left my ties around on the backs of chairs and my dental floss on the sink. So Ann met an actor with a chin like a hard, minuscule backside and an eye full of electric sparks short-circuiting away, and she had a short, sweet fling. I don't begrudge it to her. Not really.

Yes, I do. I begrudge the hell out of it.

I waved the bartender into making another round of drinks.

"Why do you still wear the arm band?" Norb wanted to know.

"For the kid, really. She's nine years old, and all I am to her is bad news. I think she connects me up with Ann's accident. Who knows? I even ran over her dog a couple of months ago, shortly before Ann's death. Didn't I tell you about it?"

"Yeah, I remember."

"Right in the dirt road that goes by our house. Not a moving thing within miles, except Agnes. That @½*&%$ dopey dog, Agnes. I think she thought the left front tire was vulcanized Ken-L-Ration. Liz was inconsolable. She's never really talked or listened to me since. But anyhow, the arm band. I want the thing to stay on as evidence that I *care*, despite the way she's been carrying on since the funeral, the malignant little wretch!"

I snickered. "Sorry, Norb, old fellow. I use words like that—malignant, gargoyle, monster child, bat girl—and I'd better wash my mouth out, because I don't really mean those words. Somewhere, in an interior organ of some sort, I love the kid. Or, if the word isn't love, then—well, at the very least, I'm *concerned* about her. I want her to be happy, because the truth is the little bloodsucker breaks my heart."

Norb and I left the Plume drunk and got drunker, and the next thing I remember is 8:45 yesterday morning in Norb's studio, and Norb sitting at the drawing board, dragging deeply at a cigarette and staring morosely at the sunshine flooding at the street below. "Hello, old man," Norb said. "God, you snore."

"Of course I do. And somebody's been at your face with the green paint."

He told me I'd been in no condition to drive home the night before, but that I'd phoned Mrs. Cleary and asked her to stay on for the night. And she'd given me one of her Irish lectures.

I shall not describe the pain I found myself in, from my lower regions to my cranium, except to say that no comparable sensation or group of sensations has been felt since the invention of ether. It was in this condition, then, that I was introduced to the camera. It stood on the file cabinet at the foot of the daybed on which I'd slept so violently all night. It was made completely of metal, with a black lacquer finish that was coming off. A leather strap ran across the top like the handle of a briefcase. The lens, which was facing away from me, was encased in a silver cone, giving the camera a faint resemblance to a lantern. Obviously, it was homemade. It was also terribly heavy and, upon close inspection, it proved to be geared for instant developing, in the Polaroid manner.

I'd bought the thing, Norb told me, for six dollars from a pawnbroker who had a shop on the east side of Third Avenue somewhere in the mid-Forties. The man had tried to sell me a battered old box camera, but I'd have none of it. "Don't you have one just as cheap, but different? Crazy?" I said.

"You mean nuts?" the man asked.

"Yah. For a nutty kid, a nutty camera," Norb said that I said.

And out had come this contraption that seemed half miner's lamp, half lunch box. It had been left with him, the pawnbroker told us (Norb said), by a thin little man with an indoor face—the face, perhaps, of a henpecked inventor who'd just lost a billion-dollar race with a large film company by only five minutes.

Oh, yes. To test the camera, I'd taken a picture of the spire of the Chrysler Building. Considering the shape I was in, the snapshot was just fine.

"*Im! Possible!*" were the words uttered by the pawnbroker when he saw the picture. And: "To tell you the truth, kid, I didn't think it'd work."

Charlie permitted his head to dip slowly forward in sleep, until his nose was snugly pressed against the margin-release button of the typewriter. Minutes later, he grunted "Huh!" suddenly, excitedly, and lifted his head from the machine. He glanced quickly to his right in time to see—or perhaps, to sketch, in his despair-logged mind—a small darting movement. The door had been opened just a bit, six inches or so, and the small hand flew from the outside doorknob the instant Charlie turned. He lurched violently across the small distance to the door, fell against it, opened it wide, and looked out. "What the hell!" he growled and, finding the cane in his hand, stalked out onto the gravel.

He was certain that he saw a pint-sized shadow far across the lawn, moving rapidly toward the house. He turned and headed back to the carport, taking fast steps up the drive to the door. The wall switch inside still lit no lights of course, and Charlie swore. From the drawer of the table that stood at the foot of the staircase he removed a flashlight and then hobbled, step by step, to the child's bedroom, the beam of the flashlight jerking to left and right ahead of him. There was no strip of illumination showing beneath the door. He walked directly across the room to the bed, keeping the flashlight beam diverted behind him and to one side so that it wouldn't awaken the girl if she was there and was asleep.

She was there. And dimly Charlie could see that she lay on her side facing him, with her lips parted slightly and her breathing coming slow and deep. Charlie placed a hand on her forehead and was surprised to find the child was quite cool. He turned off the flashlight and placed it on the desk.

"I'm an ash," he told himself, "a stupid, ignorant, selfish, frightened, unmitigated, total, and complete ash!"

And he went down the stairs again as quietly as he could. But then, once again, at the bottom of the stairs, the knowledge hit him that the child had followed him out of the room and was standing, this second, at the top of the staircase. He turned and then cursed himself for having left the flashlight behind. There was something, something the size of Elizabeth, at the bedroom door, wasn't there?

"Liz," Charlie said, barely audibly, but no response came.

And as he made his way back to the studio, he knew she was with him all the way.

Only maybe she wasn't.

Maybe it was just Charlie McLenahan's grief following him around. But whatever it was—something mortal, something imagined, something loving, or something lethal—it frightened him cold.

After he'd closed the studio door behind him, he locked it. And he had a drink. He looked at his watch. Twenty to three. There was no telling how long he had slept—three minutes or a couple of hours—because he'd already written a respectable sheaf of unnumbered pages, some filled, some half empty, without once glancing at his watch, and with no idea of his speed. He seemed to be going like a Thompson submachine gun, *zzkak zzkak zzkakkakakakak*, but maybe that was only a gin-soaked impression too. Maybe he was tapping it out in the more uncertain rhythms of a cap pistol. Tap. Tap. Taptap. Tap.

Maybe: that was the word he was tapping a moment later.

Maybe (he wrote) is a word that somehow defines my entire experience with Elizabeth. We got off to a fuzzy, maybe, start the day I met her and lifted her onto my knee and tried to give her a kiss, only to have her turn her face away so that the kiss landed somewhere behind the left ear. "Pew, you smell," she said—her first words, and I shall hang onto them always.

Of course I *did* smell occasionally of Martinis, which can sometimes give one's neighbor the impression of being downwind of an onion field. I did smell of cigarettes, certainly. And of uncared-for bachelorhood.

By and large, though, she was civil enough to me, though we never became friends, even when Ann was alive. Liz was a quiet and rather remote child. She would open up from time to time—though never, I regret, when I was present. She and Ann would horse around somewhere and when I'd enter the room—run for your lives! Bad news! Poison gas! Liz would stalk out of the room, the grand vizier stalking out of the peace conference.

She was a very religious child, as I was at her age and as, in many ways, I still am. She loved the atmosphere of church, as I did and do. She loved the nuns and the rosaries and the holy water and the confessional and the shiny linoleum everywhere. She even loved school (the creep!) and was good at her new mathematics and her ancient catechism answers. "Why did God make you?" "God made me to know Him, to love Him, and to serve Him in this world and forever in the next."

After she had thrown herself out of that second-floor window—furious, I suppose, that her mother, in death, had abandoned her—and lay grunting a long while on the grass with the wind and the pride knocked out of her, but not the fury; after her almost week-long hunger strike—a week marked by thefts from the breadbox and the deep freeze; after she had set fire to (a) her wastebasket, (b) the gardener's shed behind the house, (c) *my* wastebasket, and (d) quite unsuccessfully, the studio; and after she had run away twice and been returned twice—well, after all these raucous events had transpired one upon the other following Ann's funeral, I took this small cuckoo and occasional arsonist to see Sister Angela Marie, her teacher, and thence to Mother Paul Jude, the principal, both of whom Liz admires inordinately.

"She's ... *changeable*," Sister Angela Marie said. "She can be sullen one moment in class, and, five minutes later when the children are in church for stations, she seems almost radiant. What kind of food does Mrs. Cleary pack for Elizabeth's lunch? Perhaps her food is wrong."

Mother Paul Jude, who is not a dope, recommended psychiatry, which has been my own prescription from the beginning ("First psychiatry, then electrocution."), and told me about the nuns' pet psychiatrist, a fellow in Pound Ridge, New York, who consents to listen to children for twenty-five dollars an hour. Elizabeth has only just started her visits, of course, so there have been no reports, no findings, no diagnoses yet. Give the good old doc time, I say. Shortly after my own autopsy in the Westchester County morgue, I suspect he will find a key to the child's problem.

But I haven't mentioned the snapshots yet. I must.

Yesterday morning, the morning of the great hangover, I worked straight through at Norb Hutchinson's place. I worked all the afternoon, too, on an illustration that wasn't due at the advertising agency until today. I figured I could do the job a day in advance, deliver it, come home, and then stay at home the following day (the one I've just been through) working on a couple of book covers for a guy I know.

Anyhow, I went home, as I've recorded. Met Mrs. Cleary, said good-bye, tangled with Liz, put her to bed, as I've recorded. Then I had a few drinks because that seems to be the pattern of my life these last weeks, and slept like a grizzly bear. Leaped to the ceiling at the sound of the alarm this morning. Cooked breakfast. And . . .

"Hello, Liz."

She has this kittenish, hands-behind-the-back, let's walk-close-to-the-walls-today kind of mood about her, though she is still no more talkative than a bay scallop. She is looking for something. She is good about straightening her long black stockings and washing her dirty neck. She is on the move. Silently.

Of course! "The camera!" I exclaim, snapping my fingers.

She darts a quick, thankful look at me, though if I were to measure the wattage of that gratitude flashing there in her eye I'd give it two and a half—about enough to kindle a firefly's abdomen.

Elizabeth liked the camera. She almost—not quite—smiled when I placed it on the breakfast table in the kitchen. She circled the table once and looked at the camera closely. "I love it," she said. She tried to lift it and found it so terribly heavy she had to use two hands. "I just love it."

I suggested that she take one picture before leaving for school. She agreed. She carried the thing before her with two hands holding the leather strap, much as she would carry a pail brimming with water, and went outside. I watched her from the front door as the explosion of morning sunlight—or maybe it was the cigarette I'd just lit—set a deep, needle-point pain going in the central area of my brainpan.

She was saying, "Ah, please, let me take a picture of you, Charlie."

"Nah, my face would burn a hole in the paper." But she was (for her) so happy and so talkative that I couldn't risk a change in mood. "OK," I said, as her face began to harden, "where?"

"Back of the house, in the sun."

I stood against a section of white wall, bunching up my face like a closed fist in the early-morning sun. "I'm going to count," she said. "One."

"Don't I get a blindfold or a cigarette?"

"Two. *Three!*"

She pushed a button on the side of the machine, an action that set off a barely audible bzzzzzz-click somewhere in its middle that lasted more than a full second. The button popped back out to its normal position with the click. "There's nothing happening," she said.

I took a couple of steps toward her: "It's developing the picture. Don't worry. Whistle a song."

But her mood of delight was fast slipping away. "It's such a *stupid* thing!"

THE EVIL EYE

"Why don't you put it down on the old stump until it's ready, Liz?"

The smile was gone entirely when she looked up at me and said, carefully, "Elizabeth." She added, "I want to hold it."

It seemed half a lifetime before she tore the snapshot against the blade in the bottom of the camera and uttered her definitive comment: "But you're not *in* it!"

"Not in it?"

I stumped over to her and looked over her shoulder at the ridiculous thing. It contained nothing but a number of horizontal boards painted white—perhaps flaking just a bit—with the shadow of an eave slanting across the top left corner of the photograph. "I do seem to have a blank expression," I managed to say, despite the pang that shot through an inner pocket of my spleen. "Maybe it wasn't aimed just right, Liz," I said.

"But it was!"

She tossed the snapshot over her shoulder to the grass, as you might toss away a burned match, then placed the camera on the oak stump and walked off—or, rather, walked *out*. "It's an *ignorant* camera," she cried back at me, "and I hate it, and I hate you, and I don't want it."

"Well, that covers the situation nicely," I said, and then lifted my voice in my best quarter-deck manner: "Elizabeth! Here! Bring the camera into the house! And pick up th——"

The screen door slammed shut behind her.

We were sitting on the stump, the camera and I, when Liz drifted down the driveway on her way to the intersection where the school bus would pick her up. She never looked our way.

I shall not comment just now upon my philosophical musings or conjecturings regarding the snapshot beyond reporting that I examined it carefully and detected, beneath a clothesline hook that truly exists at this very moment in time, a rust stain on the outer wall of the house that does not. The general condition of the paint job in the picture (flaky) was a libel upon our homestead's current epidermis (smooth as nail polish). In a kind of sedate panic, I left the camera and snapshot on the stump, and, somehow, got to the studio and even managed to do some work on a jacket for a book. The hours passed, and I confess that I had a nip or two to help them along. It must have been about four o'clock that I looked up from my work to see Elizabeth crossing the lawn toward the road.

It was the first I knew that she was home from school. The camera rode on her left arm while she held the snapshot close to her face, inspecting it with an intensity you would find only in the face of a watchmaker looking into the workings of a pocket watch that has been run over by a bus. I tapped on the window with the end of the T square, and then went to the window and (This can't all be happening just a few short hours ago, can it? It can.) and opened the window all the way. I called out. "There's stuff in the kitchen. Crackers. Milk."

Without turning, she called back, "I *had* them."

"About to take another picture?"

"Yes."

"Of what?"

"Pete James."

Pete, a four-year-old with a head of tousled black hair that gives him an eternally startled look, lives down the road from us. He had appeared at the foot of the drive precisely on cue and hollered out, "Hey, Elizabeth! You wanna go froggin'?"

No, she didn't—not that minute, anyhow—but she had a better idea. *Uh*-uh, he said, he had to catch a frog for his mother. Wait, she called to him, and then said that if he, Peter James, didn't come right on over to her in sixty seconds he'd be sorry.

Pete climbed the steep lawn to the girl. Stand against the house, she ordered. You're gonna do something bad, gonna hurt, he said. No, she promised. Picture! You're gonna take my picture! Sure, and you can see it right after, she promised. *Right* after? Yup, and then she'd go frogging with him, honest. He smiled a huge, gleaming smile for the camera, his eyes tight shut. Bzzzzzz-click. OK, Elizabeth? Yes, Pete, you can relax. Let's see, huh? Pete, I *can't* go catching frogs this afternoon, I'm too busy, you go on now, get out of here, scram. I *won't* scram. Yes, you will, Peter James, you will if I have to run you off with a large rifle. I wanna see my picture. Well, you can't because I have to send the film away to be developed, to Rochester, to Kodiak, Alaska, to President Johnson. *Scram*!

She walked quickly around him and into the house, and Pete, after a moment's hesitation, came running behind her. But she was standing in the doorway holding the screen door open for him. She seized him by the face and pushed him backward onto the ground.

That final gesture of Elizabeth's had me half out of the window. "Elizabeth!"

Pete picked himself up and came crying to me, but I couldn't make out a word the kid was saying among the sobs. "Be a good boy, Pete, and go catch yourself a frog somewhere," I told him.

My spit had turned to gunpowder. But I didn't go up to Liz's bedroom because I didn't want to risk a showdown on her battlefield. It would be here, on mine. I stalked the studio room, preparing a loud speech. The speeches I make up and then do not deliver, by the way, are among the finest pieces of rhetoric in all of Western literature.

On about my thirtieth circumnavigation of the room, I detected a slight movement to the right of the drawing board and once again peered from the window. There was Elizabeth, standing in the driveway, with her bicycle just behind her on its side. She was taking a picture of the house and studio.

I forced myself to walk slowly to the open window. I forced my face and voice into a measure of passivity. "Elizabeth, come on in a minute."

She did not reply. She lifted her bicycle, placed the camera in the basket on the handlebars, coasted to the road, and began pedaling toward town. I bellowed out her name, but it was no use.

I stalked over to the house and up the stairs to her room. A snapshot, in a dozen pieces, was in the wastebasket. I brought them back to the studio with me and glued them together on a piece of Bristol board. It was the picture of a tall young man with short black hair, his eyes squinting in the sun. He was standing, as Pete had stood, before the front wall of the house, wearing a well-cut suit and a dark tie. One side of his mouth was pulled into a grin—the same pull-of-the-mouth that will transform Pete's face even now, as he concentrates on a game of skill (like pouncing upon a frog), or a repair job (like realigning the bleached-white skeleton of a snake that's gotten out of whack in a rainstorm). The young man in the picture, I was happy to note, looked sensitive, warm-natured, and well-to-do. I'd place his age at about twenty-four. And because Liz has a distant cousin of just that age, I was sure she was able to guess at Pete James's age in the picture, too, with reasonable accuracy.

"Ah, come on, Pete!" I said aloud to the picture as I stomped about the room. "When you're twenty-four, I'll be sixty," I hollered. "Sixty! A spry, waltzing, wenching sixty!"

I don't know what time it was—maybe five—when the phone rang. "Charlie? Mabel Cuthbert."

Through the tired voice I could see her tired, sweet face, with the pale freckles big as dimes on it, and her gray hair swept back into a bun, and something badly wrong with her. Some of her acquaintances think it's cancer, and I wouldn't be much surprised. She said she shouldn't be calling and telling me about anything so trivial, but——

Mabel had been cleaning a room upstairs in her house down the road when she saw Liz, acting like a bank robber, walk her bike in under the branches of a huge fir tree that's Mabel's pride and joy.

("Why, anyone could hide a water buffalo in there and get away with it," she said.) Mrs. Cuthbert was unable to resist her curiosity, so she came out of the house and peered into the tree.

Elizabeth was studying a snapshot when Mabel had come snooping into the piny lair. The girl asked her: "Mrs. Cuthbert, can you tell how old a tree is just by looking at it?"

"I don't know. What kind of tree?"

"A maple."

"If it's young, perhaps, but not if it's old."

"It's young."

"Let's see, Elizabeth."

After wrestling with a should-she or shouldn't-she decision for a painful moment, Liz handed the old girl the snapshot. The McLenahan manse, according to the photograph, was only barely recognizable, Mabel told me. Ivy grew all over the north wall and the chimney. (The place has never seen ivy in its life!— Flamingos, leprechauns, and other garden cuties paraded across the lawn in the front of the place; ships' running lights ornamented both doors; and the studio—)

"—wasn't there, was it?" I said, feeling sicker than ever.

Mabel snorted. "Exactly! But how did you know, Charlie?"

"Extrasensory perception, honey."

Where the studio had stood, a maple now grew—a tree that had been around, Mabel guessed, oh, a good fifteen to twenty years, more like twenty. The woods beyond, she said, were a little "ratty" in the picture.

"Ratty?"

"Yes, ratty," she said. "Some of the trees in the very first line are dead—long dead—and haven't been removed. And one or two of them show up black."

"Black?"

"Scorched."

And that, in essence, was her story.

Liz, "looking like the cat that ate the canary," had walked her bike onto the road and had pedaled off toward home.

As I hung up the phone, I saw Elizabeth returning—the attempt to make it all the way up the gravel drive, the slight skid, the dismounting, the abandonment of the bicycle at the door of the house. I caught her eye and waved her into the studio. She came slowly, something strangely *tight* about her, as though she were straining every fiber in her to refrain from bursting into laughter, or dancing a tarantella. I jiggled the keys in my pocket frantically in accompaniment.

THE EVIL EYE

"Elizabeth——" I began.

"Yes, Daddy?" she said, showering sparks of pure love everywhere in the room. I could have wrung her lollipop-stem neck.

"Elizabeth, I wish——"

"—that I weren't so mean to Pete?"

"Yes, well, *that* for a starter. I think it would be nice if you'd be nice to me too."

"I'm sorry, Daddy." With a *smile!*

"But I'm putting aside that particular speech for another occasion. Right now I want to make you an offer." She walked about the room as I talked, running an index finger over things. "I'm taking you to live somewhere else. New experiences. New friends. New——"

She scowled suddenly and wheeled on me. "Where?"

"Oh . . . " I wondered myself where to begin another life. "Manhattan."

"No."

"It's a different tempo. Theater. Noise. We'll go off somewhere for a while. Europe, maybe. You've never——"

"No," she said. "I'll never leave here. That's something I know." She said it flatly, with her back to me.

"Let me tell you something, small pussycat. Something important. We're leaving this house tomorrow, you and me. The day after today. And we'll never return to it. I'll have somebody else pack up for us later. Huh? We'll drive to the Algonquin Hotel in the morning. Eh? And from there on out, we'll improvise. What do you think about that?"

At the word "tomorrow" she had stiffened. Thoughts chased one another across her face like dark, medieval armies sweeping across a ruined plain. One could almost hear—cronk! crunk! clang! oof!—the clangor of the broadaxes upon cuirass and shield. But then there came a sudden terrible quiet. I think I can call it a "quiet," can't I? And, after quite a long pause, a filthy little smile caught the corners of her mouth. "All right, Daddy."

It was the small, hard smile that finished the sentence for me: All right, Daddy-o, then it will have to be tonight, won't it, old pal?

Forgive me while I groan. Ohh, my God, I'm tired. And I can't stay with this thing. I can't. Not with the last thing of all. The final snapshot. The one that cinched the whole thing. Tied it up. Turned the key. Threw the switch. Dropped the blade. Struck the spark. I need a drink. No, a cigarette. No, a drink *and* a cigarette. And then I'll tell you about death.

But Charlie hadn't even the energy to raise the bottle or light the cigarette. For a full two minutes the typewriter became his pillow again, and he would doubtless have drifted back to sleep, despite his determination to see the night through and his account completed, but a fit of coughing shook him up violently. His round, red, blue-black eyes slowly opened, and Charlie found himself staring at an image that was first colored a bright orange, then a blurred, dull, gray-black coming into sharp focus. The door. In the door, a small square window. And the window itself cut into four narrow panes. The two at the left perfectly framed the face of a child with eyes hard and dark and lifeless as coal.

As Charlie sat up, the child's face grew smaller and then disappeared altogether.

Charlie snorted, "Hnf!" and muttered drunkenly a few indeterminate words as he tried to find the end of a bent cigarette with the flame of his match. The match burned his fingers, and he catapulted it into the air. It landed on a mound of pencil sketches done on tracing paper and started a small fire which Charlie beat out with a sketch pad. He hurled the cigarette into the wastebasket. He dug a fresh cigarette from the pack and got it going without too much difficulty. "Gotta finish the job," he told himself. "Gotta gotta gotta gotta gotta fininish the jobobob." Somewhere in himself he found the strength to resume his typewritten account of his conversation with Elizabeth in the studio.

"All right, Daddy"—that's what she'd said with that small, hard smile of hers like the smile a nightclub comic throws to a heckler.

I said to her, "But you don't know how it will turn out, do you?"

"How *what* will turn out?"

"The accident."

She raised her eyebrows, meaning the look to be disarmingly quizzical.

"We know, both of us," I went on, "that there has been an accident scheduled, don't we?"

"An accident." The look was a hmm-what-have-we-here? Wary.

"And we know what kind of accident it will be."

Another small needle of light ignited in the witch girl's eyes.

"Fire." She'd formed the word with her lips, but no sound was uttered.

"Fire," I said. "Correct! Right here in the studio."

"Here."

Her conversation, you note, was not voluble, but I understand brevity of speech is common among nine-year-old patricides. Or maybe the word should be step-patricides.

"But there's something vital that we still don't know, Elizabeth. And that's what will happen to . . . " I paused.

"Elizabeth," she whispered.

"Yes again. We can't let any accidents take place, eh?—unless we know just exactly how Elizabeth will make out. Shall I take your picture? It's hardly the dinner hour yet, not even five-thirty, and we've got plenty of sunlight."

(I hear the words, but they're deep and slow, like a seventy-eight-rpm record played at forty-five.)

Now the thoughts that fled across her face were of a different sort, ending in a suspended emotion very close, I think, to despair. She nodded gravely, and we walked together to the out-of-doors.

(I see us walking together, as a bystander would, but each step takes an eternity, like the graceful sweep of a slow-motion movie.)

On the lawn, across which the trees stretched their shadows in long sloping lines to the house, I took her picture with the camera. "Say cheese," I said and got the tight little paper-clip smile. Bzzzzzz-click.

"What do you think you'll look like?" I asked as I handed her the camera. "A movie star? Or an oyster?"

"An oyster."

"Then what noise is it, Liz, that annoys an oyster, do you know?"

"*Please* shut up."

"Don't you know?"

"A noisy noise!"

"No, you're wrong. The noise that annoys an oyster is faint, ever so faint. It's the scraping sound—skkkkk!—of the oysterman's knife just beginning to go to work on her front door."

Elizabeth shivered.

"Do you hear it?" I asked her.

"Hear what?"

"The oysterman's knife. It's your last chance. I want to begin to make a real life for you. Let me do it?"

"You hate me."

"I don't anything of the kind. I love you, kitten. Here, let me throw that cam——"

She twisted away from me. "No! You hate me and you've killed everything. Everything! And I'll see the picture. I'm *going* to see the picture no matter what!"

Elizabeth stood very still with the camera held before her in both hands. The picture, when it finally appeared, was that of a young nun, just short of her thirtieth birthday or just beyond it, of the same order as that of Sister Angela Marie and Mother Paul Jude. I can't describe the young nun's face as happy, but there was a resignation in it that seemed frozen there, a calm mask over a tortured memory.

ALFRED GILLESPIE

The eyes were large, even larger than I imagined they could be, but darkly shadowed. A smile, a rather knowing smile, touched the lips. And it was the smile that did it. I knew, at that first glance, that I'd lost the war, just as surely as though some dark enemy had turned a flamethrower on me. I looked at Liz to see how the picture affected her. Her mouth twitched with excitement. In my innermost mind, I thought I detected the sound, ever so faint, of the oysterman's knife.

Death is the end of everything we know and maybe of everything else too. It's the lid coming down. It's every regret we have for failure. It's a black, asphyxiating cloud. And waiting for it is worse than waiting for pain. It's waiting for the zero, the nothing, the stopping of the intelligence that lives, like a gray shimmering pearl, somewhere behind our eyes. Death, believe me, is a lonely business. I believe in God and in eternity, but I don't (just now at least) believe in my place with Him in it. There's just the *skkk!* of the knife. And then the dark. And there's only one way to wait for it that I know. You drink. And then you drink some more. And then you

Charlie McLenahan did get to finish his account of his life and hard times with Liz—as much as he could know, that is—but with not even seconds to spare. When he became aware that the room was filled with smoke, and that, in fact, there were intimations of real red fire to his right, Charlie rolled up the forty-odd pages he'd typed into a tight cylinder and jammed them into the pocket of his robe as one would thrust a sword into a scabbard. In fleeing the studio, he fell badly once, giving his right hip a terrible wrench, and then had a devil of a job making it to the door on his elbows. The door needed unlocking, which delayed things a bit. (He'd knocked the key out of the lock and had trouble finding it.) All in all, it took him a long, wearying four minutes before he was breathing the clear, cool, almost cold night air.

He coughed a good deal as he lay on the gravel halfway down the driveway, and emitted a few indescribable noises from deep inside him. Elizabeth flew out of the house, shouting, "Daddy! Daddy!" with a shrillness that was close to hysteria. She asked him, over and over, what the matter was, but his attempts to answer came out only as grotesque wheezes and grunts. The child sobbed in apparent fear and threw her arms around him. Charlie cried a bit himself. And by the time he could get a word out, the studio was most dramatically afire. Charlie sent the child to the house to put in an emergency phone call. When she returned to him, helpless on the gravel, her eyes were still wide with excitement. She helped him to the car, so that he could move it down to the road, free of the blaze and out of the way of the volunteer firemen. Through the dark hours, they sat side by

THE EVIL EYE

side, propped against a tree by the road, watching the fire brigade hose down the blaze in the studio and in trees beyond. The flames never reached to the house.

At one point in their vigil, Charlie somehow muttered into the child's ear the fact that he, Charlie, had not had anything to do with the death of her mother; and Elizabeth, genuinely surprised at his stupidity, said that of course she knew he had nothing to do with the violent end of Ann Carmody McLenahan. A crazy old man in Central Park had done that. He'd shot her. And he hadn't even meant to.

But then——

Charlie stopped. Then why had the girl called him a murderer?

Agnes!

Of course!

Liz thought he'd killed that silly beagle bitch Agnes out of sheer wanton malice! Charlie began, very quietly, to laugh, and his shoulders shook against the tree trunk, and tears coursed down his cheeks. Liz looked at him quizzically, but he could say nothing through his exhausted giddiness. He'd tell her another time, in another place.

Then the giddiness was gone. Charlie turned to the child. Why had she been up all night, sneaking around like a ¢@$%& leprechaun?

But she hadn't, she said, and her puzzled look was entirely convincing. She'd been in bed. Asleep. His gruntings in the driveway here had awakened her and, in fact, had given her a good scare.

Charlie shook again with laughter that was not too far removed from weeping. She'd been in her room all the time! The fire had not been started by Elizabeth—it must have been his own discarded cigarette! And probably even the snapshots were only sick little flashes from his own burning imagination! Martini dreams, knitted from pure dog hair—the hair of the hair of the hair of the dog that began biting him in earnest just a few days ago, or a few weeks at the bar at the Plume.

"Show me the picture of the house," he said, almost in a whimper.

"Picture of the house?"

"Describe it to me then," he said.

"How?"

"Was there ivy? A maple tree? Santa Clauses? Reindeer? Imps? Leprechauns?"

"*Leprechauns?*"

"What, then?"

"The house," she said, shrugging. "I don't know what you're talking about, Daddy."

Charlie sighed, like a man reaching home.

There is a little to add to the story. The next day, Charlie looked everywhere for the camera, even in the ashes of the studio, but he found nothing. A couple of weeks later he put the house up for sale and took Liz off with him to New York. They lived, as he'd suggested, at the Algonquin. They went to James Bond movies, ballets, slick new musicals, even ball games. Norb Hutchinson and Charlie's other close friends at the Plume decided that the old man and his small stepdaughter were hitting it off quite well together in the big city, and Norb was extremely pleased when he learned that Charlie and Liz were sailing to Europe for the summer. Norb, of course—and everyone at the Plume—was naturally shocked to the ends of his being when he heard that, on their fourth night out from New York, while Charlie and Liz were taking a turn together, alone on the deck, Charlie fell overboard and was lost.

The little girl, in a profound state of shock, was flown back to New York from Europe and was met at Kennedy Airport by some cousins of her mother's. She lived with them only a short time, though, because she was quite unhappy, always drifting about like a new moth in a breeze. She had, they noticed with sympathy, a strange habit of holding her right arm behind her and pinching her left elbow.

In the end, the cousins gave up. They bowed to the child's entreaties and gave her over to the Church.

THE SEA DEVIL

ARTHUR GORDON

The man came out of the house and stood quite still, listening. Behind him, the lights glowed in the cheerful room, the books were neat and orderly in their cases, the radio talked importantly to itself. In front of him, the bay stretched dark and silent, one of the countless lagoons that border the coast where Florida thrusts its great green thumb deep into the tropics.

It was late in September. The night was breathless, summer's dead hand still lay heavy on the land. The man moved forward six paces and stood on the sea wall. He dropped his cigarette and noted where the tiny spark hissed and went out. The tide was beginning to ebb.

Somewhere out in the blackness a mullet jumped and fell back with a sullen splash. Heavy with roe, they were jumping less often, now. They would not take a hook, but a practiced eye could see the swirls they made in the glassy water. In the dark of the moon, a skilled man with a cast net might take half a dozen in an hour's work. And a big mullet makes a meal for a family.

The man turned abruptly and went into the garage, where his cast net hung. He was in his late twenties, wide-shouldered and strong. He did not have to fish for a living, or even for food. He was a man who worked with his head, not with his hands. But he liked to go casting alone at night.

He liked the loneliness and the labor of it. He liked the clean taste of salt when he gripped the edge of the net with his teeth as a cast netter must. He liked the arching flight of sixteen pounds of lead and linen against the starlight, and the weltering crash of the net into the unsuspecting water. He liked the harsh tug of the retrieving rope around his wrist, and the way the net came alive when the cast was true, and the thud of captured fish on the floor boards of the skiff.

He liked all that because he found in it a reality that seemed to be missing from his twentieth-century job and from his daily life. He liked being the hunter, skilled and solitary and elemental. There was no conscious cruelty in the way he felt. It was the way things had been in the beginning.

The man lifted the net down carefully and lowered it into a bucket. He put a paddle beside the bucket. Then he went into the house. When he came out, he was wearing swimming trunks and a pair of old tennis shoes. Nothing else.

The skiff, flat-bottomed, was moored off the sea wall. He would not go far, he told himself. Just to the tumbledown dock half a mile away. Mullet had a way of feeding around old pilings after dark. If he moved quietly, he might pick up two or three in one cast close to the dock. And maybe a couple of others on the way down or back.

He shoved off and stood motionless for a moment, letting his eyes grow accustomed to the dark. Somewhere out in the channel a porpoise blew with a sound like steam escaping. The man smiled a little; porpoises were his friends. Once, fishing in the Gulf, he had seen the charter-boat captain reach overside and gaff a baby porpoise through the sinewy part of the tail. He had hoisted it aboard, had dropped it into the bait well, where it thrashed around, puzzled and unhappy. And the mother had swum alongside the boat and under the boat and around the boat, nudging the stout planking with her back, slapping it with her tail, until the man felt sorry for her and made the captain let the baby porpoise go.

He took the net from the bucket, slipped the noose in the retrieving rope over his wrist, pulled the slipknot tight. It was an old net, but still serviceable; he had rewoven the rents made by underwater snags. He coiled the thirty-foot rope carefully, making sure there were no kinks. A tangled rope, he knew, would spoil any cast.

The basic design of the net had not changed in three thousand years. It was a mesh circle with a diameter of fourteen feet. It measured close to fifteen yards around the circumference and could, if thrown perfectly, blanket a hundred fifty square feet of sea water. In the center of this radial trap was a small iron collar where the retrieving rope met the twenty-three separate drawstrings leading to the outer rim of the net. Along this rim, spaced an inch and a half apart, were the heavy lead sinkers.

The man raised the iron collar until it was a foot above his head.

The net hung soft and pliant and deadly. He shook it gently, making sure that the drawstrings were not tangled, that the sinkers were hanging true. Then he eased it down and picked up the paddle.

The night was black as a witch's cat; the stars looked fuzzy and dim. Down to the southward, the lights of a causeway made a yellow necklace across the sky. To the man's left were the tangled roots of a mangrove swamp; to his right, the open waters of the bay. Most of it was fairly shallow, but there were channels eight feet deep. The man could not see the old dock, but he knew where it was. He pulled the paddle quietly through the water, and the phosphorescence glowed and died.

For five minutes he paddled. Then, twenty feet ahead of the skiff, a mullet jumped. A big fish, close to three pounds. For a moment it hung in the still air, gleaming dully. Then it vanished. But the ripples marked the spot, and where there was one there were often others.

The man stood up quickly. He picked up the coiled rope, and with the same hand grasped the net at a point four feet below the iron collar. He raised the skirt to his mouth, gripped it strongly with his teeth. He slid his free hand as far as it would go down the circumference of the net so that he had three points of contact with the mass of cordage and metal. He made sure his feet were planted solidly. Then he waited, feeling the tension that is older than the human race, the fierce exhilaration of the hunter at the moment of ambush, the atavistic desire to capture and kill and ultimately consume.

A mullet swirled, ahead and to the left. The man swung the heavy net back, twisting his body and bending his knees so as to get more upward thrust. He shot it forward, letting go simultaneously with rope hand and with teeth, holding a fraction of a second longer with the other hand so as to give the net the necessary spin, impart the centrifugal force that would make it flare into a circle. The skiff ducked sideways, but he kept his balance. The net fell with a splash.

The man waited for five seconds. Then he began to retrieve it, pulling in a series of sharp jerks so that the drawstrings would gather the net inward, like a giant fist closing on this segment of the teeming sea. He felt the net quiver, and knew it was not empty. He swung it, dripping, over the gunwale, saw the broad silver side of the mullet quivering, saw too the gleam of a smaller fish. He looked closely to make sure no sting ray was hidden in the mesh, then raised the iron collar and shook the net out. The mullet fell with a thud and flapped wildly. The other victim was an angel fish, beautifully marked, but too small to keep. The man picked it up gently and dropped it overboard. He coiled the rope, took up the paddle. He would cast no more until he came to the dock.

The skiff moved on. At last, ten feet apart, a pair of stakes rose up gauntly out of the night. Barnacle encrusted, they once had marked the approach from the main channel. The man guided the skiff between them, then put the paddle down softly. He stood up, reached for the net, tightened the noose around his wrist. From here he could drift down upon the dock. He could see it now, a ruined skeleton in the starshine. Beyond it a mullet jumped and fell back with a flat, liquid sound. The man raised the edge of the net, put it between his teeth. He would not cast at a single swirl, he decided; he would wait until he saw two or three close together. The skiff was barely moving. He felt his muscles tense themselves, awaiting the signal from the brain.

Behind him in the channel he heard the porpoise blow again, nearer now. He frowned in the darkness. If the porpoise chose to fish this area, the mullet would scatter and vanish. There was no time to lose.

A school of sardines surfaced suddenly, skittering along like drops of mercury. Something, perhaps the shadow of the skiff, had frightened them. The old dock loomed very close. A mullet broke water just too far away; then another, nearer. The man marked the spreading ripples and decided to wait no longer.

He swung back the net, heavier now that it was wet. He had to turn his head, but out of the corner of his eye he saw two swirls in the black water just off the starboard bow. They were about eight feet apart, and they had the sluggish oily look that marks the presence of something big just below the surface. His conscious mind had no time to function, but instinct told him that the net was wide enough to cover both swirls if he could alter the direction of his cast. He could not halt the swing, but he shifted his feet slightly and made the cast off balance. He saw the net shoot forward, flare into an oval, and drop just where he wanted it.

Then the sea exploded in his face. In a frenzy of spray, a great horned thing shot like a huge bat out of the water. The man saw the mesh of his net etched against the mottled blackness of its body and he knew, in the split second in which thought was still possible, that those twin swirls had been made not by two mullet, but by the wing tips of the giant ray of the Gulf Coast, *Manta birostris*, also known as clam cracker, devil ray, sea devil.

The man gave a hoarse cry. He tried to claw the slipknot off his wrist, but there was no time. The quarter-inch line snapped taut. He shot over the side of the skiff as if he had roped a runaway locomotive. He hit the water head first and seemed to bounce once. He plowed a blinding furrow for perhaps ten yards. Then the line went slack as the sea devil jumped again. It was not the full-grown manta of the deep Gulf, but it was close to nine feet from tip to tip and it weighed over a thousand pounds. Up into the air it went, pearl-colored underbelly gleaming as it twisted in a frantic effort to dislodge the clinging thing that had fallen upon it. Up into the starlight, a monstrous survival from the dawn of time.

The water was less than four feet deep. Sobbing and choking, the man struggled for a foothold on the slimy bottom. Sucking in great gulps of air, he fought to free himself from the rope. But the slipknot was jammed deep into his wrist; he might as well have tried to loosen a circle of steel.

The ray came down with a thunderous splash and drove forward again. The flexible net followed every movement, impeding it hardly at all. The man weighed a hundred seventy-five pounds, and he was braced for the shock, and he had the desperate strength that comes from looking into the blank eyes of death. It was useless. His arm straightened out with a jerk that seemed to dislocate his shoulder; his feet shot out from under him; his head went under again. Now at last he knew how the fish must feel when the line tightens and drags him toward the alien element that is his doom. Now he knew.

Desperately he dug the fingers of his free hand into the ooze, felt them dredge a futile channel through broken shells and the ribbon-like sea grasses. He tried to raise his head, but could not get it clear. Torrents of spray choked him as the ray plunged toward deep water.

His eyes were of no use to him in the foam-streaked blackness. He closed them tight, and at once an insane sequence of pictures flashed through his mind. He saw his wife sitting in their living room, reading, waiting calmly for his return. He saw the mullet he had just caught, gasping its life away on the floor boards of the skiff. He saw the cigarette he had flung from the sea wall touch the water and expire with a tiny hiss. He saw all these things and many others simultaneously in his mind as his body fought silently and tenaciously for its existence. His hand touched something hard and closed on it in a death grip, but it was only the sharp-edged helmet of a horseshoe crab, and after an instant he let it go.

He had been under water perhaps fifteen seconds now, and something in his brain told him quite calmly that he could last another forty or fifty and then the red flashes behind his eyes would merge into darkness, and the water would pour into his lungs in one sharp painful shock, and he would be finished.

This thought spurred him to a desperate effort. He reached up and caught his pinioned wrist with his free hand. He doubled up his knees to create more drag. He thrashed his body madly, like a fighting fish, from side to side. This did not disturb the ray, but now one of the great wings tore through the mesh, and the net slipped lower over the fins projecting like horns from below the nightmare head, and the sea devil jumped again.

And once more the man was able to get his feet on the bottom and his head above water, and he saw ahead of him the pair of ancient stakes that marked the approach to the channel. He knew that if he was dragged much beyond those stakes he would be in eight feet of water, and the ray would go down to hug the bottom as rays always do, and then no power on earth could save him. So in the moment of respite that was granted him, he flung himself toward them.

For a moment he thought his captor yielded a bit. Then the ray moved off again, but more slowly now, and for a few yards the man was able to keep his feet on the bottom. Twice he hurled himself back against the rope with all his strength, hoping that something would break. But nothing broke. The mesh of the net was ripped and torn, but the draw lines were strong, and the stout perimeter cord threaded through the sinkers was even stronger.

The man could feel nothing now in his trapped hand, it was numb; but the ray could feel the powerful lunges of the unknown thing that was trying to restrain it. It drove its great wings against the unyielding water and forged ahead, dragging the man and pushing a sullen wave in front of it.

The man had swung as far as he could toward the stakes. He plunged toward one and missed it by inches. His feet slipped and he went down on his knees. Then the ray swerved sharply and the second stake came right at him. He reached out with his free hand and caught it.

He caught it just above the surface, six or eight inches below high-water mark. He felt the razor-sharp barnacles bite into his hand, collapse under the pressure, drive their tiny slime-covered shell splinters deep into his flesh. He felt the pain, and he welcomed it, and he made his fingers into an iron claw that would hold until the tendons were severed or the skin was shredded from the bone. The ray felt the pressure increase with a jerk that stopped it dead in the water. For a moment all was still as the tremendous forces came into equilibrium.

Then the net slipped again, and the perimeter cord came down over the sea devil's eyes, blinding it momentarily. The great ray settled to the bottom and braced its wings against the mud and hurled itself forward and upward.

The stake was only a four-by-four of creosoted pine, and it was old. Ten thousand tides had swirled around it. Worms had bored;

parasites had clung. Under the crust of barnacles it still had some heart left, but not enough. The man's grip was five feet above the floor of the bay; the leverage was too great. The stake snapped off at its base.

The ray lunged upward, dragging the man and the useless timber. The man had his lungs full of air, but when the stake snapped he thought of expelling the air and inhaling the water so as to have it finished quickly. He thought of this, but he did not do it. And then, just at the channel's edge, the ray met the porpoise, coming in.

The porpoise had fed well this night and was in no hurry, but it was a methodical creature and it intended to make a sweep around the old dock before the tide dropped too low. It had no quarrel with any ray, but it feared no fish in the sea, and when the great black shadow came rushing blindly and unavoidably, it rolled fast and struck once with its massive horizontal tail.

The blow descended on the ray's flat body with a sound like a pistol shot. It would have broken a buffalo's back, and even the sea devil was half stunned. It veered wildly and turned back toward shallow water. It passed within ten feet of the man, face down in the water. It slowed and almost stopped, wing tips moving faintly, gathering strength for another rush.

The man had heard the tremendous slap of the great mammal's tail and the snorting gasp as it plunged away. He felt the line go slack again, and he raised his dripping face, and he reached for the bottom with his feet. He found it, but now the water was up to his neck. He plucked at the noose once more with his lacerated hand, but there was no strength in his fingers. He felt the tension come back into the line as the ray began to move again, and for half a second he was tempted to throw himself backward and fight as he had been doing, pitting his strength against the vastly superior strength of the brute.

But the acceptance of imminent death had done something to his brain. It had driven out the fear, and with the fear had gone the panic. He could think now, and he knew with absolute certainty that if he was to make any use of this last chance that had been given him, it would have to be based on the one faculty that had carried man to his preeminence above all beasts, the faculty of reason. Only by using his brain could he possibly survive, and he called on his brain for a solution, and his brain responded. It offered him one.

He did not know whether his body still had the strength to carry out the brain's commands, but he began to swim forward, toward the ray that was still moving hesitantly away from the channel. He swam forward, feeling the rope go slack as he gained on the creature.

Ahead of him he saw the one remaining stake, and he made

himself swim faster until he was parallel with the ray and the rope trailed behind both of them in a deep U. He swam with a surge of desperate energy that came from nowhere so that he was slightly in the lead as they came to the stake. He passed on one side of it; the ray was on the other.

Then the man took one last deep breath, and he went down under the black water until he was sitting on the bottom of the bay. He put one foot over the line so that it passed under his bent knee. He drove both his heels into the mud, and he clutched the slimy grass with his bleeding hand, and he waited for the tension to come again.

The ray passed on the other side of the stake, moving faster now. The rope grew taut again, and it began to drag the man back toward the stake. He held his prisoned wrist close to the bottom, under his knee, and he prayed that the stake would not break. He felt the rope vibrate as the barnacles bit into it. He did not know whether the rope would crush the barnacles, or whether the barnacles would cut the rope. All he knew was that in five seconds or less he would be dragged into the stake and cut to ribbons if he tried to hold on; or drowned if he didn't.

He felt himself sliding slowly, and then faster, and suddenly the ray made a great leap forward, and the rope burned around the base of the stake, and the man's foot hit it hard. He kicked himself backward with his remaining strength, and the rope parted, and he was free.

He came slowly to the surface. Thirty feet away the sea devil made one tremendous leap and disappeared into the darkness. The man raised his wrist and looked at the frayed length of rope dangling from it. Twenty inches, perhaps. He lifted his other hand and felt the hot blood start instantly, but he didn't care. He put his hand on the stake above the barnacles and held on to the good rough honest wood. He heard a strange noise, and realized that it was himself, sobbing.

High above, there was a droning sound, and looking up he saw the nightly plane from New Orleans inbound for Tampa. Calm and serene, it sailed, symbol of man's proud mastery over nature. Its lights winked red and green for a moment; then it was gone.

Slowly, painfully, the man began to move through the placid water. He came to the skiff at last and climbed into it. The mullet, still alive, slapped convulsively with its tail. The man reached down with his torn hand, picked up the mullet, let it go.

He began to work on the slipknot doggedly with his teeth. His mind was almost a blank, but not quite. He knew one thing. He knew he would do no more casting alone at night. Not in the dark of the moon. No, not he.

MOTIVE FOR MURDER

JOHN AND WARD HAWKINS

Everyone was very nice. They talked in whispers, did what had to be done, and made a special point of not looking at Dave Murphy, who watched it all from the padded window seat. They walked wide around the davenport where Mary, Dave's wife, lay with her face half buried in the pillows. The photographers took pictures of the little man in the shell-back chair—front and side, and then moved in to get close-ups of the white powder on the handle of the knife. The fingerprint boys kept their eyes on the woodwork, the chair arms, the glasses and bottles scattered about the room. The medical examiner came and looked and made out the removal ticket without a change of expression or an unnecessary word. Even the reporters were decent. They didn't try to steal a picture of Mary, though there were plenty of them around, and whatever thoughts they had they kept to themselves. When Mary stirred, whimpering on the edge of consciousness, Jock Dusen pulled her skirt down over her knees. Jock was precinct senior, the man in charge, and he looked as happy as if he'd been hit with an ax.

"She'll straighten us out," he said.

A couple of fingerprint men echoed that, trying hard. They'd worked second relief with Dave Murphy ever since he'd come back from the wars. They'd danced at his wedding, and now they wanted to give their friend a break—in spite of the spilled whisky, the glass that had been trampled into the rug, the smear of lipstick on the dead man's cheek.

"Do you know the guy?" Jock asked.

Murphy said, "I never saw him before."

"His name's Hamilton. Victor Hamilton."

"How'd you find that out?" Murphy asked.

Jock Dusen swore in soft amazement. "I frisked him, man," he said. "You sat right there and watched me,"

Dave Murphy wet his lips. *Murphy*, he told himself, *get the sawdust out of your head.* But it was no good. He watched the boys go through the old, old routine, and found himself remembering other rooms that had looked and smelled like this one. Second Avenue stuff, where smoke and bottles had got tangled and a party had turned into a pig-sticking. He'd been able to think down there. He'd done his job—prints, pictures, measurements, questions—but now his mind was completely numb. *Because this one's on me*, he thought. *It's my house. That's my wife over there on the davenport with a bourbon breath you could use for a cutting torch. It's my knife Hamilton's wearing between his ribs.*

He looked at the dead man, hating him. In his mind, he said, *Where the hell did you come from?* Hamilton didn't answer; Hamilton had done all the talking he'd ever do. He sat there in the shell-back chair—Murphy's chair—with his mouth open and his chin pointing down at the polished wood of the knife handle. His face was without expression, a brown and weathered face, with a gray mustache trimmed in military fashion, and eyes like gray marbles. His tweeds were freshly cleaned and pressed—old tweeds, the kind you can't buy anymore. He wore a ruptured duck in his lapel. *An ex-soldier*, Murphy thought. *You and me and ten million other guys.*

The photographers were gone now. Charlie Davis, earnest and young, picked up the bottles and glasses, working with quiet care, packing them for examination by the headquarters lab technicians. The coroner's men came and took Hamilton away, flat on his back in the wicker basket. Mary whimpered softly on the davenport, turning her face deeper into the pillows. Davis, still on his knees in the center of the room, slanted a look of question at Jock.

"Let her alone," Jock said. "We're in no hurry."

He came over and sat beside Murphy on the window seat. He was a big man, fat and untidy. He wasn't brilliant or clever, but he was an old head and he knew the answers. He'd do what he could for a brother officer and a friend. He'd foul up the routine and spend an extra hour or two waiting for Mary to wake up instead of using ice water and ammonia and a hypo. He'd hold his questions to a minimum—no lights, no shouting—and he'd limit his written report to a bare recital of the facts. But none of that would change the directness of his thought.

"Funny you don't know the guy," he said.

Murphy knew what Jock was thinking. *What I'd think*, he told himself, *if I was standing in Jock's shoes. The old and ugly story. The double-crossing wife and a party gone wrong. Kisses one minute and a blind, stabbing rage the next. A chef's knife from the wooden case on the kitchen wall—a needle-pointed, twelve-inch wedge of steel, hollow-ground and razor sharp. A drunken argument ending with a short, pushing blow. And the little man who'd come to play—the stranger with the neat mustache and the ruptured duck in his lapel—was dead in the shell-back chair.*

Murphy said, "She didn't kill him, Jock."

"I think she's awake now," Jock said.

Mary was looking at them. She had turned her head on the pillow and opened her eyes. Murphy moved, and then Jock's big hand clamped down on his leg, holding him to the window seat. Routine again. Let the suspect do the talking. They waited, and a pulsebeat hammered in Murphy's throat. Mary was small and dark—a ski-jump nose, merry eyes and a dancer's body. She'd worked the night clubs, doing a solo in the white blaze of a spotlight, until Murphy came along. She smiled now, her eyes misty with sleep.

"Hi, Irish," she said. "You're home early."

"Yes. A little," Murphy said.

He stayed where he was, sweating against the pressure of Jock's hand. Mary put her fists into the pillow and pushed herself up. Her hair fell across her eyes. She giggled, and the sound was a whip on Murphy's back.

"You didn't tell me we'd have company," she said. "I must have been asleep." She gagged, and nausea twisted her mouth. "Help me, Irish. I feel dizzy——"

"She's drunk," Jock said quietly.

Murphy said, "Or drugged."

He pushed Jock's hand away and crossed the room. Behind him, Jock said, "In the movies they get a mickey, boy. But not in a place like this." And that was experience talking. Twenty years of prying into misery and trouble and violent death. Twenty years of dirty linen and cleaning up the mess. "She's high as a kite," Jock said, with regret. "We'll check, but that's the way it is."

Murphy said, "Tell me about it, Mary."

She didn't talk—not just then. Nausea slugged her in the middle, and she bent forward, catching at him with hands that were hot and sweating. Her eyes held a numbed look. "Irish," she said, and put her face against his vest and hung on. The nausea passed and came again. She was trying to turn when Murphy scooped her up. He carried her down the hall to the bathroom, where she was suddenly and violently ill. Murphy did what he could with towels and cold compresses, while Jock Dusen watched from the doorway.

Murphy said, "You'd make a fine vulture, Jock."

"Maybe," Jock said. "But those towels go to the lab."

He saw them packed in one of Davis' cardboard boxes. He wrote the label himself: "Check for possible narcotic." Then he trudged away to make sure there was coffee, black and very hot, waiting for Mary's return to the living room. He let Murphy ask the questions there. When the uniformed stenographer opened his notebook, Jock stopped him with a growl. The stenographer went away. There were just the three of them then.

"We got maybe a half hour," Jock said. "Then one of the D.A.'s bright young men will be jumping right down our throats."

"Mary," Murphy said, "why was Hamilton here?"

"Hamilton? We don't know anyone named Hamilton, Irish."

"The little guy with the gray mustache."

"Oh," she said. "You mean the salesman. I ordered a vacuum cleaner. He had to give me a demonstration, so I'd know how to use all the gadgets. He cleaned the rug, the drapes, a chair. He was a funny little man, very fussy and very proper. I gave him a drink for doing all my work."

"Then what?" The words hurt Murphy's throat.

"I think I paid him. I started to get the money from my purse, and then—then I saw you and Mr. Dusen. And I was sick. I'm still sick, Irish. I feel drunk, but I can't be. I gave him a drink, but I didn't have anything."

Jock said, "Ask her about the knife."

"Did Hamilton get ideas? Did he make a pass?"

"No," Mary said.

"Did you fight with him?"

"Why would I? I don't fight with people."

"That set of knives in the kitchen, in the wooden case on the wall. Did you use the chef's knife to—for anything?"

"No," Mary said.

"That's all you can remember? That's everything?"

"Yes," she said. "I'm sorry I got sick."

His arm tightened around her waist. He took her to the davenport and sat beside her there. "We've got trouble, hon," he said. "Somebody used that knife on Hamilton. Mrs. Cald, from next door, came over to borrow a book. The lights and the radio were on, but you didn't answer the bell. She got curious and looked in under the blind. She saw Hamilton, saw the knife in his ribs, and ran for the phone."

He watched the trembling of her mouth. "Hamilton was a long time dead when we got here."

Mary Murphy fainted then.

Jock said, "I'll call the ambulance."

"I'll pack her bag," Murphy said.

Routine caught them up. Police Emergency, where Dave Murphy stood in a white-walled room and watched while a sleepy intern examined Mary's skull with gentle fingers, and then shook his head.

The D.A.'s man was there. "She's a pretty thing," he said; "it's a pity she's so handy with a knife." Then he saw the cold fury in Murphy's face and took a backward step. "Hey!" he said. "There's something here I don't know about!"

"She's his wife," the intern said.

Murphy heard that a dozen times in the next three hours. It followed him down the halls.

Tom Wescott, precinct lieutenant, came to stand in the door of the broom closet of an office Murphy shared with Jock Dusen. "I can't tell you how sorry I am, Irish," he said. "We'll do everything we can."

"She didn't kill him, sir."

Wescott said, "I sincerely hope you're right."

He went away before Murphy could explain that Mary had given him that set of knives to use when he played chef, and that she was desperately afraid of them. And he wanted Wescott to know Mary never drank more than one mild highball, and not even that unless Murphy was around.

Jock Dusen lumbered in, eyes red for the want of sleep. Report sheets were wadded on his clipboard: prowl car, fingerprint, lab, photo, morgue, Police Emergency. "You'd better get some rest," he said. "This's going to be rough."

"Anything new?" Murphy asked.

"Just more of the same," Jock said evenly. "We got a specialist from Mercy Hospital to examine her head. He found a bruise the intern missed, but it's small and the position doesn't help much. The doc thinks it's something she did herself, on a chair arm, maybe, or the edge of a door. The skin isn't broken and the swelling doesn't amount to much."

Murphy said, "Let's hear the rest."

Jock fixed his attention on the clip board. "The lab ran tests on the towels. No sign of any narcotic, Irish. But plenty of whisky. O'Donnell hasn't had time to make a complete report on the fingerprints yet. He did check the knife, the glasses, the bottles. The knife handle's pretty much a mess, the way they always are. He found one of Mary's—a latent thumb, on top of one of yours—clean and sharp enough, he says, to enlarge a hundred times for courtroom use. She's on the glasses and the bottles."

"Why not, Jock? She lived there."

"The thumbprint says she held the knife the way a woman would, like she was going to slice bread. That figures, if she came at him with the blade sideways."

Murphy said, "She's afraid of those knives."

"You told me that." Jock kept his eyes on the clipboard, making a point of it. "The way you see it, she was doped or slugged, or both. That means there had to be a third party around. We gave the house and the neighborhood the works. We came up empty, Irish. It looks to me like you'd better have some legal talent ready to swap punches with the D.A."

"You think she's guilty," Murphy said.

"No," said Jock. "But that doesn't matter. You can sell me, Irish. You can probably sell most of the others; they're all your friends. But you can't beat the system. Maybe that's why it's set up so a lot of guys have a hand in it. Everyone's leaned backward on this, all down the line. Everything's been checked a dozen times. The system says she's guilty, Irish. I can't help that. Wescott can't help it. It's out of our hands now. It's gone downtown to Headquarters and the D.A."

"I know how it goes," Murphy said. "I work here."

He sat there at his battered desk while the last of the reports came in. He knew the system; he was a part of it. A lot of specialists did their jobs—sprinkled powder, made cases, snapped cameras, asked questions, used scalpels and microscopes—and then filled in the blanks on a printed sheet. No imagination, guesses or emotion: just facts. The D.A. got the facts; the D.A. pulled the trigger. Hollywood didn't work that way. In the movies, now, you waded through a swarm of suspects. You were as tricky as a stripper's hips and you did a solo to get the guilty guy—in the movies. Not here. Not in Harbor Precinct. You were a plain-clothes man, second grade. You walked a million miles, talking to cab drivers, gamblers, touts and the guys who swept the streets. And when you ran into a murderer in Harbor Precinct, he was usually a ginned-up character who'd used an ax on his wife and then blubbered into the telephone.

Murphy knew the system. He knew what was coming next. He sat there quietly, his hat pushed back on hair that was not quite red, waiting for the telephone to ring. Mary was upstairs, sleeping off a hypo in a white bed in Police Emergency, with a rookie cop on the door and one of the D.A.'s men hovering in the hall. The system said she was guilty, but the system wouldn't listen to the things Dave

Murphy knew. Murphy rubbed the back of his neck and watched Jock Dusen pick up the telephone. He heard the deference in Jock's voice, and anger swelled in his throat.

"Here we go," he said harshly, when Jock had put the phone aside. "The brass whistles, and now we run."

Jock said, "Take it easy, man."

They did it very nicely. A harness cop, reduced by age and weight to the status of an errand boy, had been alerted for their arrival. He took them straight to a paneled office on the second floor of the Headquarters building. The men there were competent enough, but they were second-level brass. Resbick was an assistant chief, and John Gray was slated for the D.A.'s job when the D.A. moved into the mayor's office. They went through the motions—trained seals doing their tricks—and the rage in Murphy grew. Second-level brass. The department had decided this killing was embarrassing because it involved the wife of a department man, but wasn't really important. Gray was impatient and anxious to be gone; he let that show in his voice. Resbick was better equipped to hide his feelings. He was a granite block of a man whose deep-set eyes told you nothing.

"We're sorry as hell," Resbick said.

Gray nodded. "The D.A. asked me to express his sympathy."

Murphy sat in a big leather chair by the window and waited for the rest. He watched white clouds go dreaming down the sky while Resbick considered the broad aspects of the case. Resbick was good at broad aspects; he could talk for two weeks and never touch an important point. He talked about the newspapers. Mary Murphy was an ex-dancer. The newspapers liked killings with ex-dancers, leg art, bottles, X marks the spot, and lipstick on a dead man's cheek. Some knothead at the morgue had opened his big mouth about the lipstick. He would be disciplined, of course, but the lipstick was out of the bag and on page one. The department had asked for minimum coverage, but the papers were not eager to cooperate.

"Let them print what they want to print," Murphy said.

Gray smiled. "They will."

"Mary didn't kill Hamilton," Murphy said.

He threw that at them deliberately, trying it on for size. The second-level brass wasn't interested. Murphy could talk till his head fell off and not change a thing. But he tried. He had to try.

"Mary can't remember what happened," he said. "There's no reason to think she's lying. Plenty of people have blacked out. I did, in the Pacific. We hit the beach and the next thing I knew I was in a field hospital. We were four miles inland when I stopped one. I couldn't remember anything that happened after the barge ramp went down. I still can't remember anything. I lost half a day."

"It happens," Gray said. "In battle."

Murphy said, "My wife was slugged."

"Then the medical men are wrong," Resbick said.

"They're human. They can make mistakes." Murphy set his jaw and went on with it, "Mary worked in a nightclub, but she's no tramp. I was three weeks getting a date with her, and I was in there trying. She wasn't playing house with Hamilton. She was buying a vacuum cleaner."

Softly, Resbick said, "Jock."

"I didn't tell him," the big man said uncomfortably.

"I get all the dirty jobs." Resbick looked down at his folded hands. "Hamilton sold vacuum cleaners, Murphy. That much checks. He had business cards in his pocket. But there was no order book at your house. And no vacuum cleaner." His eyes came up. "You can see what that does to her story. We'll keep digging, of course. But I'm afraid we'll have to pull you off the case. The newspapers will be all over us if we won't."

"Because I might destroy evidence?" Murphy asked.

John Gray nodded. "Something like that."

The rest was expertly done. One brush-off, complete with handshakes and hearty assurances. The wad of report sheets went into Gray's briefcase. The D.A.'s man murmured stock regrets and went away in his expensive chalk-stripe.

Resbick said, "A good attorney might be a wise investment, Murphy. That's off the record, of course."

Then Jock Dusen and Dave Murphy were out in the street where the air was clean and cold.

"I knew it would be rough," Jock said. "But that——"

Murphy took a leather folder out of his pocket and let it fall open in his palm. He looked down at his shield, his picture. One piece of tin. One picture of a battered Irish face. A typed description: "David X. Murphy. Detective, Second Grade. Age: 34. Height: 5' 11". Weight: 175." The folder said he was a cop, a part of the system. The folder said he could walk his feet off hunting stolen bicycles while the rest of the force pinned the big rap on his wife. Murphy put the folder in Jock Dusen's hand.

"Give that to Wescott," he said. "With my love."

"Not so fast." Dusen's hand was on Murphy's arm. "You can't turn your badge in an' then go ahead and fool with this. They told you to leave it alone. They'll slam your pants in the can."

Murphy said, "She's my wife."

"I got a wife too," Dusen said. He gnawed his lower lip, thinking.

"As far as I'm concerned, you're hunting the ginzo that knocked over those service stations. It'll go on the sheet that way, Irish. But don't get in trouble. Yeah, you won't look any different in the can, if you make it wearin' a badge. How could you ask questions without your badge?"

Murphy didn't answer.

"For God's sake——" Dusen said.

Murphy held the folder and watched Dusen lumber away. Then he got a cab. He sent a lawyer to Harbor Precinct; he went home. The living room looked the way it had always looked. The department had torn it apart and put it back together. Mary would like that. The kitchen was the same, except for one knife. The knife was downtown—Exhibit A. Murphy got a bottle and a glass, and carried them into the living room. He didn't sit in the shell-back chair. Hamilton had used the chair to die in—Hamilton, a little guy who'd sold vacuum cleaners.

Murphy looked at the shell-back chair. Mary and a vacuum-cleaner salesman. Mary kissing the guy, leaving lipstick on his face. Mary getting drunk and mad, and shoving a knife in him—— No! What absolute rot that was! Anybody—anybody in the world but Mary.

He rubbed his face, trying to bring clarity to his thought. He remembered Mary saying, "Tell me, Irish, how is a guy a cop? Do you make with a magnifying glass and bloodhounds?"

"You make with facts," he'd told her. "You start with something you know for damned sure."

He knew Mary had not killed Hamilton. That was something the department didn't know; he was that far ahead of the department. He could start there. If Mary hadn't killed the man, someone else had—a third party. Man or woman? A woman might poison a man, shoot him or plant a knife in his ribs, but she'd be standing right there screaming what a louse he was. This was a man's job. Who said it was? Experience and fifty other homicides. Motive? Money or a woman. It had to be one or the other; experience said that too.

Where was the vacuum cleaner? Mary said she'd bought one and Hamilton had delivered it. The department didn't believe that. Murphy believed that, and it gave him a lead toward the motive. The killer had taken the vacuum cleaner. Who else would have? Name a guy—just one—who'd take a vacuum cleaner out of a house where a man sat with a knife between his ribs unless he'd put the knife there. So the killer had taken the cleaner. He'd killed Hamilton and taken the cleaner for a reason that had to do with money or a woman.

What about the lipstick? What about Mary being drunk? Murphy rubbed his face, breathing heavily. He wouldn't buy either one. Mary was not that kind. What was left? The killer had slugged Mary, shoved the knife into Hamilton. One out; one dead. Then the cover-up. Pour whisky down Mary's throat; paint lipstick on Hamilton's cheek. It would take a cool customer to do a thing like that, but it could be done. Hell, it had been done. Mary hadn't killed Hamilton, so it had to be that way.

Another thing. The killer had been in a desperate rush to kill Hamilton and get that cleaner. He'd done it the hard way. He'd walked into a stranger's house to do the job. Why not on a dark street? Or in Hamilton's room, waiting for him behind a door? Not only had the man been in a hurry; he'd been forced to do the job in Murphy's house. Why? Murphy didn't have the answer. He'd worry about that later.

He did have this: Strangers seldom kill each other. Ninety-nine times out of a hundred, the killer knows the victim. That was a two-way street. The victim also knew the killer. Who were the people Hamilton had known? Where had they been when Hamilton was killed? What had they been doing?

"You see how it goes," Murphy said to Mary's picture. "You go talk to people, you ask questions."

The wall clock said it was midafternoon when he left the house. He drove east across the city to a street that climbed steeply past the gingerbread mansions of another day. Proud houses once, shabby apartments now. A street of blistered paint, unkempt lawns and old men dozing in the last of the sunlight. The house with the right number was very old, very tall. Murphy climbed three flights of steps to reach the front porch. Hamilton's name was on one of a row of tin mailboxes nailed to the wall—301. His room was on the top floor. The front door was open. The front hall was dark, heavy with the odors of people and food. Something moved far back against a dim square of light. Murphy had been in a hundred such flytraps; he knew what that movement meant.

Who knows more, he asked himself, *than a nosy landlady?*

He went down the hall toward the square of light.

"Police," he said. "I want to talk to you."

"The police have been here," she said.

He showed her his shield. "They're here again."

The landlady was tall and gray, wispy hair and an air of enormous weariness. She let him into her apartment and pointed to a straight-backed chair. The chair, he knew, was for people she wanted to get rid of in a hurry. He sat down and put his hat on the floor.

"Tell me about this Hamilton," he said. "The works, good and bad. Did he drink? Gamble? Did he stay in nights or go out? Did he have women in his apartment? Men? Did he pay his rent? Everything. Start talking and I'll listen."

"How would I know so much about a tenant?" she asked tiredly. "I've got my work to do, and only one girl——"

She talked steadily for half an hour. She didn't tell him much, but what she told she told in detail. Hamilton's wife had died the year before, and he hadn't rightly got over it. He'd lived like a monk. No friends, women or men—that is, no close friends. Acquaintances, she supposed, like anybody else, but they never came to see him, and he never went out. Hamilton had been a methodical little man who paid his bills, returned the things he borrowed, and worked too hard. Too hard, that is, for a man of his size and health. He'd had no car. He'd carried those cleaners all over the North End, and when he got home, he was quite often too tired to cook a meal. Sometimes Harriet Blodgett took him something to eat.

"Blodgett?" Murphy said.

"She lives next door to him, upstairs. A nice girl."

Murphy picked up his hat. "I'll talk to her."

He climbed three flights of steeply pitched stairs. After a day's work, carrying a vacuum cleaner up those stairs must have been a back-breaker for a guy like Hamilton. He knocked on the door of 302. Harriet Blodgett let him in.

The landlady had tagged her well; she had a warm smile and a pleasant air. Thirty-odd, a girl who'd been around, but who bore no travel scars. A hostess, she told Murphy. She worked nights in a downtown restaurant. She couldn't add much to the landlady's picture of Hamilton. No friends, no enemies, no women she knew about. At least none had ever come to his apartment.

Murphy hated it, but he had to ask a personal question. "Was there anything between you two?"

She was not disturbed. "I cooked an occasional meal for him," she said. "I mended his socks, because, walking so much, they had to be darned carefully. That was all. Nothing like you mean. I guess he wasn't interested, and it's no compliment to me." Murphy thought he heard a faint note of regret.

"Well, thanks," he said.

He stopped for a look at Hamilton's apartment. There wasn't much to see—a cot, a clothes rack, a cupboard, a small electric plate, a cracked washbowl. The floor was bone white, the window sparkled—Hamilton's work, that landlady had been born tired. He opened the cupboard door on stacked underwear, towels, handkerchiefs. All very neat. He found two letter files; one business, one personal. The personal file held letters from a brother in Oregon, a friend in

Texas, but no one in the city, man or woman, had written to him. Murphy stood in the center of the room, his hat on the back of his head and mentally catalogued everything in the apartment. When he had finished, he had nothing. He went down the stairs to the street.

No friends, no enemies, he said to himself.

That left what? The people he met selling vacuum cleaners—half the city. This was going to be a beauty, a case like those Mary had ribbed him about. "Irish is working on a case," she'd tell their friends. "I don't know if she's a blonde or a brunette, but she's sure keeping him busy . . . all day and all night." This time he didn't have to call Mary and explain that he'd be late for dinner. This time he cooked his own.

Tomorrow, he told himself, *I'll check his job.*

Morning found him in the Morgan Building, in a third-floor showroom. Listening.

"Not house-to-house," the sales manager said. "I'd like to have that absolutely clear. Our people work from lists supplied by us. We give them names of prospects. They close the sales."

"And make a fortune," Murphy said.

The sales manager said, "Well, no."

He looked at Murphy, and then he looked at the shield on the counter between them. He was hearty and gone to seed. Hand-painted tie and a shirt he should have changed yesterday. Full of promises. Full of wind. He looked at the shield and sweated delicately. A fly bumbled against plate glass. Over in a corner, a girl stopped adding figures to answer the telephone.

"Mr. Richards," she said. "For you."

Murphy said, "He was stabbed. He's dead."

"A terrible thing," Mr. Richards said.

The girl said something to the telephone. Mr. Richards talked about personnel. A real problem. The ones you got you didn't want; the ones you wanted you couldn't get. Hamilton, now. An officer and a gentleman, but small. Size didn't matter, of course, but there was the sample case, the demonstrator. It wasn't really heavy, but a man like Hamilton—bad back and all—got pretty tired. He didn't have the old bounce, the old steam. A lot of sales got away.

"Bad back?" Murphy asked.

"A war wound, maybe. He didn't talk much."

"He got his demonstrator here every morning?"

"We assign cleaners to each salesman. Whenever they make a sale, they bring the deposit money in and get another new machine."

The girl told the telephone she couldn't help it if the house number was a vacant lot. But there was no use coming back. That was a good neighborhood out there and he could try next door.

"One of your sure-fire prospects?" Murphy asked.

Mr. Richards had trouble with his smile. "Sometimes we get a bad steer."

Murphy put his badge away. He felt sick. This thing was a rat race, a runaround. Maybe they had a prospect. If they didn't, they gave you names out of the telephone book. You climbed stairs and rang doorbells and made with the old college try. "Can I interest you in a vacuum cleaner, lady?" But the salesmen had districts. The wall map said so. The wall map had numbers and little red pins.

"Do they make reports?" Murphy asked.

Mr. Richards said, "Every call."

Murphy began to breathe again. Mr. Richards opened and explained the file. Daily reports. Some of the salesmen weren't to be trusted. Some of them sat in a beer hall and made things up. Hamilton let a lot of sales get away, but his reports were dependable. He wrote everything down in a small, precise hand.

"Not anymore," Murphy said.

Mr. Richards looked pained. He made unhappy sounds in his throat while Murphy checked the dates. Murphy decided to go back two days. The killer had been in a hurry; he hadn't waited two days, but Murphy'd play it safe. Two report sheets. Two lists of house numbers. Forty-five-oh-two, Van Buren Street. Forty-five-ten, Van Buren. Forty-five-fifteen, Van Buren. Murphy put the sheets in his pocket.

"No house-to-house," he said. "Nuts!"

Van Buren Street had its feet in the bay and its head in the clouds. Van Buren was ship chandlers' stores, hock shops, cold-water flats and the smell of the docks at one end; the other end was up on the crest, up there with the money, the big houses, the snob apartments and doormen who'd give a guy like Hamilton the heave-ho. The forty-five-hundred block was middle ground. Ordinary houses, swarms of kids, bicycles and roller skates. An occasional store or tavern.

Murphy parked his car and looked up the hill. Hamilton had worked the street the last two days of his life, lugging a vacuum cleaner up the steep walks, ringing doorbells. He'd put his thumb on one doorbell too many. Mary came into Murphy's thoughts then, the shadow of the wire mesh across her face. *How do you know*, Mary said. *Suppose Hamilton did see something or find something. Why did the killer let him walk away? Why did the killer wait until Hamilton came to our house?*

I'll find out why, Murphy told her.

He tried the forty-five-hundred block, up one side and down the other. "Police," he said, and held the open folder in his hand. He watched the faces; housewives, a leggy girl who should have been in school, a fat man with a beer breath and bloodshot eyes. "We're checking," he said. "A little guy tried to sell you a vacuum cleaner. We want to know what he said. What he did."

Legwork. He talked to Mary while he walked. *I'll know*, he said. *Somebody'll say too much or not enough. Somebody'll be afraid and try to cover up.*

A housewife was afraid. She looked at the folder, and the corner of her mouth began to jerk. She didn't wait for him to ask questions. "Herman's a good boy," she said. "He took that bicycle back."

Murphy tipped his hat and went away. *That's what I meant*, he told Mary, *but it'll be a place without kids. And there'll be money in it somewhere somehow.*

Murphy went up the street. "He cleaned my rugs," a giggling housewife said. "I promised to keep him in mind."

Murphy checked that number on the list. There was a star beside it. A star beside a number meant a demonstration. Hamilton had been inside the starred houses to unpack his vacuum cleaner and make his sales talk.

Skip the rest, Murphy told himself. *It's one of those.*

Six stars on the first list. Murphy talked to young women, old women, a Negro maid. Then he was climbing stairs Hamilton had climbed the last day of his life. Seven stars on the second list. Murphy moved his car up the street. He was running out of houses, out of time, and impatience piled up in him as a spring flood piles up against a dam. Two stars left. One house was new—plate glass and brick. The other was huge, built by one of yesterday's great fortunes when Van Buren Street was young. Hedges, half a block of lawn, stained-glass windows, a widow's walk and a carriage house. A window shade on the third floor was torn; the lawn needed edging along the walks.

Maybe, Murphy told himself.

The bell made a harsh jangle of sound. Murphy looked at the tightly drawn blinds and waited. He rang the bell again. There was a flutter of movement down the porch; a curtain edge had been lifted and dropped. A muscle twitched in Murphy's jaw. He leaned on the bell and let it ring in constant and insistent demand. The curtain moved again, and then feet hurried into the hall. The door snapped open against a night chain, and a full-lipped mouth twisted beneath a thin black mustache.

"Please! My aunt's desperately ill!"

Murphy took his thumb off the bell. He didn't like what he could see of this man. That didn't mean much; just now he didn't like anyone. He got the folder out of his pocket. "Police," he said, and watched the twisted mouth go flat. *Scared*, Murphy thought, but he didn't crowd it, didn't jump at conclusions. He waited, the badge cupped in his hand, and let the silence and the doubt pile up.

"But why?" the man said. "What do you want?"

He was tall and slender in brown gabardine a cop couldn't buy with a month's pay. Sweat shone on his upper lip.

"We're checking," Murphy said gently. "A little guy came by here a couple of days ago. Selling vacuum cleaners, house to house. He rang your doorbell, along with a lot of others. He got himself killed. We look into things like that."

The man said, "Oh."

His Adam's apple went up and down behind the careful knot of an expensive tie. The guy was thinking, and an honest man didn't have to think. His throat was dry. A thousand years ago, cops had hanged men who couldn't spit.

"Whose house is this?" Murphy asked.

"My aunt's—Cecilia Breckenbridge." The tall man smiled. "That chap was here. Impertinent little fellow. Rang the bell several times. Woke my aunt. I gave him hell and sent him away."

"He didn't get inside?" Murphy asked.

The tall man said, "No. Not past the door."

The tension inside Murphy let go. He thought of Mary, down at Headquarters, waiting away the hours. *You see how it works*, he told her silently. *Shoe leather and patience. Keep slugging away until you find someone who says too much. Someone who's afraid and tries to cover up. I found him, Mary. Tall and pretty and scared to death.*

"Funny," he told the tall man. "These salesmen make reports. They list every house where they make a demonstration. Your house is on the list."

The tall man wet his lips. "A mistake——"

"He didn't make mistakes about his other demonstrations. He didn't lie." Murphy left it there for a moment. "But if you want it that way, I'll check the neighborhood. People see things. I'll find someone who saw him here."

"Okay. He was here. Inside."

"Then why the runaround?" Murphy asked quietly.

The tall man was ready for that one; he was thinking faster now. "My aunt," he said. "She's—well, she's very old and it's my duty to spare her any unnecessary excitement. That's why I lied. Anyway, there's nothing she can tell you. He was here; he made his little speech. He went away."

"Sure," Murphy said. "But I've got a report to make out. Headquarters is fussy about reports. They have to be right. It's routine. We talk to a lot of people. We ask a lot of questions. What we have when we get done is a lot of people who didn't do it, and one guy who did. It's an imposition, sure. But it's better than having a murderer walking the streets. Most people are glad to help us, without seeing a search warrant, just so they can sleep nights and not worry. We're bound to be suspicious of people who don't want to help."

"My aunt's really quite ill," the tall man said.

Murphy smiled. "I can be very gentle."

The tall man worried the night chain. "It's embarrassing," he said. "But I guess I'll have to tell you what's wrong with her. Do you know what a persecution complex is?"

"I've read about them," Murphy said.

"That's her trouble. She's old and senile, and she thinks she's being kept a prisoner here. She's right, of course. If she wasn't confined here, she'd be confined in an institution. She doesn't understand that. She's outlived all her close friends, but she wonders why no one comes to see her. I can't ask anyone I know—not with her mind the way it is. That's why I let the little man in. I thought he'd help; instead, he made her worse."

Murphy said, "I see."

He removed his hat and took a step forward. The tall man let the night chain go; he had to, or have Murphy's weight against the door. There was a wide hall, a curved stairway and rich, dark paneling that had cost someone a lot of money.

Murphy asked, "Are you a Breckenbridge?"

The tall man shook his head. He was a Dolph. Harold Dolph. His aunt was Cecilia Breckenbridge, sister of John Breckenbridge, the railroad man, who had died ten years before. There'd been money once, but it was gone—stock that had vanished in '29. Cecilia couldn't understand that, either.

"So I keep the place going," Dolph said. "You know how old people are about family homes."

Murphy said he knew.

A large, locked, sliding door at the hall's end opened under Harold Dolph's key and let Murphy into a parlor. The place was crammed with old-fashioned furniture—marble-topped tables, carved chairs and whatnots. The whatnots held a lot of items that could have only a sentimental value. Framed photographs were everywhere. Cecilia

Breckenbridge was sitting in a wheel chair beside a window that looked out over the back yard. She was frail, white-haired, and younger than Murphy had expected. She looked up once, and Murphy had a glimpse of blue, tormented eyes.

"Aunt Cecilia," Dolph said, "this man is here to ask a few questions about the vacuum-cleaner salesman you saw the other day. Be a good girl and answer him." To Murphy, he whispered, "Don't say he was killed. You'll upset her." Then he moved to a place beside the old woman's wheelchair.

Murphy asked her what time Hamilton had called, how long he'd stayed and what he'd done while there. He didn't get an answer. Not a word. Cecilia Breckenbridge sat with a bent head, staring at her hands. They were fine hands. Long-fingered, beautifully formed and delicately veined with age. Dolph was trying to catch Murphy's eye and end the interview. Murphy looked at Cecilia Breckenbridge's hands, thinking. He was thinking, *Try this on for size.*

Suppose the woman was not crazy. Suppose she was afraid of her nephew because he was keeping her a prisoner. Why would he do that? Money, of course. Her money. Her family had had money, not his. And Dolph looked like a smooth, bloodless louse who could do it. If he could torture an old woman, he could kill Hamilton. Murphy wasn't sure how Hamilton fitted into the picture. He wasn't sure about a lot of things.

He said, "I'm sorry I bothered you people."

Harold Dolph showed him out. "Sometimes she'll talk and sometimes she won't," he said at the front door. "The way her mind is, it's hard to tell what to expect."

"I know," Murphy said. "But I was in, I looked and I asked questions. Now I can check this place off the list."

He drove two blocks to a drugstore and called Jock Dusen.

"I think I've spotted the man I want," he said. "How's to come out and give me a hand?"

Dusen said, "Give me the address and ten minutes."

They met around the corner from the Breckenbridge house. Murphy told him what he'd found and what he thought. Jock Dusen listened, and then he scowled.

"You could be awful wrong," he said.

"I've been wrong before," Murphy agreed. "All I want is a chance to talk to the old lady without Dolph breathing down her neck. If I'm wrong, okay. If I'm right, I want Dolph where we can make the pinch. He'll come out of there sometime. When he does, you trail the guy. I'll talk to the old lady."

"Is that him?" Jock Dusen asked.

Harold Dolph was backing a roadster out of the carriage house.

"Right," Murphy said. "Check with Precinct any time you get a chance. I'll do the same."

When both cars were out of sight, Murphy went back to the house. He had trouble getting in. No one answered the bell. One more item: Dolph and the old woman lived alone. He circled the house. The woman was not at the window, nor did she appear when he tossed a stick against it. Worried, then, he went to the back door, and used a gun butt on a pane of glass. Inside, he went straight to the parlor. Cecilia Breckenbridge was lying on the sofa. Murphy found a shallow breath and a slow pulse. He lifted an eyelid.

"Doped," he whispered.

So he was right. Dolph was keeping her a prisoner. Still, there was no place for Hamilton in that picture. Murphy felt a need for haste. Dolph had left the place in a hurry. He was getting jumpy or he had something to cover. What next? The old lady next. He found an afghan and wrapped it around the small, fragile body. He noticed her hands again. Something about them bothered him. He stared at them a long time before he knew what it was. She wore no rings. There were marks that showed she had worn rings most of her life. Murphy made a quick tour of the room, checking the photographs to find out what the rings looked like. They looked like money. Big stones in old-fashioned settings. Enough for a murder? A dollar was plenty if a killer wanted it badly enough. Rings and a vacuum cleaner.

Murphy said, "Got it!"

He gave the house a quick shakedown, top to bottom, in ten minutes—closets, attic, basement. No vacuum cleaner. There wasn't time to do a better job; he had to call in. No telephone in the house. At the drugstore again, he called Precinct.

"Dusen checked in?" he asked.

Dusen had. Harold Dolph had stopped at the Morgan Building, on Fifth. Murphy stared at the phone booth wall, scowling. Morgan Building. Wait a minute! No-house-to-house Richards was in the Morgan Building. "Call you back," he told Precinct. Dialing another number, he said, "Police speaking. Put Richards on."

Mr. Richards remembered the customer in brown gabardine. He'd come to inquire about a salesman who'd promised delivery of a cleaner. The description sounded like Hamilton but the address was wrong. The man was quite sure Hamilton's address was the wrong address. But Dolph had got Hamilton's address.

Murphy left the phone booth. He was halfway to the street, when he said, "Damn!" and went back. He called Precinct again. "Send a man and a matron to fifty-eight-forty-eight Van Buren," he said.

"There's an elderly woman with a skinful of dope in the house. Take care of her. And don't let her nephew get close."

He pointed his car toward the shabby street where Hamilton had lived. He had a mile to go, or a little less. The Morgan Building was a good six miles across the city. Luck, Murphy told himself. But it worked that way. Shoe leather and patience. Keep plugging and the breaks come. Dolph wanted Hamilton's address? Why? That was the jackpot question. Find the answer and tall-and-pretty would be down at Headquarters with a thousand-watt light in his eyes.

Mary had asked, "How does a cop work?"

This was how, Murphy thought; no magnifying glasses, no bloodhounds, no miracles. He put things together, little things. Blue, tormented eyes and the white indentations that told of rings worn half a lifetime. Torn window shades and a lawn that needed edging. Yesterday's great fortune had melted to a handful of rings. Diamonds. Tall-and-pretty was money-hungry. He needed thirty-dollar ties and suits at two-fifty a copy. Add that up and you had motive. Twenty or thirty thousand dollars' worth of motive.

He explained that to Mary as he drove: The old woman knew. She had to know. She was a prisoner—no strength, no telephone—hating tall-and-pretty the way a prisoner always hates the jailer. Doped most of the time, but aware even in her dreams that tall-and-pretty was a buzzard in brown gabardine, waiting for her to die, helping her die, so he could have those rings. Knowing he was a coward, as all birds of carrion are. Waiting. Pushing her toward death, but afraid to strip the rings from her fingers while she was still alive. Afraid someone from the great yesterdays might come to call. That's why the old woman wanted guests, why Dolph kept everyone away.

Like that, and Hamilton had come knocking at the door. A tired and harmless little guy, one of the rabbits, and tall-and-pretty decided to have a little fun. "A visitor for you, Aunt Cecilia."

And the little guy had made his sales pitch to an old woman who lived with terror, while tall-and-pretty watched. No sale, but the vacuum cleaner had snored across the rug, the metal snout of it nosing into the shadows beside the wheelchair. *She beat him*, Murphy told Mary silently. *The vacuum cleaner sucked up the rings, and tall-and-pretty didn't miss them until Hamilton was gone.*

Murphy slammed through a red light, passed a streetcar on the wrong side. Another six blocks, and then hard to the right and up the hill. There was no roadster anywhere along the street. No department car. The tall-and-pretty boy, the carrion bird, who could torture an old woman and put a knife in a harmless little man, wasn't here yet.

"He got this address," Murphy said.

He worried about that as he climbed the stairs to the shabby porch. There was an answer; there had to be. He went into the hall. Hamilton's room was three flights up—halfway to the moon for a little man whose back was bad, who'd spent his day lugging a heavy demonstrator around. What was it Mr. Richards had said? "We assign cleaners to each salesman. Whenever they make a sale, they bring the deposit money in and get another new machine." A pulsebeat hammered in Murphy's throat. A demonstrator isn't a new machine. A demonstrator is a secondhand gadget in a beat-up case.

"Pretty boy," Murphy said. "I know why."

He was running then, pounding on the landlady's door. He swore at her, and the fury in his voice drove her backward into her cluttered room. "You held out on me!" He spat the words. "I ought to throw the book at you. Hamilton had at least two cleaners here all the time. You kept still, hoping to grab one for free. Not in his room; not up and down those stairs. He kept them somewhere on this floor. Where was it?"

"The hall closet," she whispered. "He had a key."

Murphy said, "You'll give me yours . . . now!"

He found the case, scuffed and battered. The demonstrator. He yanked the cleaner out and stood it on the threadbare rug. The case he left close by. He unwound the cord. There wasn't time to plug it in; that didn't matter anyway. He heaved the coil away down the shadowed hall and moved back into the pocket of dark beside the stairs.

He had it all now. He knew what had happened. Mary had ordered a cleaner. She wasn't a prospect; she was a sure-fire sale. Hamilton had stopped here to leave the demonstrator and pick up a new machine. Tall-and-pretty, trailing him, had thought the stop was just another call. *Why not? Murphy told Mary. Hamilton went in with a cleaner, came out with one. So tall-and-pretty stayed with him all the way to our house.*

The carrion bird had closed in then, afraid the cleaner would be opened, the rings found. He'd come in the back door, through the kitchen past the wooden case of knives. He'd waited in the hall, the chef's knife in his hand.

The rest? Mary hunting for her purse, crumpling under an awkward blow. And Hamilton—the little guy, the officer and gentleman—charging out to help, charging barehanded into a twelve-inch wedge of steel.

Tall-and-pretty had to cover then, Murphy told Mary. *He heaved Hamilton into the shellback chair, trampled glass into the rug. He* gave you whisky and held your nose until you drank. He took the cleaner—the wrong cleaner—and went away.

Feet came up the front stairs now—cautious feet. The weathered floor of the porch creaked and a long shape filled the door. *Hello, tall-and-pretty.* Murphy said that in his mind. *You don't know it yet, but you're going to fall downstairs. Once for Cecilia Breckenbridge. Once for Hamilton. And once for Mary Murphy, the dark and lovely girl who married a big, dumb cop. It doesn't matter what you do. We've got you now. We'll find the other cleaner somewhere, with your prints on it. We'll find glass in the soles of your shoes. But we won't have to go that far, because you'll talk. You'll come apart as soon as we go to work on you.*

Harold Dolph was moving down the hall. He passed the cleaner, stopped and turned. He was on his knees then, fumbling with the metal fastener that held the sack in place. Dirt spilled out across his hands; the hall was full of greedy, sucking sounds. Murphy left the patch of dark beside the stairs. He stood behind the kneeling man, the tall-and-pretty boy, the carrion bird who'd put lipstick on his mouth and kissed a dead man's cheek. He looked past Dolph's shoulder to see the cold fire of diamonds, the yellow-green winking of an emerald in the dirt in Dolph's cupped hands. He heard Jock Dusen's heavy tread upon the porch. Dolph's head came up, jerked up, and fear was sick and ugly in his eyes.

"Hello, sweetheart," Murphy said.

A CABALLERO OF THE LAW

BEN HECHT

Mr. Lou Hendrix looked at the lady he had been pretending to love for the past six months and, being a lawyer, said nothing. Mr. Hendrix was a gentleman who could listen longer to female hysterics without unbending than was normal. This, he would have said, was due to his aloof and analytical mind. Then, also, the events which were taking place at the moment were of a familiar pattern.

The young lady was a nymph of the cabarets known as Brownie. Her full name was Carmen Browne. She danced, and very effectively, at the El Bravo Club, where she led the Birds of Paradise number. In this she was ravishing as a Dream of Fair Women.

Why so young and delicious a siren as Brownie should be so disturbed over the defection of Mr. Hendrix would have confused anyone who knew this gentleman or merely took a one-minute look at him. He was not Romeo, nor was he Adonis. He was a little man, with that objectionable immaculateness which reminds one, instanter, of sheep's clothing. He was one of those popinjays of the fleshpots with the face of a tired and sarcastic boy. His sideburns were a wee too long, his smile unduly persistent—like a ballet dancer's—his voice far too gentle to have deceived anyone except perhaps a woman as to his spiritual composition.

Brownie, who among her own kind was considered not only quite a reader of books but a sort of practical authority on masculine characteristics, had misunderstood Lou Hendrix amazingly. Carry on as she would now, she was no match for this *caballero* of the law who, out of a clear sky, was engaged in giving her what she called "the go-by." As her monologue of screams, epithets and sobs progressed, the lovely and muscular girl understood it all. She perceived, much too late for any use, that she had to do with as purring a hypocrite, rogue and underhanded soul as one might flush in a seven-day hunt on Broadway, which, according to the chroniclers Brownie most admired, is the world's leading water hole for human beasts of prey.

Looking around at the pretty apartment Brownie spread herself on the couch and filled her Sybaritic diggings with a truly romantic din. From the more coherent utterances of this tear-stained beauty, it seemed that she was innocent of all dallyings with a certain Eddie White, an ex-college hero. She was, wailed Brownie, being wrongly accused. Then, sitting up, her greenish eyes popping with rage until they looked like a pair of snake heads, Brownie laughed, as she would have said, scornfully, and declared that she could see through Mr. Hendrix and his so-called jealousy. He was getting rid of her because he didn't love her anymore. He was tired of her and putting her on the escalator; that was all there was to it.

To this Mr. Hendrix, thoroughly seen through, made no reply; and Brownie, announcing that she was not going to be made a sucker of, fell back on the couch, beat some cushions with her fists and shook with grief. The telephone rang. Brownie straightened on the couch.

"It's probably for you," she said.

"More likely it's Mr. White," said Mr. Hendrix.

The taunt brought Brownie to her feet.

"If it's for me, by any mischance," said Mr. Hendrix, "say I'm not here."

Brownie spoke into the phone.

"Who?" she asked. . . . "No, he's not here. . . . No, I don't know when he'll be here. . . . No, no, I don't expect him." Hanging up, she looked bitterly at Mr. Hendrix. "Your office," she said. "Always making me lie for you."

"You might have been a bit more polite," said Mr. Hendrix.

The heartlessness of this suggestion sent Brownie back to the couch and her grief. She resumed her sobs. Mr. Hendrix continued to regard her with creditable, if villainous, detachment. His heart was in the Highlands with another lassie. But even discounting that factor, Mr. Hendrix felt he was pursuing a wise course in ridding himself of so obstreperous an admirer as lay howling here. He had no use for overemotional types. They were inclined to drive diversion, which was Mr. Hendrix's notion of Cupid, out of the window with their caterwauling.

Mr. Hendrix belonged to that tribe of Don Juans, rather numerous at the Broadway water hole, who never hang themselves for love. Tears he regarded as bad sportsmanship, and heartbreak was to him plain blackmail. Beauty—and by beauty Mr. Hendrix meant chiefly those delicious and agile Venuses of the cabaret floor shows—Beauty had been put into Broadway, if not into the world, for Man's delight; certainly not for his confusion and despair. And this little barrister lived elegantly, if rather villainously, by this conception.

A number of things, all obvious to the analytical Mr. Hendrix, were now operating in Brownie's mind and making her wail: Eddie's vengeful delight at her getting the go-by; the tittering of the little group of columnists, hoofers, waiters and good-time Charlies whom she called the world; the lessening of her status as a siren—she might even be demoted from leading the Birds of Paradise number—and, through all these considerations, the nerve of the man, throwing her down as if she were some nobody! As for the pain in her heart at losing someone she had so stupidly loved and misunderstood, and at losing the foolish Broadwayish dream of wedlock she had cherished for half a year—Brownie chose not to mention these in her ravings, being too proud.

Mr. Hendrix, still preserving his finest courtroom manner of reason and superiority, watched on in silence and fell to wondering what he had ever seen in this red-headed, almost illiterate creature, with her muscular legs and childish face, to have ever considered her charming or desirable. But he was given small time to meditate this problem of idealization. Brownie, with a yell that set the base of his spine to tingling, leaped from the couch, stared wildly around, and then, emitting a series of shrill sounds, had at the furnishings of the room. She pulled a portiere down, hurled two vases to the floor, swung a chair against the wall and smashed it, beat Mr. Hendrix's framed photograph to bits against the edge of the piano, seized a clock from the mantelpiece and bounced it on the floor and was making for Mr. Hendrix's derby, which he had placed on a chair near the door, when he, with an unexpected shout, headed her off.

The barrister, defending his derby, received a blow on the side of his face that sent him spinning. A thrown object caught him behind the ear. Brownie's pointed shoes belabored his shins. He retreated. But the hysteria to which he had been coolly and analytically listening seemed suddenly to have been injected, like a virus, into his bloodstream.

It had started with the tingling in the base of his spine. Smarting from blows, and full of some sort of electric current which gave off oaths in his head, the little lawyer came at the lady, and in his hand he held, almost unaware of the fact, a large brass candlestick.

What it was that made this popinjay, so renowned for coolness, strategy and cynicism, so completely shed his character, God alone could have told; and perhaps a psychiatrist or two might also have made a guess at it. But here he was much too far gone for analysis—his own or anyone else's—charging at the lovely Carmen Browne like a bantam caveman, screaming and swinging the heavy piece of brass in the air.

There was no precedent in Mr. Hendrix's life for such a turn of events, and no hint in any of his former affairs that passion could so blind his faculties and hate so fill his heart. Yet blind he was and full of a clamorous hate that demanded something of him. From the oaths which escaped Mr. Hendrix during this preliminary skirmish with the brass candlestick, it seemed that what he hated was women; loathed and hated them with a fury out of the pit. Announcing this he swung the piece of brass, and the second swing exhilarated him the more. It had struck squarely against Brownie's head, dropping her to the carpet. Mr. Hendrix, out of breath, stood cursing and grimacing over her like a murderer.

Slowly the little lawyer's rage melted. His heart swelled with terror, and the nape of his neck grew warm. Brownie lay as she had fallen. He leaned over. Her eyes were closed. Her legs, exposed in an incongruously graceful sprawl, were inert. He put his ear to her bosom. There was no heartbeating. He stood for several minutes, holding his breath and listening automatically for sounds outside the door. The choking sensation in his lungs subsided and the cool, analytical mind that was Mr. Hendrix returned like some errant accomplice tiptoeing back to the scene of the crime.

Carmen Browne lay dead on her hearthstone. No more would she lead the Birds of Paradise number at the El Bravo Club. But Mr. Hendrix wasted no time considering this sentimental phase of the matter. He had committed a murder—without intent, to be sure—even in self-defense, looked at factually. But no, self-defense wouldn't hold. Mr. Hendrix was thinking swiftly. There rushed through his mind all the angles, holes, difficulties, improbabilities and prejudices of his case, and in less than a minute the little lawyer had put himself on trial on a plea of self-defense and found himself guilty.

Since a young man, Mr. Hendrix had always been close to crime. He had had that unmoral and intellectual understanding of it which helps make one type of excellent lawyer. In action, defending a criminal, Mr. Hendrix had always been like some imperturbable surgeon. Guilt was a disease that could be cured, not by any operation on the soul of its victim but by a process of mental legerdemain which convinced a jury that no guilt existed. Mr. Hendrix might have said that he served a cause beyond good and evil—that of extricating the victims of fleeting misadventures from the unjustly permanent results of their deeds.

Thus, far beyond most men who might have found themselves confronted by the strange and ugly dilemma of having unexpectedly committed a murder, Mr. Hendrix was prepared for his new role of criminal. He knew all the ropes; he knew all the pitfalls of the defense of such a case as this. He knew the psychology of the prosecution. And with an expert, if still slightly fevered, mind he knew the perfect details by which his guilt might be cured, the ideal evidence, persuasive and circumstantial, by which a jury could be cajoled to the verdict of not guilty.

In less than a minute Mr. Hendrix had a full grasp of his case, seeing far into its convolutions and difficulties. He set about straightening these out.

But like some dramatic critic who, after observing plays for years with subtle and intimate understanding of them, is summoned suddenly on the stage and, with the strange footlights glaring in his eyes, told to perform the part whose words he knows, whose ideal gesture and intonation he has always dreamed about, Mr. Hendrix felt the panic of debut. To know and to act were phenomena surprisingly separate. This was what delayed the cautious barrister for another minute—a minute during which Mr. Hendrix's client, with beating heart and white face, mumbled for speed, chattered even of flight.

But at the end of this second minute Mr. Hendrix had elbowed this ignominious client into a far corner of his mind, seated him, as it were, at the counsel's table with orders to keep his mouth shut, and taken charge of the case. He leaned over and looked at the clock on the floor. The dial glass was broken. The clock had stopped; its hands were at two minutes of four. Mr. Hendrix's thoughts were rapid—almost as if he were not thinking at all, but knowing. He could move the hands forward to five o'clock. He could leave the premises undetected, if possible, and attach himself for the next two hours to a group of prospective alibi witnesses, remain with them during the hours between four-ten and seven, and this would be proof that he had not been in the apartment at the time of the murder. Mr. Hendrix examined the watch on Carmen Browne's wrist. It, too, had stopped. It registered one minute after four. The two timepieces, evidently synchronized by their owner, told a graphic and substantially correct tale. At 3:58 the struggle had begun. At 4:01 the woman had been killed. He would have to set the wristwatch forward a full hour to preserve this interesting discrepancy in the stopped clocks.

The telephone rang. Mr. Hendrix straightened, not having touched either of the hour hands. He had actually anticipated a telephone ringing, and, in this anticipation, had known the ruse of the forwarded time hands was stupid. At 3:50 Carmen Brown had answered a phone call, a record of which was with the switchboard man in the lobby. Now, at 4:03—he consulted his own watch—she failed to answer. Other phone calls might likewise come before five o'clock, all of which Carmen Browne would fail to answer, thus establishing an important series of witnesses against the fact that the murdered woman had been alive between four and five o'clock; thus rendering his alibi of his own whereabouts during that time practically futile. There was also the possibility that the neighbors had heard their quarrel and noted the time of the screaming. And more than all these, the chance that someone—a maid or the building agent—Carmen Browne had been consulting him about subletting her place—might enter the room before five o'clock.

It was the hour preceding 4:01 for which Mr. Hendrix needed an alibi. He already knew its vital groundwork. At 3:50 Carmen Browne, alive, had told someone on the phone—probably Tom Healey of his own law firm—that he was not in her apartment. Mr. Hendrix's eyes had remained on his own wristwatch as his thought slipped through these pros and cons. It was 4:04. He glanced at the sprawled figure on the floor, shivered, but stood his ground. Another phase of his case had overcome him. He smiled palely, shocked at what had almost been an oversight. He must not only provide an alibi for himself but fortify it with evidence tending to prove someone other than he had done the deed. He must invent a mythical murderer—leave a trail of evidence for the sharp eyes and wits of the prosecution, leading to another—a never-to-be-found another, but yet one always present in the case.

Carmen Browne's fingerprints were on the broken clock, the smashed chair, the battered photo frame. This was wrong. It would reveal that it was Carmen who had been in the rage, smashing things, demanding something that had resulted in her murder; and this sort of situation, brought out by the prosecution, might easily point to Lou Hendrix. No, said Lawyer Hendrix swiftly, it must have been her assailant, demanding something of Carmen Browne, who had been in the rage and done the smashing and struck the fatal blow. Mr. Hendrix established this fact circumstantially by wiping Carmen

Browne's fingerprints from the objects in question with a silk handkerchief. He wiped also, and more carefully, the brass candlestick. The absence of fingerprints pointed to a certain self-consciousness on the part of the assailant after the deed, but that was both legitimate and normal. Men of the deepest passion—and there was precedent for this—remembered to obliterate evidence.

At the door Mr. Hendrix, in his hat, overcoat and gloves, paused. He repeated to himself carefully: Carmen Browne had been attacked by some suitor, jealous of her real sweetheart, Mr. Hendrix, as witness the destroyed photograph of the latter. But why hadn't she used the gun the police would find in the desk drawer two feet from the spot where her body lay? There were, of course, normal explanations to be put forward. But Mr. Hendrix did not admire them legally. For fifteen precious seconds Lawyer Hendrix balanced the issue. During this space Mr. Hendrix listened rather than thought. He listened to the prosecution pointing out to the jury that the reason Carmen Browne had not reached for this available weapon with which to defend herself was because she had not expected an attack from the assailant, because the assailant was one familiar to her, against whom she had no thought of arming herself; and even further, because the assailant, all too familiar with the premises, knew where this gun was as well as did Carmen Browne, and prevented her from reaching it. All these values pointed shadowily, Mr. Hendrix perceived, at his client. He removed the gun from the drawer and dropped it into his coat pocket. He must be careful in disposing of the weapon, and Mr. Hendrix's mind dwelt stubbornly on a dozen cases in which an attempt at post-crime evidence disposal had been the connecting link with guilt. But Mr. Hendrix assured his client firmly that he would be more cautious in this regard than any of his previous defendants had been.

With the gun in his coat pocket, Mr. Hendrix stepped out of the apartment. Now he was, he knew, purely in the hands of luck. A door opening, a neighbor appearing, would ruin his case instantly. But no untoward event happened. He had three floors to descend.

He listened at the ornamental elevator doors. Both cages were going up. Mr. Hendrix walked quickly down the three flights and, coolly now, like a gambler rather than a lawyer, rehearsed the possible permutations of luck.

He had entered the apartment at three o'clock that morning with Carmen Browne. But because it was his habit to preserve a surface air of respectability toward the attendants of the place, though he fancied they knew well enough what was going on, he had walked up to the apartment with Brownie. The switchboard operator, concealed in an alcove in the lobby, had not seen them come in, nor had the elevator boy on duty, as both were out of sight at the moment. If, now, he could leave the building with the equal but vitally more important luck of not being seen, his case would be more than launched.

The lobby was empty, but Mr. Hendrix did not make the mistake of slipping out too quickly and coddling the presumption that no eyes had observed him. He knew too well the possibility of the unexpected witness, and he paused to study the premises. The switchboard attendant, half hidden in the alcove, had his back to the lobby and was reading. Both elevator cages were out of sight. There was no one else. Mr. Hendrix stepped into the street.

Here again he stopped to look for that unexpected witness. How often, he remembered grimly, had the best of his cases been tumbled by the appearance on the stand of those aimless, incalculable human strays who had "seen the defendant." Mr. Hendrix saw two of just that type. Two women were walking, but with their backs to him and away from the apartment. A delivery truck was passing. Mr. Hendrix noticed that the driver was talking to a companion and that neither of these passers looked in his direction. There was no one else. Mr. Hendrix turned his attention to the windows across the street. Only the first three floors mattered. Identification was impossible, or at least could be sufficiently challenged, from any greater height. The windows were empty. As for the windows of the building directly over him if he kept close to the wall none could see him from these.

Satisfied with this rapid but concentrated scrutiny, Mr. Hendrix started walking toward the corner. If the triumph of intellect over nerves, of reason over the impulses of the senses may be called heroism, then this smiling, casually moving little popinjay in the black derby and snug overcoat might well be called a hero. Innocence, even aimlessness, was in his every movement and in his refusal, despite a driving curiosity to look at the time on his wrist—a telltale gesture, were it recorded by anyone—there was something approaching the loftiness of purpose which distinguished the ancient ascetics. As he turned the corner Mr. Hendrix, still unruffled, still amiably rhythmic in his movements, looked back to make sure no taxicabs had entered the street. None had.

He was now in Sixth Avenue, and he moved more briskly. He had four blocks to walk, and habit sent his eyes looking for a taxicab. But alert to every variety of witness, he shook his head and stayed afoot. He smiled, remembering that his own bed in his own apartment was unmade. He had just turned in the night before when Brownie had telephoned and asked to meet him. Thus his housekeeper, who never arrived before noon, would establish simply the fact that he had slept at home. This was unnecessary, to be sure, unless some passerby had seen Brownie and a man enter the former's apartment at three this morning.

Mr. Hendrix arrived now at a Sixth Avenue cinema palace. He looked carefully over the small crowd waiting for tickets, and then joined the line. In a few minutes he was being ushered into the roped enclosure at the rear of the auditorium. He slipped away quickly, however, and walked in the dark to the other side of the theater. He approached one of the ushers and demanded to know where he could report the loss of a pair of gloves. After a brief colloquy he was led to the office of the lost-and-found department, and here Mr. Hendrick, very voluble and affable, explained his mishap.

He was not, he smiled, usually so careless with his belongings, but the picture had been so engrossing that he had forgotten all about his haberdashery. Then Mr. Hendrix gave his name, address, a description of the missing gloves, and watched with a glow of deep creative satisfaction the time being written down on the blank form used for cataloguing such matters. "Four-eighteen," the man wrote, and Mr. Hendrix, consulting his watch, pretended to be startled. Was it that late? he demanded. Good Lord, he had had no idea of the time. It was quite a long picture. And the lost-and-found official, drawn into chumminess by Mr. Hendrix's affability, agreed that the film was a little longer than most, but well worth sitting through, to which Mr. Hendrix heartily assented.

Emerging from the movie palace, Mr. Hendrix rehearsed his case to date. The main body of his alibi was achieved. He had spent the time between 2:30 and four watching a movie. His continued presence at 4:18 in this theater was written down in black and white. He had also taken care that it should be a movie he had already seen, so as to be able to recite its plot, were he questioned in the next few hours. And he also provided a motive for seeing this particular movie. The film had to do with the character and career of a mythical state's attorney, and a newspaper friend of Mr. Hendrix who conducted a gossip column had asked him to contribute a few paragraphs from a legal point of view, carping at the improbabilities of the scenario.

Mr. Hendrix's next port of call was an elegant speakeasy. Here he had a drink, engaged in an exchange of views with the bartender, who knew him, asked the correct time, so he might adjust his watch. At 4:50 he stepped into a phone booth in the place and called his office. He inquired whether anybody had been trying to reach him that afternoon. The law clerk on duty for the firm—Tom Healey—answered as Mr. Hendrix had expected. Mr. Healey said he had been trying to find him in relation to a deposition, but had been unable to locate him. At this, Mr. Hendrix feigned a light anger. Where had the incompetent youth called? He had, said Mr. Healey, tried everywhere, even Miss Carmen Browne's apartment.

At this bit of information Mr. Hendrix, in his mind's eye addressing one of his future star witnesses, changed his voice. He grew angry, and very obviously so, for he knew the laziness of people's memory and their slipshod powers of observation. He inquired sourly if Mr. Healey had spoken to Miss Browne. On hearing that he had, Mr. Hendrix said:

"Do you mind telling me how she seemed when you asked if I was there?"

"Well, I don't know," Mr. Healey said.

"Try and think," said Mr. Hendrix. "I'd like to know."

"Well," said Mr. Healey, "come to think if it, she struck me as a little curt or upset about something."

"Ha!" said Mr. Hendrix and, to the surprise of his office underling, called the young lady a villainous name.

"I don't want you to call me up at her place anymore," he raised his voice. The clerk, Mr. Healey, said he would never do it again, but Mr. Hendrix, as though too enraged to notice this promise, continued: "I'm all washed up at that telephone number. Understand what I mean? You can just forget about it. Any other calls?"

"No," said Mr. Healey.

"O.K.," said Mr. Hendrix, and hung up the phone with an angry bang.

He walked from the speakeasy with the light step which, to Mr. Hendrix's office colleagues, always characterized a not-guilty verdict in sight. Now that the tingling at the base of his spine as well as the annoying warmth on the nape of his neck, as if a prosecuting staff were actually breathing on him, had gone entirely, Mr. Hendrix was beginning to feel not only relaxed but even amused. He could hear the prosecution falling into this little trap he had just laid.

Question: So Mr. Hendrix told you that you needn't try to reach him at Miss Browne's apartment anymore?

Answer: Yes, sir.

And Lawyer Hendrix looked winningly at the jury that sat in his mind's eye: Gentlemen of the jury, consider this. As if, having committed a crime, the defendant would be so gauche as to give himself away by some such oafish remark to a law clerk—a type of person trained to remember what he hears. Not a casual stranger, mind you, but a man with sharp and practiced wits.

Mr. Hendrix, skittering happily along the street, cleared his throat, beamed and felt a desire to laugh. He had never quite so enjoyed a case. What subtle and yet vital psychological proof of his innocence was the fact that he had just said to Tom Healey what he had; what perfect proof of the fact that he had been the victim of an obvious coincidence in saying he was washed up with Carmen Browne when she lay dead in her apartment. No guilty man would ever have said that.

From a drugstore that he was passing, Mr. Hendrix made another telephone call. He called Carmen Browne. Inquiring for her of the apartment switchboard operator, a sharp excitement stirred him. Before his eyes the image of her body, sprawled gracefully and awfully on the floor at his feet, swayed for a moment. He hoped the crime had been discovered, although there were still chances to improve his case. But the switchboard man calmly plugged in for Carmen Browne's apartment.

"She doesn't answer," he said after a pause.

"This is Mr. Hendrix calling," said Mr. Hendrix. "Has she been in at all? I've been trying to get her all day."

"Hasn't come in while I've been here," said the man.

"How long is that?" said Mr. Hendrix.

"Oh, about three hours," said the man.

"Thank you," said Mr. Hendrix, and hung up.

He had told Tom Healey he was washed up with Carmen Browne, and now he was trying to reach her, and Mr. Hendrix considered this paradox, in behalf of his client, with a smile. It revealed, gentlemen of the jury, a distracted man; a lover full of confusion as a result of—— What? "Of the fact, gentlemen," Mr. Hendrix purred to himself, "that my client was jealous of the attentions he had found out someone was paying to Carmen Browne; that he did not believe the poor girl's protestations and, driven from her side by his suspicions, was yet lured back to her by his deep love. Jealous, gentlemen of the jury, of the attentions being paid to Carmen Browne by this creature who that very afternoon had entered her apartment, and against whom Carmen Browne had defended herself until struck down and killed."

To augment this phase of the case, Mr. Hendrix returned now to the apartment building in which Carmen Browne lay murdered. He approached the switchboard operator, who greeted him by name. Here Mr. Hendrix controlled a curious impulse, that whitened the skin around his mouth. He felt impelled to ask this man whether he had noticed Mr. Hendrix in the building before, whether he had seen him during the few moments he had walked from the lobby an hour ago. Astonished at this impulse, Mr. Hendrix held his tongue for a space, aware that the switchboard man was looking at him with curiosity.

Question: How did the defendant seem?

Answer: Confused.

Gentlemen of the jury, and how would a man consumed with jealousy seem while inquiring, against all his pride, if the woman he thought was wronging him was home?

"Has Miss Browne come in since I called?" said Mr. Hendrix.

"I haven't seen her," said the man. "I'll try her apartment again." There was no answer.

"Give her this note when she comes back," said Mr. Hendrix.

He wrote on the lower part of a business letter from his pocket:

Darling: If you are innocent, don't torture me anymore. Give me a chance to believe you. I'm willing to forget what I heard, or thought I heard, over the phone. As ever,

Lou.

He placed this in a used envelope, scribbled her name on it and sealed it.

Gentlemen of the jury, can you imagine any man who had killed a woman he loved or had loved, so lost to all human reaction, so fiendishly wanton as to have written that little plea when he knew she was lying dead at his hands?

That was merely a rhetorical overtone, the human rather than evidential side of the note, but Mr. Hendrix filed it away on his memory as a bit of decoration. His alibi, Lawyer Hendrix murmured to himself, was now complete. But the secondary phase of the case needed further effort. The beauty of a case lay always in the elaborateness of diverse but corroborating detail—as if the world were crying the defendant's innocence from every nook and cranny. And happily at work, Mr. Hendrix had, lawyerlike, so far forgotten the human existence of his client as to whistle cheerily the while he turned over and re-turned over the major psychological problem in his mind.

Defense: Carmen Browne had been murdered by a man whom she refused—after, perhaps, leading him on. It might be that Carmen Browne had led a double life and was discovered in this double life by her slayer.

Ergo: Lou Hendrix, sharp-witted, observant, must suspect the existence of this other man. And Defendant Hendrix must also be jealous of him.

Witness to This: His talk to Tom Healey; his note to Carmen Browne, in the hands, now, of the switchboard operator.

And Lawyer Hendrix, with the thrill of a gambler rolling a third lucky seven, remembered at this point a third witness—a veritable star witness, beautifully, if unwittingly, prepared for her role a few days ago. This was Peggy Moore.

Miss Moore danced at the El Bravo Club as a member of the ensemble. She had been Brownie's confidante for a year. Mr. Hendrix smiled blissfully, recalling his conversation with Miss Moore less than a week ago, and recalling also her general character—one made to order for the part he was to assign her.

This young lady was a tall, darkhaired Irish lassie with slightly bulging eyes and an expression of adenoidal and not unpleasing vacuity about her face.

She was, as Brownie had frequently confided to him, a veritable love slave, a dithering creature incapable of thinking or talking on any subject other than the emotions stirred in her bosom by love or jealousy.

Some days ago Mr. Hendrix had selected this almost congenital idiot as the opening pawn in his decision to rid himself of Brownie. He had confided to Miss Moore's ears, so perfectly attuned to all tales of amorous agony, that he suspected Brownie of being still in love with Eddie White. Miss Moore's eyes had bulged, her mouth opened as if to disgorge a fishhook, and simultaneously a shrewd, if transparent, emotion had overcome her. Miss Moore, the victim of so much perfidy, had been convinced instanter of her chum's guilt and had launched at once into a series of lies, all defending Brownie's integrity and offering idiotic details of her devotion to her lawyer lover. Mr. Hendrix, intent on laying some foolish groundwork for his subsequent defection, had persisted, however, and, for no other reason than that he delighted in playing the human fraud whenever he could, had feigned sorrow and talked of woe.

Now Mr. Hendrix summoned Miss Moore on the telephone to meet him at the speakeasy he had recently quitted. He spoke guardedly, hinting at a lovers' quarrel and pretending he needed her to verify some evidences of Brownie's guilt, just unearthed. Miss Moore, full of a laudable and loyal ambition to lie her head off in Brownie's behalf, as Mr. Hendrix had foreseen, arrived in a rush.

The two sat down at a table in a corner, Miss Moore to invent innocent explanations and alibis for her chum—at which, like all other tearful addicts of passion, she was amazingly expert—and Mr. Hendrix to weave her artfully into his case.

But first Mr. Hendrix, aware of the lady's sensitivity toward all matters pertaining to love, proceeded to get himself drunk. He must be the lover stricken with jealousy and seeking to drown his pains in liquor—a characterization which this simple child and student of amour would remember only too vividly on the witness stand. Three drinks were consumed, and then, honestly befuddled from such an unaccustomed dose, Mr. Hendrix launched into cross-examination. And despite his thickened tongue and touch of genuine physical paralysis, Lawyer Hendrix remained as cool and analytical as if he were in a courtroom. He was not one to betray a client by any human weaknesses.

He put himself at Miss Moore's mercy. He must know the truth, and she alone could tell him. Otherwise with too much brooding and uncertainty, he would be sure to go out of his mind. His law practice was already suffering. He would lose all his money. Miss Moore nodded tenderly and understandingly at this saga of love woes. In reply, she could assure Mr. Hendrix that he was being very foolish to be jealous of Eddie White, because Mr. White wasn't even in town; and besides, Mr. White was engaged to marry a society girl in Newport. Mr. Hendrix sighed appreciatively at this walloping lie.

"It's not Eddie," said Mr. Hendrix; "it's somebody else. You know that as well as I. You're in her confidence. Don't try to lie to me, dearie. I caught her red-handed, talking over the phone. She hung up when I came into the room. She was making a date—and not with Eddie White."

Miss Moore paled at the thought of this dreadful *contretemps*, but kept her wits. Her chum's guilt frightened her, but at the same time she saw through Mr. Hendrix's effort to lead her astray. It was Eddie White, of course, whom he was jealous of. Miss Moore was certain of this, and Mr. Hendrix, listening to her somewhat hysterical defense of Brownie—sufficient to have convicted that young lady of a hundred infidelities, had he been interested—realized exactly what was in his companion's mind. He considered for a moment the plan of involving Eddie White—a known, hot-headed young gentleman, given to nocturnal fisticuffs in public places. But for the second time he dismissed this phase. Eddie would have an alibi, and the establishing of Eddie's physical innocence, however psychologically promising his guilt might have looked, would embarrass his client's case.

For the next hour Mr. Hendrix drank and discussed his jealousy, pleading with Miss Moore to be kind to him and reveal what she knew, and hinting at gifts in return for such service. But Miss Moore only increased the scope of her lies.

"Have you seen Brownie today?" Miss Moore finally broke off, winded.

Mr. Hendrix weaved in his seat and looked with bleary eyes at her.

"No," he said. "I don't trust myself to see her. God knows what I would do, feeling this way."

"You're just worked up about absolutely nothing," said Miss Moore, and rose. She had to toddle off to the El Bravo, where she performed during the dinner hour. Mr. Hendrix accompanied her to the door.

"Tell Brownie," he whispered, "I'll be over to the club tonight. And—and give her a last chance to prove her innocence."

"I'll give her the message," said Miss Moore, and sighed.

Alone, Mr. Hendrix returned to the phone booth. He sat down heavily and put in a call for Carmen Browne. His case was ready. He desired to hear the news of the finding of the body. An annoying tingle touched the base of his spine as he waited for the apartment switchboard to answer. He wondered how drunk he was. Drunk, to be sure, but sober enough to know exactly every phase and weigh every nuance. The moment he heard of the crime he would rush over, be detained by the police and, with the aid of his intoxicated condition, act thoroughly irrational and grief-stricken. He would hint at no alibis, reveal not a shred of his case until the coroner's inquest.

The switchboard operator finally answered. Mr. Hendrix inquired thickly for Miss Browne. He was told Miss Browne was not in. He hung up. Rising and swaying for a moment, Mr. Hendrix, at peace with the world, except for this intermittent tingle, decided on the best course. He would go to the El Bravo Club, order his dinner and wait there till Brownie's absence was noticed and a search started.

The El Bravo orchestra was rendering a dance number. The dance floor was crowded. Mr. Hendrix looked dizzily at the circling figures. He had selected a table far to the side, one of those at which the performers and their friends grouped themselves during the evening. The stuffiness of the air made Mr. Hendrix feel drowsy. Looking up, he beheld a familiar figure approaching. It was Eddie White, whom he had pleased to style the ignorant dropkicker. Mr. Hendrix smiled. He noticed tiredly that Mr. White seemed a little drunk.

The ex-college hero, still a sturdy, tanned and muscular product of the higher education, greeted Mr. Hendrix calmly. He dropped into a chair at the table and inquired, with an eye roving over the place, how tricks were. Mr. Hendrix said they were fine.

A CABALLERO OF THE LAW

There was a pause, during which the music filled the cafe with glamorous and exciting sounds.

"Didn't know you were such a movie fan," said Mr. White, apropos of nothing, and Mr. Hendrix felt himself sobering up as if in a cold shower.

"Just what do you mean?" Mr. Hendrix inquired, casually.

His companion was busy looking them over on the dance floor and offering a roguish eye to a few of the tastier numbers. Mr. Hendrix stared at him in silence and felt the tingle return to his spine.

"Saw you going to a picture this afternoon," Mr. White resumed.

"You did?" said Mr. Hendrix, and then added as if he were looping the loop: "What time was that?"

"What time?" Mr. White repeated, looking at the little lawyer with a dull, athlete's stare. "Oh, a little after four, I should say."

"You're crazy," said Mr. Hendrix, "if you think you saw me going into the movies after four. Why, I came out about twenty after four, after seeing the whole show."

"I don't care what you saw," said Mr. White. "I saw you going in at about a quarter after. I was gonna say hello, but I thought the hell with it. How'd you like the picture? Ought to be in your line—all about one of those crooked legal sharks."

In the brief space during which Mr. Hendrix was now silent, his thoughts were very rapid. Mr. White—God help Mr. Hendrix—was that most objectionable of all humans known to a legal case—the aimless stray that the prosecution was wont to drag, rabbit fashion, out of its hat to confound the guilty with. And Mr. Hendrix knew, without thinking, the full significance of this witness, Eddie White. If the defendant had been seen entering the movie theater after four, he had been seen after the murder had been committed. But that was the least damaging phase. The defendant had left the movie theater at 4:20, having lied to the attendants and told them he had spent an hour and a half in the place.

With the fact of this lie established, the prosecution could take apart piece by piece the obvious mechanism of his alibi. There was no alibi. There was no case. In fact, to the contrary, Eddie White's simple statement of the time of day—after four—revealed all the defendant's subsequent actions as those of a thoroughly guilty man, and Mr. Hendrix leaned across the table and put a hand on the athlete's arm.

"It must have been somebody else you saw," he purred.

"Listen, don't tell me," said Mr. White. "I saw you looking around, buying your ticket and ducking in."

Mr. Hendrix winced at the damning phraseology.

"I know it was about a quarter after four," pursued Mr. White, "because I had a date outside. And don't get so excited. It wasn't with Brownie."

The tingle at the base of the Hendrix spine was almost lifting him out of his seat.

"That's a lie," said Mr. Hendrix thickly.

"What's that?" Mr. White demanded.

"I said you're lying," Mr. Hendrix repeated slowly. "You didn't see me."

"Oh, that's what you said, is it?" Mr. White was unexpectedly grim. "Listen, I never liked you, and I don't take talk off a guy I got no use for. Get that."

And for the second time that day an unprecedented mood overcame the little lawyer. He made an effort to stop the words which suddenly filled his head, but he heard himself saying them and wondering confusedly who it was that was drunk—he who was listening or he who was speaking. He was telling Mr. White what a liar, numskull and oaf he was, and Mr. White stood up. Words continued, Mr. Hendrix aware that he and Mr. White were both talking at once. But the music made a blur in his ears and the El Bravo Club swayed in front of his eyes. Then Mr. Hendrix realized, and darkly, that the towering Mr. White's hand was on his collar and that he was being lifted out of his seat. The El Bravo orchestra was rolling out a jazz finale and nobody seemed to have noticed as yet the fracas taking place at this side table. As Mr. Hendrix felt himself being hoisted to his feet, a sense of nausea and helplessness overcame him. He thrust his hand into his coat pocket.

"Calling me a liar, eh?" Mr. White was growling in the Hendrix ear. He added a number of epithets.

The little lawyer saw for an instant a fist pull back that never landed. Mr. Hendrix had removed a gun from his coat pocket—a gun of whose existence in his hand he was as unaware as he had been of the brass candlestick. The gun exploded, and Mr. White, with a look of suddenly sober astonishment, fell back into a chair. The music at this moment finished with a nanny-goat blare of trumpets. No heads turned. No waiters came rushing. Shaking as if his bones had turned into castanets, Mr. Hendrix stood looking at the crumpled athlete and watched his head sink over the table.

Music started again and Mr. Hendrix turned his eyes automatically toward the dance floor. Blue and pink floodlights were shining on it, and out from behind the orchestra shell came a line of girls. White legs kicked, smiles filled the air. At the head of this chorus line, Mr. Hendrix saw Carmen Browne. She was dancing.

The little lawyer grew sick. He shut his eyes. Then he opened them. They were full of pain and bewilderment. It was no hallucination. It was Brownie. Extending under her ear at the back of her head, he saw strips of court plaster. She was alive and restored.

Mr Hendrix knew exactly what had happened. The last time he had called her apartment, the switchboard man, failing to recognize his liquor-thickened voice, had withheld the information he might have offered Mr. Hendrix—that Carmen Browne was alive, that she had summoned a doctor, that she had left the apartment.

And even as he was thinking of this tiny detail, a hundred other details crowded into the Hendrix mind. He remembered his accusations to Brownie that she still loved Eddie White; his statement to Peggy Moore last week and this afternoon that he was too jealous to trust himself; his attack on Carmen Browne, his subsequent drunkenness, his idiotic antics in the movie theater—as if he were shadowing Eddie White—what else could his rushing in and rushing out mean? Everything Mr. Hendrix had accomplished since 4:02 this afternoon pointed only at one conclusion—that he hated Eddie White; that he had almost killed his sweetheart out of jealousy over White; that, still burning with this emotion, he had tracked White down and murdered him in cold blood.

Mr. Hendrix, during these brief moments staring at the crumpled athlete, wanted to scream, so macabre did all these events strike him, but his voice trailed off into a moan. What was this insane thing he had done for his client? Exonerated him! Mr. Hendrix, still shaking, slipped down into his chair. He, Lou Hendrix, the shining legal intelligence, had, like some Nemesis, convicted himself—and not of manslaughter, which might have been the verdict otherwise, but of premeditated murder in the first degree. There was no case. No defense was possible. There was nothing left to do but to flee like some thug.

Mr. Hendrix looked at his wrist. He had twenty minutes to make the ten o'clock train for Chicago. From Chicago he would travel to New Orleans, and thence into Mexico. He had a wallet full of bills.

The side exit of the El Bravo was ten feet away. But Mr. Hendrix, struggling to get to his feet, swayed and fell forward. The dozen drinks he had so shrewdly tossed down his gullet to help him act his part joined the hideous plot he had hatched against himself. He was too drunk, too dizzy to stand up and move quickly.

They found the little barrister hunched in his seat, staring at the murdered athlete. The gun was still in his hand. Mr. Hendrix was mumbling passionlessly:

"Guilty. Guilty. Guilty."

WHEN THE WORLD WAS YOUNG

JACK LONDON

He was a very quiet, self-possessed sort of man, sitting a moment on top of the wall to sound the damp darkness for warnings of the dangers it might conceal. But the plummet of his hearing brought nothing to him save the moaning of wind through invisible trees and the rustling of leaves on swaying branches. A heavy fog drifted and drove before the wind, and though he could not see this fog the wet of it blew upon his face, and the wall on which he sat was wet.

Without noise he had climbed to the top of the wall from the outside, and without noise he dropped to the ground on the inside. From his pocket he drew an electric light-stick, but he did not use it. Dark as the way was, he was not anxious for light. Carrying the light-stick in his hand, his finger on the button, he advanced through the darkness. The ground was velvety and springy to his feet, being carpeted with dead pine-needles and leaves and mold which evidently had been undisturbed for years. Leaves and branches brushed against his body, but so dark was it that he could not avoid them. Soon he walked with his hand stretched out gropingly before him, and more than once the hand fetched up against the solid trunks of massive trees.

All about him he knew were these trees; he sensed the loom of them everywhere; and he experienced a strange feeling of microscopic smallness in the midst of great bulks leaning toward him to crush him. Beyond, he knew, was the house, and he expected to find some trail or winding path that would lead easily to it.

Once he found himself trapped. On every side he groped against trees and branches, or blundered into thickets of underbrush, until there seemed no way out. Then he turned on the light circumspectly, directing its rays to the ground at his feet. Slowly and carefully he moved it about him, the white brightness showing in sharp detail all the obstacles to his progress. He saw an opening between huge-trunked trees, and advanced through it, putting out the light and treading on dry footing as yet protected from the drip of the fog by the dense foliage overhead. His sense of direction was good, and he knew he was going toward the house.

And then the thing happened—the thing unthinkable and unexpected. His descending foot came down upon something that was soft and alive and that arose with a snort under the weight of his body. He sprang clear and crouched for another spring, anywhere, tense and expectant, keyed for the onslaught of the unknown. He waited a moment, wondering what manner of animal it was that had arisen from under his foot and that now made no sound or movement and that must be crouching and waiting just as tensely and expectantly as he. The strain became unbearable. Holding the lightstick before him, he pressed the button, saw and screamed aloud in terror. He was prepared for anything, from a frightened calf or fawn to a belligerent lion, but he was not prepared for what he saw. In that instant his tiny searchlight, sharp and white, had shown him what a thousand years would not enable him to forget—a man, huge and blond, yellow-haired and yellow-bearded, naked except for soft-tanned moccasins and what seemed to be a goatskin about his middle. Arms and legs were bare, as were his shoulders and most of his chest. The skin was smooth and hairless, but browned by sun and wind, while under it heavy muscles were knotted like fat snakes.

Still, this alone, unexpected as it well was, was not what had made the man scream out. What had caused his terror was the unspeakable ferocity of the face, the wild-animal glare of the blue eyes scarcely dazzled by the light, the pine-needles matted and clinging in the beard and hair, and the whole formidable body crouched and in the act of springing at him. Practically in the instant he saw all this, and while his scream still rang the thing leaped, he flung his light-stick full at it, and threw himself to the ground. He felt its shins and feet strike against his ribs, and he bounded up and away while the thing itself hurled onward in a heavy, crashing fall into the underbrush.

As the noise of the fall ceased, the man stopped and on hands and knees waited. He could hear the thing moving about, searching for him, and he was afraid to advertise his location by attempting further flight. He knew that inevitably he would crackle the underbrush and be pursued. Once he drew out his revolver, then changed his mind. He had recovered his composure and hoped to get away without noise. Several times he heard the thing beating up the thickets for him, and there were moments when it, too, remained still and listened. This gave an idea to the man. One of his hands was resting on a chunk of dead wood. Carefully, first feeling about him in the darkness to know that the full swing of his arm was clear, he raised the chunk of wood and threw it. It was not a large piece, and it went far, landing noisily in a bush. He heard the thing bound into the bush, and at the same time himself crawled steadily away. And on hands and knees, slowly and cautiously, he crawled on till his knees were wet on the soggy mold. When he listened he heard naught but the moaning wind and the drip-drip of the fog from the branches. Never abating his caution, he stood erect and went on to the stone wall, over which he climbed and dropped down to the road outside.

Feeling his way in a clump of bushes, he drew out a bicycle and prepared to mount. He was in the act of driving the gear around with his foot for the purpose of getting the opposite pedal in position when he heard the thud of a heavy body that landed lightly and evidently on its feet. He did not wait for more, but ran, with hands on the handles of his bicycle, until he was able to vault astride the saddle, catch the pedals and start a spurt. Behind he could hear the quick thud-thud of feet on the dust of the road, but he drew away from it and lost it.

Unfortunately, he had started away from the direction of town and was heading higher up into the hills. He knew that on this particular road there were no cross roads. The only way back was past that terror, and he could not steel himself to face it. At the end of half an hour, finding himself on an ever-increasing grade, he dismounted. For still greater safety, leaving the wheel by the roadside, he climbed through a fence into what he decided was a hillside pasture, spread a newspaper on the ground and sat down.

"Gosh!" he said aloud, mopping the sweat and fog from his face.

And "Gosh!" he said once again, while rolling a cigarette as he pondered the problem of getting back.

But he made no attempt to go back. He was resolved not to face that road in the dark and, with head bowed on knees, he dozed, waiting for daylight.

How long afterward he did not know, he was awakened by the yapping bark of a young coyote. As he looked about and located it, on the brow of the hill behind him, he noted the change that had come over the face of the night. The fog was gone; the stars and moon were out; even the wind had died down. It had transformed into a balmy California summer night.

He tried to doze again, but the yap of the coyote disturbed him. Half asleep, he heard a wild dog and eerie chant. Looking about him, he noticed that the coyote had ceased its noise and was running away along the crest of the hill, and behind it in full pursuit, no longer chanting, ran the naked creature he had encountered in the garden. It was a young coyote, and it was being overtaken when the chase passed from view. The man trembled as with a chill as he started to his feet, clambered over the fence and mounted his wheel. But it was his chance and he knew it. The terror was no longer between him and Mill Valley.

He sped at a breakneck rate down the hill, but in the turn at the bottom, in the deep shadows, he encountered a chuckhole and pitched headlong over the handlebar.

"It's sure not my night," he muttered as he examined the broken fork of the machine.

Shouldering the useless wheel, he trudged on. In time he came to the stone wall and, half disbelieving his experience, he sought in the road for tracks and found them—moccasin tracks, large ones, deep-bitten into the dust at the toes. It was while bending over them, examining, that again he heard the eerie chant. He had seen the thing pursue the coyote, and he knew he had no chance on a straight run. He did not attempt it, contenting himself with hiding in the shadows on the off side of the road.

And again he saw the thing that was like a naked man, running swiftly and lightly and singing as it ran. Opposite him it paused, and his heart stood still. But instead of coming toward his hiding place it leaped into the air, caught the branch of a roadside tree and swung swiftly upward from limb to limb, like an ape. It swung across the wall, a dozen feet above the top, into the branches of another tree, and dropped out of sight to the ground. The man waited a few wondering minutes, then started on.

II

Dave Slotter leaned belligerently against the desk that barred the way to the private office of James Ward, senior partner of the firm of Ward, Knowles & Co. Dave was angry. Everyone in the outer office had looked him over suspiciously, and the man who faced him was excessively suspicious.

"You just tell Mr. Ward it's important," he urged.

"I tell you he is dictating and cannot be disturbed," was the answer. "Come tomorrow."

"Tomorrow will be too late. You just trot along and tell Mr. Ward it's a matter of life and death."

The secretary hesitated, and Dave seized the advantage.

"You just tell him I was across the bay in Mill Valley last night, and that I want to put him wise to something."

"What name?" was the query.

"Never mind the name. He don't know me."

When Dave was shown into the private office he was still in the belligerent frame of mind, but when he saw a large, fair man whirl in a revolving chair from dictating to a stenographer to face him Dave's demeanor abruptly changed. He did not know why it changed, and he was secretly made angry with himself.

"You are Mr. Ward?" Dave asked with a fatuousness that still further irritated him. He had never intended it at all.

"Yes," came the answer. "And who are you?"

"Harry Bancroft," Dave lied. "You don't know me, and my name don't matter."

"You sent in word that you were in Mill Valley last night?"

"You live there, don't you?" Dave countered, looking suspiciously at the stenographer.

"Yes. What do you want to see me about? I am very busy."

"I'd like to see you alone, sir."

Mr. Ward gave him a quick, penetrating look, hesitated, then made up his mind.

"That will do for a few minutes, Miss Potter."

The girl arose, gathered her notes together and passed out. Dave looked at Mr. James Ward wonderingly until that gentleman broke his train of inchoate thought.

"Well?"

"I was over in Mill Valley last night," Dave began confusedly.

"I've heard that before. What do you want?"

And Dave proceeded in the face of a growing conviction that was unbelievable.

"I was at your house, or in the grounds, I mean."

"What were you doing there?"

"I came to break in," Dave answered in all frankness. "I heard you lived all alone with a Chinaman for cook, and it looked good to me. Only I didn't break in. Something happened that prevented. That's why I'm here. I come to warn you. I found a wild man loose in your grounds—a regular devil. He could pull a guy like me to pieces. He gave me the run of my life. He don't wear any clothes to speak of, he climbs trees like a monkey and he runs like a deer. I saw him chasing a coyote, and the last I saw of it he was gaining on it."

Dave paused and looked for the effect that would follow his words. But no effect came. James Ward was just quietly curious.

"Very remarkable, very remarkable," he murmured. "A wild man, you say? Why have you come to tell me?"

"To warn you of your danger. I'm something of a hard proposition myself, but I don't believe in killing people . . . that is, unnecessarily. I realized that you was in danger. I thought I'd warn you. Honest, that's the game. Of course, if you wanted to give me anything for my trouble I'd take it. That was in my mind too. But I don't care whether you give me anything or not. I've warned you anyway, and done my duty."

Mr. Ward meditated and drummed on the surface of his desk. Dave noticed they were large, powerful hands, withal well cared for despite their dark sunburn. Also, he noted what had already caught his eye—a tiny strip of flesh-colored court plaster on the forehead over one eye. And still the thought that forced itself into his mind was unbelievable.

Mr. Ward took a wallet from his inside coat pocket, drew out a greenback and passed it to Dave, who noted as he pocketed it that it was for twenty dollars.

"Thank you," said Mr. Ward, indicating that the interview was at an end. "I shall have the matter investigated. A wild man running loose *is* dangerous."

But so quiet a man was Mr. Ward that Dave's courage returned. Besides, a new theory had suggested itself. The wild man was evidently Mr. Ward's brother, a lunatic privately confined. Dave had heard of such things. Perhaps Mr. Ward wanted it kept quiet. That was why he had given him the twenty dollars.

"Say," Dave began, "now I come to think of it that wild man looked a lot like you——"

That was as far as Dave got, for at that moment he witnessed a transformation and found himself gazing into the same unspeakably ferocious blue eyes of the night before, at the same clutching, talonlike hands, and at the same formidable bulk in the act of springing upon him. But this time Dave had no light-stick to throw, and he was caught by the biceps of both arms in a grip so terrific that it made him groan with pain. He saw the large white teeth exposed, for all the world as a dog's about to bite. Mr. Ward's beard brushed his face as the teeth went in for the grip on his throat. But the bite was not given. Instead, Dave felt the other's body stiffen as with an iron restraint, and then he was flung aside without effort, but with such force that only the wall stopped his momentum and dropped him gasping to the floor.

"What do you mean by coming here and trying to blackmail me?" Mr. Ward was snarling at him. "Here, give me back that money."

Dave passed the bill back without a word.

"I thought you came here with good intentions. I know you now. Let me see and hear no more of you or I'll put you in prison where you belong. Do you understand?"

"Yes, sir," Dave gasped.

"Then go."

And Dave went without further word, both his biceps aching intolerably from the bruise of that tremendous grip. As his hand rested on the doorknob he was stopped.

"You were lucky," Mr. Ward was saying, and Dave noted that his face and eyes were cruel and gloating and proud.

"You were lucky. Had I wanted I could have torn your muscles out of your arms and thrown them in the wastebasket there."

"Yes, sir," said Dave, and absolute conviction vibrated in his voice.

He opened the door and went out. The secretary looked at him interrogatively.

"Gosh!" was all Dave vouchsafed, and with this utterance passed out of the offices and the story.

III

James G. Ward was forty years of age, a successful businessman, and very unhappy. For forty years he had vainly tried to solve a problem that was really himself, and that with increasing years became more and more a woeful affliction. In himself he was two men, and, chronologically speaking, these men were several thousand years or so apart. He had studied the question of dual personality probably more profoundly than any half dozen of the leading specialists in that intricate and mysterious psychological field. In himself he was a different case from any that had been recorded. Even the most fanciful flights of the fiction writers had not quite hit upon him. He was not a Doctor Jekyll and Mr. Hyde, nor was he like the unfortunate young man in Kipling's "Greatest Story in the World." His two personalities were so mixed that they were practically aware of themselves and of each other all the time.

His one self was that of a man whose rearing and education were modern and who had lived through the latter part of the nineteenth century and well into the first decade of the twentieth. His other self he had located as a savage and a barbarian living under the primitive conditions of several thousand years before. But which self was he, and which was the other, he could never tell. For he was both selves, and both selves all the time. Very rarely indeed did it happen that one self did not know what the other was doing. Another thing was that he had no visions nor memories of the past in which that early self had lived. That early self lived in the present; but while it lived in the present it was under the compulsion to live the way of life that must have been in that distant past.

In his childhood he had been a problem to his father and mother and to the family doctors, though never had they come within a thousand miles of hitting upon the clue to his erratic conduct. Thus, they could not understand his excessive somnolence in the forenoon, nor his excessive activity at night.

When they found him wandering along the hallways at night, or climbing over giddy roofs, or running in the hills, they decided he was a somnambulist. In reality he was wide-eyed awake and merely under the night-roaming compulsion of his early self. Questioned by an obtuse medico he once told the truth and suffered the ignominy of having the revelation contemptuously labeled and dismissed as dreams.

The point was, that as twilight and evening came on, he became wakeful. The four walls of a room were an irk and a restraint. He heard a thousand voices whispering to him through the darkness. The night called to him, for he was, for that period of the twenty-four hours, essentially a night-prowler. But nobody understood, and never again did he attempt to explain. They classified him as a sleepwalker and took precautions accordingly—precautions that very often were futile.

As his childhood advanced he grew more cunning, so that the major portion of all his nights was spent in the open, realizing his other self. As a result, he slept in the forenoons. Morning studies and schools were impossible, and it was discovered that only in the afternoons, under private teachers, could he be taught anything. Thus was his modern self educated and developed.

But a problem, as a child, he ever remained. He was known as a little demon of insensate cruelty and viciousness. The family doctors privately adjudged him a mental monstrosity and a degenerate. Such few boy companions as he had hailed him as a wonder, though they were all afraid of him. He could outclimb, outswim, outrun, outdevil any of them; while none dared fight with him. He was too terribly strong, too madly furious.

When nine years of age he ran away to the hills, where he flourished, night-prowling, for seven weeks before he was discovered and brought home. The marvel was how he had managed to subsist and keep in condition during that time. They did not know, and he never told them, of the rabbits he had killed, of the quail, young and old, he had captured and devoured, of the farmers' chicken-roosts he had raided, nor of the cave-lair he had made and carpeted with dry leaves and grasses and in which he had slept in warmth and comfort through the forenoons of many days.

At college he was notorious for his sleepiness and stupidity during the morning lectures and for his brilliance in the afternoon. By collateral reading and by borrowing the notebooks of his fellow students he managed to scrape through the detestable morning courses. His afternoon courses were triumphs. In football he proved a giant and a terror, and in almost every form of track athletics, save for strange berserker rages that were sometimes displayed, he could be depended upon to win. But his fellows were afraid to box with him, and he signalized his last wrestling bout by sinking his teeth into the shoulder of his opponent.

After college his father, in despair, sent him among the cowpunchers of a Wyoming ranch. Three months later the doughty cowmen confessed he was too much for them and telegraphed his father to come and take the wild man away. Also, when the father arrived to take him away the cowmen allowed that they would vastly prefer chumming with howling cannibals, gibbering lunatics, cavorting gorillas, grizzly bears and man-eating tigers than with this particular young college product with hair parted in the middle.

There was one exception to the lack of memory of the life of his early self, and that was language. By some quirk of atavism a certain portion of that early self's language had come down to him as a racial memory. In moments of happiness, exaltation or battle he was prone to burst out in wild, barbaric songs or chants. It was by this means that he located in time and space that strayed half of him which should have been dead and dust for thousands of years. He sang once deliberately several of these ancient chants in the presence of Professor Wertz, who gave courses in Old Saxon, and who was a philologist of repute and passion. At the first one the professor pricked up his ears and demanded to know what mongrel tongue or hog-German it was. When the second chant was rendered the professor was highly excited. James Ward then concluded the performance by giving a song that always irresistibly rushed to his lips when he was engaged in fierce struggling or fighting. Then it was that Professor Wertz proclaimed it no hog-German, but early German, or early Teuton, of a date that must far precede anything that had ever been discovered and handed down by the scholars. So early was it that it was beyond him; yet it was filled with haunting reminiscences of word-forms he knew and that his trained intuition told him were true and real. He demanded the source of the songs and asked to borrow the precious book that contained them. Also, he demanded to know why young

Ward had always posed as being profoundly ignorant of the German language. And Ward could neither explain his ignorance nor lend the book. Whereupon, after pleadings and entreaties that extended through weeks, Professor Wertz took a dislike to the young man, believed him a liar, and classified him as a man of monstrous selfishness for not giving him a glimpse of this wonderful screed that was older than the oldest Teutonic tongue any philologist had ever dreamed of.

But little good did it do this much-mixed young man to know that half of him was late American and the other half early Teuton. Nevertheless, the late American in him was no weakling, and he—if he were a he and had a shred of existence outside of these two—compelled an adjustment or compromise between his one self that was a night-prowling savage who kept his other self sleepy of mornings, and that other self that was cultured and refined and that wanted to be normal and live and love and prosecute business like other people. The afternoons and early evenings he gave to the one, the nights to the other; the forenoons and parts of the nights were devoted to sleep for the twain. But in the mornings he slept in bed like a civilized man. In the nighttime he slept like a wild animal—as he had slept the night Dave Slotter stepped on him in the woods.

Persuading his father to advance the capital, he went into business, and keen and successful business he made of it, devoting his afternoons whole-souled to it, while his partner devoted the mornings. The early evenings he spent socially, but as the hour grew to nine or ten an irresistible restlessness overcame him and he disappeared from the haunts of men until the next afternoon. Friends and acquaintances thought that he spent much of his time in sport. And they were right, though they never would have dreamed of the nature of the sport, even if they had seen him running coyotes in night chases over the hills of Mill Valley. Neither were the schooner captains believed when they reported seeing on cold winter mornings a man swimming in the tide-rips of Raccoon Straits or in the swift currents between Goat Island and Angel Island, miles from shore.

In the bungalow at Mill Valley he lived alone, save for Lee Sing, the Chinese cook and factotum, who knew much about the strangeness of his master, who was paid well for saying nothing, and who never did say anything. After the satisfaction of his nights, a morning's sleep and a breakfast of Lee Sing's, James Ward crossed the bay to San Francisco on a midday ferryboat and went to the club and on to his office, as normal and conventional a man of business as could be found in the city. But as the evening lengthened the night called to him. There came a quickening of all his perceptions and a restlessness. His hearing was suddenly acute; the myriad night noises told him a luring and familiar story; and, if alone, he would begin to pace the narrow room like any caged animal from the wild.

Once he ventured to fall in love. He never permitted himself that diversion again. He was afraid. And for many a day the young lady, scared out of at least a portion of her young ladyhood, bore on her arms and wrists divers black-and-blue bruises—tokens of caresses which he had bestowed in all fond gentleness after nightfall. There was the mistake. Had he ventured love-making in the afternoon all would have been well, for it would have been as the quiet gentleman that he would have made love—but at night he was the uncouth, wife-stealing savage of the dark German forests. Out of his wisdom he decided that afternoon love-making could be prosecuted successfully; but out of the same wisdom he was convinced that marriage would prove a ghastly failure. He found it appalling to imagine being married and encountering his wife after dark.

So he had eschewed all love-making, regulated his dual life, cleaned up a million in business, fought shy of matchmaking mammas and bright and eager-eyed young ladies of various ages, met Lilian Gersdale and made it a rigid observance never to see her later than eight o'clock in the evening, ran of nights after his coyotes and slept in forest lairs—and through it all had kept his secret save for Lee Sing . . . and now, Dave Slotter. It was the latter's discovery of both his selves that frightened him. In spite of the counter fright he had given the burglar, the latter might talk, and even if he did not, sooner or later he would be found out by someone else.

Thus it was that James Ward made a fresh and heroic effort to control the Teutonic barbarian that was half of him. So well did he make it a point to see Lilian in the afternoons and early evenings that the time came when she accepted him for better or worse, and when he prayed privily and fervently that it were not for worse. During this period no prizefighter ever trained more harshly and faithfully for a contest than he trained to subdue the wild savage in him. Among other things he strove to exhaust himself during the day, so that sleep would render him deaf to the call of the night. He took a vacation from the office and went on long hunting trips, following the deer through the most inaccessible and rugged country he could find—and always in the daytime. Night found him indoors and tired. At home he installed a score of exercise machines, and where other men might go through a particular movement ten times he went hundreds. Also, as a compromise he built a sleeping porch on the second story. Here at least he breathed the blessed night air. Double screens prevented him from escaping into the woods, and each night Lee Sing locked him in and each morning let him out.

The time came, in the month of August, when he engaged additional servants to assist Lee Sing and dared a house party in his Mill Valley bungalow. Lilian, her mother and brother and half a dozen mutual friends were the guests. For two days and nights all went well. And on the third night, playing bridge till eleven o'clock, he had reason to be proud of himself. His restlessness he successfully hid, but as luck would have it, Lilian Gersdale was his opponent on his right. She was a frail, delicate flower of a woman, and in his night mood her very frailty incensed him. Not that he loved her less, but that he felt almost irresistibly impelled to reach out and paw and maul her. Especially was this true when she was engaged in playing a winning hand against him.

He had one of the deerhounds brought in and, when it seemed he must fly to pieces with the tension, a caressing hand laid on the animal brought him relief. These contacts with the hairy coat gave him instant easement and enabled him to play out the evening. Nor did anyone guess the terrific struggle their host was making, the while he laughed so carelessly and played so keenly and deliberately.

When they separated for the night he saw to it that he parted from Lilian in the presence of the others. Once on his sleeping-porch and safely locked in he doubled and tripled and even quadrupled his exercises until, exhausted, he lay down on the couch to woo sleep and to ponder two problems that especially troubled him. One was this matter of exercise. It was a paradox. The more he exercised in this excessive fashion the stronger he became. While it was true that he thus quite tired out his night-running Teutonic self, it seemed that he was merely setting back the fatal day when his strength would be too much for him and overpower him, and then it would be a strength more terrible than he had ever known. The other problem was that of his marriage and of the stratagems he must employ in order to avoid his wife after dark. And thus fruitlessly pondering he fell asleep.

Now, where the huge grizzly bear came from that night was long a mystery, while the people of the Springs Brothers' Circus, showing at Sausalito, searched long and vainly for "Big Ben, the Biggest Grizzly in Captivity." But Big Ben escaped and, out of the mazes of half a thousand bungalows and country estates, it selected the grounds of James J. Ward for visitation. The first Mr. Ward knew was when he found himself on his feet, quivering and tense, a surge of battle in his breast, and on his lips the old war chant. From without came a wild baying and bellowing of the hounds. And sharp as a knife thrust through the pandemonium came the agony of a stricken dog—his dog, he knew.

Not stopping for slippers, pajama-clad, he burst through the door Lee Sing had so carefully locked, sped down the stairs and out into the night. As his naked feet struck the graveled driveway he stopped abruptly, reached under the steps to a hiding place he knew well, and pulled forth a huge, knotty club—his old companion in many a mad night adventure on the hills. The frantic hullabaloo of the dogs was coming nearer, and, swinging the club, he sprang straight into the thickets to meet it.

The aroused household assembled on the wide veranda. Somebody turned on the electric lights, but they could see nothing but one another's frightened faces. Beyond the brightly illuminated driveway the trees formed a wall of impenetrable blackness. Yet somewhere amid that blackness a terrible struggle was going on. There was an infernal outcry of animals, a great snarling and growling, the sound of blows being struck and a smashing and crashing of underbrush by heavy bodies.

The tide of battle swept out from among the trees and upon the driveway just beneath the onlookers. Then they saw. Mrs. Gersdale cried out and clung fainting to her son. Lilian, clutching the railing so spasmodically that a bruising hurt was left in her finger ends for days, gazed horror-stricken at a yellow-haired, wild-eyed giant whom she recognized as the man who was to be her husband. He was swinging a great club and fighting furiously and calmly with a shaggy monster that was bigger than any bear she had ever seen. One rip of the beast's claws had dragged away Ward's pajama coat and streaked his flesh with blood.

While most of Lilian Gersdale's fright was for the man beloved, there was a large portion of it due to the man himself. Never had she dreamed so formidable and magnificent a savage lurked under the starched shirt and conventional garb of her betrothed. And never had she had any conception of how a man battled. Such a battle was certainly not modern; nor was she there beholding a modern man, though she did not know it. For this was not Mr. James J. Ward, the San Francisco businessman, but one, unnamed and unknown, a crude, rude savage creature who, by some freak of chance, lived again after thrice a thousand years.

The hounds, ever maintaining their mad uproar, circled about the fight or dashed in and out, distracting the bear. When the animal turned to meet such flanking assaults the man leaped in and the club came down. Angered afresh by every such blow, the bear would rush, and the man, leaping and skipping, avoiding the dogs, went backward or circled to one side or the other. Whereupon the dogs, taking advantage of the opening, would again spring in and draw the animal's wrath to them.

The end came suddenly. Whirling, the grizzly caught a hound with a wide-sweeping cuff that sent the brute, its ribs caved in and its back broken, hurtling twenty feet. Then the human brute went mad. A foaming rage flecked the lips that parted with a wild, inarticulate cry as it sprang in, swung the club mightily in both hands and brought it down full on the head of the uprearing grizzly. Not even the skull of a grizzly could withstand the crushing force of such a blow, and the animal went down to meet the worrying of the hounds. And through their scurrying leaped the man full upon the body, where, in the white electric light, resting on his club, he chanted a triumph in an unknown tongue—a song so ancient that Professor Wertz would have given ten years of his life for it.

His guests rushed to possess him and acclaim him, but James Ward, suddenly looking out of the eyes of the early Teuton, saw the fair, frail twentieth-century girl he loved and felt something snap in his brain. He staggered weakly toward her, dropped the club and nearly fell. Something had gone wrong with him. Inside his brain was an intolerable agony. It seemed as if the soul of him were flying asunder. Following the excited gaze of the others, he glanced back and saw the carcass of the bear. The sight filled him with fear. He uttered a cry and would have fled had they not restrained him and led him into the bungalow.

James J. Ward is still at the head of the firm of Ward, Knowles & Co. But he no longer lives in the country, nor does he run of nights after the coyotes under the moon. The early Teuton in him died the night of the Mill Valley fight with the bear. James J. Ward is now wholly James J. Ward, and he shares no part of his being with any vagabond anachronism from the younger world. And so wholly is James J. Ward modern that he knows in all its bitter fullness the curse of civilized fear. He is now afraid of the dark, and night in the forest is to him a thing of abysmal terror. His city house is of the spick-and-span order, and he evinces a great interest in burglarproof devices. His home is a tangle of electric wires, and after bedtime a guest can scarcely breathe without setting off an alarm. Also, he has invented a combination keyless doorlock that travelers may carry in their vest pockets and apply immediately and successfully under all circumstances. But his wife does not deem him a coward. She knows better. And, like any hero, he is content to rest on his laurels. His bravery is never questioned by those of his friends who are aware of the Mill Valley episode.

HIT AND RUN

JOHN D. MAC DONALD

Twenty-eight days after the woman died, Walter Post, special investigator for the Traffic Division, squatted on his heels in a big parking lot and ran his fingertips lightly along the front-right fender of the car which had killed her. It was a blue and gray four-door sedan, three years old, in the lower price range.

The repair job had probably been done in haste and panic. But it had been competently done. The blue paint was an almost perfect match. Some of it had got on the chrome stripping and had been wiped off, but not perfectly. The chrome headlight ring was a replacement, with none of the minute pits and rust flecks of the ring on the left headlight. He reached up into the fender wall and brushed his fingers along the area where the undercoating had been flattened when the fender had been hammered out.

He stood up and looked toward the big insurance-company office building, large windows and aluminum panels glinting in the morning sun, and wondered where Mr. Wade Addams was, which window was his. A vice-president, high up, looking down upon the world.

It had been a long hunt. Walter Post had examined many automobiles. The killing had occurred on a rainy Tuesday morning in September at 9:30, in the 1200 block of Harding Avenue. It was an old street of big elms and frame houses. It ran north and south. Residents in the new suburban areas south of the city used Harding Avenue in preference to Wright Boulevard when they drove to the center of the city. Harding Avenue had been resurfaced a year ago.

HIT AND RUN

There were few traffic lights. The people who lived on Harding Avenue had complained about fast traffic before Mary Berris was killed.

Mr. and Mrs. Steve Berris and their two small children had lived at 1237 Harding Avenue. He was the assistant manager of a supermarket. On that rainy morning she had put on her plastic rain cape to hurry across the street, apparently to see a neighbor on some errand. It was evident she had not intended to be gone long, as her two small children were left untended. The only witness was a thirteen-year-old girl, walking from her home to the bus stop.

Through careful and repeated interrogations of that girl after she had quieted down, authorities were able to determine that the street had been momentarily empty of traffic, that the death car had been proceeding toward the center of town at a high rate of speed, that Mary Berris had started to cross from right to left in front of the car, hurrying. Apparently, when she realized she had misjudged the speed and distance of the car, she had turned and tried to scamper back to the protection of the curb.

Walter Post guessed that the driver, assuming the young woman would continue across, had swerved to the right to go behind her. When she had turned back, the driver had hit the brakes. There were wet leaves on the smooth asphalt. The car had skidded. Mary Berris was struck and thrown an estimated twenty feet through the air, landing close to the curb. The car had swayed out of its skid and then accelerated.

The child had not seen the driver of the car. She said it was a pale car, a gray or blue, not a big car and not shiny new. Almost too late she realized she should look at the license number. But by then it was so far away that she could only tell that it was not an out-of-state license and that it ended, in her words, "in two fat numbers. Not sharp numbers like ones and sevens and fours. Fat ones, like sixes and eights and nines."

Mary Berris lived for nearly seventy hours with serious brain injuries, ugly contusions and abrasions and a fractured hip. She lived long enough for significant bruises to form, indicating from their shape and placement that the vehicle had struck her a glancing blow on the right hip and thigh, the curve of the bumper striking her right leg just below the knee. The fragments of glass from the lens of the shattered sealed-beam headlamp indicated three possible makes of automobile. No shellac or enamel was recovered from her clothing. It was believed that, owing to the glancing impact, the vehicle had not been seriously damaged. She did not regain consciousness before death.

For the first two weeks of the investigation Walter Post had the assistance of sufficient manpower to cover all places where repairs could have been made. The newspapers cooperated. Everyone in the metropolitan area was urged to look for the death car. But, as in so many other instances, the car seemed to disappear without a trace. Walter Post was finally left alone to continue the investigation, in addition to his other duties.

And, this time, he devoted more time to it than he planned. It seemed more personal. This was not a case of one walking drunk lurching into the night path of a driving drunk. This was a case of a young, pretty housewife—very pretty, according to the picture of her he had seen—mortally injured on a rainy Tuesday by somebody who had been in a hurry, somebody too callous to stop and clever enough to hide. He had talked to the broken husband and seen the small, puzzled kids, and heard the child witness say, "It made a terrible noise. A kind of—thick noise. And then she just went flying in the air, all loose in the air. And the car tried to go away so fast the wheels were spinning."

Walter Post would awaken in the night and think about Mary Berris and feel a familiar anger. This was his work, and he knew the cost of it and realized his own emotional involvement made him better at what he did. But this was a very small comfort in the bitter mood of the wakeful night. And he knew there would be no joy in solving the case because he would find at the end of his search not some monster, some symbol of evil, but merely another victim, a trembling human animal.

His wife Carolyn endured this time of his involvement as she had those which had gone before, knowing the cause of his remoteness, his brutal schedule of self-assigned work hours. Until this time of compulsion was ended, she and the children would live with—and rarely see—a weary man who kept pushing himself to the limit of his energy, who returned and ate and slept and went out again.

Operating on the assumption that the killer was a resident of the suburban areas south of the city, he had driven the area until he was able to block off one large section where, if you wanted to drive down into the center of the city, Harding Avenue was the most efficient route to take. With the cooperation of the clerks at the State Bureau of Motor Vehicle Registration, he compiled a discouragingly long list of all medium- and low-priced sedans from one to four years old registered in the name of persons living in his chosen area, where the license numbers ended in 99, 98, 89, 88, 96, 69, 86, 68 and 66. He hoped he would not have to expand it to include threes and fives, which could also have given that impression of "fatness," in spite of the child witness's belief that the numbers were not threes or fives.

With his list of addresses he continued the slow process of elimination. He could not eliminate the darker or brighter colors until he was certain the entire car had not been repainted. He worked with a feeling of weary urgency, suspecting the killer would feel more at ease once the death car was traded in. He lost weight. He accomplished his other duties in an acceptable manner.

At nine on this bright October tenth, a Friday, just twenty-eight days and a few hours after Mary Berris had died, he had checked the residence of a Mr. Wade Addams. It was a long and impressive house on a wide curve of Saylor Lane. A slim, dark woman of about forty answered the door. She wore slacks and a sweater. Her features were too strong for prettiness, and her manner and expression were pleasant and confident.

"Yes?"

He smiled and said, "I just want to take up a few moments of your time. Are you Mrs. Addams?"

"Yes, but really, if you're selling something, I just——"

He took out his notebook. "This is a survey financed by the automotive industry. People think we're trying to sell cars, but we're not. This is a survey about how cars are used."

She laughed. "I can tell you one thing. There aren't enough cars in this family. My husband drives to work. We have a son, eighteen, in his last year of high school, and a daughter, fourteen, who needs a lot of taxi service. The big car is in for repairs, and today my husband took the little car to work. So you can see how empty the garage is. If Gary's marks are good at midyear, Wade is going to get him a car of his own."

"Could I have the make and year and model and color of your two cars, Mrs. Addams?"

She gave him the information on the big car first. And then she told him the make of the smaller car and said, "It's three years old. A four-door sedan. Blue and gray."

"Who usually drives it, Mrs. Addams?"

"It's supposed to be mine, but my husband and Gary and I all drive it. So I'm always the one who has it when it runs out of gas. I *never* can remember to take a look at the gauge."

"What does your husband do, Mrs. Addams?"

"He's a vice-president at Surety Insurance."

"How long has your boy been driving?"

"Since it was legal. Don't they all? A junior license when he was sixteen, and his senior license last July when he turned eighteen. It makes me nervous, but what can you do? Gary is really quite a reliable boy. I shudder to think of what will happen when Nancy can drive. She's a scatterbrain. All you can do is depend on those young reflexes, I guess."

He closed his notebook. "Thanks a lot, Mrs. Addams. Beautiful place you have here."

"Thank you." She smiled at him. "I guess the automobile people are in a tizzy, trying to decide whether to make big cars or little cars."

"It's a problem," he said. "Thanks for your cooperation."

He had planned to check two more registrations in that immediate area. But he had a hunch about the Addamses' car. Obviously Mrs. Addams hadn't been driving. He had seen too many of the guilty ones react. They had been living in terror. When questioned, they broke quickly and completely. Any questions always brought on the unmistakable guilt reactions of the amateur criminal.

So he had driven back into the city, shown his credentials to the guard at the gate of the executive parking area of the Surety Insurance Company and inspected the blue-gray car with the license that ended in 89.

He walked slowly back to his own car and stood beside it, thinking, a tall man in his thirties, dark, big-boned, a man with a thoughtful, slow-moving manner. The damage to the Addams car could be coincidence. But he was certain he had located the car. The old man or the boy had done it. Probably the boy. The public schools hadn't opened until the fifteenth.

He thought of the big job and the fine home and the pleasant, attractive woman. It was going to blow up that family as if you stuck a bomb under it. It would be hell, but not one-tenth, one-hundredth the hell Steve Berris was undergoing.

He went over his facts and assumptions. The Addamses lived in the right area to use Harding Avenue as the fast route to town. The car had been damaged not long ago in precisely the way he had guessed it would be. It fitted the limited description given.

He went into the big building. The information center in the lobby sent him up to the twelfth-floor receptionist. He told her his name, said he did not have an appointment but did not care to state his business. She raised a skeptical eyebrow, phoned Addams's secretary and asked him to wait a few minutes. He sat in a deep chair amid an efficient hush. Sometimes, when a door opened, he could hear a chattering drone of tabulating equipment.

Twenty minutes later a man walked quickly into the reception room. He was in his middle forties, a trim balding man with heavy glasses, a nervous manner and a weathered golfing tan. Walter stood as he approached.

"Mr. Post? I'm Wade Addams. I can spare a few minutes."

"You might want to make it more than a few minutes, Mr. Addams."

"I don't follow you."

"When and how did you bash in the front-right fender of your car down there in the lot?"

Addams stared at him. "If that fender is bashed in, Mr. Post, it happened since I parked it there this morning."

"It has been bashed in and repaired."

"That's nonsense!"

"Why don't we go down and take a look at it?" He kept his voice low.

Wade Addams was visibly irritated. "You'd better state your business in a—a less cryptic way, Mr. Post. I certainly have more to do than go down and stare at the fender on my own car."

"Do you happen to remember that hit-and-run on Harding Avenue? Mary Berris?"

"Of course I rem——" Wade Addams suddenly stopped talking. He stared beyond Post, frowning into the distance. "Surely you can't have any idea that——" He paused again, and Post saw his throat work as he swallowed. "This is some mistake."

"Let's go down and look at the fender."

Addams told the receptionist to tell his secretary he was leaving the building for a few moments. They went down to the lot. Post pointed out the unmistakable clues. There was a gleam of perspiration on Addams's forehead and upper lip. "I never noticed this. Not at all. My gosh, you don't look this carefully at a car."

"You have no knowledge of this fender's being bashed since you've owned the car?"

"Let's go back to my office, Mr. Post."

Addams had a big corner office, impressively furnished. Once they were alone, and Addams was seated behind his desk, he seemed better able to bring himself under control.

"Why have you—picked that car?"

Post explained the logic of his search and told of the subterfuge he had used with Mrs. Addams.

"Janet would know nothing about——"

"I know that, from talking to her."

"My wife is incapable of deceit. She considers it her great social handicap," he said, trying to smile.

"You didn't kill that woman either."

"No, I——"

"We're thinking of the same thing, Mr. Addams."

Addams got up quickly and walked restlessly over to the window. He turned suddenly, with a wide, confident smile. "Damn stupid of me, Mr. Post. I remember now. Completely slipped my mind. I drove that car over to Mercer last July. I—uh—skidded on a gravel road and had it fixed in a little country garage . . . hit it against a fence post when I went in the ditch."

Walter Post looked at him and shook his head slowly. "It won't work."

"I swear it's——"

"Mr. Addams, this is not a misdemeanor. In this state a hit-and-run killing is a mandatory murder charge. Second degree. The only way out of it is a valid insanity plea. In either case the criminal has to spend plenty of time locked up. You'd have to prove the date of the trip, show police officers exactly where you skidded, take them to the country garage, find people to back up the story. No, Mr. Addams. Not even a good try."

Addams went behind his desk and sat down heavily. "I don't know what to do. Get hold of a lawyer, I guess. All of a sudden I'm a hundred years old. I want to make myself believe that Gary bashed a fender and had it repaired on his own so he wouldn't lose his driving privilege."

"Why can't you believe that?"

"He has—changed, Mr. Post. In the last month. The teenage years are strange, murky years, if what I remember of my own is any clue. He's a huge youngster, Mr. Post. They all seem to grow so big lately. I've had trouble with him. The normal amount. If a kid doesn't have a streak of rebellion against authority in him—authority as represented by his male parent—then he isn't worth a damn. Gary has been a sunny type, usually. Reliable. Honest. He's traveled with a nice pack of kids. He's a pretty fair athlete and a B student. His contemporaries seem to like and respect him. Here's his picture. Taken last June..."

Crew cut and a broad smiling face, a pleasant, rugged-looking boy, a good-looking kid.

"He's changed. Janet and I have discussed it, and we've tried to talk to him, but he won't talk. He's sour and moody and gloomy. Off his feed. He doesn't seem interested in dates or athletics or his studies. He spends a lot of time in his room with the door closed. He grunts at us and barks at his sister. We thought it was a phase and have hoped it would end soon. We've wondered if he's in some kind of trouble that he can't or won't tell us about."

"I appreciate your being so frank, Mr. Addams."

"I can't, in my heart, believe him capable of this. But I've read about all the polite, decent, popular kids from good homes who have got into unspeakable trouble. You know—you can live with them and not understand them at all."

"Were you here in the office on the ninth?"

"Yes, if it was a weekday."

"What time did you get in?"

Addams looked back in his appointment calendar. "A Tuesday. I'd called a section meeting for nine. I was in at eight-thirty, earlier than usual. I can't believe Gary——"

"A kid can panic, Mr. Addams. A good kid can panic just as quick as a bad kid. And once you run, it's too late to go back. Maybe he loaned the car to some other kid. Maybe your wife loaned it."

Addams looked across the desk at Walter Post, a gleam of hope apparent. "It's against orders for him to let any of his friends drive it. But it could have happened that way."

"That's what we have to find out, Mr. Addams."

"Can we—talk to my boy? Can we go together and talk to Gary?"

"Of course."

Wade Addams phoned the high school. He said he would be out in twenty minutes to speak to his son on a matter of importance, and he would appreciate their informing him and providing a place where they could talk privately.

When they arrived at the high school, they went to the administration office and were directed to a small conference room. Gary Addams was waiting for them and stood up when they came in and closed the door. He was big. He had a completely closed expression, watchful eyes.

"What's up, dad? I phoned the house to find out, but mom didn't know a thing. I guess I just got her worried."

Wade Addams said, "I was going to let Mr. Post here ask you some questions, Gary, but with his permission I think I would like to ask you myself."

Walter Post had to admire the man. The answers he would get would very probably shatter a good life and, unless the kid was one in ten thousand, his future would be ruined beyond repair. Yet Wade Addams was under control.

"Go ahead," Post said.

"You have acted strange for a month, Gary. You know that. Your mother and I have spoken to you. Now I'm desperately afraid I know what has been wrong."

"Do you?" the boy said with an almost insolent indifference.

"Will you sit down?"

"I'd just as soon stand, thanks."

Wade Addams sighed. "You'd better tell us about the front-right fender on the small car, Gary. You'd better tell us the whole thing."

Post saw the flicker of alarm in the boy's light-colored eyes as he glanced sideways at Post. He had hunted a killer, and now he felt sick at heart, as in all the times that had gone before.

"You better clue me, dad. That question is far out."

"Did you repair it yourself? Were you driving or was one of your friends driving when you hit that woman? Does that—clue you enough?" he asked bitterly.

The boy stiffened and stared at his father with a wild, naked astonishment. "No!" the boy said in an almost inaudible voice. "You couldn't possibly—you couldn't be trying to——"

"To what? I'm ordering you to tell me about that fender."

The boy changed visibly in a way Walter Post had seen once before and would always remember. It takes a curious variety of shock to induce that look of boneless lethargy. Once, at a major fire, he had seen a man who believed his whole family had perished, had seen that man confronted by his family. There was the same look of heavy, brooding wonder.

Gary Addams slid heavily into one of the wooden armchairs at the small conference table. He looked at the scarred table and said in a dull voice, "I'll tell you about that fender. The fourteenth of September was a Sunday. You can look it up. You and mom had gone to the club. Nancy was off someplace. School started the next day. I played tennis. I got back about four in the afternoon, dad. I decided to wash the car. I hadn't washed it in two weeks, and I figured you'd start to give me a hard time about it any day. That was when I found out somebody had bashed the right fender and had it fixed since the last time I'd washed it. You wash a car, and you can spot something like that right away."

"But, Gary, you didn't say anything."

"If anybody'd been home, I'd have gone right in and asked who clobbered the fender. You know, like a joke. But there wasn't anybody home. And it—it kept coming into my mind. About that woman." Wade Addams had moved to stand beside his son. The boy looked up at him with a dull agony. "Dad, I just couldn't stop thinking about it. We always go down Harding Avenue. Our car matches the description. And if—if you or mom had bashed a fender in some kind of harmless way, you wouldn't have kept it a secret. I couldn't imagine you or mom doing such a terrible thing, but I kept thinking about it, and it got worse and worse. I thought I was going to throw up. And ever since then, I haven't known what to——"

"Where were you on the day that woman was hit, son?" Walter Post asked.

The boy frowned at him. "Where was I? Oh, a guy picked me up real early, about dawn, and a bunch of us went up to his folks' place at the lake and swam and skied all day and got back late."

Wade Addams spoke to his son in a strange voice. "Let me get this straight. For the last month, Gary, you've been living with the idea that either your mother or I could have killed that woman and driven away?" Walter Post could see how strongly the man's hand was grasping the boy's shoulder.

"But nobody else ever drives the car!" the boy cried. "Nobody else."

Walter Post watched Wade Addams's face and saw the fierce indignation of the falsely accused change to a sudden understanding of what the boy had been enduring. In a trembling voice Wade Addams said, "We didn't do it, boy. Neither of us. Not one of the three of us. Believe me, son. You can come out of your nightmare. You can come home again."

When the boy began to cry, to sob in the hoarse clumsy way of the man-child years, Walter Post stepped quietly out into the corridor and closed the door and leaned against the wall and smoked a cigarette, tasting his own gladness, a depth of satisfaction he had never before experienced in this deadly occupation. It made him yearn for some kind of work where this could happen more often. And he now knew the probable answer to the killing.

When Addams and his son came out of the room, they had an identical look of pride and exhaustion. The boy shook hands with Post and went back to class.

"Now we go to your house and talk to your wife," Walter Post said. "We were too quick to think it was the boy. We should have talked to her first."

"I'm glad we did it just this way, Mr. Post. Very glad. About the car. I think now I can guess what——"

"Let's let your wife confirm it."

At 3:30 that afternoon Walter Post sat in the small office of Stewart Partchman, owner of Partchman Motors. With him were Partchman and a redheaded service manager named Finnigan and a mechanic named Dawes.

Finnigan was saying, "The reason I didn't let Thompson go, Mr. Partchman, is that he's always been a reliable little guy, and this is the first time he goofs. Dawes drove him out there to bring back the Addams job, around nine o'clock, and figured Thompson was following him right on back into town, and Thompson doesn't show up with the car until after lunch. He had some story about his wife being sick and stopping by his house to see how she was."

Partchman said angrily, "So it gave him time to take it someplace and hammer that fender out, then come back here and sneak the headlamp and chrome ring out of stock and get some paint onto it."

"It was in for a tune-up," Finnigan said, looking at the service sheet on the job, "new muffler, lube and oil change. It got in so late we couldn't deliver it back out there until the next day. I remember apologizing to Mrs. Addams over the phone. I didn't tell her why it was late. She was pretty decent about it."

The mechanic said, "Tommy has been jumpy lately. He's been making mistakes."

"How do you want to handle it?" Partchman asked Walter Post.

"Bring him in here right now, and everybody stay here and keep quiet and let me do the talking," Post said wearily.

Thompson was brought in, small, pallid, worried. His restless eyes kept glancing quickly at Post. Post let the silence become long and heavy after Thompson asked what was wanted of him. At last he said, "How did you feel during those three days, while you were wondering whether she was going to die?"

Thompson stared at him and moistened his lips. He started twice to speak. The tears began to run down his smudged cheeks. "I felt terrible," he whispered. "I felt just plain terrible." And he ground his fists into his eyes like a guilty child.

Walter Post took him in and turned him over to the experts from the Homicide Section and accomplished his share of the paperwork. He was home by six o'clock. He told Carolyn about it that evening, when he was lethargic with emotional reaction to the case. He talked to her about trying to get into some other line of investigatory work and tried to explain his reasons to her.

But they woke him up at three in the morning and told him to go out to River Road. He got there before the lab truck. He squatted in a floodlighted ditch and looked at the broken old body of a bearded vagrant and at the smear of green automotive enamel ground into the fabric of a shabby coat. He straightened up slowly, bemused by his own ready acceptance of the fact it was not yet time to leave this work. Somebody was driving in a personal terror through the misty night, in a car so significantly damaged it would wear—for Walter Post—the signs and stains of a sudden murder.

THE BLACK CAT

EDGAR ALLAN POE

For the most wild, yet most homely narrative which I am about to pen, I neither expect nor solicit belief. Mad indeed would I be to expect it, in a case where my very senses reject their own evidence. Yet, mad am I not—and very surely do I not dream. But tomorrow I die, and today I would unburthen my soul. My immediate purpose is to place before the world, plainly, succinctly, and without comment, a series of mere household events. In their consequences, these events have terrified—have tortured—have destroyed me. Yet I will not attempt to expound them. To me, they have presented little but Horror—to many they will seem less terrible than *barroques*. Hereafter, perhaps, some intellect may be found which will reduce my phantasm to the commonplace—some intellect more calm, more logical, and far less excitable than my own, which will perceive, in the circumstances I detail with awe, nothing more than an ordinary succession of very natural causes and effects.

From my infancy I was noted for the docility and humanity of my disposition. My tenderness of heart was even so conspicuous as to make me the jest of my companions. I was especially fond of animals, and was indulged by my parents with a great variety of pets. With these I spent most of my time, and never was so happy as when feeding and caressing them. This peculiarity of character grew with my growth, and, in my manhood, I derived from it one of my principal sources of pleasure. To those who have cherished an affection for a faithful and sagacious dog, I need hardly be at the trouble of explaining the nature or the intensity of the gratification thus derivable. There is something in the unselfish and self-sacrificing love of a brute, which goes directly to the heart of him who has had frequent occasion to test the paltry friendship and gossamer fidelity of mere *Man*.

I married early, and was happy to find in my wife a disposition not uncongenial with my own. Observing my partiality for domestic pets, she lost no opportunity of procuring those of the most agreeable kind. We had birds, goldfish, a fine dog, rabbits, a small monkey and *a cat*.

This latter was a remarkably large and beautiful animal, entirely black, and sagacious to an astonishing degree. In speaking of her intelligence, my wife, who at heart was not a little tinctured with superstition, made frequent allusion to the ancient popular notion, which regarded all black cats as witches in disguise. Not that she was ever *serious* upon this point—and I mention the matter at all for no better reason than that it happens, just now, to be remembered.

Pluto—this was the cat's name—was my favorite pet and playmate. I alone fed him, and he attended me wherever I went about the house. It was even with difficulty that I could prevent him from following me through the streets.

Our friendship lasted, in this manner, for several years, during which my general temperament and character—through the instrumentality of the Fiend Intemperance—had (I blush to confess it) experienced a radical alteration for the worse. I grew, day by day, more moody, more irritable, more regardless of the feelings of others. I suffered myself to use intemperate language to my wife. At length, I even offered her personal violence. My pets, of course, were made to feel the change in my disposition. I not only neglected but ill-used them. For Pluto, however, I still retained sufficient regard to restrain me from maltreating him, as I made no scruple of maltreating the rabbits, the monkey, or even the dog, when by accident, or through affection, they came in my way. But my disease grew upon me—for what disease is like Alcohol?—and at length even Pluto, who was now becoming old, and consequently somewhat peevish—even Pluto began to experience the effects of my ill temper.

One night, returning home, much intoxicated, from one of my haunts about town, I fancied that the cat avoided my presence. I seized him; when, in his fright at my violence, he inflicted a slight wound upon my hand with his teeth. The fury of a demon instantly possessed me. I knew myself no longer. My original soul seemed, at once, to take its flight from my body; and a more than fiendish malevolence, gin-nurtured, thrilled every fibre of my frame. I took from my waistcoat pocket a penknife, opened it, grasped the poor beast by the throat, and deliberately cut one of the eyes from the socket! I blush, I burn, I shudder, while I pen the damnable atrocity.

When reason returned with the morning—when I had slept off the fumes of the night's debauch—I experienced a sentiment half of horror, half of remorse, for the crime of which I had been guilty; but it was, at best, a feeble and equivocal feeling, and the soul remained untouched. I again plunged into excess, and soon drowned in wine all memory of the deed.

In the meantime the cat slowly recovered. The socket of the lost eye presented, it is true, a frightful appearance, but he no longer appeared to suffer any pain. He went about the house as usual, but, as might be expected, fled in extreme terror at my approach. I had so much of my old heart left, as to be, at first, grieved by this evident dislike on the part of a creature which had once so loved me. But this feeling soon gave place to irritation. And then came, as if to my final and irrevocable overthrow, the spirit of *Perverseness*. Of this spirit philosophy takes no account. Phrenology finds no place for it among its organs. Yet I am not more sure that my soul lives, than I am that perverseness is one of the primitive impulses of the human heart—one of the indivisible primary faculties, or sentiments, which give direction to the character of Man. Who has not, a hundred times, found himself committing a vile or a silly action, for no other reason than because he knows he should *not*? Have we not a perpetual inclination, in the teeth of our best judgment, to violate that which is *Law*, merely because we understand it to be such? This spirit of perverseness, I say, came to my final overthrow. It was this unfathomable longing of the soul *to vex itself*—to offer violence to its own nature—to do wrong for the wrong's sake only—that urged me to continue and finally to consummate the injury I had inflicted upon the unoffending brute. One morning, in cool blood, I slipped a noose about its neck and hung it to the limb of a tree;—hung it with the tears streaming from my eyes, and with the bitterest remorse at my heart;—hung it *because* I knew that it had loved me, and *because* I felt it had given me no reason of offence;—hung it *because* I knew that in so doing I was committing a sin—a deadly sin that would so jeopardize my immortal soul as to place it—if such a thing were possible—even beyond the reach of the infinite mercy of the Most Merciful and Most Terrible God.

On the night of the day on which this cruel deed was done, I was aroused from sleep by the cry of fire. The curtains of my bed were in flames. The whole house was blazing. It was with great difficulty that my wife, a servant, and myself, made our escape from the conflagration. The destruction was complete. My entire worldly wealth was swallowed up, and I resigned myself thenceforward to despair.

I am above the weakness of seeking to establish a sequence of cause and effect, between the disaster and the atrocity. But I am detailing a chain of facts—and wish not to leave even a possible link imperfect. On the day succeeding the fire, I visited the ruins. The walls, with one exception, had fallen in. This exception was found in a compartment wall, not very thick, which stood about the middle of the house, and against which had rested the head of my bed. The plastering had here, in great measure, resisted the action of the fire—a fact which I attributed to its having been recently spread. About this wall a dense crowd were collected, and many persons seemed to be examining a particular portion of it with very minute and eager attention. The words "strange!" "singular!" and other similar expressions, excited my curiosity. I approached and saw, as if graven in *bas relief* upon the white surface, the figure of a gigantic *cat*. The impression was given with an accuracy truly marvelous. There had been a rope about the animal's neck.

When I first beheld this apparition—for I could scarcely regard it as less—my wonder and my terror were extreme. But at length reflection came to my aid. The cat, I remembered, had been hung in a garden adjacent to the house. Upon the alarm of fire, this garden had been immediately filled by the crowd—by some one of whom the animal must have been cut from the tree and thrown, through an open window, into my chamber. This had probably been done with the view of arousing me from sleep. The falling of other walls had compressed the victim of my cruelty into the substance of the freshly spread plaster; the lime of which, with the flames, and the *ammonia* from the carcass, had then accomplished the portraiture as I saw it.

Although I thus readily accounted to my reason, if not altogether to my conscience, for the startling fact just detailed, it did not the less fail to make a deep impression upon my fancy. For months I could not rid myself of the phantasm of the cat; and, during this period, there came back into my spirit a half-sentiment that seemed, but was not, remorse. I went so far as to regret the loss of the animal, and to look about me, among the vile haunts which I now habitually frequented, for another pet of the same species, and of somewhat similar appearance, with which to supply its place.

One night as I sat, half stupefied, in a den of more than infamy, my attention was suddenly drawn to some black object, reposing upon the head of one of the immense hogsheads of Gin, or of Rum, which constituted the chief furniture of the apartment. I had been looking steadily at the top of this hogshead for some minutes, and what now caused me surprise was the fact that I had not sooner perceived the object thereupon. I approached it, and touched it with my hand. It was a black cat—a very large one—fully as large as Pluto, and closely resembling him in every respect but one. Pluto had not a white hair upon any portion of his body; but this cat had a large, although indefinite splotch of white, covering nearly the whole region of the breast.

Upon my touching him, he immediately arose, purred loudly, rubbed against my hand, and appeared delighted with my notice. This, then, was the very creature of which I was in search. I at once offered to purchase it of the landlord; but this person made no claim to it—knew nothing of it—had never seen it before.

I continued my caresses, and, when I prepared to go home, the animal evinced a disposition to accompany me. I permitted it to do so, occasionally stooping and patting it as I proceeded. When it reached the house it domesticated itself at once, and became immediately a great favorite with my wife.

For my own part, I soon found a dislike to it arising within me. This was just the reverse of what I had anticipated; but—I know not how or why it was—its evident fondness for myself rather disgusted and annoyed. By slow degrees, these feelings of disgust and annoyance rose into the bitterness of hatred. I avoided the creature; a certain sense of shame, and the remembrance of my former deed of cruelty, preventing me from physically abusing it. I did not, for some weeks, strike, or otherwise violently ill use it; but gradually—very gradually—I came to look upon it with unutterable loathing, and to flee silently from its odious presence, as from the breath of pestilence.

What added, no doubt, to my hatred of the beast, was the discovery, on the morning after I brought it home, that, like Pluto, it also had been deprived of one of its eyes. This circumstance, however, only endeared it to my wife, who, as I have already said, possessed, in a high degree, that humanity of feeling which had once been my distinguishing trait, and the source of many of my simplest and purest pleasures.

With my aversion to this cat, however, its partiality for myself seemed to increase. It followed my footsteps with a pertinacity which it would be difficult to make the reader comprehend. Whenever I sat, it would crouch beneath my chair, or spring upon my knees, covering me with its loathsome caresses. If I arose to walk, it would get between my feet and thus nearly throw me down, or, fastening its long and sharp claws in my dress, clamber, in this manner, to my breast. At such times, although I longed to destroy it with a blow, I was yet withheld from so doing, partly by a memory of my former crime, but chiefly—let me confess it at once—by absolute *dread* of the beast.

This dread was not exactly a dread of physical evil—and yet I should be at a loss how otherwise to define it. I am almost ashamed to own—yes, even in this felon's cell, I am almost ashamed to own—that the terror and horror with which the animal inspired me had been heightened by one of the merest chimeras it would be possible to conceive. My wife had called my attention, more than once, to the character of the mark of white hair, of which I have spoken, and which constituted the sole visible difference between the strange beast and the one I had destroyed. The reader will remember that this mark, although large, had been originally very indefinite; but, by slow degrees—degrees nearly imperceptible, and which for a long time my Reason struggled to reject as fanciful—it had, at length, assumed a rigorous distinctness of outline. It was now the representation of an object that I shudder to name—and for this, above all, I loathed, and dreaded, and would have rid myself of the monster *had I dared*—it was now, I say, the image of a hideous—of a ghastly thing—of the *Gallows!*—oh, mournful and terrible engine of Horror and of Crime—of Agony and of Death!

And now was I indeed wretched beyond the wretchedness of mere Humanity. And *a brute beast*—whose fellow I had contemptuously destroyed—*a brute beast* to work out for *me*—for me a man, fashioned in the image of the High God—so much of insufferable woe! Alas! Neither by day nor by night knew I the blessing of Rest anymore! During the former the creature left me no moment alone; and, in the latter, I started, hourly, from dreams of unutterable fear, to find the hot breath of *the thing* upon my face, and its vast weight—an incarnate Nightmare that I had no power to shake off—incumbent eternally upon my *heart*!

Beneath the pressure of torments such as these, the feeble remnant of the good within me succumbed. Evil thoughts became my sole intimates—the darkest and most evil of thoughts. The moodiness of my usual temper increased to hatred of all things and of all mankind; while, from the sudden, frequent, and ungovernable outbursts of a fury to which I now blindly abandoned myself, my uncomplaining wife, alas! was the most usual and the most patient of sufferers.

One day she accompanied me, upon some household errand, into the cellar of the old building which our poverty compelled us to inhabit. The cat followed me down the steep stairs, and, nearly throwing me headlong, exasperated me to madness. Uplifting an axe, and forgetting, in my wrath, the childish dread which had hitherto stayed my hand, I aimed a blow at the animal which, of course, would have proved instantly fatal had it descended as I wished. But this blow was arrested by the hand of my wife. Goaded, by the interference, into a rage more than demoniacal, I withdrew my arm from her grasp and buried the axe in her brain. She fell dead upon the spot, without a groan.

This hideous murder accomplished, I set myself forthwith, and with entire deliberation, to the task of concealing the body. I knew that I could not remove it from the house, either by day or by night, without the risk of being observed by the neighbors. Many projects entered my mind. At one period I thought of cutting the corpse into minute fragments, and destroying them by fire. At another, I resolved to dig a grave for it in the floor of the cellar. Again, I deliberated about casting it in the well in the yard—about packing it in a box, as if merchandise, with the usual arrangements, and so getting a porter to take it from the house. Finally, I hit upon what I considered a far better expedient than either of these. I determined to wall it up in the cellar—as the monks of the middle ages are recorded to have walled up their victims.

For a purpose such as this the cellar was admirably adapted. Its walls were loosely constructed, and had lately been plastered throughout with a rough plaster, which the dampness of the atmosphere had prevented from hardening. Moreover, in one of the walls was a projection, caused by a false chimney, or fireplace, that had been filled, or walled up, and made to resemble the rest of the cellar. I made no doubt that I could readily displace the bricks at this point, insert the corpse, and wall the whole up as before, so that no eye could detect anything suspicious.

And in this calculation I was not deceived. By means of a crowbar I easily dislodged the bricks, and, having carefully deposited the body against the inner wall, I propped it in that position, while, with little trouble, I relaid the whole structure as it originally stood. Having procured mortar, sand, and hair, with every possible precaution, I prepared a plaster which could not be distinguished from the old, and with this I very carefully went over the new brickwork. When I had finished, I felt satisfied that all was right. The wall did not present the slightest appearance of having been disturbed. The rubbish on the floor was picked up with the minutest care. I looked around triumphantly, and said to myself—"Here at least, then, my labor has not been in vain."

My next step was to look for the beast which had been the cause of so much wretchedness; for I had, at length, firmly resolved to put it to death. Had I been able to meet with it, at the moment, there could have been no doubt of its fate; but it appeared that the crafty animal had been alarmed at the violence of my previous anger, and forebore to present itself in my present mood. It is impossible to describe, or to imagine, the deep, the blissful sense of relief which the absence of the detested creature occasioned in my bosom. It did not make its appearance during the night—and thus for one night at least, since its introduction into the house, I soundly and tranquilly slept; aye, *slept* even with the burden of murder upon my soul!

The second and the third day passed and still my tormentor came not. Once again I breathed as a freeman. The monster, in terror, had fled the premises forever! I should behold it no more! My happiness was supreme! The guilt of my dark deed disturbed me but little. Some few inquiries had been made, but these had been readily answered. Even a search had been instituted—but of course nothing was to be discovered. I looked upon my future felicity as secured.

Upon the fourth day of the assassination, a party of the police came, very unexpectedly, into the house, and proceeded again to make rigorous investigation of the premises. Secure, however, in the inscrutability of my place of concealment, I felt no embarrassment whatever. The officers bade me accompany them in their search. They left no nook or corner unexplored. At length, for the third or fourth time, they descended into the cellar. I quivered not in a muscle. My heart beat calmly as that of one who slumbers in innocence. I walked the cellar from end to end. I folded my arms upon my bosom and roamed easily to and fro. The police were thoroughly satisfied and prepared to depart. The glee at my heart was too strong to be restrained. I burned to say if but one word, by way of triumph, and to render doubly sure their assurance of my guiltlessness.

"Gentlemen," I said at last, as the party ascended the steps, "I delight to have allayed your suspicions. I wish you all health, and a little more courtesy. By the bye, gentlemen, this—this is a very well constructed house." [In the rabid desire to say something easily, I scarcely knew what I uttered at all.]—"I may say an *excellently* well constructed house. These walls—are you going, gentlemen?—these walls are solidly put together"; and here, through the mere frenzy of bravado, I rapped heavily, with a cane which I held in my hand, upon that very portion of the brickwork behind which stood the ghastly corpse of the wife of my bosom.

But may God shield and deliver me from the fangs of the Arch

THE BLACK CAT

Fiend! No sooner had the reverberation of my blows sunk into silence, than I was answered by a voice from within the tomb!—by a cry, at first muffled and broken, like the sobbing of a child, and then quickly swelling into one long, loud, and continuous scream, utterly anomalous and inhuman—a howl—a wailing shriek, half of horror and half of triumph, such as might have arisen only out of hell, conjointly from the throats of the damned in their agony and of the demons that exult in the damnation!

Of my own thoughts it is folly to speak. Swooning, I staggered to the opposite wall. For one instant the party upon the stairs remained motionless, through extremity of terror and of awe. In the next, a dozen stout arms were toiling at the wall. It fell bodily. The corpse, already greatly decayed and clotted with gore, stood erect before the eyes of the spectators. Upon its head, with red extended mouth and solitary eye of fire, sat the hideous beast whose craft had seduced me into murder, and whose informing voice had consigned me to the hangman. I had walled the monster up within the tomb!

THE MURDERER

JOEL TOWNSLEY ROGERS

John Bantreagh backed away from her a step on caving knees, with his gaze still on her. She looked so helpless, and somehow innocent, lying here on the meadow grass in the gray, still dawn, in front of his farm-truck wheels. In her white dress with its big red polka dots and red patent-leather belt, and her white shoes with their red heels. With her red mouth and light-brown curly hair, and her hazel eyes open.

Looking at him, it seemed like, out of dream-filled sleep, a little blankly. As she did sometimes in the early mornings, while he dressed quietly to go out and do the chores, with eyes wide open, though not yet all awake. But, of course, she wasn't. There was an opaqueness on her lenses, there was a cold dew on her face, and she was dead.

One wheel had gone over her throat and the other over her sheer-clad ankles. Her legs had hardly been hurt at all, he thought; the ground was soft, and they had just been pressed down into the mire and grass roots. Only her throat had been broken—the trachea, the larynx and pharynx, or whatever else there was in people's throats that made them live and breathe. That made them talk too. Her eyes were on him, with that look they had. But she would never say who had done it.

John Bantreagh felt as if his own throat had been crushed, as he tried to pull his gaze away, with his knees caving. As if a heavy wheel had rolled onto it, and—not like with her—had not backed away. He looked around him slowly with his reddened gaze. He had a feeling that other eyes were watching him, if not hers. But it was a lonely meadow, on a lonely road. Just dark pine woods around, and the dirt road two or three hundred yards away, beyond the tumble-down snake fence that bordered it.

His truck motor had died. He must start it and back down across the meadow to the road again. Get on back home before anyone was stirring. Let her be found by someone else. It would be hours, way off here—it might be even days. That would be too much to endure, knowing she was here. This evening, if no one had found her before then, he might suggest, just offhandedly, looking along here, as if it were something that had occurred to him without any reason. There was just so much a man could stand.

The air had lightened from dark silver to pearl. It was not full light yet, but it was no longer night. He had never known a moment so quiet and still. Across the meadow grass he could see the tracks of his truck coming in at a diagonal from the road, through the break in the fence, where the weeds were crushed down that grew in the shallow roadside ditch and along the field side of the fence. Two parallel lines, with only moderate waves in them, coming directly to where his truck stood now with its front tires almost touching her. Smooth-worn front tires, but cleated rear tires, which had left their tracks of broad, deep, transverse ridges. They were a pair he had ordered from the mail-order catalogue, and had cost a lot of money. He had got them from the freight office only yesterday morning, along with the things for Mollie and the kids, and the rest of the order; and had put them on when he got back home, with her and the kids watching him.

Just yesterday forenoon. Mollie had been rinsing out some things on the back-porch bench beside the pump, with her wrist buried in the washbasin, and soapy water splashing on the ground off the porch edge. She had paused to brush back her tendrils of damp hair with the inside of her elbow, squeezing out a handful of sand-colored fabric.

"You're proud of those tires, aren't you, John?"

"Sure am!" he told her as he knelt on the gravel unwrapping one of them. "I'll bet nobody else has anything like them in the whole county. Eight-ply, tractor tread, guaranteed for fifty thousand miles. Could have got a good-enough tire for six-fifty less apiece, maybe. But it's smart to get something that lasts, as I can see it."

"I reckon you're pretty smart, John."

"Sure am, honey. I got you."

"How long do you figure I'm guaranteed for?"

"Till death do us part," he had replied, grinning.

She had laid the sand-colored fabric down on the bench and had squeezed out a handful of something black—her dark blue blouse, it must be, that looked black because it was wet. She didn't have any black things. She didn't seem altogether pleased. The tires had cost a lot of money. Maybe she was thinking of the nice things it could have bought.

"What are you washing out, honey?" he had asked her.

"Just my rayon stockings and some old things."

"Maybe someday you'll have a pair of nylons, so you won't have to take such care of those rayons. I saw Lilybelle wearing a pair the other day. I wouldn't know, but she said they were. I guess every woman likes them."

"Does Lilybelle have nylon underwear too?"

She liked to tease him at times about Lilybelle. It was just a joke. She wasn't really jealous of Lilybelle. She hadn't any reason to be that he knew of.

"She didn't say, honey," he told her.

She had said something else then, brushing back her hair again, but he hadn't heard, having begun to pry one of the old bare-tread shoes off a rim with a mallet and tire iron. The kids had been jumping around and yelling, and she might have been reprimanding them. Vaguely, in the back of his mind, he wondered who would take care of the kids now. It was the first time he had thought of it.

His knees caved and caved. He had heard of men's knees doing that, but it didn't seem natural. He couldn't control them, though. He stiffened them, and they jerked down again as if they were only water. He planted a hand on the mudguard of his truck, taking a dragging step back toward the seat. He must start his engine and back down to the road again and go on home. Now.

There was no sound of distant barnyard roosters. It must be a good mile at least, maybe two or five, to the nearest house. If there was any wildlife in the woods around the meadow—fox, bobcat or possum—it was keeping very still.

A car was coming along the road already, though. A sedan with some early driver at the wheel. It slowed its bumping progress as it approached the break in the fence. It came to a momentary halt. The driver had seen his truck and him in the meadow, John Bantreagh thought, standing motionless. Maybe he could see the white of her dress in front of his wheels, though the truck might hide that from the road.

The car turned and came in, anyway. It drove slowly along the broad, deep, cleated tracks of his truck, approaching. That it should take the same course was perhaps inevitable, or at least expectable. Every field, however smooth, has its own hidden soft spots, waves and hummocks, and one car will tend to follow the same path across it as another, unless deliberately held to a different course. Particularly when a previous car has already made ruts at the grass roots. The driver of the approaching sedan probably didn't realize that he was flattening out those cleated and distinctive treads beneath the impress of whatever nondescript tire treads he might have himself. Perhaps he didn't notice them. Or if he did, he considered their preservation of no importance.

It wasn't important, of course, thought John Bantreagh. His truck was here, and he was here. He rested the palm of his left hand on the mudguard. His eyes burned red and sleepless. His throat was dry. His right hand hung down at his side with something in it. His truck crank, he realized. He didn't know how long he had had it in his hand. He had been quite unaware of it. He hadn't the strength now to place it back on the truck floor where he usually kept it. Not even to open his hand and let it drop into the grass.

The driver of the sedan stopped with his bumper nudging the back of the truck. He opened the door and got out. He was a big young fellow with a bronzed, square-jawed face and alert and steady gray eyes. He wore a black tropical suit, unbuttoned on an expanse of soft white shirt, black-necktied, and a black slouch hat. He overtopped John Bantreagh by four inches. His lithe, light-stepping frame had the massed weight of two hundred pounds. He was a dozen years younger than John Bantreagh—perhaps he was twenty-five. He looked fresh and well slept and newly bathed, competent and cool.

He pushed back his hat on his crisp black curls. He wore a nickeled badge, pinned to a red suspender strap over his white shirt. There was a polished walnut gun butt extruding from a black holster on his right hip, and a pair of handcuffs hanging beside it from his belt.

He gave a brief, alert glance at John Bantreagh's stained, red-eyed face and thin, shaking form. He stood looking down at the woman's body lying supine in front of the truck wheels, with his fists planted on his hips and his pectoral muscles expanded.

"What happened?" he said. "Run over?"

John Bantreagh swallowed. "Yes."

"It looks pretty much like it was deliberate," the big young fellow said quietly.

He squatted beside her, looking, not touching. With steady, alert eyes. With his alert and sleep-refreshed brain behind them.

"Name's Clade," he said. "Roy Clade, deputy, from over in Boomerburg. I was due at the courthouse this morning on a car-stealing case, and just happened to take the back road, first time in a year. Never thought I'd run into anything like this."

"No," John Bantreagh swallowed. "I reckon nobody would."

"Yep, she was murdered," the young deputy said quietly. "No two ways about it. Blood on the back of her head, matted with her hair. She was hit with a tire iron or something, and then laid on the ground when she was out cold, and the front wheels run up onto her. Know who she is?"

"Yes," John Bantreagh swallowed. "Her name's—her name was Mollie Bantreagh—Mrs. John Bantreagh—from over outside of Jeffersonville. Funny name, sounds like 'pantry,' " he said tonelessly—as he always did, to forestall banal remarks about it. "I don't know where it came from. Some say it's an aristocratic name in Scotland, but I don't know. She's—she was my wife."

"Your wife!" The young deputy shot up a quick, keen look at him. "You mean you were her husband?"

"Yes," John Bantreagh said. "That's right." He could not stop the wobbling of his knees. The dryness stuck in his throat. He rubbed his Adam's apple with his left hand to relieve the pressure on it.

"Tough!" said the young deputy, in a voice of proper sympathetic pitch. "Your wife! Gee! I thought you were just some stranger driving by. I'm not a married man myself. But your wife—she must have meant an awful lot to you. I'll bet this has hit you terribly."

"Yes," said John Bantreagh, feeling his throat. "We had our little disagreements at times, like everybody. I reckon the neighbors know. She always liked nice things a lot."

"All married people have their little battles, I expect," said the young deputy awkwardly. "It'd be kind of funny if they didn't. Gee, your wife, though! Kids, I suppose, too?"

"Three," said John Bantreagh. "Three, two boys and a girl."

"And no one to look after them now, I reckon. Tough!" the young deputy said again, with an effort at feeling. "It sure is an awful break for you, Mr. Bantreagh. Who could have done a thing like this, anyway?"

"I——" said John Bantreagh, swallowing, "I thought maybe I could get Lilybelle to look after them for a spell. She's not very fond of kids, I don't think, but she might do it for me."

"Who's Lilybelle?"

"Lilybelle Turner, lives next place down the road," said John Bantreagh, rubbing his throat. "She's only a kid herself, just nineteen, and not seeming hardly that old, with her dark curls and blue eyes. All she can think of is having a good time and loving. Mollie—

THE MURDERER

Mollie used to pretend to be kind of jealous of her, just joking. But she's a woman, anyway, and I reckon I can get her to pitch in and help with the kids, if the neighbors don't talk."

"There's always another woman, isn't there?" remarked the young deputy absently. "I mean there's always one to pitch in and help with the kids, I reckon, unless a man lives at the North Pole, when his wife goes."

But he hadn't been paying much attention to the problem, his manner indicated. He had pulled out a silver pencil and a brownish paper-bound notebook from his inner jacket pocket. He opened the notebook on his knee and unscrewed the pencil. John Bantreagh watched with dull, bloodshot eyes what he was writing.

"Mollie Bantreagh, Mrs. John Bantreagh, res. nr. Jeff'ville. Struck on back of head by tire iron or other instr'm'nt & run onto by car's front wheels. Body found by husband——"

He looked up with sharp alertness at John Bantreagh, with his pencil halted. John Bantreagh swayed. He leaned back against his truck with his crank hanging from his hand. It was coming now—the question.

"What time did you find her, Mr. Bantreagh?"

John Bantreagh let his breath seep out. He stiffened his knees. It was bound to come. But this wasn't it yet.

"I haven't got a watch," he said tonelessly. "It was just getting kind of silver light. Maybe ten minutes ago. Maybe half an hour or three quarters—I don't know. It kind of knocked me out."

"I'll put it as four forty-five," said the young deputy sympathetically. "The exact time, I reckon, doesn't make any particular difference.

" 'Found by husband at four forty-five,' " he recited as he wrote. " 'Joined by Deputy Clade at five-oh-three and scene observed. No footprints. No tire tread discernible on body; smudge on nylon stockings indication possible print had been wiped off by hand. Possible tire tracks on field obliterated by husband's car and Deputy Clade's. Implement with which struck removed by killer. No other objects apparent on scene to indicate identity.' I guess that's the story, Mr. Bantreagh."

He put away his book and pencil. He pushed his hat off the back of his head and set it on levelly again, with his frowning gaze a moment on her staring eyes.

John Bantreagh swallowed. "They're nylons?" he said.

"What? Her stockings? Oh, sure. All the women've got to have them. What did you think they were?"

"I thought they were rayons," said John Bantreagh. "The pair I got for her last Christmas. I thought they were just rayons all the time. But then tonight I figured they were nylons."

"Oh, sure," the young deputy repeated mechanically. "All the women've got to have them."

He pushed his hat on the back of his head again and stood up, taking his eye from her.

"Who could have done it?" he repeated quietly, with his fists planted on his hips, looking down at John Bantreagh's pallid face and bloodshot eyes with his keen, alert gaze, with his fresh, keen brain behind it. "Who do you suppose could have done it, Mr. Bantreagh? I mean," he explained with frowning brow, "she couldn't have been murdered for her jewels and money, because I don't reckon she had any—more than just her wedding ring that she's still got on, and maybe a couple of nickels in her coin purse or something like that. It couldn't have been just a maniac, because how could he have got her out to a lonely place like this to murder her, without her putting up some sort of a fight and screaming?

"It was some man she knew, who wanted to get rid of her. Because he was crazy about some beautiful little kid who was a few years younger than she was, maybe; and she knew about it, and was always nagging him, and stood in his way. And so he got her to ride out here with him, and he cracked her on the head with this tire iron or something that he had laid on the seat beside him handy, probably while he was making love to her, and then hauled her out and laid her down in front of his car, and ran his wheels up on her and crushed the life out of her. Figuring to drop her body in the ditch beside the road back near where she lived, like she had been struck by a hit-and-run while walking home.

"Only, after he had done it," the young deputy said, frowning at John Bantreagh, "he could see it wouldn't pass. The way her throat had been crushed would be only like she had been lying unconscious on the ground when she had been run over, just the way it had been done. There would be meadow mud and grass stains, maybe, on her dress. And maybe ten or a hundred other things that he couldn't think of at the moment, but that wouldn't let it pass. So it was murder," he said quietly, "and nothing else. And there was nothing for him to do but just leave her here, and go on home and go to sleep, like nothing had happened, waiting till somebody else happened to find her. Figuring that it wouldn't be for some hours yet, at least. And maybe days, because it was such a lonely road. Though hoping, too, that it wouldn't be too long.

"And so, as I figure it, Mr. Bantreagh, he got up quietly from where he was kneeling beside her, when he was sure that she was dead, and backed away from her, to get into his car again, that he had rolled back off her, and back it down across the meadow to the road again. Figuring that, if he had left any tire tracks, a few hours more might dim them out. Or that maybe somebody else had tires like his, or that maybe when somebody else would come along, they would roll over them with their own tracks before they had noticed them."

The young deputy pushed his hat off the back of his head and set it on again.

"Now, there's just one thing that I've got to ask you, Mr. Bantreagh."

A faint dawn breath across the dewed meadow stirred a drape of his crisp, freshly pressed black jacket as he stood looking down at John Bantreagh. It stirred the ends of the black knit four-in-hand upon his expanse of white shirt above his flat, quiet-breathing diaphragm. The skin upon his hard, young, fresh-shaven face was shiny and tight, and a little muscle rippled at the corner of his mouth, though John Bantreagh's eyes did not lift that high.

His knees—John Bantreagh's—caved, and he stiffened them. He leaned back against the windshield post of his truck, thrusting his heels against the ground. His bloodshot eyes swam, out of focus. He fingered his throat with his left hand, glancing involuntarily down. There was a deep scratch or cut across the back of his right hand, he saw, that was gripped about the crank handle. He didn't remember when he had got it, but it was still oozing. Some of the blood must have seeped stickily around onto his clenched palm, helping to glue it to the iron.

Now! he thought. What form the question would take, he didn't know. But it must come. The throat muscles of the big young deputy were still moving beneath his broad, smooth-shaven chin. He had paused only for a moment.

"Just one question, Mr. Bantreagh," he repeated. "It may seem kind of cold and brutal of me to ask it, at a time like this," he added, a little awkwardly. "But if I didn't, someone else would, anyway. And they still will, I reckon, and keep on asking it until they've found out whatever there is to know. You understand, a law officer's got his job to do, and it's just impersonal. What I mean is, Mr. Bantreagh, was there anybody that she had been going around with that you ever heard about? A boyfriend that she had, I mean—someone that she had been two-timing you with? Of course," he added, "she might have been stepping out and you not have known anything about it. That happens too. But there must have been someone, just on the face of it, because he would have been the only man in the world who would have had any cause to have done it, as sure as hell. Did she ever drop any hint to you about him, Mr. Bantreagh, as to who he was? I don't mean to seem cold and brutal."

John Bantreagh swallowed. "I know you've got to ask your questions," he said, pulling at the loose skin of his throat. "That's all right. Yes, I reckon there was"—he swallowed—"someone. She used to go down to the village two or three times a week after supper; it's only a couple of miles away. She'd tell me she was going to the free library to read magazines and books. She was always a great hand for reading. I couldn't drive her in the truck, because somebody had to stay home with the kids. I'd be asleep by the time she got home. But it seems she didn't really go to the free library at all. This fellow would pick her up on the road, and they'd go riding in his car. I only learned about it last night."

He swallowed again. He rubbed his forehead with his left hand. There was some small thing he was trying to remember. But there was much more that he wanted to forget.

"I woke up," he said tonelessly, "with one of the kids crying. He was cold, and wanted a blanket on him. Mollie always looked to their covers when she came home or got up in the night herself. But she hadn't got home yet. By the looks of the moonlight out on the yard, it looked kind of late. I held the alarm clock to the window, and it was one o'clock. I lit the lamp and put on my pants and shoes, and went out to the road in front and looked down it, but didn't see her coming. There was something white on the front porch of the Turner house a quarter mile down, but that was all.

"So I went back in and covered the kids up better, tucking them in. They sure looked cute in their new pajamas, and I wished she was there to see them. I'd got pajamas for them with my tire order that had come in the morning, pink and white stripes for the boys, and the baby's blue with white ducks on them. She hadn't seen them in them yet; she'd gone out right after supper, before I'd got them to bed. That made me think"—John Bantreagh swallowed—"of the nylons. Her birthday was tomorrow—today. Twenty-nine. And I had ordered her a pair of nylons. I figured she would like them. She had never had any.

"I had left them out in the truck in back, under the seat, to get and give her in the morning. But I thought it might be kind of nice to put them in her bottom drawer for her, where she kept her things, and kind of say something to her in the morning, joking like, that I had heard a mouse in her drawer last night, maybe it was making a nest. And she would hurry to open it and pull out all her things, and would find them at the bottom, and it would surprise her.

THE MURDERER

"So I brought them in in their envelope," said John Bantreagh tonelessly, "and opened her drawer and took out some of her things on top, the balls of socks that she generally wears, and her blouses and skirts that she had made, and a couple of starched house dresses. She kept her rayons in the drawer, I knew. But she was wearing them, I thought. I didn't know she had any other stockings." He swallowed. "But there were lots of stockings there, hid away at the bottom. A dozen pairs of them. They were the same color as her rayons, but they were smooth and slick. They had the feel of the nylons I had bought her now. And there were underthings—pink things, silk and nylon things, things with lace on them. There was even a set of black lace, step-ins and bras. They were what she had been wringing out, or others like them, when I'd been putting on my new tires that forenoon, in a little squeezed-up handful before my eyes. I don't know what there is about black lace things. They're not what a woman gets for herself. They make it seem more awful, somehow.

"I was kind of upwrought." John Bantreagh swallowed. "There was a pint out in the kitchen cupboard that her sister's husband had given me last summer when they visited, only I'm not much of a drinking man. But I got it down and took some now. I thought I'd better go and find her. I put on a shirt and coat, and put the matches up on the kitchen shelf where the kids couldn't reach them, and put out the lamp. I went out to crank the truck. I had just picked up the crank, when I looked around, and thought I saw her on the back porch behind me, among the moonlight and the vines. Only it wasn't her. It wasn't anything. It was just the moonlight moving."

John Bantreagh pulled at his throat. "I cranked the truck then," he went on, swallowing, "and got in it, and went down the road toward the village. On the Turner porch steps, just off the road, there was something white sitting. It was Lilybelle, sitting in the moonlight in her nightdress with her arms about her knees. 'Hello, Mr. Bantreagh!' she called out to me, kind of low. 'Where are you going at this time of night? What's happened to Mrs. Bantreagh?'

"I stopped." John Bantreagh swallowed. "I didn't want any gossip started. 'What do you mean, what's happened to her?' I said.

" 'I woke up and came out on the steps a little while ago,' she said. 'The moonlight was so pretty. And I looked up the road, and thought I saw somebody going into your house, like she had just got home.'

" 'No,' I told her. 'It must have been me. Mollie's been home since ten o'clock.' Not wanting to start any gossip.

" 'I love the moonlight,' Lilybelle said. 'It's so quiet and so mysterious. I saw a lamp lit in your house, and then put out again. I heard your back screen door slam, and thought I heard you say something like, "What have you been doing, Mollie?" kind of sharp and mad. Then I could hear you cranking your car. I wondered if maybe she wasn't feeling well, and you were going for the doctor.'

" 'No,' I told her. 'I guess for a minute I thought maybe she had come out on the back porch behind me. But it wasn't her. It was just the vines moving in the moonlight. I just thought I'd take a ride to set my new tires right.'

"Then"—John Bantreagh swallowed—"I don't know why, but she looked so kind of pretty, with her dark curls and her big eyes, and the moonlight silver on her nightdress and her bare feet, and I had the nylons on the seat beside me, that I'd brought back out to the truck again without knowing it; and I said to her, 'Would you like a pair of nylons, Lilybelle?' And she got up and came out to the truck, and stood up on the running board beside me and opened them.

" 'My!' she said. 'You sure know your way around, Mr. Bantreagh! What is it a bribe for? Have you murdered Mrs. Bantreagh, and you want me to keep it quiet?' "

John Bantreagh swallowed.

"Laughing," he said. "Just joking. She didn't have an idea that she was dead, of course. And she looked in the back of my truck, where I've got those old burlaps, and she said to me, 'Why, you did! You have! And you've got her body in there now, Mr. Bantreagh!'

" 'That's right,' I told her. 'No sense in trying to fool you. I hit her over the head with my truck crank because she'd been nagging me about you, Lilybelle. Now the deck's all clear for you and me. What'll it be—Niagara Falls?'

"Wanting to just take it along in stride with her." John Bantreagh swallowed. "Just joking, like a fellow does with a girl when she's pretty."

The young deputy, competent and cool, looked at him with alert and steady eyes, as gray as the dawn.

"For Pete's sake," he said, "is that all, Mr. Bantreagh? I thought you might know something about this fellow she had been stepping out with. But you don't even know for sure that there was anybody. She might have bought her stockings and lingerie stuff herself, with some grocery money that she had held out on you. Here she is dead. Somebody killed her. But all you can tell about is how you covered up your kids, and the new pajamas they were wearing, and thinking for a minute you saw her on the back porch when you were starting to crank your truck, only it was just the vine leaves and moonlight, and then some kidding conversation you had with this Lilybelle babe back and forth, to keep her from starting any gossip. But how is that telling anything about who killed her?" He shook his head with an exhalation of his flat diaphragm. "If it wasn't that it's murder, I could almost laugh," he said. "Maybe she didn't have any boyfriend. Maybe nobody killed her."

"Oh, yes, she did," said John Bantreagh tonelessly. "Oh, yes, he killed her. I drove on into the village after leaving Lilybelle. Everything was all dark and shut up, except the free library. I went in there, and the counterman was behind the counter, and a truck driver or somebody eating a piece of pie. I asked what time the free library had closed tonight. And the counterman said it had closed at five o'clock; it wasn't ever open at night.

"I said to him," he said tiredly, "had he seen a lady in a white dress with big red polka dots on it, and white shoes with her heels, with light brown wavy hair and hazel eyes, and plucked eyebrows and a red mouth, about twenty-nine? And he said there was a lady like that who sometimes came in between eleven and midnight and got sandwiches or things like that, and took them out to her boyfriend in their car, but she hadn't been in tonight. It was almost two o'clock now, he said, and so she probably wouldn't be in now.

"Then"—John Bantreagh swallowed—"the truck driver spoke up, and asked me if she lived up on Jaybird Road, and if she hung around the Swamp Run culvert bridge in the evenings, about half a mile out of town. I said yes, I reckoned she lived somewhere up that way. He said that he had seen her half a dozen times when he was going along Jaybird Road, sitting on the abutment of the culvert bridge in the evenings, like she was waiting for someone. And he had given her his horn and the high sign, only he was generally in a hurry, and there were babes like her along every road, and he could have all of them he wanted. But one time last month, he said, he had come coasting toward the culvert bridge with his engine off—there's a grade down before it, and he was a little low on gas—and he saw her sitting there, not knowing anyone was near. She was stretching out her nylon legs and tightening up her garters to some black lace things she had on. And she had looked up just as his truck rolled to her, and had smiled at him.

"It had driven him kind of wild," said John Bantreagh tiredly. "He had stopped his truck and jumped out to grab her. Just then he had looked around, and there was a car that was stopping at the side of the road, just off the culvert bridge, about twenty feet away in the shadows under the trees. There was some man in it, looking at him. He had let go of her and had jumped back into his truck again and driven off.

" 'What are you looking for her for?' he said to me. 'Are you trying to make her yourself? Brother, if I was you, I wouldn't! I'm big and plenty tough myself, and I'm not scared of anything. But there was something about that guy. . . . Your wife?' he said—I guess I must have said something—'If she was my wife, with those black lace things and that smile she had, I'd kill her!'

"So I knew." John Bantreagh swallowed. "But I had known when I found those nylons and things. I reckon I had kind of known all along, if I had thought about it. I drove around looking for her," he said tonelessly. "Along every road I came to. It was just breaking dawn when I came along the back road here. I saw something white off in the meadow, and I drove in through the break in the fence and found her. It kind of knocked me out."

The breath of dawn air across the silvered grass stirred the ends of the young deputy's black knit tie upon his expanse of snow-white shirt. He stood motionless with fists on hips. There was nothing else stirring about his hard, towering figure or about the world. Only John Bantreagh's knees, which caved and caved.

No, his knees weren't caving anymore. It was just a lingering of ceased sensation, that they still were.

"Who was he?" the calm, alert voice of Deputy Roy Clade came to him. "I guess this counterman and this truck driver wouldn't know. But what did he look like? Did they say?"

"They didn't get a look at him," said John Bantreagh tiredly. "When she had come into the Waldorf, he had always stayed in his car across the street, with his lights out in the blackness under the trees around the square. The truck-driving fellow didn't see what he looked like either. He just got scared and jumped in his truck and drove away."

"Cagey," commented Roy Clade. "He was taking care that nobody saw him with her, if he ever had to get rid of her like he did. Maybe he knew from his experience that these married ones are hard to ditch. What kind of a car did he have, did they say?"

"They didn't know the make," said John Bantreagh tiredly. "It was just a black sedan."

"Nine cars out of ten——" said Roy Clade, "nine out of ten are black sedans. I've got one myself. There's nothing in that, unless they got his license number. And they wouldn't have, if he was that cagey. He would have had his plates mudded over."

"No, they didn't get his license number," said John Bantreagh tiredly. "Nobody ever did, I reckon, that saw her with him. He was cagey, like you say."

THE MURDERER

The big young deputy shook his head. He sighed, with a quiet heaving of his diaphragm beneath his shirt.

"It's not any good, I'm afraid, Mr. Bantreagh," he said. "Nobody knows who he is, where he lives, what he looks like, the number of his car license or anything. Just this counterman and this truck driver who knew that she had been stepping out with some man that had a car, and maybe two or three more people here or around who may have seen her getting into it with him from a distance when it was getting dark, or getting out of it below the place next to yours when he brought her home. He was awful cagey. He did it, all right, I reckon. But he'll get away with it, as sometimes happens. I'm awfully sorry, Mr. Bantreagh, but I'm afraid the police have been left with nothing to go on at all."

John Bantreagh rubbed his forehead. So much—so much to forget. That he would try to forget. That he must keep from the kids forever. So much to forget, even of bright and tender things, of when he had been younger and she had been so very young, no older than Lilybelle, and all the world had been pink-colored and full of joy. He had known that he could never give her all she wanted. It hadn't been her fault that it had come to this. It had been his. If he had only been a little smarter. Though it could not be mended now. So much to forget, of shame and grief and failure. But some small, trivial thing to remember. And now he had remembered it.

"Nothing to go on, except what she told me," he said.

"What she told you?" said Deputy Roy Clade thinly. "I thought you said that she had never told you anything. That you never knew a thing about it or had the least suspicion until last night."

He stood motionless. His eyes were gray as the dawn. John Bantreagh lifted his blurred bloodshot gaze and met Roy Clade's gray eyes.

"What she told me after I had found her," said John Bantreagh. "Just before she died."

"You mean——" said Roy Clade, with the muscles moving on his face. "You mean," he said, with his eyes as gray as dawn, "that she was still alive? You mean that she told you? Why, you're crazy, you damn apple-knocking liar! She's been dead since one o'clock!"

His right fist jerked from his hip. He jerked it upward against his shoulder, with a contorted look upon his face and his mouth opening in a scream.

John Bantreagh had got his pendent right arm in motion. He had swung it, stepping in on knees swift and wiry, no longer caving, cracking the truck crank across the bones of Roy Clade's thick, strong wrist as the young deputy's fist left his hip. With his wrist against his shoulder, Roy Clade screamed.

John Bantreagh snapped his left hand forward, grabbed the gun out of its holster, dropped his crank, sidestepping. He had the gun in his right hand now, and the hammer back.

"Both hands out from your shoulders!" he said, "no use to yell at me and damn me! Heel! You know what this is. You know how it shoots. Heel, and swing your arms slowly back behind you till I have got your handcuffs on!

"Maybe she didn't tell me," he said, with a dry gasp in his throat. "But you did! Here I was beside her body, with blood on my hand, with the crank that might have been the thing that knocked her out, with my truck tracks leading right up to her, and no other tracks but them upon the field! Here I was, her husband, the first man in the world to be suspicioned, even if there was nothing to show that I had ever been around here at all! Here I was, that had drunk whisky tonight, that had given a pair of nylons to Lilybelle after she was dead! That had told Lilybelle I had killed her and had her body in my truck! That had gone in and talked to the counterman and the truck driver kind of wild, and maybe said that I would kill her when I found her—I don't know. A man gets to talking wild when he thinks of his wife and those black lace things, and his man's pride.

"Here I was, with everything saying it was me! Why, my best friends would have thought sure I'd done it! They would have figured some reason why—Lilybelle, or some argument we'd had about the kids, or about some fellow that she'd been stepping out with—wouldn't make any difference who. They would all have said that I had done it. At the least you might have asked me if I had. But you knew I hadn't done it. Only the man who had killed her himself, in all this world, would know that! No need to swear at me. Hold your hands behind you! You know what this is against your back.

"It took me a long time to figure out," said John Bantreagh tiredly. "I was knocked out. Just like a dummy. But I told you what her name was, and you pretended never to have heard it before. I didn't tell you how to spell it, though—I didn't think that you might write it down. Everybody who just hears it thinks it's spelled *t-r-y*, like 'pantry.' I always have a lot of trouble getting it spelled right. Thought sometimes of changing it myself. But you spelled it right without being told, when you wrote it down in your notebook. I've been trying to think how you knew, ever since you did.

"And other things you didn't think of, I reckon! You've got that tire iron in your car's tool kit or in your garage at home—you must still have it, you've mentioned it so often. And even if you've washed it with soap and water or kerosene, there will still be blood in the pores of the iron, that will show in some of these machines that they have these days, I reckon that you know. There will be blood on your car cushions. Maybe on the shirt and suit you wore last night.

"And you went home and slept," John Bantreagh said, "while I was out looking on every road for her all night! And got up, and took a bath, and shaved and rubbed yourself with sweet-smelling shaving lotion, and put on a clean white shirt and your crisp black suit and your black knit tie, and came on back here to park just inside the woods edge off the road, to wait for her to be discovered. Only I was already here when you came.

"There'll be the blood! There's her name, that you knew how to spell. And somewhere—yes, somewhere, when they get to looking, no matter how careful and cagey you have tried to be—there will be someone that has seen you and her together, when they go looking into it, and can tie you up in an iron way.

"Get into the back of your car! No need to blaspheme me. Kneel on the floor! I'm going to have to put some of my truck lashings around you. You're powerful, and your brain is fresh and new slept and smart. But I don't think you're going to get away. I'll try to get you to the doctor as quick as I can. I'm sorry that I had to hit so hard. I'm sorry that there'll be bumps.

"Kneel on the floor, and pray!" John Bantreagh said. "I wouldn't have ever known who you were. Nobody would have ever known about you, with nothing to start them looking into you. They would have put it on me, her husband, caught with her, caught red-handed, caught with motive, and I'd have got twenty years or life. And what would have happened to the kids is more than I can bear to think. The fear of it made my knees cave. It made me so blind that I could hardly see. If you had asked me whether I had done it, I would have fallen dead away. But it won't be that way. You told me."

He looked—John Bantreagh—at that still form lying in front of his truck wheels, with her staring eyes. "Perhaps," he said, "she helped."

PEN IN HAND

BEN AMES WILLIAMS

Man, in his goings to and fro, engraves upon the world a record of his movements. Thus the roads he builds are, in fact, inscriptions, which the wise eye may read. And these traces which his feet have etched persist with a curious stubbornness, whether they were in the beginning the broad, paved highways of the Romans or merely narrow forest tracks beaten deep by the padding feet of Indian warriors long ago. Yet unless these thoroughfares are kept in repair and tended, they will by and by begin to disappear, just as the inscription on an ancient tombstone is blurred by eroding time.

A fair proportion of the roads in Fraternity are of improved construction, broad and firm; a further number are graveled and repaired. But there are others which, save for the occasional services of a scraper to drag the contents of the roadside ditches up on the traveled way, have no care at all. And a road is like an artery or a vein: so long as traffic, no matter how thin, does flow to and fro along its length, it will retain some beat of life. But when this traffic ceases, the road begins to wither and decay. Grass grows between the wheel tracks, and alders and birches press in from either side.

You will occasionally find such a road leading to some remote hilltop in Fraternity where once upon a time there was a farm. More often than not, nowadays, of that farm no more than a cellar hole remains, and a few gnarled and neglected apple trees where partridge like to feed. But this is not always the case. There is one such byway which turns aside from the road down Muzzy Ridge; and if a traveler found this cart track and climbed tortuously for a quarter mile or so, he would emerge upon a height of land that overlooks a pond in the deep valley below, and the rising slopes of the mountain beyond.

And he would discover a neat stand of buildings there—a small white house and a shed and a barn. For this is where old Grandma Ankers—"Marm" Ankers in the local phrase—lived till these latter years alone.

She was a little old woman with a tongue that could rasp like a file, and a sharp wit to whet her tongue; and she dwelt in this house on the hill, with a horse in the barn and a cow in the tie-up, and a few chickens and a pig for only company. She was a precise old woman, scrupulously neat and clean; you would never see a chicken in her barnyard, nor a cat in her kitchen. And there was in her an indomitable courage and an independence that declined open help from any man.

Her left arm had been amputated between wrist and elbow many years ago; yet with only one hand she did all her household tasks sufficiently. And Marm Ankers had a quality that might be called morale. Though not once a week did any visitor climb the hill, there was never an afternoon that the little old lady did not dress in her best and wait in a seemly composure, ready to receive any callers who might come. Remote from the world, forgotten for the most part by the world, she nevertheless thought of herself as a part of the world and held her proud place there.

Once a week, on Saturday mornings, she harnessed her horse to the old buckboard and drove down to the store in the village, three or four miles away, to buy dry groceries and other small requirements. This was a routine from which over a period of years she did not deviate except when snow lay deep upon the ground. When this was the case, Andy Wattles used to carry her supplies from the main road up to the house. He would stop his big truck at the foot of her lane, and put on his snowshoes if the drifts required, and so make his deliveries; and out of this occasional contact there developed between these two a certain intimacy and friendliness.

Andy even managed, without her knowing it, to make sure now and then that all went well with the solitary old woman on the hill. So, though Marm Ankers thought of herself as self-sufficient and dependent on no one at all, yet she was protected too.

Saturday was her day for driving to the village; so when, on a certain Friday morning, Andy looked out through the side door of the store and saw her buckboard wheel up to the hitch rail, he was surprised, and he wondered why she had come. It is the occasion for this deviation from her routine which is to be here set down.

This Friday morning fell in late October, when the trees were stripped bare of their bright autumn foliage and the cold clasp of winter began to grip the land. The days were long and still, and small sounds rang far. The old woman who lived on the hill could look for miles across the countryside, and she liked on such days to do so; to watch the deepening shadows lengthen as the sun sank low. But the Thursday before this particular Friday was a cold day and a raw one; and she stayed indoors save when her necessary business in the barn required attendance there. Thursday afternoon she dressed in her black silk as her custom was, and sat by the dining-room window where she could watch the lane that came up from the road half a mile below the house; but no one came, and at dusk she changed into her house dress and put on an apron and lighted the lamps and took a lantern and went to the tie-up to milk and feed the cow, to pull down hay for the old horse in his stall.

She came back into the kitchen with a brimming pail of milk and poured it into the scoured, bright pans to set; and she put the milk pans away in the buttery. She filled the wood box, and chunked up the fire and made tea and toast and boiled an egg for her supper. She set the table in the dining room and brought her victuals there.

And when she came from the kitchen into the dining room with the steaming teapot in her hand, she saw, outside one of the windows, a white shadow that instantly did disappear. It was, unmistakably, a face: the face of someone who had stood outside the window, at a little distance, looking in. The face of someone who, on seeing her, quickly withdrew.

Now, Marm Ankers was not a timorous old woman, but neither was she a rash one. She had always a sum of money in the house, sufficient for her immediate needs; and this might be suspected by anyone who knew her ways, might even serve as bait to some unscrupulous one. When she saw the face outside the window, she remembered the money hidden in her bedroom; so she gave no sign that she had seen. She set the teapot on the table and went into her bedroom and took something from beneath her pillow. Then she continued through another bedroom beyond, into the front of the house. She entered the dark parlor and, herself invisible, looked out of the window there.

The night outside was dark under a cloudy, moonless sky. But there was light enough so that she could see a dark figure, half crouching, which moved across the farmyard toward the barn. This figure was no more than a shadow, and it lost itself in the shadow of the barn and disappeared. Marm Ankers was not afraid; nevertheless, she knew a certain satisfaction that her chores in the barn were done for the night. She waited awhile, but the figure did not reappear; so she came back into the dining room and slid the bolt on the shed door and drew the blinds on the windows.

Then she sat down and ate her supper quietly. Her tea had cooled, and she liked it scalding hot, but she endured the inconvenience calmly. Afterward she washed the dishes and put them all away. She thought with a faint regret that it was too bad she had no telephone, but she had discarded that instrument long ago. The continual shrilling of the bell on a party line annoyed her beyond bearing. Yet now it would have been reassuring to have a word with Andy Wattles. She felt herself incredibly isolated from the world.

But this could not be helped tonight. After a while she went to bed. Her bedroom had one window and two doors. She bolted the doors, and she lay facing the window, which was a pale rectangle in the black wall of the room. By and by she slept the faint sleep of old people; but nothing happened to disturb her, and when she awoke it was dawn.

She got up and dressed and went into the kitchen to start the fire. When she raised the blinds the farmyard was empty; the chickens in their pen behind the shed pecked at the frost-cemented ground with an empty-headed optimism. A partridge perched in an apple tree in the orchard back of the kitchen. From the parlor windows she could see nothing except the birch covert shadowed by young pines on the slope below the house.

When she had thus looked all around, Marm Ankers returned to the kitchen and saw that the wood box was almost empty. The wood was in the shed. She opened the shed door cautiously. She lifted the latch with her maimed left arm, while her right hand dropped into the pocket of her apron. But there was no one in the shed, so she went in and brought wood. She pumped a pail of water and filled the kettle on the stove. Some tramp, she decided, had taken shelter for the night in the haymow in the barn. By this time, no doubt, he was gone.

She delayed milking till after breakfast, but when she came to the tie-up, the cow looked at her with a moody resentment. Usually there were two or three quarts of milk even in the morning, but today she had trouble in getting a quart. She considered this fact thoughtfully, her shrewd old eyes darting to and fro.

When she carried the pail back into the kitchen a team was coming up the cart track from the main road. She put the pail down in the sink; and as the team stopped in the yard, she opened the kitchen door. When the man alighted, Marm Ankers stepped out on the veranda, drawing a knitted shawl about her shoulders against the cold.

"Morning, Marm," said the man. He was Levi Fee. Despite the fact that this little old woman lived far from the world, she knew her neighbors for twenty miles; for she had lived hereabouts all her many years, and so for the most part had they. Levi was a bachelor. His solitary farm was over on the slopes of the mountain, three miles beyond her own. She could even see it from her own dooryard now; a small square of white against the black growth, far away.

"Morning, Levi," she returned. He was a tall man in overalls and a heavy woolen coat, with felts and rubbers on his feet. A lean man, lank and wiry. When he unbuttoned his coat she saw, where a button on his shirt was gone, that he wore a white cotton undershirt, though the time for winter flannels had come. Also she thought Levi began to put on weight; he was heavier at the waist than she remembered.

"All right, are you?" Levi inquired.

"Why wouldn't I be?" she retorted.

But instead of replying, he asked: "Didn't see anyone around here yest'day, did you?"

"Don't many folks come this way," she reminded him.

He nodded, with a jerk of his head toward the valley below them. "Will Hedrick killed his pa down there, night before last," he explained. "And got away. The sheriff figures he went afoot. 'Lowed we'd pick him up before now, but we ain't. Thought he maybe come this way."

"Killed his pa?" she repeated. "That boy?"

"The old man had money," he pointed out. She nodded. Pop Hedrick was, in fact, notoriously rich, notoriously miserly. He had money; had, they said, the first dollar he ever earned, and all the interest that dollar had earned in the intervening years. He rented money to his neighbors, and collected the rent, and had in time the money back again—or knew the reason why. He owned a dozen farms across the hills, on mortgage deeds. Marm Ankers had known him for fifty years.

"I heerd tell Will had come home," she agreed.

"Lost his job in Boston," Levi assented. "But he didn't take kindly to farming. I was in the village Wednesday afternoon, and Andy asked me would I leave some bundles at the old man's house. So I said I would, on the way home. I pulled into the yard, and there was a light in the kitchen. So I knocked and nobody answered. So I looked in the window. There he was! Stretched acrost the floor!"

Marm Ankers drew her shawl a little tighter. "Come in and set," she told him. "I want to know."

"I'd stopped to see the old man in the morning on my way to the village," Levi explained, when they were seated beside the stove. "Owed him a piece of interest, and paid it. Will wan't around. Old Pop told me Will wouldn't ever make a hand. Said he was plumb discouraged with the boy. I always liked Pop. Wisht I'd got there in time to stop it. I might have, too, but I lost a nut off my nigh front wheel. Had a time to find it in the dark. When I got there, the old man was dead, and Will gone!"

"Did Will take the money?" she asked.

Levi shook his head.

"He didn't find it, but he'd looked for it," he assured her. "Things were tore up some, boards pulled out of the floor, and the mantel ripped off, and a brick out of the chimney and all. But he didn't find it, no. Me and Sheriff Sohier found it, yest'day morning."

"Much?" she inquired.

"Only a little over five hundred dollars," he confessed. "I 'lowed there'd be more!"

"Where'bouts was it hid?"

"That was slick too," Levi assured her. "It was behind the bed in his room. He'd loosened a corner of the paper on the wall, and glued a couple of corset steels on it so it'd hold snug down. You wouldn't hardly notice it at all, but I got to thumping the wall. You could kind of bend the wall paper up, right above the baseboard, and there was a hole in there, six inches deep and three inches high and about as wide." He added: "Guess he had the most of his money in the bank, at that. Pop was more of a businessman than people'd think. Kep' books, and always give receipts and all."

"Give you a receipt for the interest money yesterday?" she suggested.

"Certain," he assured her. He even took a worn leather wallet from his pocket and showed her the bit of paper. She put on her spectacles to read it, gave it back again. But she asked then:

"How come you're out hunting Will? That's the sheriff's job, it looks to me. And how come you know he did it?"

"He was gone," Levi pointed out. "No reason he should run away only if he did it. Shot the old man with his own gun, through the neck. Long as I was the first to see him, Sheriff Sohier wanted to know if I'd ask around, today, and see could I get any word of Will, and I 'lowed I would. I liked the old man."

Marm Ankers smoothed her apron down. But there was a lump in the pocket of the apron, made conspicuous by this gesture, so she laid her hand across this lump for concealment.

"I ain't seen hide nor hair of him," she said then.

"I just come by on the off chance he might have gone this way," Levi explained, and he rose. "I aim to ask all around. He might have showed somewhere."

"If he didn't get the money, he might wait to try again," she suggested; but Levi chuckled, shook his head.

"Wouldn't do him no good now," he assured her. "Since we found it." She followed him out on the kitchen porch to watch him drive away.

The old woman stayed on the porch, her shawl over her head, while Levi's horses picked their course down the rocky lane. Horses and wagon and Levi disappeared, but she could hear their departure after they were out of sight. She waited till these sounds were no longer audible; and then Marm Ankers turned across the farmyard to the barn.

She stood in the wide doors of the barn and looked in and all around. The horse in his stall nickered at her; the cow in the tie-up stirred.

And Marm Ankers called sharply: "Will Hedrick, you come down out of there!"

Nothing happened. She took three steps forward, looking up into the mow. And she repeated: "Will, come down!" She added: "Don't keep me standing here!"

After a long time then there was a movement in the hay. The barn was framed on timbers, weathered and old. Above one of these timbers a face appeared, and a young man looked down. The young man's eyes were haggard, and his cheek was pale and his lips were white. He looked at old Marm Ankers, and she said again, more softly:

"Come down, you young fool!"

Will Hedrick moved to obey her, and a moment later he stood unsteadily on the barn floor, in a heap of hay dislodged by his sliding descent.

She stared at him, and she asked: "What's the matter with your foot?"

"I stuck an ax into it," the boy admitted.

"You can walk, can't you?" she demanded. He nodded in a dumb fashion; and she said harshly: "Then walk yourself into my kitchen and I'll bandage it for you."

So young Will Hedrick hobbled past her, went before her through the shed into the kitchen. Behind him she exclaimed irascibly:

"You hadn't any call to scare a body to death, peeping in windows and all."

"No, ma'am," he admitted humbly.

In the kitchen she set him in a chair. She filled a basin with hot water and stripped the bloody bandage off his foot. There was a deep gash from ankle bone to sole.

"Ax slid on some frozen wood," said Will in the silence. "I couldn't see where I was hitting. It was along toward dark."

"You're a clumsy young one," she told him. "Set still! What made you run away?" She began to bathe the wound while he answered her.

"I was chopping wood down by the pond," he said. "Pop was mad at me, so I wanted to put in a good long day for him. So I worked late as I could see; and then I cut my foot, and time I come back to the house it was past dark. I couldn't move very fast this way. So when I come to the house, I heard the commotion, and peeked in the window. Sheriff was there, and Levi Fee, and two-three others. Heard them say: 'Will done it, sure!' And I could see Pop, dead on the floor. So I was scared to go in. I sneaked away."

"How come your pa to be mad at you?" she demanded.

"I went to write a letter Tuesday night, to a man in Boston, asking for a job, and I broke the point on the pen. It was the last point he had."

Her bright old eyes looked up at him. "Mad about that, was he?"

"He give me fits when he found it out," the boy confessed. "'Lowed I broke everything I touched. I offered to walk to the village and get him a new point, and he said I was just looking for an excuse not to work. Wednesday noon, that was, when I had come in to dinner. He told me to telephone from Tomer's and order some coffee and things, and a new pen point. He said Andy'd get somebody to bring 'em by the house, without my wasting half a day going to fetch them."

"Ordered some new pens, did you?"

"One," said Will. "Pop wouldn't have more. Said I hadn't any call to write letters. Said he'd do the writing for the family."

She looked at him sharply. "I dunno as I blame you for shooting him," she declared. "The miserly old hound! But why didn't you wait till you knowed where his money was?"

"I never shot him," he protested miserably. "And I knowed where he kep' his money, if it comes to that."

"Where did he keep it?" she challenged; and he said:

"Under a flap of wallpaper, in the wall behind his bed. Right above the baseboard. He'd fixed some corset steels in the wall paper to spring it down, make it lie flat."

She was bandaging his foot. She was incredibly deft with her one hand. She drew the bandage snug and secured it there.

"There," she said. "Now go on in the dining room and lie down on the sofa. I'm going to change my dress."

"I never shot pa," he insisted, while she helped him cross to the other room.

"Then you was a fool to run away," she retorted. "Lie down now, and lie still. If you start that foot bleeding again, you'll spot my floors!"

"Yes, ma'am," said Will.

She disappeared, returned in coat and bonnet. He asked quickly: "Where you going?"

"None of your business!" she said. "But you're a-staying here!" She hesitated, looked at him shrewdly. "You're still scared," she decided. "But I guess you've had enough of running away. You stay here till I come back."

"Ma'am," he whispered hopelessly, "I didn't do it."

She nodded sternly. "If I'd thought you did," she said, "I'd have done different by you. Now you lay where you be."

So young Will Hedrick was surprisingly comforted. He stayed passively on the sofa while she went out to the barn. Later, through the kitchen windows, he saw her drive away.

And this was how it happened that Marm Ankers came to the village Friday morning and spoke with Andy Wattles in the store. Later she drove home again. She found Will where she had left him there.

Early that afternoon, an automobile made its way up the lane to the farm on the hill: and this was a rare thing, and a hazardous. The car leaped and bucked on the rocky road, and the engine roared. Will heard it, and Marm Ankers heard it, and the little old woman went out on the porch to watch the automobile come into the yard.

It was Sheriff Sohier's car. The sheriff drove, and Levi Fee sat beside him, and Andy was on the seat behind. Will, watching fearfully through the window, saw them alight; saw Marm Ankers go to meet them there.

Sheriff Sohier was a slow, sure man. He passed the time of day; and he said, looking thoughtfully around:

"I'd have been here sooner, only we had to go fetch Levi. You say Will's here?"

"He's inside," she agreed. "Come in, the lot of you."

Levi said ruefully, "I feel kind of bad about this, Marm. I always kind of liked Will."

"You can tell him so," she said. "Come in! . . . Andy, you too."

So she led the way into the kitchen, into the dining room. Behind her came the three tall men.

They were all big men, and she was very small; and Will Hedrick, lying pale and weak on the sofa, stared up at them helplessly. Sheriff Sohier spoke to him.

"'Aft'noon, Will," he said uncomfortably. "I'm sorry to hear about this, son."

"He'll be all right," Marm Ankers interjected. "He's got a bad cut, but no bones broke. It'll heal up, give it time."

"I mean, about this other," the sheriff explained. He stood now beside the sofa, Levi at the foot of it, Andy by the door.

"You mean him killing his pa?" she asked; and she laughed, a strange, metallic little cackle of mirth. "It's a wonder to me sometimes," she said, "that a man can live to grow up and still be the fools most men are!"

"Yes, Ma'am," the sheriff agreed.

"And I don't mean Will," said Marm Ankers. "I mean any man. You're as bad as any, sheriff."

The officer looked at her gravely. "How come?" he inquired.

"Why, Will never done it!" she told him.

He rubbed his chin. "That so?"

"He was chopping wood, down by the pond, till dark," she explained. "Ax slipped into his foot. He had to crawl most all the way home. Time he got there, you was all there; and he heerd your talk. So he run away."

"He say so?" Sheriff Sohier asked her.

She nodded. "And he did so," she insisted. "If he'd killed his pa, would he stop afterwards to chop his foot half off?"

"The house was tore up," the sheriff pointed out. "Where he'd ripped up boards and so on, looking for the old man's money. Likely he cut himself then."

"See any blood on the floor?"

"There was blood enough," the other assured her.

"He'd have left tracks of it," she insisted, "if it was him." And she added: "Besides, he knowed where the money was. Told me where it was. Knowed all the time. He wouldn't have to look for it at all."

The sheriff clung shrewdly to his point. "He might have let on he didn't know, to fool us," he urged.

"Money wan't gone, was it?" she demanded.

The man scratched his head. "Well, maybe he took the most of it and left some. To fool us," he repeated.

She nodded. "Maybe so," she agreed. "But we can find out." She turned to Levi. "Levi, you paid the old man some money that morning. Show the sheriff that receipt Pop wrote for you."

Levi readily obeyed. The sheriff scanned the bit of paper, and

Marm Ankers asked: "How about the money you paid him, Levi? Was it there? Guess you'd know the bills, wouldn't you?"

Levi nodded. "Yes, ma'am," he declared. "It was there." He hesitated. "There was a ten-dollar bill tore half in two. I see it when we found the money." He added: "It was all there, I'd say."

And the little old woman said readily: "You see, sheriff, Will and his pa had a row that day. Will tried to write a letter the night before, and broke the pen point. It was the only one in the house, and his pa was mad at that. So next day Will telephoned to the store and ordered a new one, along with the groceries, that afternoon.... Levi, you fetched the things from the store, didn't you?"

"Yes, ma'am," Levi assured her. "Yes, ma'am, Andy here'll tell you so."

"That's right," Andy agreed.

"Pen point and all?" Marm Ankers asked, and Andy said:

"Yes, ma'am."

The old woman looked at the sheriff triumphantly, but the sheriff sighed. "Just the same," he insisted, "I guess we'll have to take Will to town. I don't see as there's anything else to do."

"I never done it," Will protested hopelessly. "I never killed pa!"

"I dunno as you did," the sheriff assented. "But, Will, all I can do is the best I see. You hadn't ought to blame me. If you didn't, I guess it'll come out in time."

"I didn't," Will said again, weakly.

And Marm Ankers spoke in irascible tones. "You're plain dumb, sheriff!" she declared. They were all save Andy grouped here by the sofa, but the old woman swung away from them now with a gesture of impatience. "There ain't a critter living as stubborn and blind as a dumb man," she declared. "A blind man could see Will never did this. He hadn't any call to. He could have took the money any time, and gone."

But Levi protested at that. "No, ma'am! Pop Hedrick kep' his eyes open. It'd take a weasel to get his money, long as he was alive. Even if you knowed where it was."

She stood now in the kitchen door. Andy had moved aside. She looked at Levi.

"A pity," she said, "you didn't get there sooner, Levi. You left the store by half-past three, but you didn't get to him, by your own tell, till after dark."

"I lost a nut off my nigh front wheel," he reminded her. "Had to walk back and look for it."

"If it wan't for that," she said, "you'd have had time to get there and pay him what you owed him and have him write the receipt before he was killed. If it wan't for that nut that you say you lost."

"I'd paid him that morning," Levi pointed out. "On the way to town."

"So you say!" she assented in a dry tone. "So you say! But the thing that sticks in my crop, Levi, how could he write that receipt for you in the morning, when there wan't a pen point in the house? How could he write it before you come along and brought the pen from the store?"

There was a sudden hush in this small room. A long, pulsing silence. Will and Sheriff Sohier looked at Marm Ankers, and so did Levi. But Andy watched Levi Fee.

And after a long time Marm Ankers said: "If it wan't for that nut falling off, you could have got there, and paid him, and got the receipt, and gone down the road, and sneaked back to see where he put the money away, and—sneaked in the house again, Levi." She said crisply: "Will says the gun was in the corner by the door, and shells on the windowsill. Pop would go into the bedroom to put the money away. He couldn't hear good. He wouldn't hear you come in. You could have been waiting for him when he come out of the bedroom. With the gun all loaded, ready. Plenty of time, if it wan't for that nut off your wagon."

The man, after a moment, laughed. "Plenty of time, yes, if it wan't for that."

"Anybody see you hunting that nut along the road?"

"Couple cars passed," said Levi Fee. "Sure."

"Who? Whose cars?"

"Didn't know them! Camden men, up gunning, likely. I'd know them again. I'll go down to Camden tomorrow and hunt 'em up, if the sheriff wants me to prove my say."

She shook her head. "It's the pen sticks in my craw!" she said.

"Maybe Pop found a pen point in the house that he'd forgot," Levi suggested. "For all I know."

The old woman looked at the sheriff. "You open the bundles, see what was in them?" she asked. He nodded, and she insisted: "See any pen point in them, did you?"

"There was a new point in the pen," he said. "On the table!"

"The pen was on the table, was it?" And she looked again at Levi. Her eyes narrowed. "Like Pop had maybe been using it right before he was killed." And abruptly she changed the subject. "Got a new undershirt, ain't you, Levi?" she asked. "How come you're wearing cotton? I sh'd think you'd have your flannels on by now."

"I got flannels underneath," he said, suddenly ill at ease.

"Thought you looked kind of puffed out, around the waist," she commented, "when I see you this morning. Kind of lumpy, under your overalls." She seemed to meditate. "Whoever killed Pop might have took some of the money, sheriff. That's what you said, wan't it? Might have tore up the house, to let on he'd looked for it and didn't find it. Might have took some money, and left some, to make it look as if he didn't find it at all." She faced Levi Fee again. "Levi, you'd be smart enough to do that. But you might be fool enough to carry the money on you. Maybe fastened onto the tail of your new undershirt. Let's see!"

The man stood for a moment rigidly. Then he laughed. "Why, Marm," he said, "if you're bent on it!"

He put his hand inside the bib of his overalls. Then he drew it out again.

But when his hand reappeared, it held an ancient pistol, thick-muzzled, ponderously deadly.

"I don't know as I've got any call to show you my undershirt," said Levi Fee, and he grinned at them all.

No one spoke, nor moved; and he backed toward the door. Toward the kitchen door, and the nearest way to the yard. He said nothing, but he watched the sheriff alertly, and Andy too.

He paid no heed to little Marm Ankers in the doorway behind him. She was too small to oppose his escape, too small and frail. He backed almost to the door where she stood, the pistol steady in his hand. He paused then.

"I didn't do it," he said. "Hadn't any hand in it. But, sheriff, you're just dumb enough to arrest me; and I don't 'low to be. You and Andy, you stay where you are. I'm leaving."

He took another step backward. But then something touched him in the spine, and Marm Ankers said crisply: "Don't turn around, Levi!"

He stood very still.

"A lone woman has to keep a gun in the house," she reminded him. "With the kind of rapscallions live around here. You just open your hand and let your gun fall."

He did not; and she whispered: "I knowed old Pop Hedrick all my life, Levi! I'd admire it if you was to make a move."

So presently there was a thump upon the floor; and then Andy and the sheriff came at swift stride across the room, and when they held him, it was Marm Ankers who said briskly:

"Now, Andy, pull his shirttail out. I want to know how right I be."

Levi did not resist them. There was no more resistance in him now; and when the thick pads of bills sewed roughly into flaps on his undershirt were revealed, she cackled gleefully.

"There!" she ejaculated. "Sheriff, I dunno what you think, but that's enough for me."

"Enough for anybody, I'd say," he agreed. "Marm, I'm obliged to you."

"You're obliged to be," she said complacently. "Now the lot of you get out of here. You've tracked mud clear across my floor."

But before they were gone Andy asked: "What about Will, Marm? Want I should help you take care of him? I can come back later on."

She looked down at young Will Hedrick, and after a moment she said:

"I've had no chick nor child that needed me this forty years. And Will needs someone now. I aim to hold on to him. You go along, Andy, and leave us be."

METHOD THREE FOR MURDER

REX STOUT

When I first set eyes on Mira Holt, as I opened the front door and she was coming up the seven steps to the stoop, she was a problem, though only a minor one compared to what followed.

At the moment I was unemployed. During the years I have worked for Nero Wolfe and lived under his roof, in the old brownstone he owns on West Thirty-fifth Street, I have quit and been fired about the same number of times, say, thirty or forty. Mostly we have been merely letting off steam, but sometimes we have meant it, more or less, and that Monday evening in September I was really fed up. The main dish at dinner had been pork stewed in beer, which both Wolfe and Fritz know I can get along without, and we had left the dining room and crossed the hall to the office, and Fritz had brought coffee and Wolfe had poured it, and I had said, "By the way, I told Anderson I'd phone and confirm his appointment for tomorrow morning."

Wolfe had said, "No. Cancel it." He picked up the book he was on, John Gunther's *Inside Russia Today*.

I sat in my working chair and looked across his desk at him. Because he weighs a seventh of a ton, he always looks big, but when he's being obnoxious he looks even bigger. "Do you suppose it's possible," I asked, "that that pork has a bloating effect?"

"No, indeed," he said and opened the book.

If I had been a camel and the book had been a straw, you could have heard my spine crack. He knew darned well he shouldn't have opened it until we had finished with coffee. I put my cup down.

"I am aware," I said, "that you are sitting pretty. The bank balance is fat enough for months of paying Fritz and Theodore and me and buying pork and beer in car lots, and adding more orchids to the ten thousand you've already got. I'll even grant that a private detective has a right to refuse to take a case with or without a reason. But as I told you before dinner, this Anderson is known to me, and he asked me as a personal favor to get him fifteen minutes with you, and I told him to come at eleven o'clock tomorrow morning. If you're determined not to work because your tax bracket is already too high, O.K., all you have to do is tell him no. He'll be here at eleven."

He was holding the book open and his eyes were on it, but he spoke. "You know quite well, Archie, that I must be consulted on appointments. Did you owe this man a favor?"

"I do now that he asked for one and I said yes."

"Did you owe him one before?"

"No."

"Then you are committed, but I am not. Since I wouldn't take the job, it would waste his time and mine. Phone him not to come. Tell him I have other engagements."

So I quit. I admit that on some other occasions my quitting had been merely a threat, to jolt him into seeing reason, but not that time. When a mule plants its feet a certain way, there's no use trying to budge it. I swiveled, got my memo pad, wrote on it, yanked the sheet off, got up and crossed to his desk and handed him the sheet.

"That's Anderson's number," I told him. "If you're too busy to phone him not to come, Fritz can. I'm through. I'll stay with friends tonight and come tomorrow for my stuff."

His eyes had left the book to glare at me. "Pfui," he said.

"I agree," I said. "Absolutely." I turned and marched out. I do not say that as I got my hat from the rack in the hall my course was clearly mapped for the next twenty years, or even twenty hours. Wolfe owned the house, but not everything in it, for the furniture in my room on the third floor had been bought and paid for by me. That would have to wait until I found a place to move it to, but I would get my clothes and other items tomorrow. Would I come for them before eleven o'clock and learn from Fritz whether a visitor named Anderson was expected, or would it be better strategy to come in the afternoon and learn if Anderson had been admitted and given his fifteen minutes? Facing that problem as I pulled the door open, I was immediately confronted by another one. A female was coming up the steps to the stoop.

I couldn't greet her and ask her business, as it was a cinch she would say she wanted to see Nero Wolfe, and I couldn't carry on with a job I no longer held by returning to the office to ask Wolfe if he would receive a caller. Anyway I wouldn't. I couldn't step aside and let her enter by the door I had opened with no questions asked, since there was a possibility that she was one of the various people who had it in for Wolfe; and, while I might have considered shooting him myself, I didn't want to get him plugged by a total stranger. So I crossed the sill, pulled the door shut, sidestepped to pass her, and was starting down the steps when my sleeve was caught and jerked. "Hey," she said, "aren't you Archie Goodwin?"

My eyes slanted down to hers. "You're guessing," I said.

"I am not. I've seen you at the Flamingo. You're not very polite, shutting the door in my face." She spoke in jerks, as if she wasn't sure she had enough breath. "I want to see Nero Wolfe."

"This is his house. Ring the bell."

"But I want to see you too. Let me in. Take me in."

My eyes had adjusted enough to the poor light to see that she was young, attractive and hipped. She had on a cap with a beak. In normal circumstances it would have been a pleasure to escort her in to the front room and go and badger Wolfe into seeing her, but as things stood I didn't even consider it.

"I'm sorry," I said, "but I don't work here anymore. I just quit. I am now on my way to bum a bed for the night. You'll have to ring the bell, but I should warn you that in Mr. Wolfe's present mood there's not a chance. You might as well skip it. If your trouble is urgent you ought to——"

"I'm not in trouble."

"Good; you're lucky."

She touched my sleeve. "I don't believe it—that you've quit."

"I do. Would I say so if I hadn't? Running the risk that you're a journalist and tomorrow there will be a front-page spread, 'Archie Goodwin, the famous private detective, has severed his connection with Nero Wolfe, also a detective, and it is thought——' "

"Shut up!" She was close to me, gripping my arm. She let loose and backed up a step. "I beg your pardon. I seem to be——You think Nero Wolfe wouldn't see me?"

"I don't think—I know."

"Anyway I want to see you too. For what I want, I guess you would be better than he. I want some advice—no, not advice exactly; I want to consult you. I'll pay cash, fifty dollars. Can't we go inside?" Naturally I was uplifted. As I had left Wolfe, and since there was no other outfit in New York that I would work for, my only possible program was to set up for myself, and before I even got down to the sidewalk here was a pretty girl offering me fifty bucks just for consultation.

"I'm afraid not," I told her, "since I no longer belong here. If that's your taxi waiting, that will do fine, especially with the driver gone." A glance had shown me that there was no one behind the wheel of the cab at the curb. Probably, having been told to wait for her, he had beat it to Al's Diner at the corner of Tenth Avenue.

She shook her head. "I don't——" she began, and let it hang. She glanced around. "Why not here? It shouldn't take very long. I just want you to help me win a bet." She sat on the landing, swaying a little as she bent. "Have a seat."

I sat down beside her, not crowding. I had often sat there watching the neighborhood kids at stoop ball.

"Do I pay in advance?" she asked.

"No, thanks; I'll trust you. What's the bet about?"

"Well"—she was squinting at me in the dim light—"I had an argument with a friend of mine. She said there were ninety-three women cab drivers in New York, and she thought it was dangerous because sometimes things happen in cabs that it takes a man to handle. I said things like that can happen anywhere just as well as in cabs, and we had an argument, and she bet me fifty dollars she could prove that something dangerous could happen in a cab that couldn't happen anywhere else. She thought up some things, but I made her admit they could happen other places too. Then she said what if a woman cab driver left her empty cab to go into a building for something, and when she came back there was a dead woman in the cab? She claimed that won the bet, and the trouble was I didn't know enough about what you're supposed to do when you find a dead body. That's what I want you to tell me. I'm sure she's wrong. And I'll pay you the fifty dollars."

I was squinting back at her. "You don't look it," I stated.

"I don't look what?"

"Loony. Two things. First, the same thing could happen if she were driving a private car instead of a cab, and why didn't you tell her that? Second, where's the danger? She merely finds a phone and notifies the police. It would be a nuisance, but you said dangerous."

"Oh, of course." She bit her lip. "I left something out. It's not her cab. She has a friend who is a cab driver, and she wanted to see what driving a cab was like, and her friend let her take it. So she can't notify the police because her friend broke some law when she let her take the cab, and she broke one, too, driving a cab without a license, so it wouldn't have been the same if she had been driving a private car. And the only way I can win the bet is to prove that it wouldn't have been dangerous. She doesn't know how the dead woman got in the cab or anything about it. All she has to do is get the body out of the cab, but that might be dangerous unless she did it just right. That's what I want you to tell me, so I won't make some awful mistake—I mean when I tell my friend why it wouldn't be dangerous. Things like where would she go to—to take it out of the cab—and would she have to wait until late at night, and how would she make sure there were no traces left in the cab."

"I see." I had stopped squinting. "What's your name?"

She shook her head. "You don't have to know. I'm just consulting you." She stuck her fingers in the pocket of her jacket, came out with a purse and opened it.

I reached to snap it shut. "That can wait. I certainly wouldn't take your money without knowing your name. Of course, you can make one up."

"Why should I?" She gestured. "All right. My name is Mira Holt. Mira with an *i*." She opened the purse again.

"Hold it," I told her. "A couple of questions. The dead woman she finds in the cab—does she recognize her?"

"No; how could she?"

"She could if she knew her when she was alive."

"She didn't."

"Good. That helps. You say she left her empty cab to go into a building for something. For what?"

"Oh, just anything. I don't know. That doesn't matter."

"It might, but if you don't know, you can't tell me. I want to make it clear, Miss Holt, that I accept without question all that you have told me. Because I am a trained detective, I am chronically suspicious, but you are so frank and intelligent and pleasing to look at that I wouldn't dream of doubting you. A man who was sap enough to size you up wrong might even suspect you as feeding him a phony, and go and take a look in that taxi, but not me. I don't even ask you where the driver is. In short, I trust you fully. That's understood?"

Her lips were tight. She was probably frowning, but the peak of her cap screened her brow. "I guess so." She wasn't at all sure. "But maybe, if that's how you feel, it would be better——"

"No. It's better like this. Much better. About this situation your friend thought up and claims she won the bet—it has many aspects. You say you didn't know enough about what you're supposed to do when you find a dead body. First and foremost, you're supposed to notify the police immediately. That goes for everybody, but it's a must for a private detective—me, for instance—if he wants to keep his license. Is that clear?"

"Yes." She nodded. "I see."

"Also you're not supposed to touch the body or anything near it. Also you're not supposed to leave it unguarded, but that's not so important because you may have to in order to call a policeman. As for your idea that all she has to do is get the body out of the cab, and where would she go to ditch it, and would she have to wait until late at night, and so on, I admit it has possibilities and I could make a lot of practical suggestions. But you have to show that it could be done without danger, and that's too big an order. That's what licks you. Forget it. However, your friend hasn't won the bet. She was to produce a situation showing that a woman cab driver runs special risks as a hackie, and in this case the danger comes from the fact that she was not driving the cab. So your friend——"

"That's no help. You know very well——"

"Shut up. I beg your pardon."

"You said you could make some practical suggestions."

"I was carried away. The idea of disposing of a dead body is fascinating as long as it's only an idea. By the way, I took one thing for granted that I shouldn't have—that your friend specified that the woman had died by violence. If she could have died of natural causes——"

"No. She had been stabbed. There was a knife, the handle of a knife——"

"Then it's impossible. A hackie letting someone else drive his cab is a misdemeanor, and so is driving a cab without a license, but driving off with a dead body with a knife sticking in it, and dumping it somewhere and not reporting it—that's a felony. Good for a least a year and probably more."

She gripped my arm, leaning to me. "But not if she did it right! Not if no one ever knew! I told you one thing wrong—she did recognize her! She did know her when she was alive! So she can't——"

"Hold it," I growled. "Give me some money quick. Pay me. A dollar bill, five—don't sit and stare. See that police car? If it goes on by——No, it's stopping. Pay me!"

She was going to panic. She started up, but my hand on her shoulder stopped her and held her down. She opened the purse and took out folded bills without fumbling, and I took them and put them in my pocket. "Staring is O.K.," I told her, not too loud. "People stare at police cars. Stay put and keep your mouth shut. I'm going to take a look. Naturally I'm curious."

That was perfectly true. I was curious. The prowl car had stopped, and a cop, not the one who was driving, had got out and circled around to the door of the taxi on his side and was opening it as I reached the sidewalk. When you have a reputation for cheek, you should live up to it, so I crossed to the door on my side and pulled it open. The seat was empty, but in front of it was a spread of brown canvas held up by whatever was under it. The cop, lifting a corner of the canvas, snarled at me, "Back up, you," and I retreated half a step, but he hadn't said to close the door, so I had a good view when he pulled the canvas off. More light would have helped, but there was enough to see that it was a woman, or had been, and that the knife whose handle was perpendicular to her ribs was all the way in.

"Good heavens!" I said with feeling.

"Shut that door!" the cop barked. "No—don't touch it!"

"I already have."

"I saw you. Beat it! No! What's your name?"

"Goodwin. Archie Goodwin. This is Nero Wolfe's house, and——"

"I know it is, and I know about you. Is this your cab?"

"Certainly not. I'm not a hackie."

"I know you're not. I mean——"He stopped. Apparently he had realized that the function of a prowl car on finding a corpse is not to argue with onlookers. His head jerked around. "Climb out, Bill. D.O.A., I'll call in." The cop behind the wheel wriggled out, and the one in command wriggled in, and I mounted the stoop and sat down beside my client, noting that she had removed the cap and apparently had stashed it.

I kept my voice low, though it wasn't necessary, for the cop was talking on his radio. "In about eight minutes," I said, "experts will begin arriving. They will not be strangers to me. Since, as far as I know, you merely came to get me to tell you how to win a bet, when they start asking questions I'll be glad to answer them if you want to leave it to me."

She was gripping my arm again. "You looked in. You saw——"

"Shut up, and I don't beg your pardon. You talk too much. Even if I still lived and worked here we wouldn't go inside because it wouldn't be natural, with policemen in a prowl car finding a corpse in a taxi parked at the curb. Oh, I haven't mentioned that—that there's a dead woman in the taxi. I mention it now because naturally I would, and naturally I would stick around to watch developments. I'm talking to keep you from talking, because naturally we would talk. I've had practice answering questions, and I know some of the rules. There are only three methods that are any good in the long run. You have strong fingers."

"I'm sorry." Her grip relaxed a little, but she held on. "What are the three methods?"

"One. Button your lip. Answer nothing whatever. Two. Tell the truth straight through—the works. Three. Tell a simple basic lie with no trimmings and stick to it. If you try a fancy lie, or a mixture of truth and lies, or part of the truth, but try to save some, you're sunk. Of course, as far as I know, there is no reason why you shouldn't just tell the truth."

"You said to leave it to you."

"Yes, but they won't. There are very few people in their jurisdiction they wouldn't rather leave it to than me, on account of certain——Here they come."

An official car rolled to a stop behind the prowl car, and Inspector Cramer of Homicide West climbed out.

If you are surprised that an inspector had come in response to a report that a corpse had been found, I wasn't. The report had of course given the location, in front of Nine-eighteen West Thirty-fifth Street, and that address held memories, most of them sour, for the personnel at Homicide West, from Cramer down. A violent death that was in any way connected with Nero Wolfe made them itch, and presumably the report had included the item that Archie Goodwin was present.

My client and I watched the routine activities from our grandstand seat. They were swift, efficient and thorough. Traffic was detoured at the corner of Ninth Avenue. A section of the street and sidewalk was roped off to enclose the taxi. Floodlights were focused on the taxi and surroundings. A photographer took shots from various angles. Pedestrians from both directions were shunted across the street, where a crowd gathered behind the rope. Some twenty city employees, in uniform and out, were on the scene in less than half an hour after the cop had made the radio call—five of them known to me by name and four others by sight. The second floodlight had just been turned on when Cramer came around the front of the taxi, crossed to the steps, mounted the first few and faced me.

"All right," he said. "Let's go in. I might as well have you and Wolfe together and this woman too. That may simplify it. Open the door."

"On the contrary," I said, not moving, "it would complicate it. Mr. Wolfe is in the office, reading a book, and knows nothing of all this and cares less. If I went in and told him you wanted to see him, and what about, you know what he would say, and so do I. Nothing doing."

"Who came here in that taxi?"

"I don't know. I know nothing whatever about the taxi. When I came out it was there at the curb."

"When did you come out?"

"Twenty minutes past nine."

"Why did you come out?"

"To find a place to spend the night. I have quit my job, so if you're determined to see Mr. Wolfe, you'll have to ring."

"You're telling me you've quit."

"Right. I don't work here anymore."

"Oh, no! I thought you and Wolfe had tried all the wrinkles there are, but this is a new one. Do you expect me to buy it?"

"It's not a wrinkle. I meant it. I wouldn't sign a pledge never to sleep here again because that depends on Mr. Wolfe's handling of a certain problem, but when I left the house I meant it. The problem has no connection with that taxi."

"Did this woman leave the house with you?"

"No. When I opened the door, coming out, she was coming up the steps. She said she wanted to see Nero Wolfe, and when I told her I no longer worked for him, and anyway he probably wouldn't see her, she said she guessed that for what she wanted I would be better than Wolfe. She offered to pay me fifty dollars for consultation on how to win a bet she had made, and we sat here to consult. We had been here fifteen or twenty minutes when the prowl car came along and stopped by the taxi, which had been standing there when I left the house, and naturally I was curious and went to take a look. The officer asked me my name and I told him. When he went to his radio to report, I came back to my client, but we didn't do much consulting on account of the commotion. That's the crop."

"Had you ever seen this woman before?"

"No."

"What was the bet she wanted to consult about?"

"That's her affair. She's here; ask her."

"Did she come in that taxi?"

"Not to my knowledge. Ask her."

"Did you see her get out of the taxi?"

"No. She was halfway up the stoop when I opened the door."

"Did you see anyone get out of the taxi? Or near it?"

"No."

"What's her name?"

"Ask her."

His head moved. "Is your name Judith Bram?"

That was no news for me, since my view through the open door had included the framed picture of the hackie and her name. As well as I had been able to tell, the picture was not of my client.

"No," she said.

"What is it?"

"Mira Holt. Mira with an *i*." Her voice was clear and steady.

"Did you drive that taxi here?"

"No."

"Did you come here in it?"

"No."

So she had picked Method Three, a simple basic lie.

"Did you have an appointment to see Nero Wolfe?"

"No."

"Where do you live?"

"Seven-fourteen East Eighty-first Street."

"What is your occupation?"

"Modeling. Mostly fashion modeling."

"Are you married?"

"Yes, but I don't live with my husband."

"What's your husband's name?"

She opened her mouth and closed it again. Then she said, "Waldo Kearns. I use my own name."

"Are you divorced?"

"No."

"Was that taxi here when you arrived?"

"I don't know. I didn't notice, but I suppose it was because it didn't come after we sat down."

"How did you come here?"

"I don't think that matters."

"I'll decide that. How did you come?"

"No. For instance, if somebody drove me here, or near here, you would ask him, and I might not want you to. No." So she also knew what "no trimmings" meant.

"I advise you," Cramer advised her, "to tell me how you came."

"I would rather not."

"What was the bet you wanted to consult about?"

"That doesn't matter either. It was a private bet with a friend." Her head turned. "You're a detective, Mr. Goodwin, so you ought to know, do I have to tell him about my private affairs just because I was sitting here with you?"

"Of course not," I assured her. "Not unless he shows some connection between your private affairs and his public affairs, and he hasn't. It's entirely up to you whether——"

"What the devil is all this?" Nero Wolfe bellowed.

I twisted around and so did my client. The door was wide open, and he was standing, his bulk towering above us. "What's going on?" he demanded.

Since I was merely an ex-employee and Cramer was an inspector, I thought it fitting to let him reply, but he didn't. Apparently he was too flabbergasted at seeing Wolfe actually stick his nose outdoors. Wolfe advanced a step. "Archie, I asked a question."

I had stood up. "Yes, sir, I heard you. Miss Holt, this is Mr. Wolfe. Miss Mira Holt. When I left the house she was coming up the steps. I had never seen her before. When I told her I was no longer in your employ, she said I would be better than you and asked to consult me. She has paid me. We sat down to confer. There was an empty taxi parked at the curb, no driver in it. A police car came along and stopped, and a cop found a dead body, female, in the taxi under a piece of canvas. I was there looking in when he removed the canvas. I came back up the stoop to sit with my client. We recessed our conference to watch the proceedings. Officers arrived promptly, including Inspector Cramer. When he got around to it, he came and questioned us. I knew nothing about the taxi or its contents and said so. She told him she had not driven the taxi here and hadn't come in it. She gave him her name and address and occupation, but refused to answer questions about her private affairs—for instance, what she was consulting me about. I was telling her that was entirely up to her, when you appeared."

Wolfe grunted. "Why didn't you bring Miss Holt inside?"

"Because it's not my house—or my office."

"Nonsense. There is the front room. If you wish to stand on ceremony, I invite you to use it for consultation with your client. Sitting here in this hubbub is absurd. Have you any more information for Mr. Cramer?"

"No."

"Have you, Miss Holt?"

She was on her feet beside me. "I didn't have any," she said. "I haven't got any."

"Then get away from this turmoil. Come in."

Cramer found his tongue. "Just a minute." He had come on up to the stoop and was at my elbow, focused on Wolfe. "This is all very neat—too damn neat. Goodwin says he quit his job. Did he?"

"Yes."

"Why?"

"Pfui. That's egregious, Mr. Cramer, and you know it."

"Did it have anything to do with Miss Holt or what she was coming to consult about?"

"No."

"Or with the fact that a taxi was parked at your door with a dead body in it?"

"No."

"Did you know Miss Holt was coming?"

"No. Nor, patently, did Mr. Goodwin."

"Did you know the taxi was out here?"

"No. I am bearing with you, sir. You persist beyond reason. If Mr. Goodwin or I were involved in the circumstances that brought you here, or Miss Holt, would he have sat here with her, awaiting your assault? You know him, and you know me. . . . Come, Archie. Bring your client." He turned.

I told Cramer, "I'll be glad to type up statements and bring them down," touched Mira Holt's arm and followed her inside, Wolfe having preceded us.

When I had shut the door and the lock had clicked, Wolfe spoke, "Since there's no telephone in the front room, perhaps the office would be better. I will go to my room."

"Thank you," I said politely. "But it might be still better for us to leave the back way. You may not want us here when I explain the situation. Miss Holt drove that taxi here. A friend of hers named Judith Bram is one of the ninety-three female hackies in New York, and she let Miss Holt take her cab—or maybe Miss Holt took it without Miss Bram's knowledge. She left——"

"No," Mira said. "Judy let me take it."

"Possible," I conceded. "You're a pretty good liar. Let me finish. . . . She left it, empty, in front of a building and went into the building for something, and when she came back there was a dead body in it, a woman, with a knife between its ribs. Either it was covered with a canvas or she——"

"I covered it," Mira said. "I found the canvas under the driver's seat."

"She's levelheaded," I told Wolfe. "Somewhat. She couldn't notify the police, because not only had she and her friend violated the law but also she had recognized the dead woman. She knew her. She decided to come and consult you and me. I met her on the stoop. She told me a cockeyed tale about a bet she had made with a friend, which I'll skip. I said somewhat levelheaded. I let her see that I knew she was feeding me soap, but kept her from blurting it out. So I told Cramer no lies, but she did, and did a good job. But the lies won't keep long. It's barely possible that Judith Bram will deny that she let someone take her cab, but sooner or later——"

"I tried to phone her," Mira said, "but she didn't answer. I was going to tell her to say that someone stole it."

"Quit interrupting me. Did you ever hear of fingerprints? Did you see them working on that cab? . . . So I have a client who is in a double-breasted jam. I'll know more about it after she tells me things. The point is, did she kill that woman? If I thought she did I would bow out quick. I would already have bowed out because it would have been hopeless. But she didn't. One will get you ten that she didn't. If she had——"

That interruption wasn't words; it was her lips against mine and her palms covering my ears. If she had been Wolfe's client, I would have shoved her off quick, because that sort of demonstration only ruffles him; but she was mine and there was no point in hurting her feelings. I even patted her shoulder. When she was through I resumed:

"——If she had killed her she would not have driven here with the corpse for a passenger to tell you, or even me, a goofy tale about a bet with a friend. Not a chance. She would have dumped the corpse somewhere. Make it twenty to one. Add to that my observation of her while we sat there on the stoop, and it's thirty to one. Therefore, I am keeping the fee she paid me, and I'm—by the way——" I reached in my pocket for the bills she had given me, unfolded them and counted. Three twenties, three tens and a five. Returning two twenties and a ten to my pocket. I offered her the rest. "Your change. I'm keeping fifty."

She hesitated, then took it. "I'll pay you more. What are you going to do?"

"I'll know better after you answer some questions. One that shouldn't wait: What did you do with the cap?"

"I have it." She patted her front.

"Good." I returned to Wolfe. "So we'll be going. Thank you again for your hospitality, but Cramer may be ringing the bell any minute. . . . We'll go out the rear. Miss Holt. This way."

"No." Wolfe snapped it. "This is preposterous. Give me half of that fifty dollars."

I raised a brow. "For what?"

"To pay me. You have helped me with many problems; surely I can help you with one. I am not being quixotic. I do not accept your headstrong decision that our long association has ended, but even if it has, your repute is inextricably involved with mine. I have never tried to do a job without your help; why should you try to do one without mine?"

I wanted to grin at him, but he might have misunderstood. "O.K.," I said, and got a twenty from the pocket where I had put the fee, and a five from my wallet, and handed them to him. Taking them, he turned and headed for the office, and Mira and I followed.

Where to sit was a delicate question, not for Wolfe—who of course went to his oversized custom-built chair behind his desk, nor for the client, as Wolfe wiggled a finger to indicate the red leather chair that would put her facing him—but for me. The desk at the right angles to Wolfe's was no longer mine. I had a hand on one of the yellow chairs, to move it up, when Wolfe growled, "Confound it, don't be frivolous. We have a job to do."

I went and sat where I had belonged, and asked him, "Do I proceed?"

"Certainly."

I looked at her. "I would like," I said, "to be corroborated. Did you kill that woman?"

"No. No!"

"O.K. Out with it. This time Method Two, the truth. Judith Bram is a friend of yours?"

"Yes."

"Did she let you take her cab?"

"Yes."

"Why?"

"I asked her to."

"Why did you ask her to?"

"Because—it's a long story."

"Make it as short as you can. We may not have much time."

She was on the edge of the chair, which would have held two of her. "I have known Judy three years. She was a model, too, but she didn't like it. She's very unconventional. She had money she had inherited, and she bought a cab and a license about a year ago. She cruises when she feels like it, but she has some regular customers who think it's chic to ride in a cab with a girl driver, and my husband is one of them. He often——"

"Your husband?" Wolfe demanded. "*Miss* Holt?"

"They don't live together," I told him. "Not divorced, but she uses her own name. Fashion model. . . . Go ahead."

"My husband's name is Waldo Kearns. He paints pictures, but doesn't sell any. He has money. He often calls Judy to take him somewhere, and he called last night when I was with her and told her to come for him at eight o'clock this evening, and I asked Judy to let me go instead of her. I have been trying to see him for months, to have a talk with him, and he refuses to see me. He doesn't answer my letters. I want a divorce, and he doesn't. I think the reason——"

"Skip it. Get on."

"Well, Judy said I could take the cab, and this evening at seven o'clock I went to her place, and she brought it from the garage, gave me her cap and jacket, and I drove it to——"

"Where is her place?"

"Bowdoin Street—number seventeen—in the Village."

"I know. You took the cab there?"

"Yes. I drove it to Ferrell Street. It's west of Varick, below——"

"I know where it is."

"Then you know it's a dead end. Close to the end is an alley that goes between walls to a little house. That's my husband's. I lived there with him about a year. I got there a little before eight and turned around and parked in front of the alley. Judy had said she always waited for him there. He didn't come. I didn't want to go to the house, because he would shut the door on me, but when he hadn't come at half-past eight I got out and went——"

"You sure of the time?"

"Yes. I looked at my watch. Of course."

"What does it say now?"

She lifted her wrist. "Two minutes after eleven."

"Right. You went through the alley?"

"Yes—to the house. There's a brass knocker on the door, no bell. I knocked with it, but nobody came. I knocked several times. I could hear the radio or television going inside—I could just barely hear it—so I knocked loud. He couldn't have recognized me through a window because it was too dark and I had the cap pulled down. Of course, it could have been Morton, his man, as he calls him, playing the radio, but I don't think so because he would have heard the knocker and come to the door. I finally gave up and went back to the cab, and as I was getting in I saw her. At first I thought it was a trick he had played, but when I looked closer I saw the knife, and then I recognized her, and she was dead. If I hadn't turned around and gripped the wheel as hard as I could, I think I would have fainted. I never have fainted. I sat there——"

"Who was it?"

"It was Phoebe Arden. She was the reason my husband didn't want a divorce. I'm sure she was, or anyway one of the reasons. I think he thought that as long as he was still married to me she couldn't expect him to marry her, and neither could anyone else.

But I wasn't thinking about that while I sat there; I was thinking what to do. I knew the right thing was to call the police, but I was driving Judy's cab and, what was worse, I would have to admit I knew who she was, and they would find out about her and my husband. I don't know how long I sat there."

"It must have been quite a while. You left the cab to go to the house at eight-thirty. How long were you gone?"

"I don't know. I knocked several times, and looked in at the windows, and then knocked some more." She considered. "At least ten minutes."

"Then you were back at the cab at eight-forty, and from there to here wouldn't take more than ten minutes, and you got here at nine-twenty. Did you sit there half an hour?"

"No. I decided to get her—to get it out of the cab. I found that canvas under the driver's seat. I thought the best place would be somewhere along the river front, and I drove there, but didn't see a good place, and men tried to stop me twice, and once when I stopped for a light a man opened the door, and when I told him I was making a delivery he almost climbed in anyway. Then I thought I would just leave the cab somewhere, anywhere, and I went to a phone booth to call Judy and tell her to say the cab had been stolen, but there was no answer. Then I thought of Nero Wolfe and you, and I drove here. I didn't have much time to make that up about the bet; just on my way here. I knew it wasn't much good while I was telling it."

"So did I." I was frowning at her. "I want you to realize one thing. I believe you when you say you didn't kill her, but it doesn't follow that I swallow you whole. For instance, the divorce situation. If the fact is that your husband wanted one so he could marry Phoebe Arden, and you balked, that would make it different."

"No." She was frowning back. "I've told you the truth, every word. I lied to you out there, but if I lied to you now I'd be a fool."

"You sure would. How good a friend of yours is Judy Bram?"

"She's my best friend. She's a little wild, but I like her. I love her."

"Are you sure she rates it?"

"Yes."

I turned to Wolfe. "Since you're helping on this, and I fully appreciate it, our minds should meet. Do you accept it that she didn't kill her?"

"As a working hypothesis, yes."

"Then isn't it likely she was killed by someone who knew that Miss Holt would be driving the cab—since Kearns didn't show, taking her away from the cab, and the radio or television was on in the house?"

"Likely, but far from certain. It could have been impromptu. Or the embarrassment could have been meant for Miss Bram, not for Miss Holt."

I returned to Mira. "How close are Judy Bram and your husband?"

"Close?" The frown was getting chronic. "They aren't close. If you mean intimate. I doubt if Judy has ever allowed any man to be intimate. My husband may have tried. I suppose he has."

"Could Judy have had any reason to kill Phoebe Arden?"

"Good Lord, no!"

"Isn't it possible that Judy, unknown to you, had got an idea that she would like to break the ice with your husband, and Phoebe Arden was in the way?"

"I suppose it is, but I don't believe it."

"You heard what I asked Mr. Wolfe and what he answered. I still like it that whoever killed her knew that you were going to drive the cab there. It's possible that Judy Bram told someone."

"Yes, it's possible, but I don't believe it. Judy wouldn't. She just wouldn't."

"It's also possible that you told someone. Did you?"

Her lips twitched—twice. Two seconds. "No," she said.

"You're lying. I haven't time to be polite. You're lying. Whom did you tell?"

"I'm not going to say. The person I told couldn't possibly have—have done anything. Some things are not possible."

"Who was it?"

"No, Mr. Goodwin. Really."

I got the twenty and ten from my pocket and a twenty from my wallet, got up and went to her. "Here's your fifty bucks," I said. "Count me out. You can leave the back way."

"But I tell you he couldn't!"

"Then he won't get hurt. I won't bite him, but I've got to know everything you do or it's no good."

Her lips twitched again. "You would really do that? Just give me up?"

"I sure would. I will."

She sighed. "I phoned a friend of mine last evening and told him. His name is Gilbert Irving."

"Is he more than a friend?"

"No. He is married and so am I. We're friends, that's all."

"Does he know your husband?"

"Yes. They've known each other for years, but they've never been close."

"Did he know Phoebe Arden?"

"He had met her. He didn't know her."

"Why did you tell him about your plan to drive the cab?"

"Because I wanted to know what he thought of it. He is a very—a very intelligent man."

"What did he think of it?"

"He thought it was foolish. Not foolish exactly—useless. He thought my husband would refuse to listen to me. Honestly, Mr. Goodwin, this is foolish. There is absolutely no——"

The doorbell rang. I had taken three steps before I remembered that I no longer worked there; then, not wishing to be frivolous, I continued to the hall and took a look through the one-way glass panel of the front door. A man and a woman were on the stoop. A glance was enough to recognize Inspector Cramer, but it took closer inspection for the woman, and I moved down the hall. Even then I wasn't positive, as the light had been dim on the picture of the female hackie in the taxi, but I was sure enough. It was Judith Bram.

It was up to me, since it was my case and Wolfe was merely helping, but he had many times asked for my opinion and it wouldn't hurt to reciprocate, so I stepped to the office door and said, "Cramer and Judy Bram. Shall I——"

"Judy!" Mira cried. "She's here?"

I ignored her. "Shall I scoot with Miss Holt and leave them to you?"

He closed his eyes. Then he opened them. "I would say no. The decision is yours."

"Then we stick. I want to meet Judy anyhow. Sit tight, Miss Holt. Never drop a simple basic lie until it drops you."

As I turned, the bell rang again. I went to the front, put the chain bolt on, opened the door the two inches the chain allowed and spoke through the crack, "Do you want me, inspector?"

"I want in. Open up."

"Glad to for you, but not for strangers. Who is the lady?"

"Her name is Judith Bram. She's the owner and driver——"

"I want to see Mira Holt!" the lady said, meaning it. "Open the door!"

I removed the chain, but didn't have to swing the door because she saved me the trouble. She came with it and darted down the hall. Seeing that Cramer, after her, would brush me, I stiffened to make the brush a bump, and he wobbled and lost a step, giving me time to shut the door and reach the office at his heels. When we entered, Judy was sitting on the arm of the red leather chair with her arm across Mira's shoulders, jabbering.

Cramer grabbed her arm and barked at her, but she ignored him.

"... and I said yes, the cab might have still been there in front when you left, but I was sure you wouldn't take it, and anyway——"

Cramer yanked her up and around, and as she came she swung with her free hand and smacked him in the face. There was too much of him to be staggered by it, but the sound effect was fine. She jerked loose and glared at him. Her big brown well-spaced eyes were ideal for glaring. I had a feeling that I had seen her before, but I hadn't. It was just an old memory—a seventh-grade classmate out in Ohio whom I had been impelled to kiss, and she had socked me on the ear with her arithmetic book. She is now married, with five children.

"That's not advisable, Miss Bram," Cramer stated. "Striking a police officer." He moved, got a yellow chair and swung it around. "Here ... sit down."

"I'll sit where I please." She perched again on the red leather arm. "Is it advisable for a police officer to manhandle a citizen? When I got a hack license I informed myself about laws. Am I under arrest?"

"No."

"Then don't touch me." Her head swung around. "You're Nero Wolfe? You're even bigger." She didn't say bigger than what. "I'm Judy Bram. Are you representing my friend, Mira Holt?"

His eyes on her were half closed. " 'Representing' is not the word, Miss Bram. I'm a detective, not a lawyer. Miss Holt has hired Mr. Goodwin, and he has hired me as his assistant. You call her your friend. Are you her friend?"

"Yes. And I want to know. She left my place around half-past seven, and about an hour later I went out to keep a date. I had left my cab out front, and it wasn't there, but I supposed——"

"Hold it," Cramer snapped. He was on the yellow chair, and I was at my desk. "I'll do the talking."

She merely raised her voice. "—I supposed a man from the garage had come and got it. I have that arrangement——"

"Shut up," Cramer roared, "or I'll shut you up!"

"How?" she asked.

It was a question. He had several choices—clamp his paw on her mouth, or pick her up and carry her out, or call in a couple of big strong men from out front, or hit her with a blunt instrument, or shoot her. All had drawbacks.

"Permit me," Wolfe said. "I suggest, Mr. Cramer, that you have bungled it. The notion of suddenly confronting Miss Holt with Miss Bram was, of course, tempting, but your appraisal of Miss Bram's temperament was faulty. Now you're stuck. You won't get the contradictions you're after. Miss Holt would be a simpleton to supply particulars until she knows what Miss Bram has said. As you well know, that does not necessarily imply culpability for either of them."

Cramer rasped with anger in his voice, "You're telling Miss Holt not to answer any questions."

"Am I? If so, unwittingly. Now, of course, you have made it plain. It would appear that you have only two alternatives—either let Miss Bram finish her account or remove her."

"There's a third one I like better. I'll remove Miss Holt." Cramer got up.... "Come on, Miss Holt. I'm taking you down for questioning in connection with the murder of Phoebe Arden."

"Is she under arrest?" Judy demanded.

"No. But if she doesn't talk she will be—as a material witness."

I was sitting with my jaw set. Wolfe would rather miss a meal than let Cramer or any other cop take a client of his from that office into custody, and over the years I had seen and heard him pull some fancy maneuvers to prevent it. But this was my client, and he wasn't batting an eye. I admit that it would have had to be something extra fancy, and it was up to me, not him, but I had split the fee with him. So I sat with my jaw set while Mira left the chair and Judy jabbered and Cramer touched Mira's arm and they headed for the door. Then I came to, scribbled on my memo pad—formerly my memo pad—tore the sheet off and made for the hall. Cramer had his hand on the knob.

"Here's the phone number," I told her. "Twenty-four-hour service. Don't forget Method Three." She took the slip and said, "I won't," and crossed the sill, with Cramer right behind.

Back in the office, Wolfe was leaning back with his eyes closed, and Judy Bram was standing, scowling at him. She switched the scowl to me and demanded, "Why don't you put him to bed?"

"Too heavy. How many people did you tell that Mira was going to drive your cab to her husband's house?"

She eyed me, straight, for two breaths, then went to the red leather chair and sat. I took the yellow one, to be closer. "I thought you were working for her," she said.

"I am."

"You don't sound like it. She didn't drive my cab."

I shook my head. "Come on down. Would I be working for her if she hadn't opened up? You told her yesterday that Kearns had phoned you to call for him at eight o'clock today, and she asked you to let her go instead of you. She wanted to have a talk with him about a divorce. How many people did you tell about it?"

"Nobody. If she opened up, what's the rest of it?"

"Ask her when you see her. Did you kill Phoebe Arden?"

From the flash in her eye, I believe she would have smacked me if I had been close enough. "Oh, for heaven's sake," she said. "Get a club. Drag me by the hair."

"Later maybe." I leaned toward her. "Look, Miss Bram. Give your temperament a rest and use your brain. I am working for Mira Holt. I know exactly where she was and what she did every minute from seven o'clock this evening on, but I'm not going to tell you. Of course, you know that the dead body of a woman named Phoebe Arden was found in your cab. I am certain that Mira didn't kill her, but she is probably going to be charged. I am not certain that the murderer tried to get her tagged for it, but it looks like it. I would be a fathead to tell the murderer about her movements. Wouldn't I? Answer with your brain."

"Yes." She was meeting my eyes.

"O.K. Give me one good reason why I should cross you off. One you would accept if you were in my place. Mira has, naturally, but why should I?"

"Because there's not the slightest——" She stopped. "No. You don't know that. All right. But don't try twisting my arm. I know some tricks."

"I'll keep my distance if you will. Did you kill Phoebe Arden?"

"No."

"Do you know who did?"

"No."

"Have you any suspicions? Any ideas?"

"Yes. Or I would have if I knew anything—where and when it happened. Did Phoebe come out to the cab with Waldo Kearns?"

"No; Kearns didn't show up. Mira never saw him."

"But Phoebe came?"

"Not alive. When Mira saw her she was dead—in the cab."

"Then my idea is Waldo—the sophisticated ape. You're not any too bright. If I killed her in my own cab while Mira was driving it, I already know everything you do and more. Why not tell me?"

I looked at Wolfe, who had opened his eyes off and on. He grunted. "You told her to use her brain," he muttered.

I returned to Judy. "You certainly would know this: Mira got there before eight o'clock and parked in front. When Kearns hadn't showed at eight-thirty, she went to the house and spent ten minutes knocking and looking in windows. When she returned to the cab, the dead body was in it. She never saw Kearns."

"But my gosh." Her brows were up. She turned her hands over. "All she had to do was dump it out!"

"She hasn't got your temperament. She——"

"She drove here with it? To consult with you?"

"She might have done worse. In fact, she tried to. She phoned you and got no answer. What's your idea about Kearns?"

"He killed Phoebe."

"Then that's settled. Why?"

"I don't know. He tried to shake her and she hung on. Or she cheated on him. Or she had a bad cold and he was afraid he would catch it. He put the body in the cab to fix Mira. He hates her because she told him the truth about himself once."

"Did you know Phoebe well?"

"Well enough. She was a widow at thirty, roaming around. I might have killed her, at that. About a year ago she started scattering remarks about me, and I broke her neck—almost. She spent a week in a hospital."

"Did it cure her? I mean of remark-scattering?"

"Yes."

"Let's finish with you. You told Mr. Wolfe that Mira left your place around half-past seven, and about an hour later you went out to keep a date. So you might have left at a quarter after eight."

"I might, but I didn't. I walked to Mitchell Hall on Fourteenth Street to make a speech at a cabdrivers' meeting, and I got there at five minutes to nine. After the meeting I walked back home, and two cops were there waiting for me. They were dumb enough to ask me first where my cab was, and I said I supposed it was in the garage. When they said no, it was parked on Thirty-fifth Street, and asked me to come and identify it, naturally I went. I also identified a dead body, which they hadn't mentioned. Is that Inspector Cramer dumb?"

"No."

"I thought not. When he asked me if I knew Mira Holt, of course I said yes, and when he asked when I last saw her I told him. Since I had no idea what had happened, I thought that was safest, but I said I hadn't told her she could take the cab and I knew she wouldn't take it without asking me."

"How well do you know Gilbert Irving?"

That fazed her. Her mouth opened and she gawked with her big brown eyes. "Are my ears working?" she demanded. "Did you say Gilbert Irving?"

"That's right."

"Who let him in?"

"Mira mentioned him. How well do you know him?"

"Too well. I dream about a lion standing on a rock about to spring at me, and I suspect it's him. If my subconscious is yearning for him, it had better go soak its head because, first, he's married and his wife has claws, and, second, when he looks at Mira or hears her voice he has to lean against something to keep from trembling. Did she happen to mention that to you?"

"No. Who is he? What does he do?"

"Something in Wall Street. Why did Mira mention him?"

"Because I made her. She phoned him last evening and told him she was going to drive your cab and why. She wanted to know what he thought of it. I want to know what motive he might have for killing Phoebe Arden."

She opened her mouth to reply, then decided to laugh instead. "Your subconscious taking over?" I inquired.

"No." She sobered. "I couldn't help it. It struck me that, of course, Gil killed her. He couldn't bear the thought of Mira's husband being unfaithful to her, it was an insult to her womanhood, so he killed Phoebe."

"Does anything else strike you? A motive for him you wouldn't laugh at?"

"Of course not; it's ridiculous. Have you finished with me?"

I looked at Wolfe. His eyes were closed. "For now, yes," I told her, "unless Mr. Wolfe thinks of something."

"How can he? You can talk in your sleep, but you can't think." She stood up. "What are you going to do?"

"Find a murderer and stick pins in him—or her."

"Not sitting here you aren't. Why don't you go and tackle Wally Kearns? I'll go with you."

"Thanks, I'll manage."

"Where did the inspector take Mira?"

"Either to Homicide West, Two-thirty West Twentieth, or to the district attorney's office, One fifty-five Leonard. Try Twentieth Street first."

"I will." She got up and was off. I followed, to let her out, but she was a fast walker and I would have had to trot to catch up. When I reached the door, she had it open. I stepped out to the stoop and watched her descend to the sidewalk and turn west. The floodlights and ropes and police cars were gone, and so was Judy's cab. My wristwatch said five minutes past midnight as I went in and shut the door. Back in the office Wolfe was on his feet, with his eyes open.

"I assumed," I said, "that if you wanted something from her that I hadn't got you would say so."

"Naturally."

"Have you any comments?"

"No. It's bedtime."

"Yeah. Since you're with me on this, which I appreciate, perhaps I'd better sleep here. If you don't mind."

"Certainly. You own your bed. I have a suggestion. I presume you intend to have a look at that place in the morning and to see Mr. Kearns. It might be well for me to see him too."

"I agree. Thank you for suggesting it. If they haven't got him downtown, I'll have him here at eleven o'clock." I made it eleven because that was Wolfe's earliest hour for an appointment, when he came down from his two-hour session up in the plant room with the orchids.

"Make it a quarter past eleven," he said. "I will be engaged until then with Mr. Anderson."

"Didn't you phone him not to come?"

"On the contrary, I phoned him to come. On reflection I saw that I had been hasty. In my employ, as my agent, you had made a commitment, and I was bound by it. I should not have repudiated it. I should have honored it and then dismissed you if I considered your disregard of the rules intolerable."

"I see. I can understand that you'd rather fire me than have me quit."

"I said 'if.'"

I lifted my shoulders and dropped them. "It's a little complicated. If I have quit, you can't fire me. If I haven't quit, I am still on your payroll, and it would be unethical for me to have Miss Holt as my client. It would also be wrong for you to accept pay from me for helping me with the kind of work you are paying me to do. If you return the twenty-five to me and I return the fifty to Miss Holt, I will be deserting an innocent fellow being in a jam whom I have accepted as a client, and that would be inexcusable. It looks to me as if we have got ourselves in a fix that is absolutely hopeless, and I can't see——"

"Confound it, go to bed!" he roared and marched out.

By eight-fifteen Tuesday morning I was pretty well convinced that Mira Holt was in the coop, since I had got it from three different sources. At seven-twenty Judy Bram had phoned to say that Mira was under arrest and what was I going to do. I said it wouldn't be practical to tell a suspect my plans, and she hung up on me. At seven-forty Lon Cohen of the *Gazette* phoned to ask if it was true that I had quit my job with Nero Wolfe, and if so what was I doing there, and was Mira Holt my client, and if so what was she doing in the can, and had she killed Phoebe Arden or not. Since Lon had often been useful and might be again, I explained fully, off the record, why I couldn't explain. And at eight o'clock the radio said that Mira Holt was being held as a material witness in the murder of Phoebe Arden.

Neither Lon nor the radio supplied any items that helped, nor did the morning papers. The *Star* had a picture of the taxi parked in front of Wolfe's house, but I had seen that for myself. It also had a description of the clothes Phoebe Arden had died in, but what I needed was a description of the clothes the murderer had killed in. And it gave the specifications of the knife—an ordinary kitchen knife with a five-inch blade and a plastic handle—but if the answer was going to come from any routine operation like tracing the knife or lifting prints from the handle, it would be Cramer's army who would get it; not I.

I made one phone call, to Anderson, to ask him to postpone his appointment because Wolfe was busy on a case, and he said sure, it wasn't urgent; and I put a note on Wolfe's desk. I wanted to make another call, to Nathaniel Parker, the lawyer, but vetoed it. For getting Mira out on bail he would have charged about ten times what she had paid me, and there was no big hurry. It would teach her not to drive a hack without a license.

At a quarter past eight I left the house and went to Ninth Avenue for a taxi, and at half past I dismissed it at the corner of Carmine and Ferrell, and walked down Ferrell Street to its dead end. There were only two alternatives for what had happened during the period, call it ten minutes, when Mira had been away from the cab. Either the murderer, having already killed Phoebe Arden, had carried or dragged the body to the cab and hoisted it in, or he had got in the cab with her and killed her there. I preferred the latter, because you can walk to a cab with a live woman in much less time than you can carry her to it dead, and also because there is much less risk of being noticed. But in either case they had to come from some place nearby.

The first place to consider was Kearns's house, but it took only five minutes to cross it off. The alley that led to it was walled on both sides, Mira had been parked at its mouth, and there was no other way to get from the house to the street. On the left of the alley was a walled-in lumberyard, and on the right was a warehouse. Neither of them seemed an ideal spot for cover, but across the street was a beaut. It was an open lot cluttered with blocks of stone scattered and piled around, some rough and some chiseled and polished. A whole company could have hidden there. As you know, I was already on record that Mira hadn't killed her, but it was nice to see that stoneyard. If there had been no place to hide in easy distance—

Three men were there, two discussing a stone and one chiseling, but they wouldn't be there at eight in the evening. I recrossed the street, entered the alley and walked through.

By gum, Kearns had a garden, a sizable patch, say forty by sixty, with flowers in bloom and a little pool with a fountain, and a flagstone path leading to the door of a two-story brick house painted white. I hadn't known there was anything like it in Manhattan, and I thought I knew Manhattan. A man in a gray shirt and blue jeans was kneeling among the flowers, and halfway up the path I stopped and asked him. "Are you Waldo Kearns?"

"Do I look it?" he demanded.

"Yes and no. Are you Morton?"

"That's my name. What's yours?"

"Goodwin." I headed for the house, but he called. "Nobody there," and I turned. "Where's Mr. Kearns?"

"I don't know. He went out a while ago."

"When will he be back?"

"I couldn't say."

I looked disappointed. "I should have phoned. I want to buy a picture. I came last evening around half-past eight and knocked, but nothing doing. I knocked loud because I heard the radio or TV."

"It was the TV. I was watching it. I heard you knock. I don't open the door at night when he's not here. There's some tough ones around this neighborhood."

"I don't blame you. What time did he leave last evening?"

"What difference does it make when he left if he wasn't here?"

Perfectly logical, not only for him but for me. If Kearns hadn't been there when Mira arrived in the cab, it didn't matter when he had left. I would have liked to ask Morton whether anyone had left with him, but from the look in his eye he would have used more logic on me, so I skipped it, said I'd try again and went.

There was no use hanging around because if Kearns had gone to call at the district attorney's office by request, which was highly probable, there was no telling when he would be back. I had got Gilbert Irving's business address, on Wall Street, from the phone book, but there was no use going there at that early hour. However, I had also got his home address, on East Seventy-eighth Street, so I hoofed it along Ferrell Street back to civilization and flagged a taxi.

It was nine-fifteen when I climbed out in front of the number on Seventy-eighth Street, a tenement palace with a marquee and a doorman. In the lobby another uniformed sentry sprang into action, and I told him, "Mr. Gilbert Irving. Tell him a friend of Miss Holt." He went and used a phone, returned and said, "Fourteen B," and watched me like a hawk as I walked to the elevator and entered. When I got out at the fourteenth floor, the elevator man stood and watched until I had pushed the button and the door had opened and I had been invited in.

The inviter was no maid or butler. She might have passed for a maid in uniform, but not in the long flowing silk number which she probably called a breakfast gown. Without any suggestions about my hat she said, "This way, please," and led me across the hall, through an arch into a room half as big as Kearns's garden, and over to chairs near a corner. She sat on one of them and indicated another for me.

I stood. "Perhaps the man downstairs didn't understand me," I suggested. "I asked for Mr. Irving."

"I know," she said. "He isn't here. I am his wife. We are friends of Miss Holt, and we're disturbed about the terrible—about her difficulty. You're a friend of hers?" Her voice was a surprise because it didn't fit. She was slender and not very tall, with a round little face and a little curved mouth, but her deep strong voice was what you would expect from a female sergeant. Nothing about her suggested the claws Judy Bram had mentioned, but they could have been drawn in.

"A new friend," I said. "I've known her twelve hours. If you've read the morning paper you may have noted that she was sitting on the stoop of Nero Wolfe's house with a man named Archie Goodwin when a policeman found the body in the taxi. I'm Goodwin, and she has hired me to find out things."

She adjusted the gown to cover a leg better. "According to the radio, she has hired Nero Wolfe."

"That's a technical point. We're both working on it. I'm seeing people who might have some information, and Mr. Irving is on my list. Is he at his office?"

"I suppose so. He left earlier than usual." The leg was safe—no exposure above the ankle—but she adjusted the gown again. "What kind of information? Perhaps I could help?"

I couldn't very well ask her if her husband had told her that Mira had told him she was going to drive Judy's cab. But she wanted to help. "Almost anything might be useful, Mrs. Irving. Were you and your husband also friends of Phoebe Arden?"

"I was. My husband knew her but you couldn't say they were friends."

"Were they enemies?"

"Oh, no. It was just that they didn't hit it off."

"When did you see her last?"

"Four days ago, last Friday, at a cocktail party at Waldo Kearns's house. I was thinking about it when you came. She was so gay. She was a gay person."

"You hadn't seen her since?"

"No...."

She was going to add something, but checked it. It was so obvious that I asked, "But you had heard from her?"

"How did you know that?"

"I didn't. Most detective work is guessing. Was it a letter?"

"No." She hesitated. "I would like to help, Mr. Goodwin, but I doubt if it's important, and I don't want notoriety."

"Of course not, Mrs. Irving." I was sympathetic. "If you mean, if you tell me something will I tell the police, absolutely not. They have arrested my client."

"Well." She crossed her legs, glancing down to see that nothing was revealed. "I phoned Phoebe yesterday afternoon. My husband and I had tickets for the theater last evening, but about three o'clock he phoned me that a business associate from the West Coast had arrived unexpectedly, and he had to take him to dinner. So I phoned Phoebe and we arranged to meet at Morsini's at a quarter to seven for dinner and then go to the theater. I was there on time, but she didn't come. At a quarter past seven I called her number, but there was no answer. I don't like to eat alone at Morsini's, so I waited a little longer and then left word for her and went to Schrafft's. She didn't come. I thought she might come to the theater, the Majestic, and I waited in the lobby until after nine, and then I left a ticket for her at the box office and went in. I would tell the police about it if I thought it was important, but it doesn't really tell anything except that she was at home when I phoned around three o'clock, does it?"

"Sure it does. Did she agree definitely to meet you at Morsini's?"

"It was definite, quite definite."

"Then it was certainly something that happened after three o'clock that kept her from meeting you. It was probably something that happened after six-thirty or she would have phoned you—if she was still alive. Have you any idea at all what it might have been?"

"None whatever. I can't guess."

"Do you think Mira Holt killed her?"

"Good heavens, no! Not Mira. Even if she had——"

"Even if she had what?"

"Nothing. Mira wouldn't kill anybody. They don't think that, do they?"

Over the years at least a thousand people have asked me what the police think, and I appreciate the compliment though I rarely deserve it. Life would be much simpler if I always knew what the police think at any given moment. It's hard enough to know what I think. After another ten minutes with her I decided that I thought that Mrs. Irving had nothing more to contribute, so I thanked her and departed. She came with me to the hall and even picked up my hat from the chair where I had dropped it.

It was ten minutes to ten when I emerged to the sidewalk and turned left for Lexington Avenue and the subway, and a quarter past when I entered the marble lobby of a towering beehive on Wall Street and consulted the building directory. Gilbert Irving's firm had the whole thirtieth floor, and I found the proper bank of elevators, entered one and was hoisted straight up three hundred feet for nothing. In a paneled chamber with a thick conservative carpet a handsome conservative creature at a desk bigger than Wolfe's told me in a voice like silk that Mr. Irving was not in and that she knew not when he would arrive or where he was. Did I care to wait?

I didn't. I left the building and went to another subway, this time the West Side; and, leaving at Christopher, walked to Ferrell Street and on to its dead end and through the alley. Morton, still in the garden, greeted me with reserve, said Kearns had not returned and there had been no word from him and, as I was turning to go, suddenly demanded, "Did you say you wanted to buy a picture?"

I said that was my idea, but naturally I wanted to see it first, left him wagging his head, walked the length of Ferrell Street the fourth time that day, found a taxi and gave the driver the address which might or might not still be mine. As we turned into Thirty-fifth Street from Eighth Avenue, at five minutes past eleven, there was another taxi just ahead of us, and it stopped at the curb in front of the brownstone. I handed my driver a bill, hopped out and had mounted the stoop by the time the man from the other cab had crossed the sidewalk. I had never seen him or a picture of him, or heard him described, but I knew him. I don't know whether it was his floppy black hat or shoe-string tie, or neat little ears or face like a squirrel, but I knew him. I had the door open when he reached the stoop.

"I would like to see Mr. Nero Wolfe," he said. "I'm Waldo Kearns."

Since Wolfe had suggested that I should bring Kearns there, so that we could look at him together, I would just as soon have let him think that I had filled the order, but of course that wouldn't do. So when I escorted him to the office and announced him, I added, "I met Mr. Kearns out front. He arrived just as I did."

Wolfe, behind his desk, had been pouring beer when we entered. He put the bottle down. "You haven't talked with him?"

"No, sir."

He turned to Kearns, in the red leather chair. "Will you have a beer, sir?"

"Heavens, no." Kearns was emphatic. "I didn't come for amenities. My business is urgent. I am extremely displeased with the counsel you have given my wife. You must have hypnotized her. She refuses to see me. She refuses to accept the services of my lawyer, even to arrange bail for her. I demand an explanation. I intend to hold you to account for alienating the affection of my wife."

"Affections," Wolfe said.

"What?"

"Affections. In that context the plural is used." He lifted the glass and drank and licked his lips.

Kearns said, "I didn't come here to have my grammar corrected."

"Not grammar, diction."

Kearns pounded the chair arm. "What have you to say?"

"It would be futile for me to say anything whatever until you have regained your senses, if you have any. If you think your wife had affection for you until she met me twelve hours ago, you're an ass. If you know she hadn't, your threat is fatuous. In either case what can you expect but contempt?"

"I expect an explanation! I expect the truth! I expect you to tell me why my wife refuses to see me!"

"I can't tell you what I don't know. I don't even know that she has refused, since in your present state I question the accuracy of your reporting. When and where did she refuse?"

"This morning—just now, in the district attorney's office. She won't even talk to my lawyer. She told him she was waiting to hear from you and Goodwin." He turned to me, "You're Goodwin?"

I admitted it, and he said to Wolfe, "It's humiliating! It's degrading! My wife, under arrest! Mrs. Waldo Kearns in jail! Dishonor to my name and to me! And you're to blame."

Wolfe took a breath. "I doubt if it's worth the trouble," he said, "but I'm willing to try. I presume what you're after is an account of our conversation with your wife last evening. I might consider supplying it, but first I would have to be satisfied of your bona fides. Will you answer some questions?"

"It depends on what they are."

"Probably you have already answered them to the police. Has your wife wanted a divorce and have you refused?"

"Yes. I regard the marriage contract as a sacred covenant."

"Have you refused to discuss it with her in recent months?"

"The police didn't ask me that."

"I ask it. I need to establish not only your bona fides, Mr. Kearns, but also your wife's. It shouldn't embarrass you to answer that."

"It doesn't embarrass me. It would have been useless to discuss it with her because I wouldn't consider it."

"So you wouldn't see her?"

"Naturally. That was all she would talk about."

"Have you been contributing to her support since she left you?"

"She didn't leave me. We agreed to try living separately. She wouldn't let me contribute to her support. I offered to."

"The police certainly asked you if you killed Phoebe Arden. Did you?"

"No. Why in heaven's name would I kill her?"

"I don't know. Miss Judith Bram suggested that she may have had a bad cold and you were afraid you would catch it, but that seems farfetched. By the way——"

"Judy? Judy Bram said that? I don't believe it!"

"But she did—in this room last evening in the chair you now occupy. She also called you a sophisticated ape."

"You're lying!"

"No. I'm not above lying, or below it, but the truth will do now. Also——"

"You're lying. You've never seen Judy Bram. You're merely repeating something my wife said."

"That's interesting, Mr. Kearns, and even suggestive. You are willing to believe that your wife called you a sophisticated ape, but not that Miss Bram did. When I do lie I try not to be clumsy. Miss Bram was here last evening, with Mr. Goodwin and me, for half an hour or more; and that brings me to a ticklish point. I must ask you about a detail that the police don't know about. Certainly they asked about your movements last evening, but they didn't know that you had arranged with Judith Bram to call for you in her cab at eight o'clock—unless you told them."

Kearns sat still, and for him it is worth mentioning. With many people, sitting still is nothing remarkable, but with him it was. His sitting, like his face, reminded me of a squirrel; he kept moving or twitching something—a hand, a shoulder, a foot, even his head. Now he was motionless all over.

"Say that again," he commanded.

Wolfe obeyed. "Have you told the police that you had arranged with Miss Bram to call for you in her cab at eight o'clock last evening?"

"No. Why should I tell them something that isn't true?"

"You shouldn't ideally, but people often do. I do occasionally.

However, that's irrelevant, since it would have been the truth. Evidently Miss Bram hasn't told the police, but she told me. I mention it to insure that you'll tell me the truth when you recount your movements last evening."

"If she told you that she lied."

"Oh, come, Mr. Kearns." Wolfe was disgusted. It is established that her cab stood at the mouth of the alley leading to your house for more than half an hour, having come at your bidding. If you omitted that detail in your statement to the police, I may have to supply it. Haven't you spoken with Miss Bram since?"

"No." He was still motionless. "Her phone doesn't answer. She's not at home. I went there." He passed his tongue across his lower lip. I admit I have never seen a squirrel do that. "I couldn't tell the police her cab was there last evening because I didn't know it was. I wasn't there."

"Where were you? Consider that I know you had ordered the cab for eight o'clock and hadn't canceled the order."

"I've told the police where I was."

"Then your memory has been jogged."

"It didn't need jogging. I was at the studio of a man named Prosch, Carl Prosch. I went to meet Miss Arden and look at a picture she was going to buy. I got there at a quarter to eight and left at nine o'clock. She hadn't come and——"

"If you please. Miss Phoebe Arden?"

"Yes. She phoned me at half-past seven and said she had about decided to buy a painting, a still life, from Prosch, and was going to his studio to look at it again and asked me to meet her there to help her decide. I was a little surprised because she knows what I think of daubers like Prosch, but I said I would go. His studio is on Carmine Street, in walking distance from my house, and I walked. She hadn't arrived, and I had only been there two or three minutes when she phoned and asked to speak to me. She said she had been delayed and would get there as soon as she could, and asked me to wait for her. My thought was that I would wait until midnight rather than have her buy a still life by Prosch, but I didn't say so. I didn't wait until midnight, but I waited until nine o'clock. I discussed painting with Prosch awhile, until he became insufferable, and then went down to the street and waited there. She never came. I walked back home."

Wolfe grunted. "Can there be any doubt that it was Miss Arden on the phone? Both times?"

"Not the slightest. I couldn't possibly mistake her voice."

"What time was it when you left Mr. Prosch and went down to the street?"

"About half-past eight. I told the police I couldn't be exact about that, but I could about when I started home. It was exactly nine o'clock." Kearns's hand moved. Back to normal. "Now I'll hear what you have to say."

"In a moment. Miss Bram was to come at eight. Why didn't you phone her?"

"Because I thought I would be back. Probably a little late, but she would wait. I didn't phone her after Miss Arden phoned that she was delayed because she would be gone."

"Where was she to drive you?"

"To Long Island. A party. What does that matter?" He was himself again. "You talk now, and I want the truth."

Wolfe picked up his glass, emptied it and put it down. "Possibly you are entitled to it, Mr. Kearns. Unquestionably a man of your standing would feel keenly the ignominy of having a wife in jail—the woman to whom you have given your name, though she doesn't use it. You may know that she came to this house at nine-twenty last evening."

"I know nothing. I told you she won't see me."

"So you did. She arrived just as Mr. Goodwin was leaving the house on an errand, and they met on the stoop. No doubt you know that Mr. Goodwin is permanently in my employ as my confidential assistant—permanently, that is, in the sense that neither of us has any present intention of ending it or changing its terms."

Kearns was fidgeting again. I was not. He said, "The paper said he had left your employ. It didn't say on account of my wife, but of course it was."

"Bosh." Wolfe's head turned. . . . "Archie?"

"Bosh," I agreed. "The idea of quitting on account of Miss Holt never entered my head."

Kearns hit the chair arm. "Mrs. Kearns!"

"O.K.," I conceded. "Mrs. Waldo Kearns."

"So," Wolfe said, "your wife's first contact was with Mr. Goodwin. They sat on the stoop and talked. You know, of course, that Miss Bram's cab was there at the curb with Miss Arden's body in it."

"Yes. What did my wife say?"

"I'll come to that. Police came along in a car and discovered the body and reported it, and soon there was an army. A policeman named Cramer talked with Mr. Goodwin and your wife. I went to the door and invited them to enter—not Mr. Cramer—and they did so. We talked for half an hour or so, when Mr. Cramer came with Miss Bram, and they were admitted. Mr. Cramer, annoyed by the loquacity of Miss Bram, and wishing to speak with your wife privately, took her away. You demanded the truth, sir, and you have it. Furthermore, I will add one item, also true. Because your wife had engaged Mr. Goodwin's services, and through him mine also, what she told us was confidential and cannot be divulged. Now for——"

Kearns bounced out of the chair, and as he did so the doorbell rang. Inasmuch as a man who might have stuck a knife in a woman might be capable of other forms of violence, I was going to leave it to Fritz, but Wolfe shot me a glance and I went to the hall for a look. On the stoop was a tall guy with a bony face and a strong jaw. Behind me Kearns was yapping, but had drawn no weapon. I went to the front and opened the door.

"To see Mr. Wolfe," he said. "My name is Gilbert Irving."

The temptation was too strong. Only twelve hours ago I had seen a confrontation backfire for Cramer, when he had brought Judy Bram to face Mira, but this time the temperament was already in the office, having a fit, and it would be interesting and possibly helpful to see the reaction. So I told him to come in, took his Homburg and put it on the shelf beside the floppy black number, and steered him to the office.

Kearns was still on his feet, yapping, but when Wolfe's eyes left him to direct a scowl at me he turned his head. I ignored the scowl. I had disregarded another rule by bringing in a visitor without consulting Wolfe, but as far as I was concerned Mira was still my client and it was my case.

I merely pronounced names, "Mr. Gilbert Irving. Mr. Wolfe."

The reaction was interesting enough, though not helpful, for it was no news that Kearns and Irving were not pals. Perhaps Kearns didn't actually spit at him because it could have been merely that moisture came out with his snort. Two words followed immediately, "You dirty——"

Irving must have had lessons or practice, or both. His punch was swift and sure and had power. It caught Kearns right on the button, and he swayed against the corner of Wolfe's desk.

To do him justice, Kearns handled it as well as could be expected, even better. He surprised me. He didn't utter a peep. The desk saved him from going down. He stayed propped against it for three seconds, straightened with his hand on it for support, moved his head backward and forward twice, decided his neck was still together, and moved. His first few steps were wobbly, but by the time he reached the door to the hall they were steadier, and he made the turn O.K. I went to the hall and stood, as he got his hat from the shelf and let himself out, pulling the door shut without banging it, and then I reentered the office as Irving was saying, "I should beg your pardon. I do. I'm sorry."

"You were provoked," Wolfe told him. He gestured at the red leather chair. "Be seated."

"Hold it." I was there. "I guess I should beg your pardon, Mr. Irving, for not telling you he was here, and now I must beg it again. I have to tell Mr. Wolfe something that can't wait. It won't take long." I went and opened the door to the front room. "If you'll step in."

He didn't like the idea. "My business is pressing," he said.

"So is mine. If you please?"

"Your name is Archie Goodwin?"

"Yes."

He hesitated a second, and then came and crossed the sill, and I closed the door. Since it and the wall were soundproofed, I didn't have to lower my voice to tell Wolfe, "I want to report. I saw his wife."

"Indeed. Will a summary do?"

"No." I sat. "It will for one detail, that eighty feet from where the cab was parked there is a stoneyard that would be perfect cover—you couldn't ask for better—but you must have my talk with Mrs. Irving verbatim."

"Go ahead."

I did so, starting with a description of her. It had been years since he had first told me that when I described a man he must see him and hear him, and I had learned the trick long ago. I also knew how to report conversations word for word—much longer ones than the little chat I had had with Mrs. Irving.

When I had finished, he asked one question, "Was she lying?"

"I wouldn't bet either way. If so, she is good. If it was a mixture, I'd hate to have to sort it out."

"Very well." He closed his eyes. In a moment they opened. "Bring him."

I went and opened the door to the front room and told Irving to come, and he entered, crossed to the red leather chair, sat and aimed his eyes at Wolfe. "I should explain," he said, "that I am here as a friend of Miss Mira Holt, but she didn't send me."

Wolfe nodded. "She mentioned your name last evening. She said you are an intelligent man."

"I'm afraid she flatters me." Evidently it was normal for him to sit still. "I have come to you for information, but I can't pretend I have any special right to it. I can only tell you why I want it. When I learned on the radio this morning that Miss Holt was in custody, I started downtown to see her, to offer my help, but on the way I decided that it wouldn't be advisable because it might be misconstrued, as I am merely a friend. So I called on my lawyer instead. His name is John H. Darby. I explained the situation and asked him to see Miss Holt, and he arranged to see her and has talked with her, but she won't tell him anything. She even refused to authorize him to arrange bail for her. She says that Archie Goodwin and Nero Wolfe are representing her, and she will say nothing and do nothing without their advice."

I touched my lips with a fingertip, the lips that Mira had kissed. I was blowing the kiss back to her. Not only had she put my name first but also she had improved on my suggestion by combining Method Three and Method One. She was one client in a thousand. She had even turned down two offers to spring her.

"I'm not a lawyer," Wolfe said, "and neither is Mr. Goodwin."

"I'm aware of that. But you seem to have hypnotized Miss Holt. With no offense intended, I must ask, are you acting in her interest or in Waldo Kearns's?"

Wolfe grunted. "Hers. She hired us."

I put in, "You and Kearns agree. He thinks we hypnotized her too. Nuts."

He regarded me. "I prefer to deal with Mr. Wolfe. This is his office."

"You're dealing with both of us," Wolfe told him. "Professionally we are indiscrete. What information do you want?"

"I want to know why you are taking no steps to get her released and what action you intend to take in her interest. I also want you to advise her to accept the services of my lawyer. He is highly qualified."

Wolfe rested his palms on the chair arms. "You should know better, Mr. Irving; you're a man of affairs. But before I gave you an inch, let alone the mile you ask for, I would have to be satisfied that your interest runs with hers."

"But I'm her friend! Didn't she say I am? You said she mentioned me."

"She could be mistaken." Wolfe shook his head. "No. For instance, I don't even know what you have told the police."

"Nothing. They haven't asked me anything. Why should they?"

"Then you haven't told them that Miss Holt told you on the phone Sunday evening that she was going to drive Judith Bram's cab?"

It got him. He stared. He looked at me and back at Wolfe. "No," he said. "Even if she had, would I tell the police?"

"Do you deny that she did?"

"I neither deny it nor affirm it."

Wolfe upturned a palm. "How the devil can you expect candor from me? Do you want me to suspect that Miss Holt lied when she told us of that phone call?"

"When did she tell you?"

"Last evening, here. Not under hypnosis."

He considered. "All right, she told me that."

"And whom did you tell?"

"No one."

"You're certain?"

"Of course I'm certain."

"Then it won't be easy to satisfy me. Assuming that Miss Holt fulfilled her intention and took the cab and arrived with it at Mr. Kearns's address at eight o'clock, and combining that assumption with the fact that at twenty minutes past nine the cab was standing in front of my house with a dead body in it, where are you? Miss Bram states that she told no one of the arrangement. Miss Holt states that she told no one but you. Is it any wonder that I ask where you are? And specifically where you were last evening from eight o'clock on?"

"I see," Irving took a breath, and another. "It's utterly preposterous. You actually suspect me of being involved in the murder of Phoebe Arden."

"I do indeed."

"But it's preposterous! I had no concern whatever with Miss Arden. She meant nothing to me. Not only that, apparently whoever killed her managed to get Miss Holt involved—either managed it or permitted it. Would I do that?" He made fists and shook them. "Damn it, I have to know what happened! You know. Miss Holt told you. I have to know."

"There are things I have to know," Wolfe said dryly. "I mentioned one—your movements last evening. We have it from your wife, but I prefer it from you. That's the rule, and a good one—get the best available evidence."

Irving was staring again. "My wife? You have seen my wife?"

"Mr. Goodwin has. He called at your home this morning to see you, and you had gone. Your wife wished to be helpful. You know, of course, what she told him."

"Did she tell him——" He stopped and started over. "Did she tell him about a phone call she made yesterday afternoon?"

Wolfe nodded. "And one she received. She received one from you and made one to Miss Arden."

Irving inclined his head forward to look at his right hand. Its fingers bent slowly, to make a fist. Apparently something about the operation was unsatisfactory, for he repeated it several times, gazing at it. At length his head came up. "My lawyer wouldn't like this," he said, "but I'm going to tell you something. I have to if I expect you to tell me anything. If I told you what I told my wife, you would check it, and it won't check. I know Miss Holt drove Judy Bram's cab there last evening. I know she got there at five minutes to eight and left at ten minutes to nine. I saw her."

"Indeed. Where were you?"

"I was in a cab parked on Carmine Street, around the corner from Ferrell Street. I suppose you know what her purpose was in driving Judy's cab?"

"Yes. To talk with her husband."

"I had tried to persuade her not to. Did she tell you that?"

"Yes."

"I didn't like it. There isn't much that Kearns isn't capable of. I don't mean violence; just some trick like getting her out of the cab and going off with it. I decided to be there, and I phoned my wife that I would have to spend the evening with a business associate. I was afraid if I took my car Miss Holt might recognize it, so I got a taxi with a driver I know. Carmine Street is one way, and we parked where we would be ready to follow when she came out of Ferrell Street. We were there when she arrived, at five minutes to eight. When she came back, nearly an hour later, she was alone. There was no one in the cab. I supposed Kearns had refused to let her drive him, and I was glad of it."

"What then?"

"I went to my club. If you want to check I'll get you the cab driver's name and address. I rang Judy Bram's number, and I rang Miss Holt's number three or four times, but there was no answer. I supposed they were out somewhere together. And this morning I heard the radio and saw the paper." He breathed. "I hope to heaven I won't have to regret telling you this. If it contradicts anything she told you, she's right and I'm wrong. I could be lying, you know, for my own protection."

I was thinking, *If so, you're an expert.*

Wolfe's eyes, at him, were half closed. "It was dark," he said. "How could you know there was no one in the cab?"

"There's a light at that corner. I have good eyes and so has the driver. She was going slow, for the turn."

"You didn't follow her?"

"No. There was no point in following her if Kearns wasn't with her."

"What would you say if I told you that Miss Holt saw you in your parked taxi as she drove by?"

"I wouldn't believe it. When she drove by, arriving, I was flat on the seat. It was dark, but I didn't risk her seeing me. When she left she didn't drive by. Carmine Street is one way."

Wolfe leaned back and shut his eyes, and his lips began to work. Irving started to say something, and I snapped at him, "Hold it." Wolfe pushed his lips out and pulled them in, out and in, out and in. He was earning the twenty-five bucks I had paid him. I had no idea how, but when he starts that lip operation the sparks are flying inside his skull.

Irving tried again. "But I want——"

"Hold it."

"But I don't——"

"Shut up!"

He sat regarding me, not warmly.

Wolfe opened his eyes and straightened. "Mr. Irving"—he was curt—"you will get what you came here for, but not forthwith. Possibly within the hour, probably somewhat later. Tell me where I can reach you, or you may——"

"Damn it, no! I want——"

"If you please. Confound it, I've been yelped at enough today. Or you may wait here. That room has comfortable chairs—or one, at least. Mr. Goodwin and I have work to do."

"I don't intend——"

"Your intentions have no interest or point. Where can we reach you?"

Irving looked at me and saw nothing hopeful. He arose. "I'll wait here," he said and headed for the front room.

Having turned my head to see that Irving shut the door, I turned it back again. "Fine," I said. "We're going to work."

"I'm a dunce," he said. "So are you."

"It's possible," I conceded. "Can you prove it?"

"It's manifest. Why did that policeman stop his car to look inside that cab?"

"Cops do. That's what a prowl car is for. They saw it parked with the hackie gone and, while that's nothing strange, they thought it was worth a look. Also it was parked in front of your house. He knew it was your house. He said so."

"Nevertheless, we are dunces not to have questioned it. I want to know if that policeman had been prompted. At once."

"It's a point," I admitted. "The papers haven't mentioned it. I doubt if Cramer would——"

"No."

"I could try Lon Cohen."

"Do so."

I swiveled, dialed the *Gazette* number and got Lon. Wolfe lifted his receiver to listen in. I told Lon I wanted something for nothing. He said I always did and usually got it, but if what I was after this time was an ad under Situations Wanted, I would have to pay.

"That was just a dirty rumor," I said. "I am permanently in Mr. Wolfe's employ—permanently, that is, in the sense that I may still be here tomorrow. On our present job we're shy a detail. If you'll supply it, I'll give you something for the front page if and when. We don't know whether the cop who stopped to uncover Phoebe Arden's body in the taxi had been steered or was just nosy. Do you?"

"Yes, but I'm not supposed to. The D.A. is saving it. He may release it this afternoon. If he does, I'll call you."

"We need it now. Not for publication, and we wouldn't dream of quoting you. We're just curious."

"I'll bet you are. I wish I got paid as much for being curious as Wolfe does. O.K. It was a dialed phone call to Canal six, two thousand. Probably a man, but it could have been a woman trying to sound like a man or the reverse. It said there was a taxi standing in front of Nine-eighteen West Thirty-fifth Street with a dead woman in it. As you know, that address has been heard from before. The sergeant radioed a prowl car."

"Has the call been traced?"

"How? Modern improvements. But you'd better ask the D.A."

"A good idea. I will. Many thanks and I won't forget the front page." I hung up and swiveled. "I'll be damned. Where can we buy dunce caps? For a passerby to see it he would have had to open the door and lift the canvas."

Wolfe's lips were tight. "We should have done that hours ago."

"Lon may not have known hours ago."

"True. Even so, get Mr. Cramer."

I swiveled and dialed. It wasn't as simple as getting Lon Cohen had been. Cramer was in conference and couldn't be disturbed. I was hacking away at it when Wolfe took his phone and said, "This is Nero Wolfe. I have something that will not wait. Ask Mr. Cramer if he prefers that I deal with the district attorney."

In two minutes there was a bark, "What do you want?"

"Mr. Cramer?" He knew darned well it was.

"Yes. I'm busy."

"So am I. Is it true that Miss Holt refuses to talk without advice from Mr. Goodwin or me?"

"Yes, it is, and I was just telling Stebbins to get Goodwin down here. Then I'm going——"

"If you please. Mr. Goodwin and I have decided that it is now desirable for Miss Holt to answer any questions you care to ask—or that it will be after we have had a brief talk with her. Since I must be present, and I transact business only in my own office, it will be pointless for you to send for him. If you want her to talk, bring her here."

"You're too late, Wolfe. I don't need her to tell me that she drove that cab to your address. I already know it. Her prints are on the steering wheel and the door and other places. You're too late."

"Has she admitted it?"

"No, but she will."

"I doubt it. She's rather inflexible. I regret having called you to the phone to no purpose. May I make a request? Don't keep Mr. Goodwin longer than necessary. I am about to conclude a matter in which he has an interest and would like him present. I wanted Miss Holt here, too, but since I'm too late I'll have to manage without her."

Silence—prolonged.

"Are you there, Mr. Cramer?"

"Yes. So you're going to conclude a matter."

"I am. Soon afterward Miss Holt and Mr. Goodwin and I will talk not by your sufferance but at our will."

"Are you saying that you know who killed Phoebe Arden?"

" 'Know' implies certitude. I have formed a conclusion and intend to verify it. It shouldn't take long. But I'm keeping you. Could you do without Mr. Goodwin until, say, four o'clock? It's half-past twelve. By then we should have finished."

Another silence, not quite so long. "I'll be there in fifteen minutes," Cramer said.

"With Miss Holt?"

"Yes."

"Satisfactory. But not in fifteen minutes. I must get Judith Bram and Waldo Kearns. Do you know where they are?"

"Kearns is at his home. He said he would be if we wanted him again. Judith Bram is here. I'll bring her along, and I'll send for Kearns. Now."

"No. People have to eat. Will you lunch with us? And Miss Holt?"

"I will not. Did you ever skip a meal in your life?"

"Many times when I was younger, by necessity. Then I suggest that you arrive with Miss Holt at two o'clock, and arrange for Miss

Bram and Mr. Kearns to come at two-thirty. Will that be convenient?"

"By heaven! Convenient!"

A click. He was off. We hung up. I said, "Probably Irving eats too."

"Yes; bring him."

I went and got him. He marched to Wolfe's desk and demanded, "Well?"

Wolfe's head slanted back. "I forgot, sir, when I said possibly within the hour, that lunch would interfere. It will be a little longer. I have spoken with Inspector Cramer, and he will arrive with Miss Holt at two o'clock. We shall expect you and your wife to join us at two-thirty."

His jaw was working. "Miss Holt will be here?"

"Yes."

"Why my wife?"

"Because she has something to contribute. As you know, she had an appointment with Miss Arden which Miss Arden did not keep. That will be germane."

"Germane to what?"

"To our discussion."

"I don't want a discussion. I certainly don't want one with a police inspector. I told you what I want."

"And you'll get it, sir, but the method and manner are in my discretion. I give you my assurance without qualification that I am acting solely in the interest of Miss Holt, that I expect to free her of any suspicion of complicity in the murder of Phoebe Arden, and that I shall not disclose what you have told me of your movements last evening without your prior permission. Confound it, do I owe you anything?"

"No." His jaw was still working. "I'd rather not bring my wife."

"We'll need her. If you prefer, I'll arrange for Inspector Cramer to send for her."

"No." He sighed. He looked at me and back at Wolfe. "All right. We'll be here." He wheeled and went.

Five of the yellow chairs were in place facing Wolfe's desk, three in front and two behind those, and Mira was in the one nearest to Cramer. I had intended the one at my end for her, but Cramer had vetoed it, and since she was his prisoner, I hadn't insisted. Of course, he was in the red leather chair, and the uninvited guest he had brought along, Sergeant Purley Stebbins, was seated at his right, with his broad burly shoulders touching the wall.

Mira looked fine, considering. Her eyes were a little heavy and the lids were swollen, and her jacket could have stood washing and ironing, and the corners of her mouth pointed down, but I thought she looked fine. Wolfe, seated behind his desk, was glowering at her, but the glower wasn't meant for her. It was merely that he had had to tell Fritz to advance the lunch hour fifteen minutes, and then had had to hurry through the corn fritters and sausage cakes and wild-thyme honey from Greece and cheese and blackberry pie, with not enough time to enjoy it properly.

"Was it bad?" he asked her.

"Not too bad," she said. "I didn't get much sleep. The worst was when the morning passed and I didn't hear from you." Her head turned.... "Or you, Mr. Goodwin."

I nodded. "I was busy earning my fee. I wasn't worried about you because you had promised you wouldn't forget Method Three."

"I kept my promise."

"I know you did. I'll buy you a drink anytime you're thirsty."

"Get on," Cramer growled.

"Have you been told," Wolfe asked her, "that others will join us shortly?"

"No," she said. "Here? Who?"

"Miss Bram, Mr. Kearns, and Mr. and Mrs. Gilbert Irving."

Her eyes widened. "Why Mr. and Mrs. Irving?"

"That will appear after they arrive. I thought you should know that they're coming. They'll soon be here, and we have two points to cover. First, I need a question answered. When you drove away from Ferrell Street last evening, and meandered in search of a place to dispose of the corpse—don't interrupt me—and finally drove here, did you at any time suspect that you were being followed by another car?"

Her mouth was hanging open. "But you—you——" she stammered. Her head jerked to me. "Did you know he was—what good did it do to keep my promise?"

"A lot," I told her. "Yes, I knew he was. Everything is under control. Believe me, I would rather lose an arm than lose the right to ask you to promise me something. We know what we're doing. Shall I repeat the question?"

"But——"

"No buts. Leave it to us. Shall I repeat the question?"

"Yes."

I did so, omitting the "don't interrupt me."

"No," she said.

"Proceed," Wolfe told me.

I knew it would have been better to have her closer. She was six yards away.

"This one is more complicated and more important. During that drive, from Ferrell Street to here, are you certain that another car was not following you? There are various ways of making sure of that. Did you use any of them?"

"No. I never thought of that. I was looking for a place——"

"I know you were. All we want is this—if I told you that a car was following you all the way, what would you say?"

"I would want to know who it was."

I wanted to go and pat her on the head, but it might have been misconstrued. "O.K.," I said. "That's one point. The other one is simple. Tell Inspector Cramer what you told us last night, including the phone call to Gilbert Irving to tell him that you were going to drive Judy's cab." I looked at my wrist. "You only have fifteen minutes, so reel it off."

"I won't," she said. "Not until you tell me why you're doing this."

"Then I'll tell him. You'll know why after the others get here. I'll tell you this; someone tried to frame you for murder and this is payday. Anyway there's not much left, now that he knows you drove the cab here with the corpse in it. Would we have spilled that if we didn't have a good hold? Go ahead."

Wolfe put in, "Don't interrupt with questions, Mr. Cramer. They can wait. . . . Yes, Miss Holt?"

She still didn't like it, not a bit, but she delivered, starting with Sunday evening. She left gaps. She didn't say that Judy had given her permission to take the cab, merely that she had taken it, and she didn't mention the phone call to Irving; since I had already mentioned it, that didn't matter. The main thing was what had happened after she got to Ferrell Street with the cab, and she covered that completely; and when she got to where she and I had sat on the stoop and talked, Cramer began cutting in with questions. I will not say that he was interested in tagging me for obstructing justice than he was in solving a murder case, as I don't like to brag, but it sounded like it. He was firing away at her, and Sergeant Stebbins was scrawling away in his notebook, when the doorbell rang and I went to answer it. It was Waldo Kearns. When I took him to the office, he went to Mira without so much as a glance for the three men, and put out a hand.

"My dear wife," he said.

"Don't be ridiculous," Mira said.

I can't report whether he handled that as well as he had handled the right cross by Irving because the bell rang again, and I had to leave them to admit Judy Bram. She had an escort, a Homicide dick I only knew by sight, and he thought he was going to enter with her, and I didn't, and while we were discussing it she slipped in and left it to us. We were still chatting when a taxi stopped out front and Mr. and Mrs. Irving got out and headed for the steps. The dick had to give them room to pass, and I was able to shut the door on him without flattening his nose. Since it was quite possible that Irving's appearance would start something, I entered the office on their heels.

Nothing happened, Mira merely shot him a glance and he returned it. Kearns didn't even glance at him. The newcomers stood while Wolfe pronounced their names for Cramer and Stebbins and told them who Cramer and Stebbins were, and then went to the two chairs still vacant, the two nearest my desk. Mrs. Irving took the one in front, with Judy between her and Mira, and her husband took the one back of her, which put him only a long arm's length from Waldo Kearns.

As Wolfe's eyes moved from right to left, stopping at Mira, and back again, Cramer spoke. "You understand that this is not an official inquiry. Sergeant Stebbins and I are looking on. You also understand that Mira Holt is under arrest as a material witness. If she had been charged with murder, she wouldn't be here."

"Why isn't she out on bail?" Judy Bram demanded. "I want to know why——"

"That will do," Wolfe snapped. "You're here to listen, Miss Bram, and if you don't hold your tongue, Mr. Goodwin will drag you out. If necessary, Mr. Stebbins will help."

"But why——"

"No! One more word and out you go."

She set her teeth on her lip and glared at him. He glared back, decided she was squelched and left her.

"I am acting," he said, "jointly with Mr. Goodwin, on behalf of Miss Holt. At our persuasion she has just told Mr. Cramer of her movements last evening. I'll sketch them briefly. Shortly after seven-thirty she took Miss Bram's cab and drove it to Ferrell Street and parked at the mouth of the alley leading to Mr. Kearns's house. She expected him to appear, but he didn't. At eight-thirty she left the cab, went through the alley to the house, knocked several times and looked in windows. Getting no response, she returned to the cab, having been gone about ten minutes. There was a dead body in the cab, a woman, and she recognized her. It was Phoebe Arden. I will not——"

"You fat fool!" Judy blurted. "You're a fine——"

"Archie!" he commanded.

I stood up. She clamped her teeth on her lip. I sat down.

"I will not," Wolfe said, "go into her thought processes, but will confine myself to her actions. She covered the body with a piece of canvas and drove away. Her intention was to dispose of her cargo in some likely spot, and she drove around in search of one, but found none. I omit details—for instance, that she rang the number of Miss Bram from a phone booth and got no answer. She decided she must have counsel, drove to my house, met Mr. Goodwin on the stoop and gave him a rigmarole about a bet she had made. Since he is vulnerable to the attractions of personable young women, he swallowed it."

I swallowed that. I had to, with Cramer sitting there.

"Now," Wolfe said, "a crucial fact, I learned it myself less than three hours ago. Only a few minutes after Miss Holt and Mr. Goodwin met on the stoop, someone phoned police headquarters to say that a taxi in front of this address had a dead woman in it. That is——"

"Where did you get that?" Cramer demanded.

Wolfe snorted. "Pfui. Not from you or Mr. Stebbins. . . . That is proof, to me conclusive, that the murderer of Phoebe Arden had no wish or need for her to die. Phoebe Arden was killed only because her corpse was needed as a tool for the destruction of another person—a design so cold-blooded and malign that even I am impressed. Whether she was killed in the cab, or at a nearby spot and the body taken to the cab is immaterial. The former is more likely, and I assume it. What did the murderer do? He or she—we lack a common pronoun—he entered the cab with Phoebe Arden the moment Miss Holt disappeared in the alley, coming from their hiding place in the stoneyard across the street. Having stabbed his victim—or rather his tool—he walked up Ferrell Street and around the corner to where his car was parked on Carmine Street. Before going to his car he stood near the corner to see if Miss Holt, on returning to the cab, removed the body before driving away. If she had, he would have found a booth and phoned police headquarters immediately."

Cramer growled, "What if Kearns had come out with Miss Holt?"

"He knew he wouldn't. I'll come to that. You are assuming that Kearns was not the murderer."

"I am assuming nothing."

"That's prudent. . . . When Miss Holt turned the cab into Carmine Street and drove on, he followed her. He followed her throughout her search for a place to get rid of the corpse and on to her final destination, this house. Some of my particulars are assumption or conjecture, but not this one. He must have done so, for when she stopped here he drove on by, found a phone booth and made the call to the police. The only other possible source of the call was a passerby who had seen the corpse in the cab as it stood at the curb, and a passerby couldn't have seen it without opening the door and lifting the canvas." His eyes went to Cramer. "Of course, that hadn't escaped you."

Cramer grunted.

Wolfe turned a hand over. "If his objective was the death of Phoebe Arden, why didn't he kill her in the stoneyard—they must have been there, as there is no other concealment near—and leave her there? Or if he did kill her there, which is highly unlikely, why did he carry or drag the body to the cab? And why, his objective reached, did he follow the cab in its wanderings and at the first opportunity call the police? I concede the possibility that he had a double objective—to destroy both Miss Arden and Miss Holt—but if so, Miss Holt must have been his main target. To kill Miss Arden, once he had her in the stoneyard with a weapon at hand, was simple and involved little risk; to use her body as a tool for the destruction of Miss Holt was a complicated and daring operation, and the risks were great. I am convinced that he had a single objective—to destroy Miss Holt."

"Then why?" Cramer demanded. "Why didn't he kill her?"

"I can only conjecture, but it is based on logic. Because it was known that he had reason to wish Miss Holt dead and no matter how ingenious his plan and adroit its execution, he would have been suspected and probably brought to account. I have misstated it. That's what he did. He devised a plan so ingenious that he thought he would be safe."

Purley Stebbins got up, circled around the red leather chair, and stood at Waldo Kearns's elbow.

"No, Mr. Stebbins," Wolfe said. "Our poor substitute for a common pronoun is misleading. I'll abandon it. If you want to guard a murderer, stand by Mrs. Irving."

Knowing that was coming any second, I had my eye on her. She was only four feet from me. She didn't move a muscle, but her husband did. He put a hand to his forehead and squeezed. I could see his knuckles go white. Mira's eyes stayed fixed on Wolfe, but Judy and Kearns turned to look at Mrs. Irving. Stebbins did, too, but he didn't move.

Cramer spoke, "Who is Mrs. Irving?"

"She is present, sir."

"I know she is. Who is she?"

"She is the wife of the man whom Miss Holt called on the phone Sunday to tell him she was going to take Miss Bram's cab, and why.

Mr. Irving has stated that he told no one of that call. Either he lied or his wife eavesdropped. . . . Mr. Irving, might your wife have overheard that conversation on an extension?"

Irving's hand left his forehead. He lowered it slowly until it touched his knee. I had him in profile. A muscle at the side of his neck was twitching. "To say that she might," he said slowly and precisely, as if he had only so many words and didn't want to waste any, "isn't saying that she did. You have made a shocking accusation. I hope——" He stopped, leaving it to anybody's guess what he hoped. He blurted, "Ask her!"

"I shall. . . . Did you, madam?"

"No." Her deep, strong voice needed more breath behind it. "Your accusation is not only shocking, it's absurd. I told Mr. Goodwin what I did last evening. Hasn't he told you?"

"He has. You told him that your husband had been prevented by a business emergency from keeping a dinner-and-theater engagement with you, and you had phoned Phoebe Arden to go in his stead, and she agreed. When she didn't appear at the restaurant, you rang her number and got no answer, and then went to another restaurant to eat alone, presumably one where you are not known and plausibly would not be remembered. After waiting for her at the theater until after nine o'clock, you left a ticket for her at the box office and went in to your seat. That sounds impressive, but actually it leaves you free for the period that counts, from half past seven until well after nine o'clock. Incidentally, it was a mistake to volunteer that account of your movements, so detailed and precise. When Mr. Goodwin reported it to me I marked you down as worthy of attention."

"I wasn't free at all," she said. "I told Mr. Goodwin I wanted to help and——"

"Don't talk," her husband commanded the back of her head. "Let him talk." To Wolfe. "Unless you're through?"

"By no means. . . . I'll put it directly to you, madam. This is how you really spent those hours. You did phone Phoebe Arden yesterday afternoon, but not to ask her to join you at dinner and the theater. You told her of Miss Holt's plan to drive Miss Bram's cab in an effort to have a talk with her husband, and you proposed a prank. Miss Arden would arrange that Mr. Kearns would fail to appear and, if he didn't, Miss Holt would certainly leave the cab to go to his house to inquire. Whereupon you and Miss Arden, from your concealment in the neighboring stoneyard, would go and enter the cab, and when Miss Holt returned she would find you there, to her discomfiture and even consternation."

"You can't prove any of this," Cramer growled.

"No one ever can, since Miss Arden is dead." Wolfe's eyes didn't leave Mrs. Irving. He went on, "I didn't know Miss Arden, so I can't say whether she agreed to your proposal from mere caprice or from an animus for Miss Holt, but she did agree and went to her doom. The program went as planned without a hitch. No doubt Miss Arden herself devised the stratagem by which Mr. Kearns was removed from the scene. But at this point I must confess that my case is not flawless. Certainly you would not have been so witless as to let anyone have a hand in your deadly prank—either a cab driver or your private chauffeur. Do you drive a car?"

"Don't answer," Irving commanded.

"Yes, she does," Judy Bram said, louder than necessary.

"Thank you, Miss Bram. Apparently you can speak to the point. . . . Then you and Miss Arden went in your car and parked it on Carmine Street—away from the corner and in the direction Miss Holt would take when, leaving, she made the turn from Ferrell Street. You walked to the stoneyard and chose your hiding spot, and when Miss Holt left the cab, you went and entered it. It is noteworthy that at that point you were committed to nothing but a prank. If Miss Holt had suddenly returned, or if anyone had come close enough to observe, you would merely have abandoned your true objective—a disappointment, but no disaster. As it was, you struck. I am not a moralizer, but I permit myself the comment that in my experience your performance is without parallel for ruthlessness and savagery. It appears that Miss Arden was not merely no enemy of yours; she was your friend. She must have been, to join you in your impish prank; but you needed her corpse for a tool to gratify your mortal hatred for Miss Holt. That was——"

"Her hatred for Miss Holt," Cramer said. "You assume that too?"

"No, indeed. That is established. . . . Miss Bram. Speaking of Gilbert Irving, you said that when he looks at Miss Holt or hears her voice he has to lean against something to keep from trembling. You didn't specify the emotion that so affects him. Is it repugnance?"

"No. It's love. He wants her."

"Was his wife aware of it?"

"Yes. Lots of people were. You only had to see him look at her."

"That is not true," Irving said. "I am merely Miss Holt's friend, that's all, and I hope she's mine."

Judy's eyes darted at him and returned to Wolfe. "He's only being a husband because he thinks he has to. He's being a gentleman. A gentleman doesn't betray his wife. I was wrong about you. I shouldn't have called you a fat fool. I didn't know——"

Cramer cut in, to Wolfe, "All right, if that isn't established, it can be. But it's about all that's established. There's damn little you can prove. Do you expect me to charge a woman with murder on your guess?"

You don't often hear a sergeant disagree with an inspector in public, but Purley Stebbins—no, I used the wrong word. Not "hear," "see." Purley didn't say a word. All he did was leave his post at Kearns's elbow and circle around Irving to stand beside Mrs. Irving, between her and Judy Bram. Probably it didn't occur to him that he was disagreeing with his superior: he merely didn't like the possibility of Mrs. Irving's getting a knife from her handbag and sticking it in Judy's ribs.

"There's nothing at all I can prove," Wolfe said. "I have merely exposed the naked truth; it is for you, not me, to drape it and arm it with the evidence the law requires. For that you are well equipped: surely you need no suggestions from me; but, item: Did Mrs. Irving get her car from the garage yesterday evening? What for? If to drive to a restaurant and then to a theater, in itself unlikely, where did she park it? Item: The knife. If she conceived her prank only after her husband phoned to cancel their engagement, which is highly probable, she hadn't time to contrive an elaborate and prudent plan for getting a weapon. She either bought one at a convenient shop, or she took one from her own kitchen; and, if the latter, the cook or maid will have missed it and can identify it. Her biggest mistake, of course, was leaving the knife in the body, even with the handle wiped clean; but she was in a hurry to leave, she was afraid blood would spurt on her, and she was confident that she would never be suspected of killing her good friend, Phoebe Arden. Other items——"

Mrs. Irving was up, and as she arose her husband did, too, and grabbed her arms from behind. He wasn't seizing a murderer: he was being a gentleman and stopping his wife from betraying herself. She jerked loose, but then Purley Stebbins had her other arm in his big paw.

"Take it easy," Purley said. "Just take it easy."

Mira's head dropped and her hands came up to cover her face, and she started to shake. Judy Bram put a hand on her shoulder and said, "Go right ahead, Mi. Don't mind us. You've got it coming." Waldo Kearns was sitting still, perfectly still. I got up and went to the kitchen, to the telephone extension, and dialed the *Gazette* number. I thought I ought to be as good at keeping a promise as Mira had been.

Yesterday I drove Mira and Judy to Idlewild, where Mira was to board a plane for Reno. Judy and I had tossed a coin to decide whether the trip would be made in the Heron sedan which Wolfe owns and I drive, or in Judy's cab, and I had won. On the way back I remarked that I supposed Kearns had agreed to accept service for a Reno divorce because now it wouldn't leave him free to marry Phoebe Arden.

"No," Judy said. "It's because his wife was a witness in a murder trial, and that wouldn't do."

A little later I remarked that I supposed she had stopped dreaming about a lion standing on a rock about to spring at her.

"No," she said. "Only now I'm not sure who it is. It could even be you."

A little later I remarked that if the state of New York carried out its program for Mrs. Irving, who was in the death house at Sing Sing, I supposed Mira would get back from Reno just in time for a wedding.

"No," Judy said. "They'll wait at least a year. Gil Irving will always be a gentleman."

Three supposes and all wrong. And still men keep on marrying women.

TEXT CREDITS

"The Master of the Hounds" by Algis Budrys. Reprinted by permission of Russell & Volkening, Inc. "The Hammer of God" by G.K. Chesterton. Reprinted by permission of Dodd, Mead & Company, Inc., from *The Innocence of Father Brown* by G. K. Chesterton. Copyright 1910, 1911 by The Curtis Publishing Company. Copyright 1911 by Dodd, Mead & Company. Copyright renewed 1938 by Frances B. Chesterton.

"The Dream" by Agatha Christie. Copyright 1937 by Agatha Christie Mallowan; copyright renewed © 1964 by Agatha Christie Mallowan. Reprinted from *The Regatta Mystery and Other Stories* by Agatha Christie, by permission of Dodd, Mead & Company.

"The End of Devil Hawker" by Sir Arthur Conan Doyle. Reprinted by permission of Jonathan Clowes, Ltd., London.

"Motive for Murder" by John and Ward Hawkins. Copyright 1947 by The Curtis Publishing Company. Copyright renewed © 1975 by John and Ward Hawkins. Reprinted by permission of Brandt & Brandt.

"Method Three for Murder" by Rex Stout. Copyright © 1960 by The Curtis Publishing Company. Copyright © 1960 by Rex Stout. Reprinted from *Three at Wolfe's Door* by Rex Stout, by permission of Viking Press.

The stories in this collection appeared in *The Saturday Evening Post* in the following years: "Secret Service" by F. Britten Austin, 1919. "The Master of

TEXT CREDITS

the Hounds" by Algis Budrys, 1966. "October Corn" by Sigman Byrd, 1935. "The Hammer of God" by G.K. Chesterton, 1910. "The Dream" by Agatha Christie, 1937. "The End of Devil Hawker" by Sir Arthur Conan Doyle, 1930. "The Evil Eye" by Alfred Gillespie, 1966. "The Sea Devil" by Arthur Gordon, 1953. "Motive for Murder" by John and Ward Hawkins, 1947. "A Caballero of the Law" by Ben Hecht, 1933. "When the World Was Young" by Jack London, 1910. "Hit and Run" by John D. MacDonald, 1961. "The Black Cat" by Edgar Allan Poe, 1843. "The Murderer" by Joel Townsley Rogers, 1946. "Pen in Hand" by Ben Ames Williams, 1933. "Method Three for Murder" by Rex Stout, 1960.